The
TIMEKEEPER'S
MOON

ALSO BY JONI SENSEL

The Farwalker's Quest

The
TIMEKEEPER'S
MOON

JONI SENSEL

BLOOMSBURY

NEW YORK BERLIN LONDON

Published by Bloomsbury Books for Young Readers
175 Fifth Avenue, New York, New York 10010

Library of Congress Cataloging-in-Publication Data
Sensel, Joni.
The timekeeper's moon / by Joni Sensel. — 1st U.S. ed.
            p.   cm.
Sequel to: The Farwalker's quest.
Summary: Summoned by the moon to embark on a dangerous journey,
thirteen-year-old Ariel Farwalker, knowing she must obey or risk
destruction, sets out with her guardian, Scarl, to follow a mysterious
map to an unknown entity called "Timekeeper."
ISBN: 978-1-59990-457-3
[1. Fantasy. 2. Adventure and adventurers—Fiction.] I. Title.
PZ7.S4784Tim 2010   [Fic]—dc22   2009016690

First U.S. Edition March 2010
Drawings by Yelena Safronova
Typeset by Westchester Book Composition
Printed in the U.S.A. by Worldcolor Fairfield, Pennsylvania
2 4 6 8 10 9 7 5 3 1

All papers used by Bloomsbury U.S.A. are natural, recyclable products
made from wood grown in well-managed forests. The manufacturing processes
conform to the environmental regulations of the country of origin.

For the writing friends
traveling the path with me

The
TIMEKEEPER'S
MOON

CHAPTER 1

Thunder Moon Madness

The moon refused to hush or come down, so Ariel Farwalker was forced to climb up.

She kicked aside her blankets and abandoned her straw mattress. Ariel slipped through the dim hallways of Tree-Singer Abbey to its great wooden door, the cool flagstones soothing the itch in the soles of her bare feet. Lifting the latch, she pulled the door open, soundlessly this time. She didn't want to disturb her friends' sleep. Not again.

Arise, walker. Hither. The full moon kissed Ariel's face, but its silvery voice needled her. *Arise. Hasten. Late, late.* Despite its name, Thunder Moon shone from a sky free of clouds, and rather than growling, it hissed. Its voice, stealthy and barbed as a porcupine quill, pierced her thoughts, caught there, and pulled. Dragged from her bed by that moon, Ariel thought she knew how the tide felt.

She hurried outside and along the stone wall to a corner. Her nightgown fluttered in the brisk mountain breeze, which was cool even though it was summer. Moonlight drenched Ariel and gleamed on the abbey. Although she did not have the talent for speaking with trees, the Tree-Singers' grand hall had become her home over the past year. Tonight, instead of shelter, the rough-hewn stone building could serve as her stairway to the moon.

She fitted her strong fingers and toes into the quoins' deep mortar joints and hoisted herself up. Her muscles complained, but she pushed them. Although she was only thirteen, Ariel was a Farwalker—the sole member of a trade once thought extinct—and she'd endured a great deal more strain in earning that name than she could face climbing a familiar stone building. The danger would never have stopped her, but if she hadn't been so desperate to quiet the moon, she would have recognized the folly in her risky ascent.

The moon whined and wheedled, urging Ariel to hurry. *Hear, walker. Heed.* Each word tugged at her feet, which throbbed restlessly even as she crept up the wall. Although usually friendly, the stones of the abbey nipped, too, their sharp edges biting into her soles.

Ignoring the sting, Ariel gained the cornice. The overhang stymied her for only a moment. She gripped the stone gutter and hung there from both hands, her feet dangling. With a kick, she swung them up onto the slate tiles. As they so often did, her feet found a way of their own, and her sturdy legs levered her onto the roof.

She huddled there briefly, catching her breath, and then rose unsteadily to her feet. The slant made her teeter. Emptiness yawned between Ariel and the earth, twenty-odd feet below and swirling with moon shadows. A pine scent wafted over the meadow to tickle her stubby nose and twine in her dark, blunt-cut hair. Her soles, slick now with blood, slid on the smooth slate with each step. But Ariel's attention fixed again on the moon.

That round, silver face looked almost as far away as before. It leered at her failure to reach it.

Half only, half only. Unripened. Undone. The syllables circled and blurred, their insistence more clear than their meaning. *Hurry.*

"I'm trying!" Ariel scanned for the best route to the peak of the roof. As a Farwalker, she was accustomed to letting her feet lead her wherever she needed to go, without thinking too much about it. Her skills did not seem to be helping now, though. Of course, her farwalking usually took place on earth.

As she searched for firm footing, a glimmer below caught her eye. She eased toward the end of the roof and looked down.

The moon also shone below her.

One full moon taunted her from above, in the southeastern sky, but another swam on the surface of the abbey's stone well. With an insight twisted by exhaustion and moonlight, Ariel realized she could reach her goal that way instead. A few running steps and a leap would plunge her into that wavering light. The moon's sly face would burst as it received her, silver droplets a balm for her aching head and stinging feet. The moon, which had tormented her all spring, would shut up—and Ariel might finally sleep.

"That's better," she murmured. "I'll meet you."

She gauged the distance to the well and backed along the gutter, working out the angle and how many steps she could take before launching herself off the edge. Four long strides and a good kick should do it.

Running feet pounded below. Zeke Stone-Singer burst into the abbey's dirt yard. Despite the darkness, Ariel could tell it was her friend not only by his lanky silhouette, but also by his speed.

"Ariel!" Zeke whirled and peered up. "What are you doing on the roof? You might fall!"

An exasperated grunt escaped her. "I was trying so hard to be quiet! I didn't mean to wake you, Zeke. Sorry."

"You didn't. The stones woke me. They're worried about you. Now come down!"

Ariel scowled. No one but Zeke could have heard such a warning from stones. It wasn't always convenient to have a best friend with his unique talent.

To her greater dismay, another dark figure joined Zeke. Her friend must have roused Scarl, the man who served as guardian to them both. Scarl's limp had prevented him from arriving so swiftly, but he'd not come empty-handed. He clutched a dark bundle.

Zeke pointed her out. "There," he said, as if Scarl Finder couldn't have found her quickly enough by himself. Few things eluded a Finder who sought them.

"It's okay," Ariel called down to them. "Go back to bed. I've just got to hush the moon, that's all. And then I can—"

"Ariel, hear me."

She flinched at the snap in the Finder's usually muted voice.

"Stop right where you are," Scarl ordered. "Sit down."

Distant trees murmured. Something wasn't right, Ariel knew. It wasn't just that she'd disturbed her friends' rest yet again. Scarl sounded upset. Ariel hadn't heard that tone from him in a year, not since they'd discovered the Vault and its treasures hidden there at the abbey. She'd almost forgotten how sharp Scarl's voice could be when he raised it.

Still, his command echoed dully compared to the whisper slicing down to her from the sky: *Half done, whole undone . . .*

done undone . . . and die. She didn't have to understand for the last word to scare her. It wasn't the first time the moon's whisper had threatened.

"Don't be mad at me, Scarl," she said faintly. "Please. But I can't."

"She's sleepwalking or something." Zeke's moon shadow jittered behind him, drawing Ariel's attention upward again.

"I don't think so. Ariel!" Scarl cursed when she didn't respond.

"What should we do?" asked Zeke. "Should I ask the stones to help somehow, or—?"

"Here, take this. Quick."

Their frantic voices drifted to Ariel from a distance. She was caught in the moon's skewed stare, one of its round eyes looking on from the sky while the other stared up from the well. Her feet didn't just itch now, they burned—and only reaching one moon or the other could cool them. Neither moon was quite right. One was too distant, the other too wet. But—

Heed now. The moon pulled harder than uncertainty, harder than pain. To silence it, Ariel shoved herself into a run.

Zeke cried out below. A rush of the babble he sang to stones followed. As if moved by his voice, the roof—the whole world— slipped sideways. Ariel's bloody feet skidded from beneath her before she could jump. Her legs pumped, but only on air. Her left side slammed against slate, cold and unyielding against her temple and cheek, and tears sprang to her eyes. Her body slid toward the edge of the roof. The view around her rushed sideways, a blur of shadows on darkness. Thunder Moon whirled, flitting beside her like a bright butterfly.

As it danced in her peripheral vision, that light traced a pattern, stark white on black. Too complex to be chance, the pattern struck a chord of recognition deep inside her—a note even louder than the siren call of the moon.

She didn't have time to consider its meaning. Every nerve shrieked of danger. A mountain lion might survive such a drop, but even a sturdy girl like her would not escape without broken bones—or much worse. Ariel's hands and legs fought for purchase, but the roof was too steep, the slate tiles and her own feet too slick.

Zeke's singing grew louder, and—almost too late—the stones of the abbey responded. They set loose a dozen slate tiles, which slid under Ariel like a sled down a snowbank. At the gutter, the tiles caught on the lip, jammed, and backed up in a pile. The jumble halted Ariel's skid, but only for a moment. As her hands swept for a grip, any grip, on the roof, the mound of slates shifted beneath her and came unstuck to flip over the brink.

Ariel nearly tumbled down with them, but by then she'd found the gutter herself. She clung with one hand and the crook of an elbow as her legs and torso swung into space.

Her screech split the night. Slates struck below her and shattered.

"Hang on!" Scarl shouted. His advice seemed both unneeded and hopeless.

"I don't think I—" Ariel's bent arm gave way and slipped off. The clenched fingers of one hand trembled with effort while the other scrabbled to regain a hold—and failed.

Ariel dropped through black dread. Perhaps she passed out for an instant. When the night steadied around her, she blinked, surprised to see Scarl's face over hers.

"—okay?" he asked. "What hurts?"

She raised her head. Her backside and one thigh ached, and

her soles still burned, but no part of her howled. Her arms and legs were all tangled in Scarl's, though, with both of them sprawled on the ground.

"You caught me?" She began to sort out her limbs.

"I'd call that a stretch." Scarl sat up and shoved a tangle of blanket out from between them. "But you dangled just long enough for us to get beneath you with a blanket. That broke your fall."

"And all of my fingers, I think," Zeke said. Standing nearby, he nursed both curled hands to his chest.

"And nearly my heart," said a thin voice. Ariel turned. Ash Tree-Singer, the abbey's grizzled master, hobbled closer. The noise must have awakened him, too, and he'd come out in time to see Ariel plummet. "I was sure you or Scarl would be terribly hurt."

"I don't know yet that I'm not," Scarl said. He folded and unfolded his legs, stretched his long back, and ran a shaky hand through his nutmeg brown curls. "Whew."

"I'm sorry," Ariel whispered, aware now of what she'd done. The ground beneath her pressed hard on her bones. "I know it was dumb to climb up there." She didn't mention her impulse to jump. Her friends might not have noticed the gleaming reflection in the well. More than her climb, that imposter moon and her urge to reach it confirmed just how crazy her thoughts had become.

Zeke toed shards of slate scattered around them. They clinked cheerfully.

"Oh, tell them I'm sorry, too, Zeke!" Ariel said. "Tell them I—" She fought a surge of ridiculous tears.

He shrugged. "Rocks like to slide. And they don't really mind breaking. You would mind. I'm sure glad they warned me."

"Were you dreaming?" Ash asked Ariel. "I know you've been struggling to sleep."

"No." Blinking hard, she tipped her head to stare up at the moon.

Scarl caught her chin in his fingers and drew her gaze back toward his. "Enough moon fever, Ariel," he said. "It's not funny."

"I'm not doing it on purpose!"

"I realize that. But that's why we need to get to the bottom of it. And I can tell you've been keeping something from me. I don't know why, and I don't care. Spill it. Anything—*anything*—you think might be the problem. We're not going back inside until you do."

Ariel yearned to unload some of her burden on Scarl. More than twice her age, the tall, taciturn Finder was the nearest thing she had to a father. They'd certainly faced other trials together. But his temper sometimes surprised her, and she couldn't bear to have it directed at her. Fear stuck the words in her throat.

He snapped his fingers. "I mean it."

"It . . . it started this spring." Ariel gulped. "Promise you won't hurt me or send me away?"

"You know better," Scarl said. "I won't promise not to tie you to your bed, though. Not until I hear a better idea."

Nausea churned in Ariel's stomach. She'd heard stories of lunatics being bound, buried, and bled in attempts to cure them. The worst cases were sometimes set adrift on the sea in the fear that their madness might otherwise spread.

Her queasiness must have shown on her face. Scarl touched her arm. "Forget I said that. We'll work it out. What started in spring?"

Ariel mumbled into her lap. "The moon started gnawing on me."

"Gnawing?" Zeke hunkered closer to hear.

"Not just any moon, though," Ariel whispered. "March's moon. Full. Back home, we had a name for March full moon."

Zeke sucked in a breath. Ariel peeked up. Scarl's narrowed eyes told her that he, too, knew which name she meant.

Death Moon.

CHAPTER 2

Death Moon Disturbing

Hesitantly, Ariel told her friends how she came to be moonstruck. At first, the March moon had only kept her awake. It pried around the edge of her window to shine in her eyes, and it glowed behind her eyelids when she closed them. Even after Death Moon began waning, the thought of it troubled Ariel's mind. It didn't matter if clouds masked the sky. It didn't help to close her eyes before the dwindling moon rose. She tossed under her blanket for longer and longer each night before sinking, exhausted, into darkness.

At last, that sinister moon died of starvation. Thaw Moon started growing, but it didn't bring Ariel any relief. Her feet started tingling, especially when she lay awake. Soon the sensation grew to an itch. She recognized it then as an impulse to walk, but her restless legs did not seem to know which way to go. Sometimes they wanted to pace in the Great Room. Other times, she circled the abbey and gazed toward the south, watching for birds and wishing summer would come. She rubbed her feet with herbs from the Tree-Singer's garden and hid them under thick socks, ashamed of how raw she had scratched them. Soon Ariel haunted the hallways at night and stumbled around groggy all day. Ash brought her warm goat milk on many evenings, but it never helped.

As soon as the weather grew kind, Ariel had talked Scarl into a farwalking trip. They'd headed west to the coast because she had a message to share with Fishers there. Not even those with the most seaworthy boats ventured far beyond their own harbors; travel had become a lost art that few besides Ariel dared. Last fall, though, she'd inspired a few brave Fishers to try it. They needed to know that their boats would be given safe haven, and they offered the same in return. Bearing that message, Ariel had set forth with purpose. A long string of seaside villages welcomed and heard her before she and Scarl came home. The journey eased her itching soles, as she'd hoped, and strengthened her confidence in her new trade. It did little, however, to improve her sleep.

She began hearing the moon's voice immediately upon their return to the abbey in May. *Sssow, walker*, the Planting Moon had called in a sly, somehow threatening whisper. *Sow seeds, sow, hole, heed . . . halves and whole.* Ariel had helped plant the vegetable garden, but the moon had not been appeased. Berry Moon followed in June, the name sweeter but the slithering voice just the same.

"Nothing stops it," Ariel moaned, confessing now to her friends under the July Thunder Moon's baleful eye. "Not stuffing my head in my pillow, or plugging my ears, or . . . or crying. I have tried and tried to sing to the moon, like Zeke does with the stones. I listen and ask questions and beg. Nothing changes. I hear it now even during the day."

"Why didn't you tell me?" Scarl asked. "I just thought growing pains were keeping you up."

"And I assumed mice and rabbits were raiding my herbs," added Ash. "I knew you'd been restless, but I didn't know it troubled you every night."

Ariel shrugged, miserable. The voice had seemed proof of madness, or at least a failing she'd been loath to admit. As proud as Ariel was of her trade, which had been wholly lost until she had revived it, her skills clearly had limits. She could find her way from one place to another in a world where almost no one strayed out of the villages in which they'd been born. She could soothe wary men not accustomed to strangers and recall messages without tangling their details. But Ariel could not satisfy the insistent moon. It spoke to her as "walker," so it must want something to do with her trade. Yet she couldn't imagine where the moon meant her to go, or what to do, or why she needed to hurry. If a trip to the moon had been possible, she would have set off with pleasure. But not even a Farwalker could walk to the moon.

Unfortunately, ignoring her madness had only freed it to grow. She did not share this part with her friends, but tossing in her bed, with her eyelids squeezed tight against the stabbing moonlight, sometimes she'd opened them not on her familiar stone room but on the rafters of her family's cottage back in Canberra Docks. More than once Ariel had joyfully embraced her mother, who was not dead after all, and regaled her with an incredible dream filled with Finders, kidnapping, and murder. Then Ariel had skipped to the front door of the cottage, only to fall over the threshold and land with a painful jolt on her bed in the abbey. These flashes of a home that was lost were not merely dreams, she was certain. On the contrary, it was Ariel's life at the abbey that began to feel unreal. Her dreams and her life—the past and the present—became tangled, each blurring the other until she'd nearly lost track of the boundary.

She'd nearly lost her senses completely. Sitting in the dirt now outside the abbey with Scarl, Ariel eyed the stone well and shuddered. A jump to the well from the roof would have silenced more than the moon. If she hadn't broken her skull on the rim, undoubtedly she would have drowned.

She squirmed to escape a rattling chill. "Can we go back inside now? I don't like Old Moonface staring down while it hisses at me."

Scarl cocked his head and gazed up. "Do you hear it even now?"

"Yes. Nagging." Ariel rose, putting weight gingerly on her feet. Her raw soles complained, but she could hobble.

Scarl stood carefully, too, and followed her and Zeke toward the door. He turned to Ash, who trailed them all with concern on his face. "This moon song," Scarl said. "Is it something Tree-Singers understand?"

Ash shook his gray head. "Coyotes and wolves are the only creatures I know that speak with the moon."

Scarl cast Ariel a thoughtful glance. "They're not the only ones touched by its tides, though."

"Sounds to me like you've gone moon-loony," said Zeke. He winced at Scarl's look of warning.

Ariel moaned. "I know."

"Nonsense." Scarl held the door as they entered the abbey. "Just because we don't understand doesn't mean we should let superstition defeat us."

Their footsteps echoed in the gloom of the hall, reminding Ariel of an echo she had not heard but glimpsed. She'd recognized something in that jiggling flash of moon as she'd fallen.

An insight of panic, perhaps, or a glimmer of life's mystical Essence as she flirted with death, it struck her as a hint—a key to whatever the moon had been trying, for so many nights now, to tell her.

Ariel kept her voice low, not wanting to wake those still abed. "I think it must be some Farwalker thing I'm just not getting." It was not easy to be an apprentice with no master to learn from. Ariel sometimes envied other young people, who all had help honing their skills.

She added, "Were you ever confused, Scarl, when you were first learning to find?"

"Confused, yes," he replied. "Tormented, no. This doesn't sound like a budding instinct to me. Especially since you've led us well each time you've tried. Your farwalking talents are already sound."

"Yeah, but . . ." She struggled to pull her hunch into words. "My moon trouble has something to do with the map."

"What map?" Scarl frowned.

"The one you don't believe is a map."

"Ah," he said. "That."

A year had passed since they'd found it, yet the flash of intuition during Ariel's fall tonight had thrust the map into her mind. Its importance hovered just beyond her understanding, elusive as the night shadows in the abbey's silent hall.

"I want to go look at it," she told Scarl. "Come with me?"

"Of course."

"If you'll be puzzling a while, I'll fetch you some tea," Ash said, pausing at a corner. "Chamomile, in the hope that you'll sleep yet tonight." He waved aside their thanks but regarded Ariel gravely. "If you don't mind, Ariel, I may also consult the cherry tree in the courtyard. Perhaps she will offer an insight."

Ariel gulped, uncomfortable about causing a fuss and apprehensive about what Ash might learn. The trees did not bother with trivial matters.

"Please, Ash," Scarl said in her silence.

His robe swishing, the old Tree-Singer disappeared into the gloom. Ariel hurried on toward the mapstone, trying to outpace the silvery voice that could only be drowned by her footsteps.

CHAPTER 3

Thunder Moon, Full on the Map

Ariel's heart rose when she spied the formidable door that had long hidden the Vault. It reminded her that even things that were frightening were not always what they appeared. Though this door had initially scared her, a treasure had awaited behind its dark face.

If that had not been proof enough, she could never forget how terrified she'd once been of Scarl. She'd first met him last spring, far away in the village where she was born. Ariel had found a remarkable prize in a tree: a telling dart, one left over, it seemed, from a time that had passed. At first, she and Zeke had marveled over the dart without understanding that it carried a message for her. Nobody knew where it had come from, who had sent it, or why. Then two threatening Finders, Elbert and Scarl, had arrived at her home in Canberra Docks. Ariel, who had never seen strangers before, feared them more when she realized they'd come for her dart. They stole not just the dart but Ariel, too, kidnapping her and dragging her far from her home.

Only after great trials did she learn that the dart had been intended for her all along, that it called her to discover her lost farwalking trade and the Vault. Others had received darts, thirteen in all, one person from each of the trades. But powerful men had conspired to hide the darts' message and to kill any Farwalker that her dart might reveal. When the edge of a knife pressed to Ariel's throat, one of her kidnappers surprised her by leaping to her defense. Acknowledging his true purpose—to locate the Vault—Scarl had helped her defeat those who wanted her dead. It had taken a while for Ariel to trust him, and they both had lost people they loved in the fight. But together, with Zeke's aid, they'd obeyed the dart's summons to discover the source of a legend.

The Vault lay concealed in the abbey, on the underside of the Tree-Singers' largest stone floor. The reverse of each flagstone was painted with stories and drawings from a time long ago, before the great plague of blindness, when writing was common and everyone knew the meanings of symbols. The stones had hidden this treasure through a time of great darkness, keeping it safe. Recovered at last, it offered lost knowledge and hope that the world sorely needed.

Although she didn't understand most of the symbols herself, Ariel had known at once that the design on one of the stones was a map. She and Zeke had been crouching near Scarl beneath the Great Room's vast windows that day. The air buzzed with spring light and the thrill of their find.

While the Finder struggled to overturn an unusually stubborn flagstone, another not much larger than a robin's nest had drawn Ariel's eye. Pleased to spot one she could manage alone, she'd curled her fingertips around it and flipped it.

"Look, Scarl," she'd called. "This one's different from the rest. It's a map."

He abandoned his work to peer closer. "It can't be."

"Sure it is," she replied, surprised he couldn't see it. Though overlapped in confusion, the lines and circles painted on the rock's belly spoke to the Farwalker as if she had seen them before. She thought they looked like wandering paths.

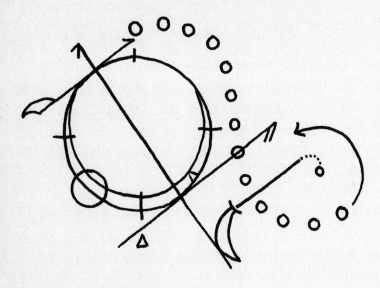

She tapped the design's largest part, a double hoop with marks at the points of the wind. "Isn't this north, south, east, west?"

Scarl shook his head, his curls catching the sun. "I know that's what it looks like, but none of the lines start from any fixed points. There aren't any landmarks—no mountains, no rivers—and the arrows point in all different directions. It can't be a map if you can't find yourself on it."

He turned to Zeke, who'd been examining other newly flipped stones. "Will you try, Zeke?"

Zeke approached. "It looks like tangled sailboat rigging to me," he said. But the Stone-Singer ran his hands over the flat, gritty surface. A few notes of a guttural song fell from his lips. Ariel held her breath, trying to imagine the stone's voice grating in her mind, as it did in Zeke's.

"She's right," Zeke agreed after a moment. "It is a map."

"Told you so." Ariel poked Scarl.

"But a map of what?" Scarl protested. "To and from where?"

"The stone said, 'The map speaks for itself,'" Zeke replied.

"Not very well," grumbled the Finder. "Nothing on it makes sense. How is anyone supposed to follow it?"

Swiping blond hair out of his eyes, Zeke tried again before he shrugged and gave up.

"The stone just keeps repeating that it's out of time," he told them. "'You began in the middle. You should leave.' That's all it will say."

Ariel huffed. "Leave? We just got here." Not all of the stones were giving Zeke useful clues about the drawings they bore, but none of the rest had been rude. "And like a rock has something better to do? Sorry we're bothering it."

"I don't know what it means," Zeke added. "I'm just telling you what it said."

Scarl thanked him for trying and turned to Ariel. "You knew it was a map. Think it's some Farwalker tool?"

"It might be." At that point, her Farwalker trade was still so new, she'd had little idea what it entailed. "But so far, I haven't needed a map. My feet find the way by themselves to wherever I want to go."

"Does it make you want to walk?"

"Nope," she said brightly. "It makes me want to eat." The map's largest circle reminded her of a pie, fresh and ready for slicing, and she'd seen a Tree-Singer baking that morning.

With a chuckle, Scarl had set the mapstone aside in the

sunshine. "Go fatten up a bit, then. If we ever figure out where it leads, you may need it."

Since then, Ariel had eaten all the pie she could want, but she was no closer to being too stout. Throughout the previous summer and fall, she'd walked hundreds of miles, spreading the news that the Vault had been found. She'd discovered, to her delight, what her revived trade entailed: connecting villages that had become isolated, bearing goodwill and gifts, and guiding bold travelers to places they needed to go. During the long mountain winter, Storians who had returned with Ariel to the abbey slowly deciphered the marks on the flagstones. They didn't understand everything yet, but their work was gradually unveiling forgotten secrets and tools.

Only the strange map remained completely baffling. The Storians had set it aside in defeat. Scarl still mulled it over occasionally, but Ariel had nearly forgotten about it—until now.

Reaching to push open the Vault's imposing door, she summoned a weak smile for Scarl and Zeke. Her body still ached from her fall off the roof, and with the moon muttering to her of things only half done, the last thing she needed was another enigma. But her friends had helped her solve difficult puzzles before.

She led them through the Great Room's long shadows and hush. Moonlight spilled in through the windows, gleaming on the new floor that Scarl had helped the Tree-Singers place. The original flagstones were now spread on tables, where their symbols could be copied to linen. Swaths of fabric were easier to carry and share.

One stone, of course, sat apart from the rest. Ariel spied the mapstone on an unused back table. Moonlight glinted off its white and red markings. She traced the arcs and lines with a finger. The cool, gritty surface tingled her skin.

"So . . . is it just the roundness that makes you connect this to the moon?" Scarl asked. "Or this little crescent down here?"

"No." Ariel tried to keep the frustration out of her voice. Scarl was trying hard not to patronize her, she could tell, but his doubt leaked through. "It's not that simple," she added. She knew the strange patterns somehow charted a journey. But one to the moon? Even she doubted that.

Her fingertips found something her eyes had missed until now. Her hand froze over the stone.

"Oh! Look here." She traced a Farwalker sign, **ᤰ**, that lurked in the design. It was lopsided, true, but once she'd recognized her trade mark, she couldn't unsee it again.

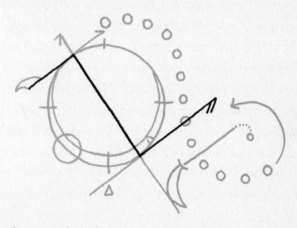

Scarl grunted and bent closer. "How could I not have noticed that before?"

"Maybe the moonlight is helping," Zeke offered.

Ariel spied something else. She drew Scarl's attention to the tail end of the Farwalker's mark. Seen alone, that part of the drawing looked like the brass dart that had drawn them together and eventually brought them here.

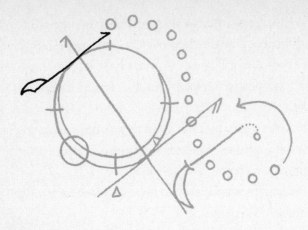

"Think that's a telling dart?" Ariel asked with a shiver of both excitement and dread. The dart that had found her last spring had known Ariel's trade before she did. It had prompted both wondrous and terrible events. A second dart she'd discovered had led to the Vault. The mere likeness of a third felt like one ominous message too many.

"Hmm." Scarl sounded uncertain. "Drawings and symbols and map all in one?"

"Tell me to shut up if you want," said Zeke, "but, Ariel, are you sure you're not finding those patterns because you *want* to see them? Like faces in clouds or designs in the stars?"

"Perhaps," Scarl agreed. He rubbed his stubbled jaw. "Perhaps not."

"More like voices from moons," Ariel said. Feeling a new kinship with the stone, she lifted it into her arms. A quiver ran through her legs. They wanted to walk. But to where?

As she'd done once with her telling dart, she simply gazed at the marks she did not understand and then asked her feet where they meant her to go.

Hither . . .

This time, the urging wasn't a voice but a tangible impulse tugging her feet toward the door and, beyond that, the southeast. Ariel smiled. This sensation she knew. It resembled the itch that had plagued her for months, but, at last, it came with a direction.

"I need to make a cloth copy," she said, hugging the mapstone. "Scarl, can we leave in the morning?"

His eyebrows rose. "Where are we going?"

"Farwalking. Southeast." A thought struck her. "Toward tonight's moonrise."

"There's a small matter of bloody feet." He pointed. Dark footprints had followed behind her.

"Oh." Ariel turned up one sole. The sting of her cuts, forgotten, awoke.

"I don't think my hands are going to work for a few days, anyway." Zeke raised swollen fingers. His skin shone tight and white in the moonlight, dark bruises creeping out from his joints.

"Oh, Zeke! I'm so sorry!" Ariel's eyes stung with remorse. But a colder pressure throbbed from the stone at her chest. *Now, now,* it urged her, its weight and rough edges insistent. And the moon, which had briefly been silent, whined again in her ears. *Haste, walker, haste. Halves lost, whole lost, halves, whole, heed, haste.*

She groaned and dumped the stone on a table as if it had bitten her. "I need to leave right away, though! Something bad is going to happen if—"

The door swung open. Ash entered, a bowl in his hands.

"Calm down," Scarl told Ariel. "Let's tend a few wounds, and then we can talk about what to do next. Ash, we probably need bandages more than the tea."

"The water's not hot yet." Ash set down his bowl. "I brought bruise-bane compresses for Zeke." He began winding Zeke's left hand with a damp linen strip. The boy gritted his teeth.

Ariel forced her uneasy legs forward so she could help bind Zeke's other hand.

"I'm afraid I also bring a message," Ash added. "The trees seem to be in cahoots with your moon."

CHAPTER 4

Thunder Moon Midnight

Ariel stood frozen while Ash hurried to explain his upsetting remark.

"The cherry cannot, or will not, advise you on this matter," he told her. " 'Trees have helped too much already,' she said. It's not like her to give such an evasive or callous answer. When I pleaded for clarification, she said this: 'A circle of ancients expects her. They perform a vast favor, but they can't wait much longer, or all she has done will be undone. Send her now.' "

Ariel spun to Scarl. "See? I have to leave. There's nothing to talk about, unless you won't go with me this time."

The Finder's jaw tensed. He stared at the floor and then reached to Ash's bowl for another wet cloth.

"We're halfway to morning already," he told Ariel. "Leave Zeke to Ash. Either sit on a table so I can clean up your feet, or I will put you atop one myself."

She obeyed. The bruise-bane stung her cuts, but it helped her ignore the moon's silver whisper.

As he bound her soles, Scarl said, "You'll probably be sore, but the wounds aren't so bad. We'll take another look and decide what to do in the morning."

"Leaving is what we have to do in the morning."

His grip on her right heel tightened.

"Ow."

His fingers relaxed, but his stern face did not. As their eyes met, he repeated, "We'll decide in the morning." But he broke the gaze first to finish wrapping her feet.

Relieved to have a plan, whether Scarl agreed yet or not, Ariel replied, "All right. We'll see." She refused to return to her bed, though, until he'd copied the mapstone. Quick with a brush, he complied without comment. Then they slept in what little was left of the night.

The hours may have been short, but Ariel awoke refreshed for the first time in months. Still, her fingers trembled as she dressed. She knew which direction to go, but not who or what she would find, how far away—or whether the effort would silence the moon.

Determined to start that morning, she gathered clothes for her pack. Glancing about for things she might need, she spied her broken knitting needle on the windowsill. It bore the marks from her telling dart, which she had carved there so she could have a copy. Ariel liked keeping it close, but she also feared losing it, so she usually left it safe at the abbey.

Debating whether to take it this time, she was struck by a quirk of the marks. One spot had been left conspicuously blank.

She rushed with it into the hall and found Scarl and Ash speaking in low tones together.

"I had to help him in the outhouse and into his clothes," Ash was saying. "He didn't want me to tell you, but—"

"Scarl!" Ariel hurried to them. "I think I might know what's half done!"

"Not breakfast." Ash smiled. "It's ready when you are."

"Thank you," she said hastily, and in the same breath told Scarl, "The cherry warned of things being undone last night. And the moon talks of something half done, halves and wholes. There is one thing, in all that has happened, that seems kind of half done to me." She raised her needle. "When I first found my telling dart, we didn't know who it was meant for or where it had come from. Nobody knew there was a Farwalker left, or that the dart might have been sent to me. And the mark for whoever had sent it was blank. Now we know I was supposed to receive it. But the half that's still undone—"

"Who sent it." The distance in Scarl's eyes told Ariel he no longer saw her.

"Maybe I need to find out." She added the words she knew would convince him. "Whoever sent it might have more darts. Other goods from the past. Or even another whole Vault."

"Another Vault seems unlikely," he said. "But the sender—"

"Could be somebody old." Pleased with that idea, Ariel nodded. "That's why I need to hurry. So we can meet them, and learn from them, before they leave the world."

Scarl's brow wrinkled in doubt. "The idea is tempting," he said. "But your mapstone was created a long time ago. How could it lead to a sender living now?"

Ash cleared his throat. "Your sender may not be human."

Scarl said, "A machine?"

The Tree-Singer smiled. "I was thinking a tree. Even one of Zeke's stones. But"—he turned to Ariel—"why would any of this make you hear a voice from the moon?"

"I don't know," she admitted. "Unless I am going daft."

Scarl folded his arms and studied the floor between them. "I think, Ariel, it's unwise to hope for too much. But I suppose we need to follow your feet and find out." Over her hurrah, he added, "How are they feeling this morning?"

"Fine," she said, exaggerating. "I'm already half packed."

"I don't suppose we could eat breakfast first?"

"Guess we'd better," she said. "It might be the best one we get for a while."

She returned to her room to stuff extra socks in her bag and pad the insoles of her boots with goose down. She tested the cushioning through different gaits as she followed her nose toward the warm smell of breakfast. Her legs might move slowly the first couple of days, and she was glad their packhorse could carry her gear, but her feet were not overly sore.

Zeke skidded up behind her as she joined Scarl at the table. "You can't go without me," he said.

Ariel hated her answer, but she pushed it out. "I'm sorry, Zeke, really. I'll miss you. But we've gone without you before." Unlike Scarl, Zeke often remained at the abbey, helping decipher the flagstones. Ariel always set out with less cheer when Zeke stayed behind, but their reunions made up for the loss.

Zeke scowled. "This is different."

"I know, but—"

"Zeke." Pointedly Scarl eyed the boy's bandaged hands.

"I'll be better tomorrow. Or the day after." Zeke's voice cracked, and Ariel winced.

"I wish I could wait, Zeke," she whispered. "I can't."

"We'll be all right without you," Scarl added.

Zeke's eyes blazed. "Are you sure? I'm the one who woke *you* last night!"

Taken aback, Scarl returned the boy's stare. "I'll do my best, Zeke."

"Will you keep her safe, though?"

Ariel wanted to remind them she was still in the room. She asked, "Safe from what?" She had told them about the moon's constant torment, but not everything it had said. *Death, dwindle, die . . .* Menacing words echoed in her mind.

"Do you know something I don't?" Scarl grabbed Zeke's wrist. "Have the stones warned you?"

Zeke dropped his gaze. He slumped onto the bench. "No. I already asked. They agree she should go. In fact . . ."

"In fact what?" Scarl growled.

"They told me I won't be a Stone-Singer long if she stays."

Scarl released Zeke in surprise. Ariel recoiled, too.

"Why not?" she asked. "They'd stop speaking to you?"

"No, I don't think that's it. It's more like something would fail. You, I guess. I'm not sure." Zeke groaned. "The more upset I get, the less I understand them. They said almost exactly what the cherry tree did, though: she's had help enough. But I'm worried. For us both. Please wait so I can come, too."

Ariel and Scarl shared a glance. Scarl spoke for them jointly. "You've only convinced us not to delay, Zeke."

"Let me come now, then. I don't need hands to walk."

"You can't even put on your boots," Ariel said.

Scarl spoke more firmly. "No. Stay here and heal. You saved her from breaking bones last night. This time, that has to do."

Ariel rose to throw her arms around Zeke. "I'll find a feather each day and puff it into the air when we camp," she murmured into his neck. "When you see feathers here, you can pretend they're from me."

"No, stones," he said. "Throw a stone or stomp bedrock

every single day. The vibration will travel, and I'll ask them to keep track as you pass."

Ariel agreed, but her smile was forced. He had the advantage. The stones she trod on could indeed report to Zeke about her. She'd have no news of him until she returned home at last.

Nor did she know how long that might take. When she thought of the map, her feet wanted to lead her, but they had never been able to tell her how far. The moon below the horizon remained quiet this morning. Its silence implied it approved of her plans.

Still, she could not forget its recent threats: *Hasten, hasten, heed both halves. Dally, dawdle . . . and die.*

CHAPTER 5

Thunder Moon Waning

Ariel knew she was treading the right path when the moon ceased to hound her. At first she caught up on lost sleep, curling into her wool blanket the moment she finished her supper. After a few days, she sat up with Scarl until moonrise, which came later each night. Gibbous and waning, July's Thunder Moon seemed to melt in defeat.

Her sense of victory faded the following week as Ariel realized what day approached. She couldn't suppress a grumble when her fate became clear: she would pass her fourteenth birthday in a swamp.

"I'm sorry, I had hoped we'd reach some village by today," Scarl told her that evening in the waterlogged twilight. "No way to celebrate your First Day here, I'm afraid. We're lucky to have a dry place to sleep." Stirring up the coals of their campfire, he added a few chunks of peat, the only fuel he had found. The weather was too hot and sticky for burning, but neither of them liked raw potatoes, and that was about all they had left.

"It's okay." Ariel sighed. "I'm the one who led us this way." They'd loaded their packhorse, Willow, and headed southeast from the abbey. Although she'd never ventured far in that direction before, any qualms about it had fled when she'd realized that the heaviest line on her map also pointed that way. Looking at it together over campfires at night, she and Scarl had decided the small mark at the tail of that line, which resembled the Tree-Singers' trade mark, perhaps represented the abbey. In the fortnight since their departure, however, they'd encountered only one tiny village, and they'd left solid ground days ago. Fully healed, Ariel's feet drew her relentlessly forward, despite stumbling through muck. But she was starting to wonder if the moon simply wanted to drown her.

She poked their potatoes with a stick to see if either was soft yet. "It's not such a bad First Day," she said, with more cheer than she felt. "I don't like mosquitoes singing the song in my ear, but being able to sleep is a pretty good gift."

The Finder sat back against a crumbling log and flicked one hand uselessly at the bugs. "I guess you won't need the one I have for you, then?"

A cry of surprise and delight escaped her. "Oh! Yes, I do! Please?"

"I don't know." His amused eyes found hers through the smoke. "Perhaps we should wait until we can celebrate with poppers and a First Day pudding. Or even until we return to the abbey, so Zeke and the others can watch you open it, too."

At Zeke's name, Ariel sagged. "Aw, you're probably right." She jabbed her stick into the coals. "I wish you hadn't told me, though. I hate waiting."

A grin lit Scarl's shadowy face. "Patience is not one of your virtues."

"Kindness is not one of yours."

He chuckled. "I didn't know you thought I had any virtues

at all. But Zeke has already seen it. I offered to wait, but he knows you pretty well. He said that letting you have it right away would be another present from him."

"As if he were with us," Ariel murmured, wishing he were. She'd been careful to toss a stone for him at least once a day.

"Exactly." Scarl rummaged in his pack.

Ariel flushed with gratitude for her friend and a prickly love for the Finder. Having helped, indirectly, to make her an orphan, Scarl had vowed to protect and accompany her for as long as she needed. But battles of will weren't uncommon, and neither had expected the affection that had grown up between them.

He pulled out a small packet wrapped in linen and tied with a frayed but familiar ribbon. Ariel couldn't place it.

"Happy First Day," Scarl said as he presented the package to her. "Joy and discovery."

At the traditional sentiment, Ariel squirmed in excitement. She turned the bundle over, savoring its texture in her hands. Firm lumps shifted inside, tantalizing. She pulled off the ribbon.

The gift had not one but two linen wrappings. The inside of the first bore three lines of symbols marked in brown paint.

She glanced up at Scarl. He nodded. "You can read it."

She'd been learning basic symbols for more than a year, but they didn't stick in her head as well as they might. Haltingly, she read aloud, "'A girl with so many stories needs a few story beans.'"

"Beads," he corrected.

"Oh! Especially since I lost mine!" she exclaimed. Some weeks ago, she'd misplaced the green glass bead she always wore as a necklace. She'd taken it off for a bath and forgotten to put it back on right away. It must have gotten mixed up with the laundry or rolled away into a crack. Ariel and her friends had scoured the abbey in vain. Even using his Finder's glass, Scarl hadn't been able to find it.

"This isn't the first time I've failed," he had told her. "But I'm very sorry to fail on something that means so much to you."

With a pang now for her lost treasure, Ariel bent to finish the note.

" 'Happy First Day,' " she read. She faltered, unsure about the remaining two symbols. The very last looked enough like a Finder's mark to be Scarl's name. The one before that, $\bigvee^{\rho}$, was pretty but unfamiliar.

"I don't know these," she said. "This one looks like the symbols for 'boy' and 'girl' put together."

A twitch in Scarl's face gave away a hint of discomfort. "The mark for love," he murmured. "It says, 'Happy First Day. With love, Scarl.' "

Ariel almost didn't need to open the rest of the package. He'd never before expressed such tenderness. Once or twice he had hugged her, but mostly the Finder focused on the practical matters of keeping her well fed and safe. He filled the roles of both trade master and parent better than Ariel would have expected. Still, the wounded corner of her heart that cried for her mother's embrace or the doting care of a father had never fully healed. This unexpected sentiment from Scarl made it throb.

Too overwhelmed even to smile—in fact, closer to tears— she crawled around the fire to nestle herself against her care- taker's ribs. Despite the heat, he rested his arm loosely over her shoulders.

"Open it," he urged.

Wanting to stretch the moment as long as she could, Ariel first folded the note and wrapped it with the ribbon. The ribbon's faded color finally hit home: she'd worn it around her neck for a year.

"Hey, is this—" She turned an accusing stare on him.

He bit back a smile.

She fumed. "You told me you'd never lie to me!"

"First Day secrets don't count."

With a dirty look, Ariel tore through the folds of fabric. Her green bead lay inside amid a small mound of glass and other materials.

"You're awful!" she cried. "I can't believe you let me think this was lost! You must have stolen it in the first place." She shoved away from his side, glaring.

"No, I didn't take it." He chuckled. "I just didn't return it right away when I found it."

"So you're giving me a First Day present that's already mine." She sniffed. "That's still pretty awful."

His face fell. "Well, I tried to improve it. I thought— I'm sorry."

His distress jabbed at her heart. Only then did her exasperation thin so she could clearly see what lay in the cloth. Ariel lifted the green bead from the others around it. Instead of being strung alone on a ribbon as before, it dangled from a fine satin lanyard. Along the cord on both sides hung smaller beads of ebony and pinewood, sea pearl and amber, dragon's tooth, silver, and what Ariel suspected was gold. She gasped.

"Forgive me," Scarl said softly. "I didn't mean to ruin it for you. Here, I'll put it back on your ribbon." He held out his hand for the bead.

"No, no. I just didn't get it at first." She drew it beyond his grasp. Firelight glinted off the metals and shone through the glass. She'd never owned anything nearly so grand. "It's fantastic, Scarl. Did you craft it yourself?"

Warmth returned to his face. "I had help from Allcrafts in several places we've traveled. And opinions from Zeke. Don't miss this, though."

He pointed. With the necklace removed, several sparkling chunks of glass remained in the linen. Broken shards from some old jar or vase, they gleamed in pale green and gold to echo her large bead.

"A skilled Flame-Mage should be able to melt those into beads, too," Scarl explained. "Or a bracelet, something to go with your necklace. And people in that last village shared rumors of Flame-Mages somewhere past the swamp. If we ever escape it."

Even fourteen thanks did not seem enough, but Scarl made Ariel stop there. Limp with amazement, she asked him to tie the satin cord around her neck before she rested against him once more. She fingered the new beads on her necklace.

"Where did you get them all?"

"Found the glass." He hesitated. "The beads came from my grandfather's story abacus."

Shared memories of hardship and sorrow slid over them both like a blanket. Scarl rarely spoke of the past, but Ariel knew that some of the losses they'd endured together had hurt him more than he let on. The limp he'd gained in an accident showed. Most of the other wounds didn't.

She brushed her cheek against the rough cloth of his shirt.

"Do you know the beads' stories?" she asked. When he nodded, she added, "Will you tell me one?"

"Which would you like?"

Ariel tucked her chin to study the beads. The oblong of ebony wood caught her eye.

"How about this one?" she asked.

Scarl regarded the bead and then looked back at the fire. "Perhaps not that one tonight. Second choice?"

Ariel studied him. He could hold his face powerfully blank, though.

"Any one. You choose." She could pester him about the ebony bead's story some other time.

He told her the tale that belonged to the pearl. Although the words involved selkies and seawater, the pearl, round and white, drew Ariel's thoughts back to the moon. No bright eye shone on them that night; the moon's thin, waning sickle would not rise until nearly dawn. Even a slivered moon pulled on the sea, though, and perhaps that pull echoed in pearls. Long after they'd each retreated to their blankets and Scarl had fallen asleep, Ariel fingered her necklace and felt the moon tugging on it and on her.

Once she even thought the pearl sang in response, a silvery chime tickling her skin. To her relief, it whispered no words— but it did seem to urge her to hurry.

CHAPTER 6
Thunder Moon Gone

Ariel hated the feeling of slime between her toes. Scarl limped straight through the swamp water most of the time, sometimes probing ahead with his walking stick, but Ariel hopped between tussocks of grass when she could. The treacherous ground prevented them from riding the horse; it was too unpleasant to fall when he stumbled.

"I'm not sure I want to meet any sender who can't live on dry land," Ariel said. The swamp had stretched on for days, and even clusters of trees stood shin-deep in water. "He's probably a toad."

"I'd like to know such a toad," Scarl replied. "He might talk. And it would not be the first time you'd led us to something that others considered a myth. Are you content that we're still aligned with your mapstone?"

Ariel reached into her pocket. While her fingers squeezed the cloth copy, she relaxed her eyes' focus to better feel the intent of her feet. They kept splashing forward.

"Yes," she grumbled. "This is the right way. Stinky or not."

She tried to make the best of squishy socks by working them into new verses for her Farwalker's song:

Walk with the wind and sun;
Moon whispers, calling.
Hurry, *it says to me,*
Hasten and come.

Hurry through slimy mud,
Moon finally silent.
Walk where the mapstone leads.
What lies ahead?

What lies ahead of us?
Who is the sender?
Feet splashing, I'll go learn
Why I should come.

"Clever tongue," Scarl said. "Passing your First Day has not changed your talent for song."

Ariel soaked in his praise, and her fingers found her necklace. She tried to gauge whether she felt any older. Her body had begun changing lately, sometimes in startling ways, but without any increase in poise. She felt neither wiser nor more graceful, and she was still prone to behavior that others called foolish. Almost nobody but Scarl took her seriously.

She glanced sideways at him. "Don't laugh at this, okay? But how old were you when you finally felt grown-up?"

Scarl considered, his gaze on his splashing feet. "You may not like my answer," he said.

"Tell me anyway."

He drew a heavy breath. "I was seventeen the first time I kissed Mirayna."

Ariel dipped her head to cover surprise. Scarl normally

dodged any mention of the woman he'd once hoped to marry.

"That made me feel grown-up, all right," he continued. "But I don't think I really grew up until she died in my arms."

Ariel winced. Losing people she loved hadn't made her feel grown-up. Death always made Ariel feel smaller and younger than ever.

"Perhaps not even then," Scarl added. "My responsibility to you afterward played a role. I don't know. Maybe people keep growing up all along. Or we never do, really, until we cross the bridge out of the world."

"That's not what I meant." Ariel sighed. She hated to remind him of sorrow, and the unexpected results of her question seemed proof that she'd never grow out of her thoughtless tongue.

"I did warn you," he replied. "Take my first answer, if you like: seventeen."

She slogged through the water. Three more years sounded like an awfully long time. She watched Scarl out of the corner of her eye, trying to picture him at seventeen.

Her curiosity twitched. "When's your First Day, Scarl? You've never said."

He didn't look up from his path. "Oh, nobody kept track of the days way back then." He peeked up at her startled reaction and grinned. "November 11."

"Hmm. Fall child." She recited a rhyme:

Hard but warm the winter child,
Spring born, brightest of them all.
Summer baby, light and mild,
Flecked with frost the child of fall.

"That fits you," she told Scarl.

"Think so? Well, you may be light, but you're hardly mild."

She couldn't argue. "Zeke was a spring child, though. That one's true."

"He is a sharp one," Scarl agreed. "Anyway, you know the version that parents tell summer children they wish would be milder. There's another way to say it."

"There is? What?"

"Summer baby, wise but wild."

Ariel smirked.

Scarl nodded. "I think the seasons guide us more than we—" His feet stopped and he cocked his head.

"What?" As their eyes met, his idea jumped to her like a spark. "Winter, spring, summer, fall." Ariel plucked the map-stone cloth from her pocket and spread it flat against Willow's ribs, staring at the double circle marked with the four points of the wind. A strange assurance resonated inside her.

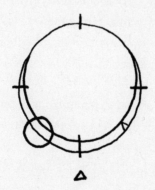

"It's not just directions." Ariel poked the small Flame-Mage's triangle at the bottom. "I thought this was for south, 'cause it's hot there. But summer is fiery, too."

"The cycle of seasons." He swept his finger around from the

top to the smaller hoop strung on the larger ones like a bead. Following his motion, Ariel chanted the months in her head. A shiver ran under her skin.

"August?" She'd been born July 21. August was only nine days away.

"Or May," he replied. "Depending on which way around the circle you go. It's probably not an exact month, anyway. The marks are more likely solstice and equinox days, so it'll be off by almost a fortnight."

Ariel frowned. "It's now," she insisted.

"Why do you say so?"

She drilled her fingertip into the solstice mark for summer. "Solstice, June 21." She moved it. "July 21." The smaller circle began there and spanned to her next touch: "August 21. Equinox in September."

He murmured appreciatively.

"But why didn't whoever painted it just use the symbol for August?" she added. "They didn't have to make it so hard."

"Calendars can change," he explained. "And the names of months, too, especially over long generations. But the sun moves the same in the sky now as ever. Didn't your Storian teach you that?"

With a flare of anger, she slapped at a mosquito drilling her skin. The map made her feel stupid enough without questions like that.

Scarl renewed his study. "So it's not just a map. It's a calendar, too."

"A map of places *and* times. When to go." She remembered the moon's whispers about being late. Thoughts of the moon helped her spot something else.

"I hope our bearing line doesn't indicate time or distance as well," Scarl said, "from one side of a year to the other. And beyond."

Ariel grimaced. "Even a Farwalker would dread a trip that long."

"It might only be the diameter of the year's circle. . . ." Scarl glanced up and squinted, calculating. "That would be a hundred . . . roughly a hundred fifteen days? Plus the stretches outside the circle? Or a hundred fifteen miles, perhaps. But we've already come farther than that. Curse the mapmaker for not giving us measures."

"We definitely haven't gone too far," Ariel told him. "I can always feel in my feet when we get where we're going, until I start thinking about someplace else. But three or four months—we'd drown in the sea if we walked in one direction for that long! Wouldn't we?"

Scarl snorted. "Perhaps your sender's a whale." He tapped the long chain of dots swooping away to one side:

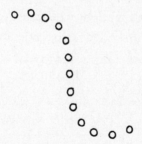

"Or these could be days. I like that idea better. A fortnight? We'd be almost there." He counted. "No. Only thirteen. Not months, then, either. Something else."

Ariel waved her free hand, fending off biting bugs. She had an idea about those thirteen dots, but she wasn't sure how to broach it with Scarl.

"We'd better move on before we're both eaten," he said. "More to think about, though."

Content to muse for a while, Ariel tucked the map away, and they led the horse forward again.

An eel slithered out from between Ariel's feet.

"Eek!" Jumping sideways, she slipped to one knee. Water slopped over her thighs.

"Don't panic, it's only a mudtail." Scarl yanked her back to her feet. They watched the eel retreat, the swamp's surface rippling in its wake.

"Ugh." Scowling, Ariel tried to scrape slime from her legs before giving up and splashing ahead. "If this gets much worse, I might have to try riding Willow."

Scarl halted. He pointed ahead to a large stand of cypress dripping with moss. "Perhaps you can just climb a tree."

It took Ariel a moment to see what he meant: the cypress trees held more than moss. Ladders reached into their shadowy branches. Square, unnatural shapes poked from behind gray-green veils, and dots of firelight winked through the gloom like trapped stars. As Ariel stood staring, sounds drifted out, too— splashing, a clunk, a shrill human voice. A village rose there before her, concealed by trees and plunked smack in the midst of giant stink cabbages and rot.

CHAPTER 7

Moonless Welcome

A ruckus arose as voices called through the trees that strangers had arrived. As she and Scarl sloshed forward, Ariel realized the buildings weren't squatting in the mud but clinging partway up the trees, lashed to trunks and resting on branches. She could have walked beneath all but a few. Most of the structures were little more than a floor, though, with boughs draped overhead against rain. Ariel could look up and see the tree dwellers gazing back in uneasy surprise.

She wondered if there might be someone among them who knew what a telling dart was and had sent some. If so, nothing in their rustic appearance gave it away. Her feet wanted to linger, however, even though it was barely midday. Ariel took that to mean she was meant to arrive here. She smiled.

Somber men splashed to meet them and usher them up a ladder onto an empty platform. Ariel guessed it must serve as the village's commons, and, indeed, a curious crowd soon hovered around her and Scarl. She could hear the swishing of others arriving below. Willow, left hitched at the base of the ladder, drew as much attention as the human visitors did.

The people, though they waded daily in mud, were more artful than some Ariel had met. They wore simple shifts of linen or hemp, but the men were clean shaven, the women twisted their hair in intricate patterns, and both draped themselves with delicate chains of snail shells or seedpods.

A robust woman with a garland in her hair bustled up. She glanced at Ariel but extended both hands toward Scarl, palms up, the way women reach for babies. Her face cramped with worry.

"I hardly know how to greet you," she said. "It's been long and long since a stranger appeared here."

Scarl barely hesitated. He and Ariel both were becoming adept at figuring out unfamiliar gestures of greeting. He placed both his hands in the woman's.

"Well met," he said. "We come in goodwill."

She studied him, gripping his palms as if feeling through his skin whether to believe him. A smile broke onto her lined face.

"Welcome," she said. "I'm Lamala Judge."

Ariel realized why the woman had invited a clasping of fingers. Judges could spot lies at a glance, and the good ones could sense deeper trouble or truth through a touch.

Lamala flapped a hand at the village. "This is Skunk, but perhaps you know that. Or can smell it. It's not us! It's the cabbage."

Ariel smothered a giggle.

"We're grateful for your welcome," Scarl said. "I'm Scarl Finder."

"A Finder—that explains it," said Lamala. "What made you want to find us?"

"Not me." Scarl tipped his head. "Ariel Farwalker."

The woman's eyes widened as she released his hands to reach for Ariel's.

A tingle passed between them at the touch. Lamala's smile shriveled and dismay darkened her eyes.

Ariel's heart flopped. As she opened her mouth to ask what was wrong, the Judge shook herself—or was that a shiver? She recovered her smile, squeezed Ariel's hands, and let go.

"A Farwalker! I must say, that's a fresh one on me." Lamala turned back to Scarl. "Your daughter?"

"You might say so."

His words, which were more truth than fact, warmed Ariel's heart. So did Lamala's knowing nod. Ariel decided she must have misunderstood the woman's fleeting expression.

"Farwalkers are no more," said a man behind Lamala.

Another voice suggested, "Prove it."

"She doesn't have to prove it." Scarl's eyes flashed. He'd grown sore to this common reaction. "If you're not interested in what a Farwalker can share with you, we'll go elsewhere."

Ariel touched his arm. This was no ordinary farwalking trip, and she couldn't just leave. But it seemed rude to start asking questions about senders or mapstones without first sharing the news of the Vault. Their reactions to her so far implied they knew no more about it than people anywhere else. Besides, she rather enjoyed proving herself. She reached into her pack.

"No, no. Please don't mind them." Lamala cast a glare over her shoulder at the hecklers. "She got here, didn't she?" Turning back, she added, "We just thought Farwalkers had passed from the world. Surely you understand?"

"It's all right." Ariel pulled a fanged skull, as big as a shoe, from her pack. It drew a collective gasp as she brandished it over her head.

"Have you heard of a place where these swim in the sea?" she asked the crowd. "They're called wolf eels, and if you think this is ugly, you should see one alive. I can tell you about them, if you like. The seacoast where they live is just one of the places I've walked to." Curious questions and at least one apology filtered to Ariel's ears.

"That walloped them," said Lamala. "But before you start yarning, let's tend first things first. Are you hungry? If not, we're eager to hear what has brought you."

Scarl turned to Ariel. "The usual?" he murmured. "Or . . . ?"

She consulted the skull in her hands, not sure how to proceed. The eel's toothy grin bolstered her confidence. She took charge.

"I have important news to share with you, and gifts from afar," she told the villagers. "Will you gather at sundown, when your day's work is done, to hear me?" She was hoping for a few hours alone before then so her feet could lead her to whatever had drawn her here.

"Forget sundown," said Lamala, "unless you're too tired. Curiosity will slay us by then. Our work can wait. If we feed you our best, will you sit down and talk to us now?"

Ariel couldn't deny her. The Judge announced a picnic on the spot, and the villagers retreated to gather snacks and more people. Resigned, Ariel watched the commons fill and soon caught the excitement of her usual farwalking duties. Adults who'd only heard rumors of faraway places asked whether monsters lurked beyond the swamp. Children dared one another to approach her, jostling until they tumbled off the platform with a splash. Lamala directed the bustle, bombarding her guests with food and positioning favored villagers around them.

"Does Skunk have a Flame-Mage?" Scarl asked. "It's not urgent, but if so, we'd like to meet him or her."

The reminder of her birthday gift shot a thrill through Ariel. Lamala scanned the crowd for the Flame-Mage.

"He's not feeling well today," said a clear voice. "But I'd like to be met in his place, if I may."

"Ah, that'll do," said Lamala. She drew a slender young woman, not many years older than Ariel, through the crowd. "Meet Sienna, first apprentice to our master Flame-Mage."

Tall and striking, Sienna stood proudly above most of the other villagers. Her long hair, a glowing paprika that Ariel had seen only in sunsets, wound in complicated plaits at the base of her neck. Like everyone in Skunk, her feet and legs were bare to midthigh, but her velvety shift fit her snugly. Sienna eyed Ariel.

"So you're a Farwalker." Her voice hinted of challenge.

"So you're a Flame-Mage," Ariel replied. "I have a job for a Flame-Mage, if you think you can do it."

Sienna stared back, unflinching. Suddenly she smiled and took Ariel's hand.

"Oh, we can talk about that later." She pulled Ariel down to sit where they stood. "There isn't much fun in Skunk," she added in a whisper. "You might be sorry you came. But I'm glad. Tell me what a Farwalker does, and where you come from."

Pleased by the quick thaw, Ariel chattered with Sienna while everyone ate. She was midway through a description of Tree-Singer Abbey when Sienna interrupted.

"Your necklace." Sienna reached toward Ariel's throat and then faltered. "Gorgeous. Can I touch it?"

Ariel nodded, unable to hide a proud blush.

"Where did you get it?"

"My Storian back home gave me this bead," she said, pointing out the green one. "Scarl strung the rest for me."

Sienna's deep gaze bounced to Scarl. "How sweet."

Ariel giggled. She would never have placed that word on Scarl herself. "It was a First Day present," she explained. "I need a Flame-Mage to make something else to go with it. I've got the glass."

"Easy." Sienna waved off the topic. She posed questions about Scarl until Ariel got her talking of fire. Sienna told of burned fingers, singed eyebrows, and sizzling hair.

"That's why I have to keep my hair tied up," she said, stroking her plaits. "You could say it picked my trade for me— my Da still calls me Firetop—but it sure doesn't help. If I wasn't careful, it would be shorter than yours. Which is nice, by the way. Bouncy. Want me to braid the longest bits for you?"

Ariel realized how many eyes were upon her. Their meal complete, the people of Skunk watched her, whispering and fidgeting.

"Maybe later," she told Sienna. She rose.

In the instant hush, Ariel's heart sped and an anxious lump formed in her throat. She took a deep breath and reminded herself that nobody could criticize her performance because they'd never had a Farwalker visit. Besides, forces greater than whim or fortune had sent her. She felt the map cloth through her pocket and glanced at Scarl, who nodded encouragingly.

She repeated her name for late arrivals and began. "I'll start with a gift." Delivering was her favorite part of being a Farwalker; it always helped her get past the jitters. She reached for and dug in her pack, glad it still held the spoils of her last trip.

"Does Skunk have a Healtouch?" she asked.

A thin man waved from near the edge of the platform.

Ariel tossed him a packet. "Medicines from Tara Healtouch of Conkor," she said. "I can tell you later what each is good for.

She would be grateful if you can trade anything to help coughing or the cramping disease."

"Well, bite off my nose and spit in my brainbox! I believe
perhaps I can."

Ariel blinked past his unusual exclamation. "Um . . . okay.
Also, there's a village called Esme that very much needs a Healtouch, if you have an older apprentice who's willing to go."

"Tell them we'll trade a Healtouch or just about anything
else for some good-looking husbands for our daughters," called
a woman. The crowd laughed.

"Do they have to be good-looking?" Ariel asked.

"Oh, they're joking," Lamala told her.

"No, we're not," said the woman who'd spoken. "If she's a
Farwalker, she can carry that message."

"I will." Ariel nodded. She pulled a small, white puff from
her pack and displayed it. "Is there anyone here, an Allcraft or
a Kincaller maybe, who knows how to make fabric from butterfly cocoons?"

Only puzzled looks answered.

"I know, it sounds weird," she added. "But I met someone
who swears her great-grandmother did, and she'd like to learn
how. The sample she showed me was pretty amazing."

She tucked the cocoon back into her pack and riffled its
contents. "Let's see . . . you don't have someone named Camity
Allcraft here, do you?"

An older woman swapped uneasy glances with her neighbors. "I'm Camity," she said.

"Truly?" Ariel had asked the question before without ever
getting a positive answer. "Did you have a sister named
Annabelle Windmaster?"

"Why, yes! But I haven't seen her since we were young,"

Camity said. "The wind loved her so much that one day it plucked her right into the sky."

Ariel slipped a bit of lace from her pack. "It must have dropped her eventually, in a place called Integra. I don't know if you'll recognize this, but it was the best memento her husband could give me." The lace passed through the crowd toward Camity, along with Ariel's sad smile. "Annabelle left the world last year, but she never forgot you. If you'll come see me later, I'll tell you more."

Wonder lit Camity's face. Sorrow slowly dimmed it, but she reached eagerly for the lace.

Her nervousness forgotten, Ariel went on for several more minutes, handing out crop seeds, small gifts, and messages. Her work grew with every village. Pleas from places in need of a Healtouch or Storian crowded her memory. Nobody had responded yet, except to extend sympathy, but Ariel looked forward to a day when some brave apprentice would step up to say, "I'll go. Take me."

The people of Skunk offered Ariel plenty of other reactions, of course, mostly gaping mouths, questions, and good-natured jokes. But their eyes never left her. Only Sienna didn't pay much attention. Instead the young woman's gaze rested mostly on Scarl. Too busy to wonder, Ariel finished her deliveries by passing a pinecone to Skunk's Tree-Singer.

"Pine seeds from Tree-Singer Abbey," she said. Once she'd convinced the listeners that the abbey was no myth, she added, "That brings me to even bigger news. The Vault has been found. At the abbey." She'd learned that people believed her sooner if she didn't mention that she'd found it herself.

Voices erupted. Over the hubbub, Ariel explained that what had been found was not jewels or gold but lost knowledge. She

handed out several rectangles of linen with symbols and drawings on them, including a copy of the primer that had introduced her to reading. Skunk did not have a Storian, or at least
none who went by that name, but Lamala and several elders
took the sheets eagerly and promised to begin learning and
teaching the rest.

With her routine duties done, Ariel gnawed her lower lip,
debating what to say next. "And now I hope to learn something
from you," she told the crowd. "I'm looking for someone or
something that sent me a telling dart. Do you know what that
is?" She wished she could show them. Her original dart had
been stolen, but Storians at the abbey had been studying the
dart she'd found later. In her rush to leave, she hadn't thought
to retrieve it.

It didn't matter. Most of the adults had heard of the device,
even though they'd never seen one.

"There were a lot of darts, actually," Ariel explained. "Someone mysterious sent them last spring. I've been hoping to find
that sender."

Though the villagers exchanged hopeful looks and deferred
to the elders, it quickly became clear that no one could offer
much help. Ariel's heart sank. This wouldn't be as easy as she
might have hoped.

"So the sender's not here?" she said, mostly to herself.

Scarl spoke up. "Do you have anything remaining from old
times? Perhaps even something so odd or confusing that no one
can say what it is?"

After a few more blank stares, a voice in the crowd said,
"Well, there's Tattler, ain't there?"

CHAPTER 8

Moonless Day

A few people laughed. A little girl squealed, "Don't let Tattler get you!" and pressed herself into her mother's ribs. Others clucked to soothe her, shaking their heads.

"Don't go off on that twaddle," Lamala said scornfully. "The girl didn't tramp all this way for Tattler."

"She golly well might have," the Healtouch replied. "If she's after old junk from back-when times. That's all we've got from them days, anyhow."

"It's not even here," Lamala said. "It's not ours."

"What's Tattler?" Ariel asked, both alarmed and intrigued.

Nobody answered. Villagers avoided her glance. At last Lamala told her, "It's a hoodoo far away on the edge of our swamp."

"T'ain't a hoodoo," muttered the person who had first spoken. "It's a beast."

"Hoodoo?" Ariel repeated. Every village had its own favorite words, but Skunk's were beginning to feel like another language.

"A strange rock formation," Scarl told her, glancing at Lamala for confirmation. "Spooky, sometimes. The blowing wind shapes them and howls through them as if they were haunted."

"Spooky is right." Lamala cast a sympathetic look toward the cowering girl and then glared at certain adults. "Fools use it to frighten young children. Not that any of us have ever seen it, mind you—"

"'Cause it ain't so close as the edge of our swamp," declared someone else. "My grandpappy went a-hunting it once. He used to say it stood nigh on the edge of the world."

"Just as well," said Lamala. "We don't need it closer. But it creeps into stories told on long winter nights."

"What are the stories?" asked Scarl.

The Judge tilted her head toward the smaller children. "Later, perhaps. They're the kind that give nightmares. I'm not sure why you'd want to go see it." She smiled. "But then, I'm not sure why you'd want to come to Skunk, either."

"Kind hospitality," Scarl replied.

"And new friends," Ariel added with a shy nod to Sienna. She tried to ignore the real reasons, the questions clamoring in her mind. With her curiosity burning about Tattler, however, she couldn't resist one last attempt. She drew her map from her pocket and showed it. "Tattler's not on this drawing, is it?"

"They say Tattler looks like a giant bug," said Sienna. "Legs everywhere, antennas, teeth. Your drawing looks more like a game of marbles to me."

"Do you recognize anything on here?" Ariel pivoted so the whole crowd could see. "A landmark, a pattern you know . . . something that represents Skunk? Because I think it's a map."

Bemused heads shook all around.

"Well." She sighed. "If you think of anything, please let me—"

She happened to glance toward Lamala. Their hostess had bowed her face toward her lap, but the dread in her expression stopped Ariel's tongue.

Scarl also had noticed. A tiny shake of his head warned Ariel not to pursue it just now.

"Let me know," Ariel finished. Despite a spike of concern, she stuffed the linen back into her pocket and grinned. "I'll stop talking now, before your ears fall asleep. Anyone who might want to answer the trade requests I told you about, or give me a message to carry, or help with the work at the abbey, please come and see me about it."

"Allcrafts especially, for the abbey," Scarl said. "We need someone who can start trying to make the tools drawn on the stones."

"I could take you there, of course," Ariel added. "I guide people, too."

She heard those habitual words and hurried to amend them. "I mean . . . I can't take you right now, but I could come back for you later. If you're not too much trouble." At the group's laugh, she smirked along with them, but she meant what she'd said. Two of the Storians she'd led to the abbey had whined and complained so much that Ariel had threatened to leave them. Scarl always preached patience, but they'd both become more careful. They did their best to scare off people who didn't seem hardy enough for the trip.

Amid a chorus of thanks, Ariel bowed like a performing Fool and plopped down to a seat.

Lamala's voice broke through the babble. "We'll try to repay you for all that you've brought us." Her face shone, free of the qualms there moments before. "I'm sure we can offer gifts for you to take elsewhere. But is there anything you need for yourself?"

Ariel most wanted to hear about Tattler, but she understood why she had to wait.

"We can always use food that will keep," Scarl said.

"And a few more dry socks," Ariel added.

Lamala turned to her neighbors. "You hear that? Let's show them there's more here than swamp gas and bugs. So the next village will hear more of Skunk's generosity than its scent."

Ariel laughed. "I wouldn't—"

"Don't waste your breath, girl," said Lamala. "We make up for it, that's all. The swamp does have advantages, though they might not be apparent."

The villagers agreed. With much chatter and smiling, they began to mill and disperse.

Ariel eyed Lamala and exchanged a meaningful look with Scarl. She reached for the map in her pocket.

With a quick gesture, he stopped her. "Later," he murmured. "Alone. You have admirers first." He tipped his head toward the people edging forward to meet her.

So Ariel allowed new friends to touch her, share their names, and thrust sweet treats into her hands. When Skunk's Tree-Singer asked to hear more of the abbey, Ariel took the chance for a trade. She described Zeke and promised to tell the Tree-Singer everything she wanted to hear in exchange for any news the trees could relay about Zeke. Other villagers clamored for details about wolf eels or the place she came from. For a while, the attention was pleasant. But soon the press of bodies and voices made Ariel feel hemmed in. She still didn't know why she'd been drawn here, and the frustration made her jittery. Her eyes roamed between villagers and over their shoulders, longing to escape, if just for a moment.

Her restless gaze struck a boy standing near the top of the ladder as if he'd just arrived. Dark hair fell around his fine features and onto his shoulders. Circlets of feathers set off the lean lines of his bare arms and calves. Her age or a bit older, he was so bronzed by the sun that he could have been carved from wood. Ariel was certain he'd never been part of the picnic, but he watched the commotion now hungrily.

Their eyes met. Startled, he backed up a step—and promptly fell off the platform.

Ariel exclaimed, afraid he'd be hurt. Before she could move through the crowd toward him to check, his head poked back up over the edge. Water dripped from his hair, the drops glinting—not unlike his pale green eyes, which were startling against his dark skin.

He smiled wryly, twitched his eyebrows at her, and again disappeared below.

Sienna caught Ariel's arm. "You said you had glass you wanted worked?"

Ariel glanced back toward the boy, but it was too late to ask why he alone didn't come say hello like everyone else. She shook off her curiosity.

"Let me see it," Sienna continued. "Shards or sea glass?"

Ariel hesitated. The moon couldn't possibly have prodded her to Skunk merely for this, but she might as well trade with a Flame-Mage while she could.

"You're still an apprentice, aren't you?" she asked.

Sienna looked down her nose. "I'm eighteen, and glass was the first thing I made my master teach me. Candles and hearth coals are boring. I'll show you my work, if you don't believe me."

"I believe you." Ariel turned quickly to her pack. She knew what it was like to have her trade questioned.

Sienna studied Ariel's shards of glass. "What do you want of it?" she asked.

"Can you make me a bracelet—not beads, but a band?"

"I can, but it will be too thin," said Sienna. "It'll break the first time you bang it on a tree or a ladder. Beads will be stronger."

Ariel slumped. "I wanted something more special than beads."

"Here's another idea, then." Sienna held the glass against Ariel's dark locks. "Yes. Let me make clips for your hair. I can get two out of this. The glass catches the light and reflects your pretty eyes. And they won't break—unless you bang your head often." She winked. "Come, let me show you in my looking glass."

Ariel needed only a glance to know that the Flame-Mage was right. She admired the bright glints on her hair and tried not to see the old scar below, on her left cheek.

"Can you do it right now?" Ariel asked.

"Tomorrow. It will take a while to make the pit hot enough."

"What can I trade you?" Ariel scanned the platform that belonged to Sienna's family. It overflowed with clothing, bedding, and goods.

"Your necklace."

"No!" Ariel's fingers flew to her neck. "That's not a fair trade."

"Just teasing." Sienna flashed a smile. On coarser lips, it might have looked cruel.

"Scarl is a really good Finder," Ariel said. "He'll find for you, if you don't have a message you want me to carry."

Sienna gazed thoughtfully into the trees. "Let me think about it," she said finally, tucking the broken glass into Ariel's hand. "We can talk in the morning."

Ariel could tell by the look on her face that the Flame-Mage knew exactly what she wanted in trade. She just wasn't ready yet to declare it.

CHAPTER 9

Moonless Judging

Ariel returned to the common platform to find it empty, apart from Lamala fussing over where the guests should sleep for the night.

"We'll be comfortable here, if we won't be in somebody's way," Scarl assured her.

"You must have something to cushion the floor," Lamala insisted. She called to several children who stood below, petting the horse. "Go collect hare's ear," she told them. "Enough for two beds. Hurry, now!"

"Not from rabbits, I hope," Ariel said.

Lamala laughed. "Tender heart, are you? Don't fret. It's a weed."

Scarl caught Ariel's eye. They were alone with Lamala for a moment. Ariel took a deep breath and braced herself for the loss of Lamala's smile.

"Lamala?" She licked her lips. "Um . . . I was wondering . . ." She looked to Scarl for help.

His voice low, he said, "We're looking forward to hearing stories once the young ones are abed. But there is another thing, if I'm not mistaken, that you could provide us in trade. Would you handle the drawing that Ariel showed earlier? Tell us what you make of it as a Judge."

The woman drew back, misgivings creasing her brow. "Oh . . . isn't there something else I could do for you or have done? I'm not sure I want to do that."

"Why not?" Ariel asked.

Lamala squirmed. "I know your intentions are honorable, but . . ." She laid her hand along Ariel's cheek. "I mean no insult, dearling, and I'm grateful you've come. When I greeted you, though, I was taken aback. If you had not been breathing and warm, I would have said I'd touched a corpse."

She hurried past Ariel's wince and a choked sound from Scarl. "I've not met a Farwalker, ever, and I assumed it was simply your trade—back from the dead, as it were—that carried such clamminess with it. Then I saw your eel skull and thought perhaps I'd felt that death through you. But when you pulled out that cloth . . ." She shuddered and exhaled heavily. "It's like a stench on it."

Ariel unstuck her tongue from the roof of her mouth. "My map leads to . . . death?" Was she too late already, and the sender had gone from the world? What would that mean for the Vault, or for Zeke? A shiver raced over her skin, defying the sticky heat.

"No, no. I cannot say that," Lamala said. "I don't understand it at all."

"It's a copy of something quite old," Scarl said. "Are you sure—"

"I know, I know." Lamala groaned. "I wish I could say that explained it. It won't. Old Tattler feels like a nighty-night story next to this."

"Do you think they're related?" he pressed.

"I certainly hope not. I'd be much more afraid of our own heeber-jeeber in that case."

They stood together in silence. Lamala looked from Scarl to Ariel and sympathy softened her face. She sank to her knees and held out her hand. "Give it over, then, Ariel. If you can carry it, I ought to be able to judge it for you. Perhaps I'll be reassured, after all."

They joined her on the floor. Ariel gave her the crumpled linen. Lamala smoothed it between her palms and tipped her head, her eyes distant.

"I would not have called it a map, if you had not," she said. "To me it feels more like . . . an open hole." She cast Ariel an apologetic look. "I almost said a grave, but that isn't quite right. It has the same shadow of loss, but also a promise of filling up. Fixing. Planting . . . yes. Sowing. Which should be a good thing." She shook her head. "And even death leads to new starts, so I cannot fathom why this disturbs me so much. I'm quite sure I'm not judging it clearly. I don't know why. It's almost as if it's not really here. Just a shadow."

Ariel grasped for an explanation that could offer some comfort. "Because it's a copy?"

"No. Because it's a hole. I can't tell you much better than that." She looked at the drawing. "Yes. You see? Round holes spilled across it. If I were to guess, I might say the drawing represented a well. But a dangerous one with no bottom."

Ariel flinched, struck hard by a memory of the moon in the well at the abbey. "There's not a well like that here, is there?"

Lamala grunted. "Heavens, no. We only dig wells during droughts."

A babble of approaching voices signaled the children's return.

"Thank you for your judging," Ariel murmured. Scarl echoed her.

Lamala offered the map to the Finder. "I'd feel better if you carried this," she told him. "She's young for such a burden. In fact, I'd ask you to burn it, if I thought you would listen. But I can feel the pull it has on you both."

Ariel reached for the cloth. "It's mine," she said softly. "I'll bear it." She tucked it away.

"How long can I keep you here, safe, then?" Lamala asked. "You're more than welcome for as long as you like."

Ariel closed her eyes and posed the question to her feet. Since she and Scarl had arrived, she'd been distracted by excitement and the hope that her quest for the sender might end here. Now, turning inward, she felt the urge to keep moving southeast. Skunk was a waypoint, not a goal. Her heart sank.

She opened her eyes and parted her lips to speak.

Not yet. Linger. Gather.

Ariel gasped and tipped her face toward the sky. She could not see through the cypress and vines, but the waning moon should not be visible at this time of day, anyway. Still, it had spoken, hidden or not.

"What's wrong?" Scarl asked.

"Nothing," Ariel said. "Just thinking. We'll stay tonight . . . ?" She couldn't prevent her voice from rising in a question. "And maybe tomorrow?" But the sky did not comment.

"No longer," she added, more comfortable obeying her feet than a lunatic voice. "And then we'll continue southeast."

She gritted her teeth when Lamala pleaded with them to stay for a week. Scarl cut short her pressure with a polite but no-nonsense refusal. Grateful, Ariel promised herself she would tell him that the moon had begun muttering again. Later. Or . . . maybe only if it happened again.

Lamala's errand boys and girls hauled up armloads of rushes. One side of each rush was lined with cottony fluff. Piled with the soft sides turned up, they would make well-cushioned beds. While the Judge supervised their arrangement, Ariel climbed down from the platform with Scarl, who wanted to make sure Willow had forage. They discovered that a son of Lamala's had already taken charge of the horse, leading him off to a rise where his hooves could dry out.

"I'm going to wander around," Ariel said. "I'd like to find a big rock I can stomp on for Zeke."

"Ariel, before you go . . ." Scarl scanned the vines around them and Ariel realized he was hunting for words. When he found them, he said, "I'm troubled by Lamala's sense of your map. I'm not sure it's wise to continue."

"But . . ." The Judge's words had frightened her, too, but she hadn't considered turning aside from her path. "We have to."

"No, we don't. I'll be honest. I'm concerned about the Vault and the threat of your work somehow coming undone, and I'd love to meet anyone, human or not, who could have sent out the darts. But I'm more worried I won't be able to protect you from whatever lies ahead."

"You can't protect me forever," she whispered.

"I can try. But does that mean you still want to keep going?"

"No." Her voice hitched. "I just don't have any choice. The cherry, Zeke's stones—you heard what they said. Besides, if we go home, I'll go crazy at night, like before. I . . . The moon just spoke again, Scarl. For the first time since we left. Like it's creeping up on me the moment we stop." She took a steadying breath and added more firmly, "My feet want to keep going, whether I do or not. And you always say I should listen to them."

He ran his hand along his jaw, his face grim, but he nodded. "All right. I trust your farwalking sense. But I wanted to pose the option, at least."

"I wish we had one." A scary thought flared in her mind. "Thanks for sticking with me."

"Don't think you've grown so old as that. I wouldn't allow you to do it alone. I'm not sure I should even let you out of my sight."

"I'll be okay," she said. "Honest."

Scarl studied her briefly. "Don't go far. Watch out for snakes."

Snakes were the least of Ariel's worries. She hadn't found a single answer here, only more questions. Many of her trips had stretched longer than this one, but none before had been driven by fear. She wished she knew for certain that Zeke was all right. She couldn't forget the warning that his trade might be at risk.

She asked the first person she met if Skunk had any boulders. When the answer was no, she let her feet guide her. Perhaps they'd lead her instead to whatever the moon felt she ought to gather. Her first impulse was to splash away from the village in the same direction she'd been traveling before, but when she resisted, her feet only meandered below the platforms. She never found even a small rock, but eventually she passed a thicket where a young boy was picking bog-berries.

He waved shyly. She waved back.

A thought struck her. "Hey," she called out to him. She stepped nearer. After learning his name, she lowered her voice and asked, "Do you know the story of Tattler?"

Connor glanced both directions before nodding quickly. A spike of guilt slid through Ariel.

"Never mind," she said. "I don't want to get you in trouble."

He shook his blond tangles, beckoned, and whispered, "Come on."

She followed him into the shelter of an overhung bough. He turned solemn eyes on her and said, "Everyone knows Tattler, and I'm too big for nightmares. I'll tell you."

"Don't leave anything out."

By the time Ariel left Connor, she'd heard all she thought she needed to know about Tattler.

CHAPTER 10

Moonless Night

The tangled branches and vines over Skunk sped the nightfall. In the darkness, Ariel could barely see the figures on the common platform. A candle in a clay bowl between them cast more shadows than light. She recognized Scarl by his shape, but only the voices told her Lamala was among those who sat talking with him.

"Ariel," Scarl called. "We've been waiting for you."

"You wanted to hear about Tattler," said Lamala. "I hope you won't be disappointed. I probably made too big a fuss." As Ariel joined them, she added, "Wyn can tell you the story. He's got the best voice for spooking."

Wyn, a grizzled Reaper hardly larger than Ariel, rubbed his hands together. He leaned forward over the candle to speak directly to her. Lit from below, his weathered face hung eerily in the dark.

"Time was," he began in a low, raspy voice not much over a whisper, "a giant lived on the edge of the swamp. Tattler, folk called it, half live thing, half mountain. If you were foolish enough to go see for yourself, you'd meet a beast with four legs twice as tall as a tree, three bug-eyes that stare out over the swamp, two funnel ears sharp as those on a bat, and a sting like a whole swarm of bees."

Ariel feigned interest in case he could make out her face. She'd heard stories of giants and monsters before. What she'd heard about this one sounded completely made up. The telling darts were real, and so was whatever had sent them—not any beast with three eyes.

"Time was," Wyn repeated, "Tattler was friendly, and it used those big eyes and ears to watch over folks. It kept us all safe. But something went wrong. Some claim the moon burnt out Tattler's eyes. Others say Tattler went blind in the war, just like everyone else. A few say it died of old age. That one's not true. Tattler still listens, but now it's gone mad, and it listens for the footsteps of children to eat. Any who wander too far in the swamp. It eats every part but their eyeballs and teeth. Those it sends home with a slingshot. Even if it can't manage to catch you and eat you, it tattles. It whistles so loud we can hear it in Skunk, so we know some young scamp has been wandering. It likes to hear the sound of behinds being whupped."

Despite her disappointment that this monster was fake, Ariel laughed. Connor hadn't mentioned that part.

"It isn't so funny when the backside is yours," Wyn said sternly, but she did not miss his wink.

"Time was," he continued, "before the earth grew so wet, Tattler sometimes came here. But Tattler doesn't like water, so it never strays this deep into the swamp anymore. It stays on the edge of the world by itself. Make sure you stick close to where you belong, too. When the wind's right, you might hear it whining, 'cause it's hungry for someone to eat. And the last person from Skunk who went to meet it never showed up again."

Wyn crossed his arms and leaned back, letting his warnings sink in.

"You see?" Lamala said. "It's little more than a bugaboo tale to make children behave."

Scarl pursed his lips, giving it more consideration than Ariel expected. "It contains a few interesting details, though."

"You don't really think the darts were sent with a slingshot, do you?" Ariel tried to keep the scorn from her voice.

The silence before he answered told her she hadn't succeeded. "Of course not. But most stories hold kernels of truth."

"Oh, I've no doubt there's something out there," Lamala said. "Or there was. A hoodoo for the wind to sing through, most likely, maybe even one with a frightening face. Or a granddaddy tree, though our Tree-Singer won't hear of that. But the rest of the story is nonsense."

Ariel couldn't hold her tongue. Wyn had barely mentioned the most frightening part of what Connor had told her. She asked casually, "What about the crazy woman?"

The candle flickered in silence.

"Who told you that?" Lamala asked.

"She's right," someone said. "That part isn't nonsense."

Lamala fussed with her hands. "It doesn't bear mentioning, either."

"It might," Scarl prompted.

"It's shameful," said Lamala. "It's the reason we don't have a Storian here. While I was a tot, we still did. Her name was Vi Storian, and she told the most wonderful tales about old times and the flood that created the swamp. But when disease took her husband and daughter at once, her mind broke. Sometimes she ranted and screamed at the moon. She scratched herself until she bled. Her apprentices got scared off and took up other trades. At last the Judge before me decided Vi had to go. They forced her out of the village. Some fool ran his mouth about sending her to Tattler so the two could be mad together, and in her confusion, she took up those words. She vowed she would go and be eaten so her ghost could take vengeance on Skunk. She's the one in Wyn's story who never came back."

"She said if she wasn't eaten, she'd tame it and send it to eat us instead," Wynn added. "You can see we're still here."

"Vi should be, too," said Lamala. "That's no way to treat somebody crazy from grief."

Ariel was glad no one from Skunk knew that she had heard the moon speak. Clearly not all were as kind as Lamala.

"What did Tattler do before it went mad?" Scarl asked. "Besides watch over people."

"If you ask me," huffed Lamala, "its name should have been Gossip. We've got a few of those taking Tattler's job, and sometimes I'd like to send them away, too."

Wyn chuckled. "That's a righteous Judge talking. We don't rightly know, but they say it sent messages telling folks what it saw, and it passed along secrets it heard from afar. That's how it can tattle on wandering kids. . . ."

Wyn went on, but Ariel's ears had stopped working. She heard only the echo of one phrase: "It sent messages." Connor had not mentioned that, either.

Scarl turned toward her. In the dark, she couldn't see his expression, but softly he said, "That might be a slingshot worth seeing."

The conversation moved on to other topics, other stories. Ariel stared at the candle, lost in thought, until Skunk's Tree-Singer joined them to complete their earlier trade.

"You'll still need to tell me all you can of the abbey," said the soft-spoken woman, whose first name was Raven. "My chattiest cypress couldn't say much about it except to assure me it stood in a grand forest of trees, far off on a mountain, and that nothing now troubled the Tree-Singers there." Encouraged by that news, since surely it meant Zeke was untroubled, too, Ariel was unprepared for what Raven said next: "The trees are more interested in you. The cypress would not tell me why, but they're definitely watching you pass and awaiting your actions—I suppose because a Farwalker's so strange nowadays, don't you think?"

Ariel doubted the trees' interest was quite so mundane, but she ignored the self-consciousness that rushed over her and repaid Raven by describing the abbey in depth. When her voice tired and Scarl offered to add a few details, Ariel thanked them both, said good night, and crawled to the nearest bed. She stretched out to settle her whirling emotions. The day had been too full of mountains and valleys, surprises and letdowns, confusion and hope. She felt as exhausted as if she'd actually been climbing.

The hare's ear was soft, though. Ariel's turmoil ebbed. Growing sleepy, she curled toward the voices floating out of the dark, glad they all came from people and not from the sky. Now and then she caught a word about the Vault or a phrase from a story she knew—or one she had lived.

Something behind her in the dark touched her arm.

With a squeak, she brushed at her shoulder and spun. Rushes scattered as she scrambled away from whatever had touched her.

The nearby voices halted.

"Ariel? All well?" Scarl called.

Her eyes fought to identify the large shadow that had crept

up behind her. She imagined Tattler, come to eat her, or at least a great snake. But when the shape coalesced out of the gloom, the green-eyed boy she'd seen earlier was crouching before her. She couldn't imagine how he'd drawn so close without making a sound. His teeth flashed in a smile. Her heart resumed, thudding.

Footsteps approached, led by Scarl's uneven gait.

"It's all right," she said as he dropped his hand on her shoulder.

"Oh, don't be startled," said Lamala, who had also come to investigate. "That's only Nace, my youngest. The one taking care of your horse. He's got a Kincaller's heart, and he's a bit of a wild creature himself."

The boy thrust Ariel a shallow basket draped with a cloth. She lifted the fabric. Fat, hairless caterpillars squirmed beneath.

"Ugh!" She shoved it back toward the boy.

Dismayed, he shook his head and refused to take it. Instead he blew on the uncovered worms. At once, the basket glowed as though filled with coals. Ariel and Scarl both exclaimed.

"Fire worms?" Scarl asked. "I've heard tales." He reached for the basket.

Lamala stepped in and took it instead. "Go on, Nace," she said kindly. "Girls aren't as fond of crawling things as you are."

His face fell. Nace whirled and vanished into the dark.

"Wait," Ariel said, too late.

"He meant to give you a night-light, I'm sure," Lamala told her. "But he doesn't understand other people very well sometimes."

Ariel gazed after him. Kincallers understood animals best. Their instincts helped them tend goats or chickens or bees for their trade. She'd always found such skills impressive, and she wished she hadn't recoiled from his gift. "Why won't he say hello?"

"He can't, I'm afraid, not like regular folk, and he's been teased enough to be skittish." Lamala smiled sadly. "I thought myself lucky to have a baby who never cried until I realized, at last, that he couldn't. Nace can't speak. He's a good lad, though. You needn't fear him."

Ariel felt a rush of sympathy. One of the Tree-Singers in the abbey chose not to speak except to the trees, but that wasn't the same as being mute whether you liked it or not. Silence seemed a cruel prison. She determined that, before she left Skunk, she would press Nace's hand in a silent hello.

"We can set this by the ladder to light your way if you need the privy before sunrise," said Lamala. She stepped away with the basket.

Ariel jumped to catch her. "I'd like to keep it by me," she said.

Lamala blinked. "You would?"

Ariel nodded. "I just never saw glowing caterpillars before. The glowworms in sea caves back home are as tiny as hairs, and they wink out if you make any sound."

With a shrug, the woman returned the basket. "Don't put 'em too close to your head," she warned. "As soon as dawn breaks they'll all crawl away, and you don't want them squirming into your hair by mistake."

Ariel stirred the worms with a fingertip. The touch inflamed them and left a trace of glow on her finger. She held it up in wonder and then looked back into the dark.

"Thank you, Nace," she called, hoping he was still near enough to hear. "I do like them." She hesitated. "Maybe I'll see you tomorrow."

She turned back toward her bed. The worms lit the amusement on Scarl's face.

"What?" she asked. "I think they're nice."

His grin gave way to a chuckle, but he said only, "You're right." He peered into the basket again before rejoining the other adults.

Ariel mounded her bedding once more, but as she lay down, she remembered Zeke's rocks. After failing earlier, she'd nearly forgotten.

She wiggled to retrieve a pebble from a small stash in her pack. She'd plucked them from a sandbar two days ago in case she had trouble finding more later. They were small, but she hoped Zeke would understand. Rocks were heavy.

Unfortunately, a pebble thrown here was more likely to drown than to vibrate the earth. Ariel squeezed the lump in her fist, a knot as unyielding as the distance between her and Zeke. She flung the rock off the platform, but did not hear it land.

Voices murmured nearby, though, as soothing as wavesong. Ariel lay back and fell asleep in the worms' eerie glow.

When she checked the basket the next morning, the glowworms had indeed left it empty—except for one pebble. Ariel told herself it must have been under the worms all along.

CHAPTER 11

New Dog Moon, Invisible

Get up, sleepy! We have goodies for you!"

In the filtered morning light, Ariel rubbed her eyes clear of sleep. Six or eight bouncing kids and several adults broke into a loud song about being born under a toadstool. Sienna was among them. Nace wasn't.

"I thought you might like to celebrate late," Scarl told her when the song ended. "Since you've only been fourteen for two days."

She grinned and allowed herself to be served pancakes with fruit, which were as tasty as any First Day pudding. Once the food had been eaten, Lamala prodded Sienna.

"Show Ariel some fun on the swing," she said. "Before she puts on clean clothes."

Sienna rolled her eyes, but the other kids whooped and scattered eagerly from the platform.

"You don't think it's fun?" Ariel asked the older girl.

"You might," Sienna replied with a long-suffering sigh. "Come on."

They squelched along a trail to a hollow where the swamp

deepened into a pond. A rope hung from a high tree branch. Kids swarmed the branches below. When they'd climbed high enough, they swung on the rope, screamed with glee, and splashed into the water. They emerged dripping with muck.

A little mud didn't scare Ariel. She hoisted herself into the tree, glad she'd left her map safe in her pack. When she reached a small jumping-off platform built partway up, new friends crowded around to instruct her. They argued about whether it was more fun to stand in the loop tied at the bottom of the rope or to sit on the knot just above it.

The first time, Ariel gritted her teeth. She swooped into space and almost back to the tree before convincing herself to let go. The dunking felt the way fruit tasted, both explosive and sweet. Her second flight left her dizzy and giggling. She'd just taken the rope for her third turn when she spied Nace perched in another tree nearby. A small green snake coiled through his fingers as he watched.

"Hello, Nace," Ariel called.

He raised a hand from the snake in greeting.

"Want a turn?" she asked, twitching the rope.

He considered before he set his snake loose and swung down from his branch.

"Nace is the best," said Connor at Ariel's side.

"He should be," said Sienna, who stood below looking indulgent and bored. "He's been doing it since before you were born. He's only three years younger than I am."

"You're just jealous because you can't do tricks like he can," Connor retorted.

"Hardly." Sienna sniffed. "This is kid stuff."

Busy calculating that Nace was just a year older than she was, Ariel let the insult slide off.

The kids parted for Nace's arrival. His expression thoughtful, he did not smile, but his eyes met Ariel's warmly. He took the rope with a twitch of his eyebrows like the one he'd given her yesterday.

She watched as he climbed to the next higher branch and stuck one foot through the loop. He jumped—but only held the rope for an instant. By the midpoint of the swing, Nace was hanging upside down. His hair swept the water. As his body swung up the far side of the arc, he kicked free of the loop and somersaulted into the pond.

Ariel closed her gaping mouth as Nace emerged with a grin. She knew he'd been showing off for the stranger, but it had been a spectacular trick. The crowd clapped and cheered.

"I want to try that," Ariel said.

Connor scoffed.

Others took turns. Once Nace returned to the platform, Ariel reached for the rope and slipped her foot through the loop as he had.

Nace grabbed the rope to stop her. He made warning gestures.

"I won't hurt myself," she protested.

"Yes, you will," called Sienna from below. "One boy broke his collarbone and a girl nearly drowned copying Nace. He's not supposed to show off in front of the little kids."

Nace shot Sienna a look of annoyance.

Ariel's legs quivered, but she set her jaw. "Can't you teach me?" she asked.

Looking dubious, he lifted a palm to say, *Wait*. He pondered. Then he tugged the loop back off her foot. She stamped her boot in frustration.

He grinned and tapped his temple: he had an idea.

Nace put his bare foot through the loop and then reached to pat his back.

"Piggyback, Nace means to say," Connor told Ariel.

Nace reached toward her, inviting her into the curl of his arm.

She hesitated only an instant. Grabbing Nace's shoulder, she boosted herself onto his hip, more sideways than piggyback. Like a clumsy possum baby, Ariel clung and tried not to think just how much she was touching this boy or how he felt under her limbs.

"You're crazy," called Sienna.

"Hold tight?" Ariel asked.

Nodding, Nace wrapped his free arm around her waist, clamping her to his ribs so snugly it frightened her. Finally he tipped his head toward the pond, eyebrows lifted: *Ready?*

Her heart in her throat, Ariel kept her eyes on his face. The water would look too far down. She swallowed hard and gave him a nod.

"If you die," Sienna asked, "can I have your necklace?"

Nace winked at Ariel and shoved them both from the tree.

If even a second passed before Nace dropped his hold of the rope and they flipped head-down together, Ariel didn't feel it. Gripping him fiercely, she tried to watch the green blur, but her eyelids clamped shut by themselves. A screech pushed between her clenched teeth. Just as her courage caught up with her body, Nace kicked the rope free. They dropped. Entangled by Ariel, he strained to spin them so they didn't land on their heads. Water gulped them. They jolted against the muddy bottom, and Ariel let go to splash toward the air.

They both erupted from the pond. She was laughing almost before she could breathe. "That was great!"

His silence disconcerted her until she saw his pleased grin.

Nace retraced their fall with his hand, slamming his palms together and whistling a note of amazement.

Understanding perfectly, Ariel couldn't smother her giggles as she asked, "That didn't hurt, did it?" She knew he'd taken most of the impact and probably a knee or elbow from her.

He shrugged.

"Want to do it again?"

He shook his head hard enough to scatter droplets, and he raised one finger: *No. Once was enough.* But his grin widened.

Still flushed with adrenaline, Ariel beamed. "Okay. Thanks, though."

"Swing me, Nace! Swing me!"

Ignoring the chorus of pleas, he grabbed Ariel's hand and led her toward shallower water.

Much more aware of his hand than her feet, she stumbled twice. Nace kept her up. He dropped her hand just before they reached the other kids, but Ariel could feel his fingers wrapping hers long after he'd let go.

She took several more turns on the swing, but they felt tame after riding with Nace. He lingered near the other kids, helping the smaller ones haul the rope back to the tree. Ariel caught him watching her, though. Twice he dropped his gaze right away, as if backing down was a habit. The third time, it was Ariel who could not hold the look. His pale eyes burned hers.

The next time she glanced toward him, he was gone.

Deciding that dry clothes sounded better than another swing, she collected Sienna to return to the commons. The older girl shook her head at Ariel's mud-drenched condition.

"You should try it," Ariel told her. "It's like flying."

"I've done it, thank you." A smile softened Sienna's sarcasm. "I'm too old for that."

Ariel snorted. "I'm never going to get too old for fun."

"You'll just change your mind about what's fun." Sienna studied Ariel. "You think Nace is cute, don't you?"

Ariel blushed, but she couldn't halt the grin that popped onto her face. "Kinda."

"Watch out for him." The older girl glanced around for observers and lowered her voice. "He's not normal."

That was obvious, Ariel thought. "He's been nice to me."

"He's spooky," Sienna replied. "There's more wrong with him than his voice."

"Like what?"

Making a face, Sienna shook her head.

Impatience kindled in Ariel's chest. "Either tell me what it is or stop talking about him."

Sienna stared. Then she laughed and slid an arm around Ariel's shoulder. "Sassy girl. Never mind. You won't be here that long. I'm glad you came, though. This place needed excitement."

Mollified, Ariel returned her smile. Yet as she climbed the ladder to retrieve her dry clothes, Sienna's words twisted into her heart. Ariel was planning to leave the next morning. Tattler—or something—awaited. But to some inarticulate yearning inside her, tomorrow sounded rather too soon. The conflict was not hard to figure out, either. The Farwalker anxiously wanted to leave. The girl who had twined fingers with Nace didn't.

CHAPTER 12

Dark Dog Moon and Tides

Ariel wasted no time in grabbing dry clothes from her pack.

Loading his pack with the food they'd been offered in trade, Scarl canted his head at her grubby condition. "Looks like you enjoyed that," he said.

She grinned. "I sure did."

"Want to stay longer?"

The chance for more time with Nace sparkled before her, but only for a moment. Her smile faded. "I thought you wanted to see Tattler. It might be the sender."

"It might, and I do, if it still exists and isn't out of our way. It may be only a hoodoo, as Lamala suggested, but it sounds as though its reputation grew before the war, so it might tattle on the past a bit, too." He plucked his Finder's glass from his shirt pocket and waggled it between his fingers. "But I can find Tattler, whatever it is, by myself. You could stay here. Where I know you'll be safe."

Ariel's head began shaking before his words sank in completely. "Forget it, I'm— Hey, we should have thought of that sooner! Your Finder's glass could help with the map! You could just find the sender. Or at least our place on the—"

"I've tried, Ariel. Before we ever left the abbey. And again this morning, while you were gone."

Her jaw dropped. "It didn't work?"

With a rueful chuckle, he said, "I know you think I can find anything, and I appreciate that, but it's not true. Some part of me has to know what I'm seeking. And it has to be tangible. I can't find ideas."

"Couldn't you just find 'the place where the map leads'?"

He shook his head. "I told you, I've tried. Besides, I'm not convinced it's a place. It could be an event or a task. Don't forget the map is a calendar, too. And the hardest thing about finding is not to seek the wrong thing. If I make a false assumption, I could lead us astray. Badly. Farwalking seems to be a better trade in this case."

Ariel had to admit that her map was more than a route to a place. Her brief excitement faded. "Aw."

"I understand your frustration, believe me," he told her. "The more I look at your map, the more it mocks me. I can't get us to answers any faster than you can, but I could go investigate Tattler. Make sure it's no hazard. Perhaps rule it out. It also lies to the southeast, where we've been headed."

"It does?"

"I believe so."

That almost seemed proof Tattler waited for her. Tempted regardless to stay here and play, she struggled with her sense of responsibility, her reluctance to be parted from Scarl, and, not least, an uncomfortable awareness of time passing too fast.

Reminded of time, she said, "Oops. I forgot Sienna is waiting for me."

"Think about it," Scarl said. "You don't have to decide until morning."

Ariel retreated to the ground with her clothes and a knot of mixed feelings. To her surprise, Sienna had not given up and departed.

"Is everything all right?" the older girl asked.

"Yes." Ariel sighed. "It's just hard to be a Farwalker sometimes." She ducked behind a wide cypress to change.

When she stripped off her muddy garments, she groaned. Her drawers were spotted with menstrual blood. She always lost track of the days when they traveled, and her monthly period had surprised her again.

Sienna heard her groan. "What's wrong now—forget something? I'll get it for you."

Slipping her clammy trousers back on momentarily, Ariel emerged, her cheeks burning. "That's all right, I'll get it." Dropping her voice, she confided, "It's hard to be a girl sometimes, too."

"Ah," said Sienna. "I know what you mean."

She followed Ariel back onto the platform. Thankfully, Scarl paid them no mind as he worked, and Ariel found her clean rags near the bottom of her pack.

"That's what you use?" Sienna asked. "Those raveled old things?"

Heat rushed to Ariel's face. She mumbled, "What else?"

Sienna planted her hands on her hips and turned to the Finder. "Scarl? You remember Camity Allcraft? Ariel had a message for her yesterday."

Ariel hissed, "Sienna! What—"

Scarl glanced up. Ariel wanted to crawl into her pack. The best she could do was to cross her arms and hide her rag in the crook of her elbow.

"Of course," Scarl said.

"She lives on the second-to-last platform that way." Sienna pointed. "And she makes very nice bleeding garments. Go trade her some finding to get a few for Ariel."

Mortified, Ariel turned her back so she wouldn't have to see his expression. Sienna's bossy order burned in her ears, and she braced for awkward questions, if not a rebuff.

"All right," Scarl said. His boots tromped across the platform and dropped below.

Astonished, Ariel peeked up.

"What's with you?" the older girl asked. "Is it kept a secret where you come from?"

"Not exactly, but . . ." Ariel floundered. "Well, actually, yes. Pretty much."

"Silly," Sienna declared. "What do they think, everyone is a boy and babies come from storks?"

"No. From mermaids." Ariel giggled, her embarrassment boiling out. "We're all really fish. You can tell by the way we kiss." Seized by mad whimsy and desperate for some other subject, she puckered her lips to kiss the air like a fish.

"Oh, yeah? Well, this is how fish kiss around here!" Sienna flapped her wrists at her shoulders, sucked in her cheeks, and attacked. Ariel squealed and dodged. By the time Scarl returned, both girls were lying helplessly on the platform, shaking with laughter.

"I'm sorry I missed the joke," he said, handing Ariel a soft bundle.

Behind him, Sienna pursed her lips for a kiss, and that was enough to send Ariel off again.

Scarl continued over her peals. "Camity was happy to trade those for your message."

"Thank you for going," she gasped.

"Yes, thank you, Scarl," added Sienna. Her brilliant smile held no discomfort at all.

"No trouble." Before he turned back to his gear, he added, "Come talk to me, Ariel, when you're not busy and your giggles stop being contagious."

Her laughter stopped short.

"I'd better go check on the fire pit," said Sienna. "I'll come back soon, and we can chat more about your hair clips."

Ariel finished changing her clothes and hovered below the platform, stalling, before drawing a difficult breath and climbing back up. She might as well get it over with.

Scarl sat cleaning Willow's bridle. He slid aside his work to accommodate her. She knelt awkwardly.

"This isn't the very first time you've bled, is it?" he asked.

Ariel studied the planks near her knees and shook her head.

"Good, because I don't know much about it. Sienna can help, though, obviously. I—" He reached to tip her chin up. "Don't look so ashamed."

She tried to meet his gaze but could not.

"All right," he said. "I can see this is not a topic you want to discuss. But let me mention one thing. There's a tradition that says a woman can divine on the days that she's bleeding. Do you know of it?"

"No."

"They say the moon whispers into your thoughts then," Scarl explained. "Not everyone believes it, but the moon seems to speak with you anyway, and it was often my experience with Mirayna that those stories were true."

"Really?" Curiosity nudged aside some of Ariel's discomfort. "Like what?"

"Her intuition was strongest and she always did her best crafting then. And she first knew she was sick—"

Scarl looked away. He flexed his fingers as if to work out a cramp that Ariel knew gripped his heart, not his hand. After exhaling at length, he went on. "Other things as well. Dreams about things that hadn't happened yet, then did. We had a terrible argument once when she told me I already had a daughter borne by somebody else. I didn't believe that one." His gaze returned pointedly to Ariel. "Not at the time. But I'm sure she glimpsed the future."

"Wow," Ariel breathed, wondering if her mother had known any such stories.

"Yes," he agreed. "It often scares men, which is why some places treat your bleeding as Canberra Docks must have. But I'm glad to use it, if we can. You might study the map again with that power in mind. Perhaps you'll divine something to reassure me."

"Actually, I already noticed something that might be a hint from the moon." Ariel retrieved her map and unfurled it. "Lamala called these dots 'holes.' You said they couldn't be months because there were thirteen, not twelve. But that's not the only way to count months. Women count months with the moon—thirteen full in one year, thirteen new in the next."

"Mm. Could be." His fingers tapping, Scarl counted from the top to the moon pierced by an arrow: ". . . six, seven, *eighth* moon."

"August, in most years," she said. "I told you so. Full moon, I suppose. Wouldn't you draw the arrow through the space between dots for a dark moon?"

He nodded. "It points to a day, then. Not just a month. A day marked by August's full moon."

"The Dog Moon."

Scarl glanced skyward. "Let's see, the July moon must be getting thin. . . ."

"Dark moon tonight." Fighting a blush, Ariel added, "The bleeding almost always starts then."

"Ah. So we've got two weeks."

Ariel thought wistfully about lingering in Skunk. But they had no idea how far away Tattler might actually be.

"Two weeks until what, though?" Scarl continued. "Something happens? Something stops? Or something needs to be done? And why does it matter?"

A chill ran through Ariel. Skunk's fetid smells and overgrown vegetation pressed too tightly around her. In a flash of panic, she jumped up. Her legs wanted to run.

Concern flooded Scarl's face. He reached toward her. "Ariel, what? Did you just glimpse some answer to my questions?"

"No. The swamp air just smothers me, that's all." Her voice trembled. "I need to get away for a walk. I feel trapped."

She hurried away, but she felt Scarl's frown on her back as she went.

CHAPTER 13

Dog Moon and Decisions

Ariel nearly trampled Sienna, who was just mounting the platform.

"The pit is hot enough for me to make your hair clips," said the Flame-Mage.

Ariel brightened. Her walk could wait until they'd worked out the deal. "Did you think of something fair to trade?"

"Yes." Sienna's eyes darted toward Scarl. She squared her shoulders and announced, "I want you to take me when you leave here. As far as the next village, at least."

Ariel choked. "What for?"

"I'm eighteen and I want to get married." A plaintive note slipped into Sienna's voice. "And have a baby. There is nobody in Skunk for me to marry except little boys who still have to grow up or men who are too closely related to me."

"But I don't know where we're going next," Ariel said. "I want to keep walking southeast, but there might not be any village that way. Nobody here thinks anything's out there except Tattler."

"Fairy tales don't scare me," Sienna replied. "Are you going to walk off the edge of the world?"

Ariel fidgeted. "I don't think so."

"Of course not. So you'll have to arrive somewhere eventually. That'll do."

"There may not be anyone there who is better."

"There has to be," Sienna insisted. "At least I won't be cousins with anyone there, and they'll all be new and interesting, not people I'm bored with. Even if there's nobody I want to marry, I'm a good Flame-Mage. I can trade for food and somewhere to sleep."

Shaking her head, Ariel said, "How about this? I'll come back for you before I go home and take you somewhere I've already been." Ariel ignored the muttering fear that she might not return from this particular trip. "Somewhere nice. Before winter. Okay?"

"No. Now. That's the trade for the hair clips." Sienna's face hardened. "Do you want them or not?"

Ariel gave Scarl a look of dismay. He was watching, his features so blank that she knew he thought ill of the idea but was trying not to show it.

"Don't look to me," he said. "It's your decision. Whether we both leave tomorrow or not."

"I was thinking of staying a bit longer in Skunk," Ariel explained to Sienna. It wasn't quite true, but she hoped it might dissuade the Flame-Mage.

"Fine. I'll go with you as soon as you leave."

"It could be weeks before we arrive anywhere, though. You'll have to walk the whole way." Ariel described blisters and biting insects and storms, as well as the chance they might run low on water or food.

"It'll be worth it," Sienna said. "I'll bring anything you say I need. I'll make a fire every night and every morning, if you want, and I'll cook for you, too. I won't complain a word. Ask my master. He'll tell you—I've never groused about burns or anything he set me to do."

Ariel huffed air into her bangs. "Just a minute."

She approached Scarl to whisper with him. He heard her concerns, nodding, and he reminded her that she could also talk to Sienna's master about working the glass, or find another Flame-Mage somewhere else. He remained adamant, however, about leaving the choice to her.

And she very much wanted the hair clips that Sienna had helped her imagine.

Ariel's fingers rose to worry her necklace as she struggled with the decision. Something tickled the back of her mind. It wasn't the voice of the moon but an intuition, contrary to all common sense, that she should agree to the deal.

Ariel turned back to the Flame-Mage. "The next village, whatever and wherever it is."

"Anywhere that's not here," Sienna said.

"If you change your mind after we leave, you find your way back by yourself."

Scarl raised his eyebrows at that, but Sienna nodded. "All right. But I won't."

"Okay."

Sienna whooped and drummed her feet on the platform. "I'm so excited! It'll be fun."

"I guess it might," Ariel allowed, catching Sienna's enthusiasm.

"I promise it will. Thank you." Sienna graced Scarl with her smile as well, repeating her thanks.

He only waggled his head with an expression that said, "We'll see."

Sienna turned quickly back to Ariel. "So we leave tomorrow, or later, or what? Tomorrow's not too soon for me."

An image of Nace rose in Ariel's mind, and the hand he'd held tingled, but she hadn't forgotten the map, either. Or a Tattler to find in two weeks. She nodded. "Yes. Early."

Her decision not to stay here in safety while Scarl sought Tattler didn't please him much, either. But he said nothing.

"Where's your glass, then?" Sienna asked. "I've got to start now to finish properly."

Ariel retrieved it and handed it over. Watching Sienna depart, she imagined leaving Skunk with her the next day. The uncertainty of what lay ahead weighed upon her. Reluctant to face it or make preparations, she spurted away to escape for her long-delayed walk.

After charging blindly down the ladder, she headed in a direction she hadn't explored yet. A sharp whistle stopped her. When she looked around, Nace was waving at her from a distance. He crooked a finger at her: *Come here*. His other arm cradled a bundle.

Willingly Ariel gave up on her walk. As she caught up with Nace, he gestured for her to follow.

"Where are we going?" She didn't expect an answer but couldn't help wondering aloud.

He turned toward her. Hesitant, he tapped a finger near his eye.

"To see . . . ?"

Beaming, he nodded and added a few other quick gestures she couldn't begin to interpret.

"To see . . . something." She sighed.

His smile sank.

Ariel stepped forward. "Okay, let's go."

Nace tipped his head to ponder her. Ariel wished she could hear his thoughts even more than she wished he could speak.

He reached for her hand, watching her face to gauge her reaction. At first she thought he was trying another way to communicate with her. When she realized he meant only to hold it, her heart quickened, pumping heat to her face. But she didn't pull her fingers away. His grin returning, he led her on.

This time, their hands weren't muddy, but Ariel's quickly grew sweaty. She groaned inwardly, certain Nace must think she had a squid attached to her wrist rather than fingers. Her skin felt so fishy she didn't realize his palm was as sweaty as hers.

They passed Willow, tethered on drier ground. Nace clucked to the horse, earning a whinny, but did not pause. After another short distance, he released Ariel's hand to put one finger to his lips, telling her to be quiet.

Slowly they crept to the edge of a clearing. A litter of fox kits scampered about a hollow log while Mama Fox yawned in the sun.

Ariel crowed under her breath. The mother fox jerked her snout toward them. Nace whistled softly, a few notes repeated. Her ears flicked, but she didn't get up. One careful step at a time, Nace drew Ariel forward. Not far from the log, he sank to his knees in the grass, pulling her with him.

The mother fox slowly relaxed, and the kits wrestled and gnawed on each other. Nace grinned at Ariel's muffled giggles.

He unwrapped the bundle he'd tucked under his arm. Ariel could smell the melon before the cloth fell away. With it were cold meat and honeycomb. He tapped his stomach and pointed at her: *Are you hungry?*

Ariel didn't need to be hungry to eat melon or honeycomb. She nodded eagerly.

They nibbled and watched the fox babies. Although she enjoyed them, Ariel's gaze kept straying to Nace. With a few whispered yes-or-no questions, she learned that the honeycomb came from a hive he tended himself. Her praise made him glow.

Silence rested between them again. Ariel wanted to scratch it.

"When we were swinging this morning," she said, "and you wanted me to jump on piggyback, the kids understood the movement you made." He shrugged, and she continued. "Will you teach me more of your words?"

He licked melon juice from his fingers for so long, she feared she'd offended him. But at last he pointed to the foxes and repeated the gesture he'd made earlier when she'd asked where they were going. This time, Ariel understood it as a reference to pointed noses and ears.

"Fox," she said. He nodded.

They spent a few minutes on easy signs for their food, the grass, and their clothing. Most were obvious with the things there before her. Ariel quickly realized, however, that ideas or actions would be much harder to put into gestures.

When he ran out of items nearby, he stopped, his face no longer bright. She didn't push for more. Instead of helping her talk with him better, their efforts had mostly sharpened the gulf between them.

With regret, Ariel reached to squeeze his forearm. "Thank you," she said. "I'll try to remember all those."

She let go, but Nace caught her wrist and drew her hand back. He traced designs on her palm. Ariel's breath stopped. It felt as though he were singing to her hand.

Goose bumps rippled through her, without sign of abating, until at last she slid her hand from his grasp. His touch was even more delicious than the honeycomb, but too overwhelming.

"Nace, I—," she began, not sure whether an apology or explanation would follow. His green gaze shot up to meet hers, and his fingers leaped to still her lips.

Two things instantly struck Ariel. The first was the startled look in his eyes, as if she'd silenced him and not the other way around. The second was an old memory of Scarl hushing her thus—and how utterly different the Finder's curt motion had felt. Nace's touch was intended not to tame her but to keep her in the wild.

Their eyes locked. Neither breathed, but Nace did not lower his fingers. Instead they slid, light as feathers, to trace Ariel's mouth. They stayed to travel the scar on her cheek and follow it back to her lips. He watched his fingertips move as if they belonged to somebody else.

Engulfed in invisible fire, Ariel parted her lips to say something, with no idea what. Accordingly, nothing came out.

Nace caught his own lower lip in his teeth.

That scared her. Fingers on lips were startling enough. Two sets of lips were a kiss. On the brink of a territory she'd never explored, Ariel faltered. She shrank back an inch.

Nace's fingers hovered and dropped. His gaze followed. He studied the grass between them, his hair falling forward to veil his expression. His breathing, and hers, sounded too loud in the silence. Unsure whether he was hurt or angry or something else altogether, Ariel said the only words that might work regardless.

"I'm sorry!"

Still flooded with fizzing sensations, she jumped up and fled.

CHAPTER 14

Dark Dog Moon's First Night

What amazed Ariel most was how Skunk and Scarl and everything else could still be the same when she felt so different.

She'd run all the way back to the village and then paced below the common platform, shaking. She climbed up only when Scarl called down to ask if that was her splashing around. Carefully she peeped over the top of the ladder. She expected him to take one look and see that she'd held hands with a boy she'd thought, for a moment, might kiss her.

Scarl only asked if she was hungry. Dumbfounded, she shook her head and sank down near her pack, hoping she looked busy with it, when in fact she was staring at the gray wood beneath and seeing nothing. She relived the last hour and worried about the next time she saw Nace.

Scarl went off on some errand. With the platform to herself, Ariel could swoon and fret freely. She thought of Sienna. She jumped up to find the Flame-Mage, wanting to share what had happened. She dropped back to her seat almost as fast. Sienna had spoken ill of Nace.

When Scarl returned, Ariel watched him anxiously. She longed to tell someone about the astonishing things she'd just felt, but she didn't know how he'd react.

"Scarl?" When he gave her his attention, she couldn't make her mouth go any farther except to add, "Nothing."

He raised one eyebrow at her. "That's a little hard to believe." She shook her head impatiently.

"Okay, well . . . my ears will work later, too." He studied her. "Change your mind about staying? You can."

She could. She could eat another picnic with Nace and splash with him through the swamp again, fingers knit. She could tell him to kiss her, if that's what he wanted.

A pained laugh escaped her. She could never do that. The mere idea made her tremble. Besides, she feared the moon would start niggling again. Would Nace look at her differently if he knew she heard a voice from the sky?

"No, I can't. I can't stop here, Scarl. We have only two weeks."

He wanted to reassure her, to convince her to stay. She could see it in his face. But when he finally spoke, he said only, "And Sienna?"

Ariel wrinkled her nose. "That'll be all right, I think. I know it's odd, but I want her to come."

"Hmm. I suppose she can't be any worse than that fellow from Ajian."

The unfortunate Storian of whom Scarl spoke had been so nervous about leaving home that he'd counted each step aloud and hiccuped the whole way to the abbey. Remembering, Ariel snickered and mimicked his hiccup. That made her laugh. Soon, for the second time that day, irrational mirth overtook her.

Scarl shook his head in wonder. "The moon does something to you, that's clear. I'll try not to be so amusing."

Laughing harder, she managed, "Please!"

Gasping, Ariel lay back on the platform to stare at the sky and ponder how she had lost all control of her body. As her giggles leaked out, though, so did her unsettled feelings. Thoughts of Nace still made her quiver, but she began looking forward to walking again. Tattler might be a giant as well as the telling darts' sender, and she could lead them to meet it. Farwalking she knew, understood, and was good at—unlike holding hands with a boy or having to tell him good-bye.

Nearly everyone in Skunk came by that afternoon or evening to wish Ariel and Scarl a good journey. Several brought gifts. Others asked the Farwalker to carry messages or small items to trade. Nowhere among the visitors did Ariel spot Nace. Kept busy, she slipped away only briefly to check for him at the tree swing. It hung silent and still. He wasn't tending their horse, either.

"I haven't seen him since this morning," said Lamala when Ariel plucked up the nerve to ask. "He's like that. Disappears for long stretches. I don't worry."

Ariel considered a return to the foxes' clearing. The possibility of meeting him there alone made her feel too weak.

As night fell, Sienna's voice rose up the ladder. "Hail above." She ascended partway. "Am I interrupting?"

"No," Ariel replied, eager for distraction. "Oh! Did you bring my hair clips?"

But Sienna stepped up empty-handed. Ariel held her breath, afraid Sienna might have goofed and ruined the glass.

"They're perfect, just wait till you see them," the Flame-Mage told her. "But they have to cool slowly. I'll get them for you right before we leave."

She peppered Ariel with questions about what to pack. By the time Sienna left to prepare, Ariel wondered how much sleep the young woman would get.

Ariel neglected her own bed until late, too, in the hope that one more visitor might still appear. At last, though, stuck between disappointment and relief, she tossed another pebble for Zeke and dropped to her blanket to untie her boots. Sleep overcame her as irresistibly as her laughing fits had. She never twitched when Scarl finally pried off her second boot and tucked her blanket around her.

If she could, she would have invited Nace into her dreams, but it was Scarl who appeared there. He was crouched in the lane outside her mother's cottage, and distantly Ariel knew it was being at home, not Scarl's presence there, that was wrong. His Finder's glass glinted in his palm. Wondering what he was seeking, she came up behind him and peeked over his shoulder.

Like amber could trap insects, the glass in his palm held a flickering, crimson flame.

"Oh!"

At Ariel's noise, the fire leaped beyond the bounds of the glass. She and Scarl both flinched. To trap it, the Finder clenched his fingers so hard the glass crunched and blood or liquid flame oozed from his fist. He spun toward Ariel. She cringed, expecting his anger.

"That's all right." He opened his bloody hand to drop the shards of his glass. No fire remained. "The moon will lead you, if you listen."

The tinkling of the glass as it fell hurt her ears. Ariel clapped her hands to them.

The jolt knocked her awake. The shadows of boughs overhung her, as they so often did, and the newborn Dog Moon could offer no light, but Ariel knew where she was. The wooden platform was hard through the hare's ear. Its solid reality brought her relief. Scarl's dark figure was stretched out not far away, his blanket rumpled alongside him and his slow breathing nearly as familiar as her own.

With her nightmare still glittering behind her eyes, she raised her fingers to the glass in her necklace. Finding the cool droplet of her largest green bead, her fingers fanned to encompass the rest.

No other lumps met her fingers. Instead she felt only her warm neck and the string holding the bead.

Her hand patted . . . slid . . . clutched at her throat. Only the one bead, the original, remained on her necklace. She sat up with a jerk and then whimpered, afraid the motion might have scattered beads that had somehow come loose. Was that the clatter of them bouncing away, or just the rustle of her bedding? Ariel's free hand swept through the hare's ear, rattling more, before a small fact pierced her growing panic: the bead she still possessed hung from a ribbon, not the satin cord Scarl had given her. Moreover, her necklace had not come untied. She could feel the knot's pressure against the back of her neck as she tugged on the bead from the front.

"What?"

Ariel jumped. Scarl's shadow hunkered beside her. She saw a wink of starlight off his knife blade.

He added, "Somethin' crawl on you? Bite?" Though his voice was heavy with sleep, he grabbed her arm, preparing to yank her to safety if necessary, and his grip felt plenty alert. "Sounded like you were thrashing."

Ariel moaned. "No."

His hold on her relaxed. "Nightmare?" She'd told him about the unsettling dreams in which she'd slipped so surely back to her old life in Canberra Docks, the past bright and sharp around her until she stumbled or turned a corner to find herself instead in the abbey.

She fumbled for the right answer. "No, my necklace is gone!"

"It came untied?" He put away his knife and patted the reeds around them. "I'm not usually so feeble with knots. But we'll find it in the—"

"No, look!" She grabbed his hand and pulled it to the single bead still around her neck.

His fingers found it, alone. Both his hands rose then, following the ribbon to meet behind her neck, then back down. His head cocked.

"How'd you manage that?"

"I don't know. Am I still dreaming?"

"Not unless I'm sharing your nightmare. Maybe Zeke was right and you are moving about in your sleep."

"You would have heard me sooner. I can hardly roll over without waking you."

"We could have used your glowworms tonight. Just a minute." He turned and rummaged in his pack. A spark caught his tinder and, from there, a small candle. Ariel's hands rose to dash at her eyes before he lit her tears.

Scarl turned with the light and grunted. "Now, my fingers are not so dull as that!"

At his expression, Ariel clapped one hand back to her

necklace—her new one, intact, every bead in its place. A sound that was half sob and half laugh burst from her. Scarl lifted the candle so close to her chin that her bangs wafted in its heat. He touched the necklace again, too, and scowled at her.

Anticipating him, she protested, "It wasn't me! You felt it, too. It was just the one bead!"

"How'd you switch it so fast?"

"I didn't. It changed. Like a shadow chased away by your light."

He studied her face.

"I don't know how," she added, "but it did." She pressed the beads to her skin as if to embed them. "I'm just glad my new one is back."

He blew out the candle. In the fresh dark, they both felt her necklace, fingers tangling along the beads. There was no mistaking them.

"Well . . . ," Scarl said at last. It sounded as though he meant to keep speaking, but he simply set the candle aside. "Best try to sleep again, I suppose."

Neither of them really succeeded.

CHAPTER 15

Dog Moon, Slender Crescent

Ariel's only disappointment with her hair clips was that Nace didn't see her wearing them. Affixed to thin folds of metal, they slid snugly into her hair, their luster as perfect as Sienna had promised. They coordinated well with her necklace, which had ceased any tricks. Yet only a few early risers had a chance to admire them, since Ariel led her companions away from Skunk just after dawn. The horse had been hitched at the base of the platform, bridled and waiting, and her heart tripped when she saw him. But Nace did not appear in the small crowd that came to see the visitors off.

Sienna's family made up most of the well-wishers. Though her mother cried, Sienna never wavered. She'd carefully followed Ariel's packing instructions, and Willow flattened his ears at the unusually large load that was lashed to his back. Once the Flame-Mage's tools were secure, Scarl took up his walking stick and the travelers marched away to a chorus of goodwill and good-bye.

Once they'd passed beyond the network of trails around Skunk, Ariel paused to adjust their course into the wilds. She let both hands flit to her head, fingering the newly shaped glass there as she felt for the call of her feet.

"Confused already?" Sienna asked. "You're not going to get us lost, are you?"

"Hush, Sienna," Scarl said. "That isn't confusion."

Sienna walked silently next to Ariel for a long time after that. Ariel stayed quiet as well, wishing she'd had a final look into Nace's eyes. Soon, though, she felt a burst of relief at moving southeast again, and her natural cheer surfaced.

She asked Sienna about local flowers and birds as they passed. The Flame-Mage's replies were all short and subdued. Finally Ariel tucked an arm through Sienna's.

"Why won't you talk?" she asked. "This was supposed to be fun."

"I don't want to make Scarl mad again," Sienna murmured.

Ariel laughed. "You haven't seen him mad, believe me. If he gets sick of hearing us, he'll just drop back out of earshot. He does it with my friend Zeke and me all the time."

Sienna asked about Zeke, so Ariel told her how he heard stones, just as Tree-Singers heard trees, and how he ran across meadows with the abbey's herd of goats, and how he'd hurt his hands helping to save her from a fall. The conversation flowed more freely from there. The older girl enjoyed showing off her knowledge of things that would burn. She told funny tales about people in Skunk, and she listened appreciatively when Ariel sang her Farwalker's song. Ariel made up a verse for Sienna:

Walk toward the morning sun,
Guiding Sienna.
New friends make travel fun:
Walk, talk, and laugh.

By the end of the day, Scarl indeed lagged with the horse, keeping the girls just in sight, but Ariel felt as though she'd known Sienna for weeks. When they passed a boulder, they kicked it together to send Zeke a joint greeting.

Later, while the two waited at a likely camping spot for Scarl to catch up, Sienna said, "I think you're pretty, so don't take this wrong, but how'd you get that scar on your cheek?"

Ariel sobered at the memory of the standoff that might have ended her life, if Scarl had not proven to be more than he'd seemed.

"Somebody cut me," Ariel told her.

"On *purpose?* With a knife?"

Ariel nodded. "I've got one on my arm, too." She pushed up her sleeve to show it.

Briefly speechless, Sienna finally huffed, "I'd like to smack whoever did it, if I ever meet 'em."

While Ariel appreciated Sienna's indignation, she could imagine what Elbert Finder might have done to a young woman who slapped him.

"You can't," she said quietly. "Scarl killed him."

Sienna's eyes widened. "Seriously?"

Ariel nodded.

"He must really love you," the older girl murmured. "Tell me the story?"

Looking away, Ariel shook her head. She didn't like to relive those days—especially not this close to bedtime.

"I understand." Sienna turned and studied Scarl as he approached through the trees.

"Don't be afraid of him, though," Ariel said. The Flame-Mage didn't answer.

When he reached them, Ariel took a close look at Scarl's

face. The sun wasn't very low yet, but she could tell by the sheen in his eyes that he'd limped enough for one day. His bad foot often forced him to rely on Willow late in the day, but when the horse already bore a heavy load, Scarl became reluctant to add to the burden by riding. He bristled when nagged, though, so Ariel had become skilled at reading his eyes and his gait when deciding whether to push on or stop.

"I thought this might be far enough for Sienna's first day," she told him.

"I could go a little farther, if you want," Sienna said.

Ariel shot her an annoyed look, but Scarl agreed with Ariel's choice of a campsite.

Fortunately, he didn't have to move much that evening. True to her word, Sienna took charge, creating a cheerful fire and a dinner of fried eel. She grew a bit bossy, Ariel thought, but the results were impressive.

"A lot better than Scarl's cooking." Ariel giggled and slurped her last bite.

"I should hope so," Sienna replied.

"I'll remember that, Farwalker," he said. "But I have to agree."

Finally Sienna, too, could rest near the fire. She pulled her hair loose to brush it. Ariel envied those flaming red locks, which glowed radiantly in the firelight.

"You're so pretty, I bet lots of men will want to marry you," she told Sienna. "Wherever we get to. Don't you think, Scarl?"

"Likely," he agreed.

"You really think so?" Sienna directed her question straight to Scarl. Ariel felt a twinge of exclusion.

He nodded, shifting his eyes from Sienna to the fire.

"Will I want to marry *them*? *That's* the question," she mused.

They watched the flames flicker. Ariel yawned, but it was not even dark and too early for sleep.

"How 'bout a story, Scarl?" she asked. "You haven't told me the story of the ebony bead yet."

"You keep asking for it at night," he replied. "It's not good for bedtime."

"Is it scary?" Sienna asked.

He shrugged. "It's just . . . grim."

"Why did you give me a bead with a grim story?" Ariel asked.

He took her more seriously than she'd intended. "That's well wondered. Hmm. Partly because I wanted a dark one alongside the sea pearl, but . . . only partly."

"Tell it," Ariel pleaded. "Sienna will let me snuggle against her if it's too awful. Won't you?"

"Of course." Sienna smiled. To Scarl, she added, "I'm really curious now. Please?"

Scarl gave in. He settled more comfortably on the ground and said, "In a place far away, when the world was young—"

"Don't you say 'Once upon a time' to start a story?" Sienna asked.

Scarl just looked at her.

"Don't interrupt him," Ariel murmured. "He's practically a Storian."

"Sorry," Sienna said. "I thought they all started that way."

With a slight emphasis, Scarl said, "In a place far away, when the world was young, the bridge between life and death did not stretch nearly so long as it does now, and things living and dead sometimes crossed to the side where they didn't belong."

Ariel shivered. Perhaps he'd been right about not telling this story at night.

"After a long month of trouble," Scarl said, "the people of the village nearest the bridge decided to post a guard to keep the dead from coming across. But nobody wanted the task. After much argument, a young Reaper agreed to stand watch if someone else would take his place in a fortnight. Two guards, he said, could trade back and forth so neither spent all of his time in the shadows."

"Sounds fair to me," Ariel said. Sienna shot her a glance, but Ariel knew the difference between interrupting and participating.

Scarl nodded. "It was fair, but nobody else volunteered. Finally a very old woman, a Healtouch, grumbled, 'Shame on you all. But I will relieve the first guard in two weeks.'

"So the Reaper took up his post, turning back all manner of spirits and haunts, and he slowly lost his fear of the dead. Still, he greatly looked forward to the end of his fortnight. Unfortunately, the old woman died the day before his turn would be up. As she went to leave the world by the bridge, the young man saw her coming.

" 'You're early,' he told her.

" 'No,' she replied. 'Someone else will relieve you. Let me pass.'

"But, too eager to leave, the Reaper didn't recognize that she was no longer living. She could have just waited and then gone on her way once he left, but even in death the old Healtouch worried about leaving the bridge wholly unguarded. So she struggled with him and toppled them both off the bridge."

"To what?" Ariel asked. "What's between life and death?"

"Flame," whispered Sienna.

To Ariel's surprise, Scarl agreed. "Flame."

They all gazed at their fire. It reached and chortled and grinned.

"Love and hate," Scarl continued. "Or love and evil, some say—"

"Some say the flame is the Essence," Sienna protested meekly.

"Some do," Scarl said.

"Oh! The sparks in the sea, in snow, in your glass"—Ariel grabbed the largest bead in her necklace—"in my Storian's bead once? *That* Essence?"

"Yes. In the sea, in the sky, in your heart, in your eyes—all are flecks of the same fire, consuming as it creates."

Ariel gazed upward into the dark and wondered if the hiss of the moon might be the sizzle of the Essence burning within it. She'd not heard it for a couple of days, not since its one cryptic whisper in Skunk. She must have gotten whatever it thought she needed to gather.

"Anyway," Scarl went on, "when the young man and the old woman fell, the flame rose and swallowed the bridge. Time stopped, because no one could leave the world without crossing the bridge. And none could be born, either, because the unborn must cross the same bridge. The sun and moon froze in place. When the flame finally receded, a hole had been burned not just in the bridge but between life and death. A hole right through time."

"A hole." Ariel hugged herself and shimmied closer to the fire. Lamala had described her map as a hole and talked about death and new beginnings, too. When Scarl met her gaze, his eyes told her he was mindful of the Judge's words, too.

As Sienna's mouth opened with questions, Scarl quickly

went on with the story. "The villagers tried to repair the hole, but it couldn't be fixed. Anything near it fell in and was lost. Flames boiled up through the breach, and demons sometimes rode on those flames. Of course, with demons afoot, no one else would stand guard. Instead, they put clever barriers on their end of the bridge, hoping to keep the dead and the demons where they belonged.

"Today that bridge is too daunting for most souls to cross more than twice, first to enter the world and later to leave. Ghosts rarely return to haunt the living these days." He glanced at Ariel, who'd once befriended one. "A few, but not many. Demons, who tend to be lazy, don't relish the trip. And very few of the living try to cross and return. If they're not afraid of demons, they're afraid of the hole. Those who claim to have ventured partway always mention a light—the glare of flame through that hole.

"And this story belongs to your black bead, Ariel, because ebony is the only wood that won't burn." He glanced at the Flame-Mage to see if she cared to dispute it. She didn't. "And they say ebony wood forms the bridge. That's why it looks blackened and scorched. It has one end in life and one end in death, and it has already been through the flame."

The fire crackled.

"Well," said Sienna at last, "I bet no Flame-Mage tried fixing that hole."

Scarl chuckled. "Perhaps not. But you'd have to find the bridge first. Not easy to do."

"You can find it for me," she quipped. "Then I'll fix it."

The reflective look on his face stirred unease in Ariel's heart. "Have you sought it, Scarl?" she asked softly.

"It's a story," Sienna said. "I was joking."

Scarl stared into the coals. "I thought about it for a while." His eyes flicked to Ariel and his lips twitched in a humorless smile. "That's one thing I believe I could find, if I tried. But I don't think it's meant for the living to find."

At her worried expression, he smiled again, this time with warmth. "Besides, you're still young to be farwalking all by yourself."

"You'd better never find it and cross it without me, at least," she said, shaken. "You promised to stay by my side."

"As you choose," he confirmed.

Sienna squirmed, clearly feeling left out. "I liked that story. It wasn't so grim."

Neither Ariel nor Scarl argued. But Ariel gave Scarl a weak smile to apologize for Sienna's words, if not her presence.

He shrugged one shoulder.

Watching their silent communion, Sienna drooped. "I think I'll lie down," she said with a sigh. "I'll try to rise first to wake up the fire."

"No need," Scarl told her. "We ate well tonight. Let's make some distance tomorrow."

With a twinge of sympathy for Sienna, Ariel rolled into her blanket alongside her and reached to pat her arm.

"You might hear strange animals in the night," she whispered. "Don't be scared."

"If you aren't, I won't be," Sienna replied. "Snuggle up if you have nightmares."

"I will."

Ariel didn't sleep at all for a long while, though. She lay staring up at the sky. The moon could not have been more than a bright eyelash tonight, and by now it had already set. The silent stars winked like holes pricked in the night. Fingering her ebony bead, Ariel wondered again why Scarl had strung it into her necklace. It occurred to her that her beads all had holes more surely than either her map or the sky did, but that notion did not soothe her, either.

CHAPTER 16

Dog Moon and Secrets

When Ariel awoke, Sienna was sitting alongside her, stretching herself alert. Smiling, the Flame-Mage observed, "The stars fell on you last night." Handfuls of tiny white flowers had been sprinkled across Ariel's blanket.

"Oh, pretty," Ariel said. "Thank you!"

"I didn't do it," Sienna replied. "Must have been Scarl."

Startled, Ariel spied him tending Willow not far away. He'd never done anything like that before, but perhaps it was a final First Day surprise. She hated to scatter the blossoms, but reluctantly she got up.

Sienna lagged, replaiting her hair. "I feel like I'm braiding bugs into my hair," she complained. "You sleep on the ground so much, I can see why you chop yours."

"Scarl's got a knife," Ariel said. Sienna's look of horror made her laugh.

Ariel's smile lingered as she stuffed her feet into her boots and went to meet Scarl, who was returning from the horse. She didn't initially notice his wrinkled brow.

"Thank you," she told him shyly.

"For what?"

She gestured toward her blanket. "The flowers."

He glanced that way and shrugged. "Don't thank me. Sienna must have picked them for you. Tell me, though, Ariel—am I a bit mad? What does this look like to you?"

He showed her a dark knit cloth crushed in his hand.

"It's a hat, isn't it?" As the words left her lips, though, she realized why he frowned. "Oh—*your* cap? Your old one? I thought you lost that in the Drymere last year!"

His fingers kneaded it. Sand showered out. "I did. But it was in my bag this morning, alongside my socks. You're not having me on, are you? Concealing it all this time?"

"No, not me. I—" She started. Her hand flew up to check her necklace for the third time in two minutes. Finding it safe, she looked again at the flowers. "Could Misha be back? Playing tricks on us both? I haven't seen him since we found the Vault, but . . ."

Scarl shivered. Ariel considered Misha a friend, but the Finder had never been comfortable with the abbey's teen ghost. "I might rather be mad. Did he ever bring physical objects before?"

Ariel shook her head. Yet she could think of no other explanation. The abbey's Tree-Singers thought that once Misha's work in the Vault had been found, his spirit had moved on. Perhaps they were wrong.

Uneasy, she opened her own pack to stuff in her blanket. A wad of yellow cloth inside caught her eye. Her heart swelled, blocking her voice. Although she felt as if she'd found something dead in her bag, she reached in and drew the cloth out.

"That's a pretty skirt," said Sienna from nearby. "You're not going to wear it here in this muck, are you?"

"S-S-Scarl?" Ariel turned with the skirt held at arm's length. He didn't recognize it. She had to remind him that he'd ripped up this skirt to bandage the wound on her arm that had so long since healed. Now here it was, whole and unbloodied, as if that day had never happened. Reeling, Ariel dropped the skirt to shove up her left sleeve. The familiar scar filled her with a perverse relief. The earth seemed to have whirled so that nothing could be trusted to remain in its place. But her own skin, at least, hadn't changed.

Scarl gazed apprehensively into the empty air around them.

"Misha?" Ariel called. "Mark something with your handprint, will you? Please?" That was how the ghost had announced his presence before.

No answer came. Ariel put off Sienna's questions and they quickly left camp. Over the older girl's protests, Ariel left the skirt behind. It stirred old aches too much. Besides, it was too wrong to abide.

Later, as her shock faded and walking brought her calm, Ariel told her new friend about some of her encounters with Misha. At first, Sienna's eyes widened, but Ariel recognized the moment her credulity snapped.

"You and Scarl both tell good tales," said the Flame-Mage with a wink. Ariel did not bother to argue.

By midday they'd finally left swamp muck behind. They traveled through wooded uplands busy with birdlife and cooling breezes, the latter welcome after the stifling swamp. Now and then they glimpsed sweeping views that made Ariel's heart soar and helped her forget the strange morning. Born near the wide sea, she always felt smothered in close habitats. In contrast, Sienna clutched Ariel's arm the first time they paused on a hilltop overlooking a distance.

"It's so . . . empty!" Sienna exclaimed. "I feel we could fall in and vanish! Is it like this everywhere?"

"Pretty much," Ariel said. "I mean, sometimes there's mountains or sand dunes or plains. The things growing are different. But almost all of it's wild."

"You're even braver than I thought," Sienna replied. "All this space, with no people . . ."

"Not many, at least," Scarl said. "We rarely walk less than a week between villages."

Ariel admired the swells in the land, listening to the wind's swirling song. "I like it. No hint of Tattler, though." Her feet pulled her along, but she asked to be sure. "You don't think we've passed it, Scarl, do you?"

"No. I don't think it's close, but I can feel it ahead."

"Honestly, Scarl?" asked Sienna. "I was sure Tattler was only made up."

"I could be wrong," he replied, "but unless Ariel changes course, I expect to find something. She never leads us to naught."

Ariel jigged in excitement. It had to be the sender, at last!

Scarl misunderstood her squirm. "I don't think we need to be nervous, though. Cautious, perhaps."

"Oh, no," said Sienna. "Not with you here to protect us."

Ariel swallowed a snicker. With her feet drying and the sender finally within reach, she was in too bright a mood to tease Sienna for fawning. Instead, she peered ahead for some glimpse of her goal. If Tattler was truly a giant, they should be able to see it from afar.

Having chatted so much on the previous day, she and Sienna had exhausted the easiest talk. Accustomed to Scarl's quiet company, Ariel didn't mind swaths of silence, but Sienna grasped for topics. She told Ariel stories she knew, sighed about the dirt on her shift, and prodded the Farwalker into describing other places she'd been.

"Do you like secrets?" Sienna asked slyly, late in the day. They'd still seen nothing of Tattler. "I'll tell you one if you'll tell me one."

Ariel mulled it, not sure she had any. She thought about the meadow with Nace, but chose something less risky.

"It's not really a secret," she told Sienna, "but you know how I said the Vault had been found? I'm the one who found it. We stopped saying so unless people ask, because lots don't believe it. Since I'm just a girl."

"You're not 'just a girl.' But they think Scarl found it instead?"

Ariel nodded. "Or some other Finder. He gets mad either way. It's easier just to skip that part."

"You could say the Tree-Singers found it. People would believe that."

"That'd be lying, though."

Sienna didn't seem particularly troubled.

"So what's your secret?" Ariel prompted.

Sienna glanced sideways at Ariel and then over her shoulder to make sure Scarl wouldn't hear. "Secret, now. Promise?"

Ariel nodded impatiently.

Tipping her head close, Sienna whispered, "I'm going to kiss Scarl the first chance I get. And I bet I can make him want to marry me, too."

Ariel stopped in her tracks.

Sienna laughed. "See if I don't." She flipped her braid over her shoulder. "But don't worry, I won't take him from you. He can still act like your father. But I'll be his wife. By the time we get to the next village, he won't want to leave me. You and I can be friends forever!"

Ariel's lungs refused to work until she glanced back at Scarl—*her* Scarl. His familiar form reassured her that nothing had changed except words in the air. She knew him. Sienna didn't. The Flame-Mage was spouting nonsense.

"Who knows," Sienna added, "maybe I'll even meet your little ghost at the abbey."

Her glib tone helped Ariel force her feet forward. Sienna hardly knew what was real and what wasn't. Still, the older girl smiled like a cat with a mouthful of mouse, and Ariel fretted for the rest of the day.

Sienna's secret was hardly a shock by itself. Ariel didn't think Scarl was handsome, but she loved him. It wasn't hard to imagine someone older wanting to marry him. What troubled her was the chance that Sienna's scheme could succeed. Confidence oozed from the lovely young woman beside her, and the strange events of recent days seemed proof that Ariel didn't understand the world as much as she thought.

Her eyes grew sharper on both her companions. She noticed details she hadn't before—Sienna's legs, for instance. The young woman's shift, short enough to avoid mud in Skunk, here in the uplands simply looked daring. Moreover, it stayed mostly clean, and Ariel saw for the first time how dirty she let herself get. Sienna avoided splashes and smudges with a great deal more success, her longer limbs gliding while Ariel's tromped.

Over the next several days, Sienna continued to be solicitous to her and Scarl both, cooking, washing dishes, and tending the fire, as she'd promised. But her skill with the fire began to look boastful, her every move crafted to earn attention.

When Sienna let down her hair to brush it, Ariel suppressed a glare. The brushing took forever. Hidden meanings now lurked in other tasks, too. Did Sienna's fingers linger when she handed Scarl his food? Did she bend closer when she took back his bowl, did her voice change when she asked him a question? Ariel thought so. And the sickle moon seemed to agree, its sly grin getting broader each evening as it dropped to the west.

Sienna kept trying to pretend that nothing had changed. Ariel sometimes forgot that it had, and they giggled together like they had on the first day. More often, their conversations were curt. Sienna's company, once pleasant, annoyed Ariel. She could see in Sienna's eyes that the older girl knew it and her feelings were hurt. Soon it was no wonder that Scarl received nearly all of the Flame-Mage's smiles.

When she could, Ariel stayed near him—so near he tripped over her twice, the second time with a curse. Tattler, on the other hand, receded before her as though running away. Each dawn she arose full of hope that today they would meet it. Each evening that hope drained away, leaving chagrin in its wake. Scarl had to assure her so often that it still lay ahead that he finally told her not to ask him again. Ariel resented her feet for not knowing how far it would be, and she groused about the people in Skunk who had made it sound close.

Only one thing cheered Ariel's days. Every morning, a handful of flowers lay strewn on her bed. At first she suspected Sienna of trying to earn back her friendship, perhaps picking blossoms in the middle of the night after waking up too full of water. Like Scarl, Sienna staunchly denied it. Ariel looked for Misha in her dreams, but the ghost never visited her there as he once had. Though the mystery seemed harmless enough, several times Scarl sat up late, trying to witness the elusive shower of blossoms, but he never managed to do so. Ariel tucked petals into her pockets and stopped mentioning it because she did not want it to end—and she awoke every morning to dread, afraid to see blossoms on Sienna's blanket instead.

Her walk turned into a trudge. Too aware of the beauty walking beside her, Ariel didn't notice her path or the scenery as much as she otherwise might. Then one afternoon, not long after they'd rounded the shoulder of a slope, Scarl tapped her and pointed. A patch of white gleamed on a ridge farther ahead and off to the side. Ariel shaded her eyes to gaze at it.

"It's August," she murmured. "That white spot can't be snow."

"Where? Oh!" Sienna stared, too.

Scarl said, "It's too big for a cliff goat, and too smooth and bright to be daisies. Could be a sheer face of stone reflecting the late sun."

"It could be," Ariel replied. Her excitement simmered harder for being so long denied. "But it's not."

She led them on, faster, without mentioning a tiny doubt: why hadn't Tattler appeared dead ahead? Ariel focused harder on her feet than she had for a while, but their preferences seemed muffled. Whether she stepped to the left or right of stumps and briar patches did not seem to matter as it usually did. Once the land's humps and hollows obscured the far-off gleam she was sure must be Tattler, Ariel had to slow. Her feet tried her patience, contradicting themselves on what seemed to be a zigzagging route, first more to the south, then more east, back and forth. She would have preferred to climb out of the dells and follow the ridgelines, keeping that white patch in view, but she didn't dare question her feet, which had saved her from cliffs and impassable slopes more than once.

When at last a fresh vista opened, a tall silhouette rose against the evening sky like a steeple stretching into the heavens. Ariel had once seen a Storian's house with a tower and a bell hung inside it. This spire went much higher. The white patch they had seen from afar was some part jutting out near its top. The whole thing listed a bit to one side. Still far away but now directly ahead, it towered over the hillside, at least three trees tall.

"It almost looks like a snag, with most of the branches broken off," said Sienna.

"Too big," Ariel said. "It's more like a ship's mast with the rigging all tangled, but it's way too tall for that, too."

"I'd say we've spied Tattler," Scarl said. "Do you suppose it's spied us?"

Sienna fidgeted with her braid. A similar unease wormed through Ariel. The pale, round shape near the silhouette's top resembled an eye more than a bell in a steeple.

She refused to acknowledge her fear. "If it is the sender," she declared, "it probably knew we were coming. Let's go find out."

If they'd been birds, they might have reached it before dark. They weren't. Reluctantly Ariel decided to camp. She wanted to sleep where she could gaze toward Tattler, but Sienna protested.

"I'm surprised it's real," said the Flame-Mage. "I still don't believe it will eat us, but I don't think I can sleep with it staring at me all night long, either."

Scarl agreed. "We know nothing about it but threatening rumors," he told Ariel when she grumbled. "It's probably harmless, but we might as well shelter from it while we can." He picked a campsite in the lee of a slope that blocked their view forward as well as any view Tattler had back toward them.

Though his reasoning was sound, Ariel couldn't overlook whose side he'd taken.

As far as she knew, the kiss Sienna wanted had not occurred, but she'd seen the young woman trying to bring it about. Noticing Scarl rubbing his bad foot one evening, Sienna had offered to do it for him. Though he'd refused, Ariel had braced herself for a time when he might accept.

Something even more upsetting took place the night they camped hidden from Tattler's view. Ariel was darning a sock by the firelight when she happened to glance up. Sienna bustled nearby, draping damp clothes over a bush so they'd dry. The last time Ariel had noticed, Scarl had been admiring the stars. Now earthly beauty attracted his gaze: when Sienna turned her back, his eyes traveled the young woman's form.

Ariel nearly let out a screech. She'd not seen Scarl ogle anyone like that, including Mirayna, whom he would have wed if she had not left the world.

As she fought to control a rush of dismay, Scarl shifted his focus to the fire, nudging a stray coal safely back to the middle. Oblivious, Sienna came to sit in the circle of light with her hairbrush. Scarl paid her no mind, but Ariel hadn't imagined the subtle interest he'd shown a moment before. Sienna may not have earned a kiss yet, but she'd succeeded in attracting his attention in a way Ariel could not. She feared he wouldn't—couldn't—have enough for them both. And in a choice between one and the other, Ariel didn't see how she could win.

Turning away from her companions, Ariel abandoned her darning and curled into her blanket without saying good night. Only holding her breath kept the tears in.

The moon, now having reached its first quarter, hadn't spoken to her since before they'd left Skunk. But the advice it had last given her there—*linger, gather*—kept Ariel wakeful a long while that night. Sienna could not be what she'd needed to gather from Skunk, could she? The moon must have meant the knowledge Ariel had gleaned about Tattler, or, if not, perhaps the messages or gifts she'd received there were important. Certainly Ariel didn't need Sienna, hair clips or no. She refused to believe that Scarl might.

CHAPTER 17

Dog Moon at First Quarter

Twice that night, Ariel was awakened by a burning throb in her left forearm, as though the limb had fallen asleep worse than usual. Each time, she checked her necklace—a new habit—and then cradled her arm to her belly and rubbed it until the pain faded. When at last her eyes opened on morning, a stripe of blood stained her sleeve.

Gasping, she shoved the fabric up to her elbow. She found no blood beneath; her scar creased her forearm, snugly healed if not smooth. She probed it to be sure and then slid her cuff back in place. The red swath, still damp, lay precisely over her scar.

"You must have had a nosebleed last night," said Sienna, noticing from nearby. She wrinkled her own slender nose. "And wiped with your sleeve in your sleep."

"I guess so," said Ariel faintly. She touched the base of her nose but found no evidence there, nor on the sweater she'd used as a pillow. She ignored the alarming but unlikely idea that Tattler had somehow attacked her. The bloody sleeve seemed more akin to the eerie appearances of her old necklace

and skirt—remnants from another journey that somehow under-
lay this and were themselves bleeding through.

When she rushed to show Scarl her sleeve, though, he, too,
blamed a nosebleed. He put a cup of warm tea in her hands.
"Here. Slow yourself down. I know a few things have happened
that don't make much sense, but let's not see phantoms behind
every tree. It'll be harder to spot the true hazards. You haven't
seen Misha, have you? Other than the flowers?"

Preoccupied, she'd barely noticed them this morning. She
shook her head.

"Then the simplest answer is probably correct."

Ashamed, she hastily washed her sleeve before breakfast.
The blood, not yet dried, came out readily enough, but the cold
water made her arm ache in a familiar way she tried to ignore.

"For heaven's sake, why don't you wash the whole shirt
and wear something else?" asked Sienna when she saw Ariel
dripping.

"Why don't you mind your own business?" Ariel replied. "If
I brought as many clothes as you did, we'd need a whole
'nother horse."

"I was going to offer something of mine." Sienna turned
away with a flounce. "But forget it."

An apology flickered in Ariel's mind, but before it got
farther, Sienna raised her voice to call, "Scarl, let me get you
more tea."

Dismissing her guilt, Ariel stalked in the other direction.

Although the visible reminder was gone, Ariel thought of her
arm for several hours that morning. The pain she'd felt through
her sleep reminded her of the nightmares that had swept her too
tangibly into the past. It occurred to her that her wound, like her
necklace and skirt, were not just from her past, but specifically

from her very first farwalking trip—which had begun with her telling dart, which in turn had been launched by the sender. Maybe Tattler was somehow responsible for sending these strange waking dreams. Ariel didn't believe they were dreams, not at all, more like souvenirs from events she would rather forget, but they kept ambushing her when she awoke as if they'd followed her back from her sleep. Since they were growing more unsettling as the travelers drew nearer the giant, Ariel would be reluctant to close her eyes in its shadow. Scarl may have been right about camping under its gaze.

As they progressed toward it, Tattler played hide-and-seek, looming larger at each sudden view. It gave no sign of wanting to eat them. Despite awkward angles and lines reminiscent of a praying mantis, it gradually took shape as a beast built by man. Ariel could clearly see legs, spread and planted to support the tall steeple, but Tattler's flesh was a lattice.

"Oh!" she said, once her eyes made out the blue sky through the holes. "Back home, we had this big metal tree. That's what we called it. It wasn't so tall, just a tangle of limbs, and the men broke off pieces for tools." The quick thrill of recognition dwindled to vague disappointment. "This isn't the same, is it, Scarl?" She couldn't see how a big metal tree could send darts.

"Clearly both were created before the Blind War," Scarl said. "But I saw what was left of your metal tree, and I don't think their purposes could have been much the same. Looks to me like Tattler's main work was to hold aloft its eyes and its ears."

Most of those organs—though clearly metal, not living—had fallen. One had caught in the lattice; others had burst at Tattler's feet in a tangle of dented pieces, torn mesh, and wires. The gleam of white they'd first spied still hung aloft, round and protruding at Tattler's top. Its front bulged, bringing to mind a wide eye. Other parts were shaped more like odd funnels or the seashells Ariel had once held to her ear to hear the rush of the sea. High above the ground, overlooking the landscape in every direction, these devices indeed could have caught whispers on the wind or spied on distant events. Ariel could imagine the metal beast relaying those secrets, passing them on through some inscrutable machine talk more complex than bats' eerie locator sense or even the telling darts' magic. Although not made of flesh, Tattler's ruined organs still seemed gory, and the gaze of the remaining eye made Ariel's skin crawl.

Sienna hung back. "It's creepy."

Ariel had to agree. One of the legs had collapsed on itself, which is why the whole tilted, and other parts of the lattice were crumpled or stuck out in unnatural directions. Dismayed by the obvious damage, which boded ill for her search for the telling darts' sender, she said, "It looks dead. If it was ever alive."

"Your telling dart wasn't alive," Scarl said, "but it could still act. Some things—especially things from the past—have powerful energies other than life."

"Not just from the past," said Sienna. "Fire, too."

"Or rabbit snares, I suppose." Right away, Ariel wished she hadn't thought of a trap.

"Fire doesn't make you feel like it's watching you, though," Sienna added.

Nobody argued.

Ariel's unease grew. Still, she'd led them a good distance along the base of the slope Tattler stood on, expecting to turn and climb up soon, before she realized she wasn't just nervous. Something important was wrong with her feet.

She stopped and stared, not at the giant above, but at the gentle meadows sloping away to the south. She turned back to Tattler.

"I don't want to go up there, Scarl," she said.

To her surprise, he said, "Good. You plunge too readily into situations that should scare you. Why don't I climb up alone, just to start? We have a few hours of daylight to spare."

"No, you don't get it! It's not being scared. My feet don't want to go there." She'd changed course yesterday after spotting Tattler from a distance. Now, if she focused on it, her feet were willing to scramble up toward it. Otherwise they inclined considerably more to the south. "We're practically past it," she added, "but they want to keep walking that way and around—" Her voice broke. "Like Tattler's not where we're going at all." The weight of more miles ahead, and less knowing, crashed down upon her. She'd been so ready for the path and the mystery to end.

Scarl turned a wistful look up at Tattler.

"Fine by me," said Sienna. "Let's find a nice creek for a bath."

"Are you sure your feet aren't simply taking an easier route up the hill?" Scarl asked.

"I thought that's what they were doing twenty minutes ago," Ariel said. "But if there was a reason we couldn't march straight up the slope, by now we could see it." She sank to the ground. "I thought this was it. I thought we'd be done! How far away could the stupid sender still be?"

Scarl extended a hand to help her back to her feet. "Take heart. We've gone much farther before. I should have tempered your hopes about Tattler. Or for that matter, finding a sender at all." When she ignored his hand, he let it fall to his side. "But while we're so close, I'd still like to explore this. Would you be comfortable resting and waiting an hour or two for me? Or do you want to take Willow ahead with Sienna, and I'll catch up tonight?"

Neither appealed. In fact, his offer made Ariel feel both cowardly and lazy.

"Ooh." Sienna wrung her hands. "I don't want to get that far ahead of you, Scarl. We might need you."

Ariel groaned and pulled herself back to her feet. "I guess I—"

A screech drifted down to them on the wind. Their faces turned up. The sound thinned and broke, jiggled, and repeated more sharply.

"Is that some kind of bird?" asked Sienna.

Scarl must have caught the words first. He cast Ariel a worried look precisely as she recognized what the voice above kept repeating: "Farwalker! I seen you! I seen you! 'Zat you?"

CHAPTER 18

Dog Moon and Legend

Willow's reins were in Ariel's hands before she realized it. Scarl whirled and began climbing, digging his walking stick into the slope.

"Wait!" Ariel said. "I'm coming, too."

He didn't stop. "No. Stay until I know who that is. Your feet may have headed away to protect you."

Ariel ignored him, but to coax the horse along, too, she had to switchback up the hill rather than scramble straight up. Sienna floundered behind.

"You still down there? You coming?" screeched the voice from above.

"Yes!" Ariel shouted.

Scarl turned, probably deciding whether to stop her by force. He chose instead to cut her off and pull the reins from her hand. "At least keep behind me. Help Sienna. Stay close."

They clambered through thick brush and up the dry, crumbling slope. The warbling voice did not come again, but they heard clattering gravel above, and shortly they found a thin path worn in the dirt. Slipping and scrambling, they crested a rise to a wide, stony landing. A metallic whine greeted them. Their heads tipped back in awe.

Tattler straddled the landing and them, its feet splayed amid clumps of witch broom and gorse. Entire houses could have huddled in the space underneath and, indeed, the remains of a stone building sat against one of the feet. What looked like an enormous plate—a fallen piece from above—lay amid the rubble of one wall. One latticed leg had a tree growing up through it, or that leg also would have sagged and twisted to increase Tattler's list. But the crisscrossing lines and jagged, crimped metal imparted the air of a mean dog made all the more dangerous because it was crippled.

Movement caught Ariel's eye. Long, narrow flags fluttered from the lowest portions of lattice. Their movement added a dry rustle to Tattler's steady keening, which changed pitch with the breeze. Looking closer, Ariel recoiled. The flags were not strips of fabric or woven grass, but dozens of rattlesnake skins.

"Eeeeeee!" A bent figure darted from behind the shack and scurried up Tattler's nearest leg like a spider. "Don't hurt me!" Pegs, spaced along the lattice like handles, seemed to help, but in places the owner of the voice simply clambered up the lattice itself. Reaching a height well over their heads, the apparition paused and peered down. Wild white hair swirled around a face as wrinkled and brown as a walnut. Tattered snakeskins flapped and dangled below, more like kelp stuck on a rock than true clothing.

"An old woman!" Ariel said. "Isn't it?" She had to be eighty years old, maybe more.

Scarl said, "I suspect it's—"

"Stay away!" With remarkable speed, the withered crone scrambled higher. "Stay away, man. Tattler will eat out your eyeballs! It will!"

Involuntarily Ariel glanced toward Tattler's head. Neither teeth nor a mouth was apparent.

"I hope not," she said, her voice cheery and unthreatening. "I'm Ariel. Hello. Who are you?"

Although the woman gazed down with mistrust, she eased slightly lower. Her head cocked. "Fa-a-ar . . . walker." She might have been calling a lost pet. "Farwalker. Come."

Hearing her name on this madwoman's tongue made Ariel shiver. It put her in mind of another troubling voice from the moon.

Sienna spoke up. "Vi? Is your name Vi Storian?"

The woman straightened. She smoothed her hair and a smile crept onto her face.

"Brilla? I knew you'd come back to me! I've been waiting." She began climbing down. "Come, come. Let me look. All grown now, are you?"

"You know her?" Ariel whispered as Vi worked her way back to the ground.

"No, I just guessed," said Sienna. "She was sent away long before I was born. And Brilla was the name of her daughter. The dead one."

"Yes, all grown-up and lovely, surrounded by friends." Reaching Tattler's base, Vi hurried toward them. "Weren't there another? A shadow behind. I saw the Farwalker coming, and her friend, and her shadow—oh, I knew you would come! Hoo! Brilla, my Brilla. From your toddling days you had a Farwalker in you. I knew it, I saw—" She halted in confusion and her gaze bounced between Ariel and Sienna.

She tipped her head straight back, mouth gaping, to stare overhead. "Are you sure? The small one?" She eyed Ariel. "No, no. She can't be the one. My Brilla's the Farwalker girl."

"I'm a Farwalker," Ariel told her. "My name is Ariel, though." Sienna introduced herself, too.

Scarl remained silent, but Vi squinted at him in mistrust. "Oh, I see you, too. You stay distant, you hear? Just like the other."

Ariel wondered what "other" she meant. Not done ranting at Scarl, Vi seemed to answer her thought.

"You stay near that horse. Horse backsides, the lot of 'em. Men." She spat in the dust. When her face turned back up, she beamed again. "But I'm glad my Farwalker came."

She shuffled forward, arms raised to embrace Sienna. The Flame-Mage stiffened, shot Ariel a desperate look, and whispered, "What do I do?"

Ariel wasn't eager to step forward into that hug, either. As Vi drew within a few feet, though, she gasped. Her arms dropped and she stared at Ariel's neck. "Story beads! I had a— Hey, did you steal those? Did you steal 'em from me? Are those mine?"

Ariel drew back, one hand protecting her necklace. But Vi only cackled. The angry pucker smoothed from her face.

"Silly! You're right. I had my own once, strung with plenty of stories. Let's see if I know all of yours . . ." She crept closer, one trembling finger pointing out beads. "Move your hand for a peek, there's a girl. Flame . . . and death. Love and loss. Riches and jealousy, yes, yes. And hiding there, quietlike, fail-safe. Of course!" She clapped her hands like a child. "A good abacus! A good one for traveling with a Farwalker, sure." She raised her gaze reproachfully to Ariel's eyes. "As neck beads, though, they'd wear better on Brilla, not her friend the Storian's apprentice."

"But I'm not a—," Ariel said.

"Never mind. It's still good. Smart girl to bring a Storian with you, young one or not." Vi patted Sienna's arm approvingly. "You'll need her, since I've gotten too old to go. Especially with stories like those, all balanced on the point of a needle. A pin. Oh, maybe a dart. That's pointy, too."

Ariel started. "Do you know about telling darts? Did you send some last year?"

Vi ignored the question, busy lifting both arms and one foot to wobble on the other. She looked like a decrepit heron. "Balanced on tiptoe and ready to fall." Sadness crossed her face, and she put her foot down to gaze up. "Like my Tattler friend."

Keeping his voice soft, Scarl asked, "Can you tell us a story, old mother? One of Tattler, perhaps?"

"Or darts?" Ariel added.

"Stories . . ." Vi sighed. "It's been so long since I told a story. To any but Tattler, that is. Oh!" She reached toward Sienna. "I have one you must hear, though. Will you listen?"

She ignored all responses until Sienna, nudged by Ariel, said, "We all will."

"Good, good. Let me sit and collect my thoughts a bit first. All this gabble and clamber is aching my bones." She turned and shuffled toward the stone shack, but she called over her shoulder. "Tie up that horse. And that man—if you can, you should tie him up, too. And watch yourself close in the rocks. Rattlers like Tattler, and— Ooh." She spun back to them. "You bring me some food? Nice swamp food? Not snakes?"

"Yes," Ariel told her. "We're happy to share."

Vi cheered and disappeared into her shack.

Ariel looked at Scarl. "She's awfully crazy."

He nodded. "There's insight in her insanity, though. She knows your trade."

"No, she doesn't! She's got me mixed up with Sienna!" She wouldn't have minded so much if her trade had been lost to Scarl instead.

"The knowledge is confused with memories of her daughter, who probably looked and dressed more like Sienna. But she was struggling with that. Her comment about the dart might be chance, but it's curious. And her Storian skills are still strong." He tapped a bead on her necklace. "She put an interesting name to one of your beads that I wouldn't have thought to give it: fail-safe."

Ariel bent her neck to look at the bead, carved from white wood. "What's it mean?"

"It's a way to make certain that things turn out all right even if something goes wrong. Mistake-proof is another word for it. Because the bead is fire-pine wood. Do you know fire pines?"

"Pine trees, sure," Ariel said. "I've never heard of fire pines."

"I have," said Sienna.

"I grew up near a stand," Scarl said. Willow jostled him, restless. "Here, come with me. You might need to pretend to tie me." He led the horse to the nearest of Tattler's feet and hitched him within reach of a few tufts of grass. As he knotted the reins, he explained: "The trees in the story are crotchety elders. But real fire pines also live very long lives, and they don't like to be crowded by hungry young trees. So they grow cones every year, but their cones cannot open. The seeds remain trapped, and the cones drop to be buried under needles and moss—until a wildfire comes along. Then the heat of trees burning opens the cones so the seeds can finally sprout in the ash and replace the trees killed by the fire."

"They use fire as a tool, same as us," said Sienna. "Just like cooking mud-clams until they pop open."

Scarl nodded. "It gives fire pines a fail-safe—a way to stop seedlings unless something's gone wrong, and in that case, to allow them to grow."

"Pretty smart," Ariel said. "Even if the old trees sound kind of mean."

"Well, the moral of the story is not to think you're so clever that you can't be surprised by unforeseen events." He glanced toward the stone shelter. "Or by Storians who've gone slightly mad. I'll be interested in what Vi can tell us."

Ariel sighed. "If it makes any sense."

"Would you rather keep walking now?" he asked. "I'd like to learn more about Tattler yet, but I haven't forgotten the reason we're here."

"I wish I could forget." Ariel's feet wouldn't let her, but for the first time in her life she wasn't sure she still wanted to follow their lead. The wreck over their heads might once have performed feats—maybe even shooting telling darts into the air—but she couldn't believe it had done so as recently as last spring. Vi, too, was a wreck, and meeting a mad sender might be worse than finding none. Ariel felt no closer to her goal now than two weeks ago.

Scarl awaited her decision. She shrugged. "We might as well hear Vi's story. And give her some decent food. I don't want to sleep here tonight, though."

"Neither do I," said Sienna. "Tattler's whining is creepy. Not to mention all the dead snakes. I am hungry, though. I'll start a fire and cook something better than rattler."

While Sienna worked, Scarl poked around Tattler's fallen eyeballs and ears and collected small parts to take back to the abbey for study. He tried to ask Vi's permission beforehand, but returned after peeking in through the doorway.

"She's asleep," he reported. "Snoring like a bear."

"It wears you out to be crazy," said Ariel. "I know."

Rousing herself, she climbed a ways up one of Tattler's legs. In some ways it was easier than climbing a tree because the pegs and the lattice were all the same distance apart. The view was lovely, and she could imagine Vi watching them approach and concluding that travelers meant a Farwalker led them. In that way, Tattler truly had spied them from afar. With its metal warm from the sun, Ariel also would have liked to sit and gaze for a while. But nothing about Tattler's sharp edges was comfortable, so she didn't linger.

As she started back down, dizziness overcame her. She clamped her hands tight. The metal thrummed and flexed under her hands. It had to be the wind—had to be—but in a moment of panic she feared Tattler was not as dead as it appeared. Her whole body tensed and she pressed every limb to the lattice.

Scarl called her name in alarm. His voice drifted distantly up from the ground. Blue sky pivoted around her. Was she falling? Yet she could still feel the metal pinching her palms, pressed to her body, and biting the soles of her boots.

Ariel shut her eyes, hoping to stem the vertigo. The voices calling her name came from above, below, and then behind her, proving, it seemed, she was tumbling. The whining of the wind through the lattice softened to the shush of tree boughs in wind, and Ariel would have sworn that one of the voices calling along with Scarl's was Zeke's.

Then, just as Zeke had done on the day she'd climbed his tree, a hand clamped on Ariel's ankle.

CHAPTER 19

Dog Moon Over Tattler

Zeke! He'd grabbed her, but how? Ariel's eyes flew open once more, but she saw neither Zeke nor a tree. Vi's wrinkled face peered aslant into hers.

"No, no," Vi scolded. "You ain't known Tattler so long as I have. You don't know which joints are weak and will bend."

Barely daring to breathe, Ariel turned her head. She hung upside down, clinging to a section of lattice that had sprung free and sagged toward the ground.

"Come this way. I gotcha." Tugging and nudging, Vi helped her reach a sturdier section. Ashamed of being rescued by such an old woman, but grateful, Ariel tried not to lean on her much.

Once her balance had been recovered, she hurried down, careful to follow Vi's winding lead. Scarl awaited not far from the ground, his face tight. He backed away as they approached and Vi began shooting him suspicious looks.

"That was too nearly a fall," he said when Ariel's feet at last touched the earth.

Vi shook her finger at him. "You oughtn'ta chased her up there, that's all."

"I'm okay." Dizziness still pulled at Ariel, though. She held her eyes wide against it, unblinking, and sagged against Tattler's frame.

Waving Scarl off, Vi scurried around her. "Come, come, Tattler's sorry. Old and broken, but sorry. Didn't mean to give you a scare. We can't help our bad bones, none of us. Oh! I know. Tattler's got a present for you." She sniffed the air like a dog. "Is that food?"

On wobbly knees, Ariel followed the old woman to Sienna's small fire. "Rice with cattail root," the Flame-Mage announced.

Ariel ate only a few bites, but Vi eagerly took the remains of her share and a goodly portion of Scarl's. Vi's manners had not improved in her solitude, that was certain. Rice flew from the gaps in her teeth. As they ate, Scarl asked gentle questions about Tattler, but direct answers were rare. Vi talked mostly of it singing to her under moonlight, winking at her with one eye, and calling the snakes, keeping them lulled so she didn't get bitten or starve.

"And treasures," Vi announced. "Tattler helps me find treasures from back-when. I'll show you. And give you one, too." She trundled off to her shack and returned, cupping a collection of junk at her chest. She laid it in the dust at their feet.

Ariel scrambled to her knees when she spied the tail of a telling dart. She slumped back to a seat soon enough. Vi had pieces of several, but none whole.

"Do you have so many here because Tattler sent them?" Ariel asked with a flicker of hope.

"Tattler? Ah, ha ha ha!" Vi slapped one hand to her cheek and tipped her head up to share the joke with the giant. "Your master ain't teaching you right," she said, "and I'm too old to take an apprentice. But even a young 'un like you ought to know that only folks could send darts. Like arrows, they needed a bow to shoot off from. And the bowstring is inside your head." She pressed a grimy fingertip to Ariel's forehead and nudged. "A purposeful thought, that's what sends 'em. No brainbox, no darts. Tattler's got eyes and ears, and sings pretty good, too, but I live in his brainbox. I can tell ya, it's empty."

"You, then," Ariel pressed. "Have you ever sent some?"

"How old you think I am? Two hundred or so? No darts flying in my lifetime, Storian girl. My master saw one, or that's what he said, but he was prone to fish tales. His master, more likely. But here. You take this." She tucked a dirt-crusted dart missing its tail into Ariel's hand. "Tell your master to learn you better about the back-whens." She paused. "Oh. You don't got a master. *Tsk, tsk.*" She shook her head. "It's worse than I thought. Well, you come back when you're done with the Far-walker, and I'll try to help."

Ariel looked down at her lap to hide her disappointment, which seemed deeper alongside her brief moment of hope.

"Now, Brilla, this one's for you." Vi reached into her pile and drew out a corroded metal disc that appeared to be murky glass on one side. She presented it to Sienna.

"Thank you. It's very, uh, pretty." Sienna held it so Ariel could see.

Ariel exclaimed and Scarl did, too. On the round, pale face beneath the scratched glass, notches marked the four winds. Three dark lines, one an arrow, lay in the circle. The combination reminded Ariel vaguely of her map. As Sienna turned it, the pointers skittered and shifted inside, loose.

"Is it a toy?" Sienna asked. "You jiggle it to line up the arrows?"

"No, no," Vi said. "Timepiece."

"Like a sundial," Scarl explained, "but much more precise. We've a diagram of one at the abbey. The arrows are supposed to be fixed in the center. If it weren't broken, they would track the hour of the day."

"No. That's wrong," declared Vi. Scarl gave her a startled look, but she only plucked the timepiece from Sienna's fingers. "Not you." She passed it to Scarl. "You. Man or not, you're a help to the Farwalker, and Tattler says she has a timekeeper already."

"I do?" Ariel asked.

"I . . . I *do?*" Sienna echoed, trying to help.

Vi only nudged her and cackled as if they were sharing a joke. Ariel wondered if the old woman meant the moon.

"I'm grateful," Scarl told her. "Perhaps with help I can get it working again. But are you sure you want to part with it?"

"Bah," Vi told him. "It's nothing. Is it time for the story?"

"Don't I get a present?" Sienna asked.

Vi shook her head. "You get the story."

"Now would be good," Ariel said grimly. "We need to go before dark." Sooner would be even better.

"Yes, yes, can't keep you long. My Farwalker's got to get moving. But this is important. The first time I heard it, I knew my daughter would need it. You'd be the one, yes golly, none too soon." She patted Sienna's knee. "Not here, though." Her head whirled as if she were checking for eavesdroppers. "The brainbox. We should go hide in there. There are some who would crush out this story."

Ariel's first thought was for the Forgetting, a time in which people worked to get rid of all trace of the old days and ways. Tattler itself had likely survived only because it stood so remote from known villages. Indeed, the frightful legends about it may have been attempts to discourage interest. As she pondered this, though, Ariel's eyes reminded her that Vi was half crazy. Who knew whether anything she said could be trusted?

The old woman led them all to her shack. Reluctant to enter, Ariel paused at the doorway. Except for rock rubble and a mound of snake skulls, the shack was as Vi had said: empty.

"Yes, this'll do," said Vi. "Sit here, sit here. We can pretend we're all inside the Vault."

With a sharp intake of breath, Ariel rushed to obey.

Vi stood in the center, folded her gnarled hands, and looked down at her feet. "This story is called Noah's Fail-Safe," she warbled, "and I've lost the bead I had for it. My girl Brilla wore it sewn on her dress when they buried—" She shook her head impatiently. "Noah's Fail-Safe," she repeated. "But I call it Brilla's Proof. You'll see why."

Raising her head, Vi scanned her audience, her gaze coming to rest on Sienna. When she continued, her voice held a rousing vigor that took Ariel aback.

"There once was a wise man named Noah, before the Blind War. Noah liked to poke about in the swamp, and on one of those pokes he heard a voice out of nowhere. Noah wasn't a Tree-Singer, mind you. The trees never spoke to people before the blindness, but he heard a voice just the same."

"I know a story about Noah," Ariel whispered to Scarl, "but it's different from this."

"Shh. Later."

Vi narrowed her eyes to hush them. "The voice might have been trees. Or Tattler. Or my friend the moon." She shot Ariel a sly smile. "You hear the moon, too. Tattler says so."

Ariel stared back, disturbed that a madwoman knew such

things about her and even more chilled to hear she and Vi had something in common.

Vi cackled. "Anyhow," she continued, "the voice said destruction was coming. And Noah was doomed. But he could help ease the doom for some others. He could put all he knew, or as much as would fit, in a Vault. It had to be simple, because the most learned folk might not survive. It had to be hidden, and he had to work fast. But most important, Noah needed to make sure his Vault couldn't be found until it was safe—not before. Not before the destruction and fighting were over. Not before folks could work together again and do right with what it contained. And it couldn't be found just by accident, either." She looked from one listener to the next. "The voice told him how."

"How?" Ariel asked, when Vi didn't go on.

Pleased, the Storian nodded. "Ah, but nobody knows. That's how Noah made his Vault mistake-proof. Wise as he was, even he didn't understand all he did. But the folks back-when were clever in the ways of the Essence, and the voice guided him, too. They say the Vault can't be found . . . until it is found. You probably heard that and thought it was just a mind teaser, like the one about the sound of a single hand clapping."

Not having heard either saying, Ariel glanced at her companions. Only Scarl murmured agreement.

"It's no mind teaser, that. All of us have to show that we're ready to find the Vault first. But the proof, don't you know, is hidden away in the Vault. So even if it's found by good luck and chance, there's more to be done. Because good luck and bad luck are not that far apart. That's another way Noah was clever. His fail-safe used the power of the number thirteen— good luck or bad, right or wrong, renewal or death. All or nothing, that is. If we don't prove we're ready, the thirteen will flip and the Vault will be hidden again."

Vi clasped her hands and gave Sienna a smug smile. "And my Brilla will prove it. Or find it. Or both. I've known it since the night of her birth. Plus, any fool can see the Vault's been lost much too long. If we don't find it soon, we'll never understand what it holds anyhow. It won't speak any language still cousin to ours."

"But . . ." Sienna glanced to Ariel for guidance. "The Vault's already been found."

Vi's satisfied look dropped. "Has it? By you?"

"Um, not exactly," said Sienna while Ariel bit her tongue.

Barely waiting for her answer, Vi said, "You must be off on the proof, then! Heavens." She paced, pulling a wisp of hair to her teeth to gnaw it. "Hard to tell what it is, 'cept it ain't visiting me. You'd best go to the Vault first. Some help will be there."

Ariel and Scarl exchanged a look. She reached into her pocket before she realized the map was folded away in her pack.

Vi flapped her hands at them and then yanked a snakeskin from her body to flick it like a whip. Its rattle buzzed. "Go, go! If you're proving, there's no time to waste! No daughter of mine is going to fail the proof! Find more help, if you need it! Storians, Judges, men! Oh, if only I weren't so old. Or had friends! Or if Brilla . . . if only I'd kept Brilla safe." She sank to her knees. Dully, she added, "Or we aren't ready yet, and we won't be. Them men driving me out like a rat surely weren't. I was so certain that girl was special . . . was fated . . . The Essence was on her like stink." Vi covered her face with her hands. "Now I only have Tattler. Only Tattler and me. And busted back-whens. It's all broken."

Tattler's keening rose and fell overhead. Sienna extended a comforting hand. "Poor Vi—"

At her touch, the old woman shrieked. "Not you! No! Brilla!" She dashed out.

Stunned into silence, the others followed, expecting to find her nearby. When she didn't appear shortly, they searched. Ariel considered venturing up Tattler just a short way to spot her from above. That's when they finally spied her: Vi had climbed up to the giant's remaining eye. She slumped there like rags among whatever rigging kept the eye suspended. No amount of shouting drew her attention. Neither did waving the map. Despite the daunting height, Ariel suggested she take it to Vi, but Scarl was too worried she'd fall. So was she. He contemplated it briefly himself, but Ariel doubted his limp would allow it, and they both feared that a man approaching might upset Vi even more.

The sun dropped near the horizon without the slightest stir from the old woman. The half-moon appeared over Tattler, too. The sight of it convinced Ariel they needed to leave.

"Perhaps we should wait until morning," Scarl said. "Dawn might bring her down."

"It might not," Ariel fretted, "and we'll have lost that much more time." After hearing Vi's story, nonsense or not, she was more frightened than ever of dallying, and her feet jittered to be on their way.

"You said we wouldn't sleep here," said Sienna. "I won't be able to. Please?"

Scarl rubbed his forehead. "She may not have been much help with the map, anyhow. No other Storians have been."

As they gathered their gear and the horse, Ariel asked, "You think she'll be all right?"

"She has been for long years before us," Scarl replied. "And if not, the bridge out of the world may actually bring her more peace."

Nonetheless, he left half their food and his blanket behind. When Sienna questioned the wisdom of such generosity, he assured her he could find more to eat and sleep wrapped in his coat.

"You can share my blanket, then, if you like," Sienna told him. Ariel choked, but Scarl replied that since it was summer, he'd be comfortable enough.

Eager to change the subject, Ariel asked him what he thought of Vi's astonishing story. They'd barely had a chance to discuss it.

"There are many legends about the creation and location of the Vault," he said as they tramped down the hill into the dusk. "I thought I knew them all, and none turned out to be true. But I've never heard that one."

"She might have made it all up," said Sienna. "In the Noah story I learned in Skunk, Noah's a Tree-Singer and what he saves is tree seeds from the flood that created our swamp."

"My Noah was a Kincaller," Ariel said, "but he had a flood, too. He got away with animals on a boat. He did a mistake-proof thing, too, though. The only creature he let loose at first was a bird, and he didn't free the rest until the bird showed him that the land was safe and growing again."

"The name Noah may be stuck to anyone who protects valuable items from harm," Scarl told them.

Ariel laughed without humor. "Maybe *he* sent the darts, like he sent out his bird. But if so, I don't think we'll find him alive."

"The rest of what Vi said interests me more," Scarl said.

"The idea of a fail-safe, proving our worth. Especially given your sense that you need to hurry."

"What if it's true?" With movement now soothing Ariel's antsy feet, she wondered if the decision to leave had been right.

Scarl blew a long breath. "It's hard to imagine how the Vault could become hidden again—a great earthquake or landslide? I suppose it could happen."

Ariel gulped, imagining an avalanche crushing the abbey and everyone in it.

"A story can't cause an earthquake," said Sienna.

"Other forces can," Scarl replied, "and it would not be the first time the world has concerned itself with a Farwalker's business."

Ariel moaned. "I wish it would help more! How can I prove anything when I don't even know where we're going or what we'll find when we get there?"

Scarl's look of sympathy made her feel worse. "The same way you found the Vault in the first place, I suppose. Trust the powers behind you and follow your feet."

Easy for him to say, Ariel thought. He didn't know how the weight of worry numbed her feet in her boots.

CHAPTER 20

Dog Moon, First Quarter Spilled

Ariel lay blinking at eight knobby brown legs weaving slowly through the dew-covered grass. Only gradually did sleep evaporate from her, leaving the awareness that she was watching one too many grazing horses.

Alarmed, she sat up. The usual flower blossoms scattered around her, unnoticed.

"Shh. Don't spook him." Scarl's whisper stopped the cry in her throat. Sienna was still sleeping nearby, but beyond their fire's dead ashes, the Finder lay propped on one elbow in the gray predawn light.

He added, "You see him, then, yes?"

Ariel looked back and recognized the second horse, smaller and darker than ham-boned old Willow. They hadn't seen Orion for more than a year, not since he'd run off from a poor hitching near Tree-Singer Abbey. Scarl still spoke fondly of his first horse now and again, and as the previous winter had approached he'd repeatedly tried to find him. He'd concluded that Orion either was long gone or had fallen prey to a mountain lion. Now here he was, munching grass and snuffling, muzzle to muzzle, with Willow.

"He found us?" she breathed. "After all this time?"

"I'm not . . . sure about that," Scarl said, his whisper contorted.

Soon Ariel saw why. At first, Orion looked as sturdy and sleek as she remembered. But as the light rose and the horses strayed farther apart, Orion dulled and became indistinct, his legs lost in waving grass stems, as if he might only be a trick of morning mist.

"Is he a ghost?" she asked. The idea that Misha may have taken a mount seemed preferable to other conclusions, but it couldn't prevent her from stealing a quick glance at her arm. No blood.

"One way to find out, I guess." Scarl stood. "Orion."

Both horses threw up their heads at his voice. Orion's nostrils flared, and he snorted, uncertain. The breeze lifted his mane. He nickered and stepped toward Scarl. The sound or motion broke some spell. Between one footfall and the next, he was gone.

Scarl exclaimed, glanced to Ariel for confirmation, and hurried toward the remaining horse.

Ariel rose to follow. "Be careful!" She feared one or both of them might cross a misty threshold and disappear, too.

They found no such passage, only Willow, who rubbed his face against Scarl in greeting.

"Like my cap," Scarl said. "Here one moment, and the next just a memory again."

"Your cap's gone now, too?"

"Has been for a couple of days."

Ariel checked for hoofprints, but the soft earth was so pocked it was impossible to tell if one horse or two had marked it. When she looked up, Scarl was striding back toward their beds.

"Good morning," said Sienna, emerging from her blanket. "What's going on?"

To Ariel's delight, Scarl ignored and stepped past her.

"Horse stuff," Ariel told Sienna. "Aren't you going to build a fire for breakfast?"

Sienna's tentative smile slipped. "Of course."

Scarl lifted a bridle from the tree branch where he'd draped it last night. He inspected it. By the time Ariel reached him, he'd replaced it and folded his arms to await her.

She fingered the leather. It looked an awful lot like a bridle she'd once been tied up with.

"I hope I can make that fit Willow," Scarl growled. "Since Willow's is no longer here."

"It can't be Orion's!"

"You tell me, then! Whose is it? It's too small for Willow's great lunking head!"

Startled by his tone, she met his eyes.

He looked away. "Forgive me. It's easier for me to be angry than . . . the alternatives. If Misha's pulling pranks, I wish you'd get him to stop. It's too uncanny for me."

"I don't think it's Misha." Ariel rubbed the scar on her arm. "It's more like we're crossing our own path, somehow finding old tracks." That such tracks could be objects and creatures, however, particularly since they'd never come this way before, was almost too frightening to consider. What if their old enemy, Elbert, appeared next?

Scarl exhaled at length. "Leave it to you, Farwalker. Can I take another look at your map?"

She obliged him, and he sat with it next to the fire that Sienna already had dancing.

Sienna welcomed him, and him alone, with a smile and an empty cup. "Here, I'll have tea for you shortly," she said. "I'm boiling oats with dried berries. Sound good?"

Absently Scarl agreed.

Ariel leaned in to regard the map with him, recognizing something they shared that Sienna could not. Their postures recalled her dream in which she'd peeked over his shoulder, not at the map but into his glass and the flame licking there. She'd never mentioned that particular nightmare to Scarl.

"I don't see how we could be going backward or over ground we've trodden before," he said. "It's crazy to even consider. But there are plenty of lines here that curl back on themselves. I wish I understood this thing. It vexes me more every day."

Ariel rubbed the heel of one hand against the other, wrestling with an idea that made her nervous and yet tantalized her because it, too, would exclude Sienna. "What if we looked into your Finder's glass together?"

"Together?"

"Why not? Maybe the sparks that appear inside when you use it would—I don't know—show us a picture or something to help us."

"Never tried anything like that." He shrugged. "But I'm willing." He asked Sienna how long they had until breakfast.

"Twenty minutes," she said, stirring her oats. "Don't be so impatient, Scarl, dear. I just started."

Ariel flinched at the endearment. Scarl drummed his fingers on his leg. The tiny sign of annoyance rewarmed Ariel's heart.

"We might as well," he told Ariel. "I don't expect much, but that should be plenty of time to find out."

He retrieved his glass from his gear, tumbled it in his palm, and then offered it to her.

"It's yours," she protested. "You hold it."

"No." He folded her fingers around it. "This was your idea. You hold it and I'll . . . I'll try to help you."

She cupped the cool disk in both hands like a splash of water. Scarl sat opposite her on the ground. Uncertainly, he reached one palm to cradle her knuckles as if her hands were his glass. Sienna watched with interest from the fire.

"Ready?" Ariel asked.

He snorted. "I guess so."

His hesitancy gave her unexpected confidence. "Think of where the map leads," she said. "Or when. The map's end point, whatever it is—the darts' sender, some fail-safe thing, treasure . . . the moon . . ."

They both gazed into the glass. At first Ariel felt nothing, just as she had the one time he'd helped her try finding. Reminding herself that her initial attempt had partly succeeded, she redoubled her focus. She waited to see sparks in the glass as before.

Instead, she experienced a small, internal jolt, like a door bolt in her head sliding back.

"Our destination," she breathed. "Show us."

Scarl sucked a breath through his teeth. His free hand rose to press his fingertips between his eyes. Ariel thought he must also have felt that internal click.

Not letting her stare into the glass waver, she whispered, "Are you all right?"

"Keep going," he muttered. "There's something there."

Encouraged, she bent her will upon the glass, pouring herself into the lens in her hands. Scarl, the fire, and breakfast all faded. A fine thread of light shot through the glass and through her. The unbolted door had cracked open.

She pushed the door open farther.

A brilliant flare pulsed from the glass. Briefly blinded, Ariel heard Sienna gasp.

When the light softened and the spots cleared from her vision, she no longer saw a glass in her hands. Its cool weight on her palm and Scarl's warm fingers both had fallen away, and she found herself somewhere else altogether. The spray of a thunderous waterfall misted her skin. Standing at its base, she tipped her face toward the top and saw only white water. A surge in the flow high above curled out like spindrift from the sea. Unable to move, Ariel watched it shimmer and spiral outward, then down. Too late, she realized it would collapse over her, and it wasn't so delicate, either. Water slammed into her and battered Ariel to the ground.

Choking, she forced herself upright and pried her eyes open. No river was falling at her. She hadn't moved from her spot in the dirt, but the glass in her hands had split exactly in half. Scarl remained seated before her, fingertips still pressed to his forehead. Pain cramped his face.

"Scarl?" She coughed.

He didn't answer. Sienna called both their names and advanced.

"Stay there," Ariel ordered over her shoulder. She repeated Scarl's name, her voice hitching higher.

"I'm all right," he mumbled, moving nothing, his eyelids still clenched. Her ears barely caught his tight voice. "Are you?"

"Yes." Her head hurt, but not as much as Scarl's must have.

Her face was wet, though. Drawing her fingers from his, she dropped the broken glass to wipe her cheeks. The moisture might have been waterfall spray. She guessed it was more likely tears.

She added, "But we broke your glass."

He didn't react for a frightening moment, but at last he inhaled more deeply and cracked open his eyes. His pupils were so dilated Ariel couldn't see the brown iris around them.

"That was . . . not what I expected." His voice remained low. "I don't think we'd better do it again. Did we learn anything?"

"There's a waterfall," she said. "A big one. I don't know how far, but I've got to get there as quick as we can." It was all she could do not to jump up and run toward it. "It's a good thing my feet want to walk to it, since you can't find it with your glass ruined. Sorry." She poked at the shards.

Scarl rubbed both hands over his face. "I can get along without it," he said. "If my head will stop roaring."

Ariel touched his wrist. "Your eyes look funny. Are you sure you're okay?"

"No, I'm not sure. I'm just hoping it will be worth it."

Maybe it was some hidden instinct from her Healtouch mother, but touching him reassured Ariel that he would be fine.

"It will be worth it," she replied. "Now I'll recognize it. I—"As if the knowledge had trickled in through a crack, she knew the waterfall's name. A shiver ran through her, a muddle of excitement and dread. "Oh, Scarl. The waterfall is Timekeeper."

"I don't—"

"Timekeeper! When Vi said I already had one, I didn't get it. But remember my telling dart? The summons said, 'Come take up this challenge no later than Beltane. Timekeeper is counting.' *That* Timekeeper! I never knew what it meant. It's the falls!"

He winced as her volume increased. "I . . . I can't think right now, Ariel. Give me a few minutes, will you?"

"Please tell me you're both all right!" Sienna crossed to them.

With an impatient nod, Ariel scooped up the broken Finder's glass and curled against the base of a tree. Keeping one eye on Scarl, she pondered what they might find at the falls—assuming they arrived there in time.

After she'd found the Vault, she'd given the message on her dart no further thought. Beltane, the first day of May, had just passed and the deadline seemed no longer needed. So the date had receded back into the year as nothing more than the mark for spring planting. But both the deadline on the dart and the moon's insistence on speed now made more sense if the Vault truly did have a fail-safe. May first might have been important not because it mattered when she located the Vault, but because she still had to discover the mapstone and begin following it. She had a limited time to prove that the opening of the Vault had been no mistake.

Ariel tried not to swoon. The search for the Vault had nearly killed her, Scarl, and Zeke, too. If this trip turned out to be half so dreadful, she wasn't sure she could bear it. Yet whatever remained to be done as proof that people deserved the Vault's contents might very well be even worse.

Resistance surged through her, squelching her dire thoughts. Perhaps people *weren't* ready or clever enough for the contents of the Vault, but, if so, it would not be because Ariel Farwalker got too scared to try. Grimly, she gazed at the sky and wished for a glimpse of the moon or even the chime of its voice. She wanted to check just how far it had waxed. Not much more than a week could be left, though, before the full Dog Moon marked on her map. If she hadn't reached Timekeeper by then, she might welcome madness. It would be better than learning that her discovery of the Vault had been in vain or, more awful still, that people she cared about at the abbey had left the world because of her failure. But surely the trees would give warning if the land were to heave violently enough to bury the Vault!

It took Ariel a moment to remember that the threat from the moon hanging over her own head if she failed was not madness but death. And since he traveled with her, perhaps she'd put Scarl at risk, too.

For the first time, she rejoiced that Zeke had not joined them. She trusted his stones to protect him, wherever he was, more than she trusted herself. Wistfully she fitted the two halves of Scarl's glass together and hoped she had the strength for what lay ahead.

It was closer to lunchtime than breakfast before the trio started walking that day. Scarl felt better after two hours' rest with his feet up. It took another hour to adjust the horse bridle so Willow could wear it. Until that was done, Sienna hovered over Scarl like a vulture. Ariel found a few painkilling plants, which Sienna yanked from her hands to infuse into smelly teas she insisted on serving the Finder herself. Ariel sat fuming and studying the map, trying to spot a waterfall on it. The wave of small dots looked like water to her, but she and Scarl had already decided those were the months of the moon.

As Ariel stole baleful looks at Sienna, however, the driving impulse to get to the waterfall waned. She dreamed instead of stumbling on cottages, cows at pasture, or a fishing hole crowded with boys. For as much as Ariel wanted to reach Timekeeper, the journey would seem easier without a certain rock in her boot. She longed to encounter a village and get rid of Sienna while she still could.

CHAPTER 21

Dog Moon, Waxing Bright

I can't fix it. I'm sorry." Sienna had asked to see the broken halves of the Finder's glass not long after they finally left camp. Now she handed them back. "I could fuse it easily enough back home, but not here."

The trees had given way to a high plateau where tall grass whipped their legs. Its baked summertime scent swirled around them. They had room to walk abreast, and at first Ariel had taken the middle. But Sienna kept slipping into the center herself. Ariel figured the broken glass was just one more excuse.

"No matter," Scarl said, dropping the pieces back into his pocket. "Perhaps when we get where we're going."

"What happened to break it?" Sienna asked tentatively. "I mean, I saw the flash, but what were you trying to do?"

"I'm not sure." He looked past Sienna to Ariel. "Tell me what you experienced with the glass, if you would. From the start."

The hot wind lashed at Ariel as she recalled the strange impressions and feelings. Sometimes struggling to find the right words, she relayed everything she could remember from the click of the door bolt to the water on her cheeks at the end.

"Was it like that for you?" she wondered.

"Nothing like that," Scarl said. "Hmm. How can I . . . Well, finding a person or object over a great distance—like I found you and your telling dart last year, for instance—always puts me in mind of a ladder. I often can't say where the thing is, but I know where to find the next rung and the next. I feel closer. So I simply move up one rung at a time until I'm near enough to reach for the thing itself."

"That's what it felt like to you?" Ariel asked. "Climbing a ladder?"

"No. This was more like descending the ladder. Toward . . . I don't know. Darkness. Except I knew you were on the ladder above me and I was trying to hold it steady for you. I think what you felt as a click to me felt like being jostled or . . . as if you had stepped on my fingers on a rung. And when I perhaps foolishly told you to keep going, you came down so fast you knocked me all the way to the ground. I wasn't sure I was going to stay conscious."

Ariel winced. She could feel Sienna's reproachful eyes on her, but she knew Scarl would reject any apology offered. She only murmured, "I'm glad I had a door instead."

"It felt like your doorway went through my head. I just can't imagine where it took you, or how. I'll be interested in seeing this waterfall—Timekeeper, you say?—myself. If we come upon it."

"Is there a waterfall on your map?" Sienna asked.

"I don't think so," Ariel grumbled.

"Don't be so sure," Scarl said. "Is your map in your pocket?"

"My pack."

"Never mind, then, we don't need to stop. Look." He plucked a dry grass stem, broke it into three bits, and arranged them on his palm: ⫻. His bent thumb kept them from being snatched by the breeze. "One of the arrows on the map ends like this."

"The one that goes through the August full moon," Ariel said.

"It's a symbol with a number of meanings, depending on what is around it," Scarl told her. "The most common are related to power and movement. But it can also mean waterfall."

Ariel crowed and flashed Sienna a victorious smile.

"I've peeked at your map, though, over your shoulders," said the Flame-Mage. "I don't remember the mark you're talking about, but we started going southeast. Today we're mostly going south. None of the lines go south, do they?"

With effort, Ariel stopped herself from checking the position of the sun. "Shut up, Sienna. What do you know about it?"

Wounded anger glinted in Sienna's face, but she pressed her lips and held her tongue.

Scarl's eyebrows rose, too, but he told Sienna, "Sometimes she has to find a path around hazards and rivers. A Farwalker's feet can't always keep to a straight line. Besides, the map is complex. The falls may be a symbol, like in a dream, not real water."

"It was real," Ariel insisted. "I saw it. I got wet. And I know where I'm going."

He tipped his head to study her. "All right, no need to get angry."

"I'm not angry." Veering away, Ariel yanked seed heads from grass stems and flung them to the wind.

"Just cranky as a gator," said Sienna, not quite under her breath.

Ariel ignored her. When she thought no one would notice, she eyeballed the sun and headed more toward the east. Though she tried to stretch her thoughts toward the waterfall she knew lay ahead, they soon drifted back to Sienna and Scarl. Silently she urged her feet to find a village soon.

At first the murmur came softly, so softly Ariel thought she heard only the chortling breeze. The words were few and sporadic, uncertain. That evening, she looked for the moon. Barely past its first quarter, it sailed high overhead, where it seemed to feel her notice. The whisper repeated and grew louder: *Heed, walker, heed.*

A chill rattled through her. "I *am* heeding," she said. "I'm coming, aren't I?" The bulging half circle said nothing more.

Passing through rolling hills buzzing with stink-flies, Ariel and her companions walked into August. Ariel barely noticed the flies. Worries preyed upon her instead: the map, the Vault, Zeke . . . even Vi. But what felt like life-or-death problems sometimes faded before another that was smaller but right there before her each moment: whether Sienna was winning Scarl's affection and how life might change if the Flame-Mage stayed with them forever.

With so much clamoring in her mind, and given conflicting instructions—the nearest village, the map, or Timekeeper, wherever it was—her feet lost their focus, just as they had after she'd first seen Tattler. With the tower visible in the distance, she'd let herself be guided by her eyes and her assumptions about the sender, instead of attending the actual pull of her path. Similarly, Ariel kept walking now, unaware of the indifference creeping into her legs. This time her wits were too dulled by fretting for her to notice.

Early on the third afternoon since they'd left Tattler, Scarl halted them midway through a sunlit wood. Aspens quaked all around them, and at first Ariel thought he merely wanted to rest and admire the dappled forest. He'd been eyeing the trees thoughtfully for some time. She inhaled the leaves' sweet pungency, grateful that Sienna kept her mouth shut for once. The breath left her in a rush when Scarl unlashed their packs from Willow and pulled them to the ground.

"Are we camping already?" she asked.

He nodded. "I think we should, for today. You know why?"

Ariel studied Willow, the shimmering aspens, Scarl's face, and, briefly, Sienna, without spying a clue. "Not really."

Scarl licked his lips and glanced at Sienna as if wishing she weren't standing there. He gestured to a dead tree not far ahead.

"We passed that snag several hours ago," he said quietly. "I would have said something sooner, but the sun's been so nearly overhead, I wasn't sure until I saw that again. We've gone in a circle, Ariel."

Sienna rolled her eyes, but Ariel's gaze fell to the ground. Distracted and no longer feeling her way, she'd missed the moment her feet had abandoned the challenge of taking her two different places at once—toward her goal but away from Sienna.

"I'm sorry! I—" She choked.

Scarl put a hand on her shoulder. "It's not a disaster. Let's just relax and start fresh in the morning."

She nodded mutely.

All three silently unpacked and then fidgeted, unsure what to do with themselves. It was too early to eat. Ariel wanted to escape by herself but feared she might make matters worse by getting lost from the camp. More importantly, she didn't want to give Sienna and Scarl time alone.

"Since Sienna's fires are so nice to sit by, and we'll likely burn one a long while tonight, I'll go collect wood," Scarl said. "Ariel, why don't you come help? Sienna's been gathering more than her share."

Ariel frowned. He jerked his head, encouraging her, before he turned and slipped into the trees.

"Well, I'll help if you won't." Sienna got up. "We will need a lot, stopping so soon."

"No." Ariel dashed after Scarl.

She caught him quickly. He shifted what he'd already gathered so both his arms could be filled.

"Load me up," he said.

She stacked dry sticks into his outstretched arms.

Once they'd fallen into a rhythm, Scarl said, "I've been thinking back, Ariel, and I wonder: Was there something that troubled you when we used my glass the other day? Something you saw or felt that we didn't discuss?"

"Huh? No." It hadn't even been on her mind.

"You didn't find more blood on your sleeve, did you? Or anywhere else?"

She shook her head, grateful the answer was no.

He waited until he could catch her eye. "Then what's wrong?"

She stared at him. "I blew it today, and we don't have time for mistakes!"

"Besides that." His look penetrated too deeply.

Ariel ducked her head. "Nothing. That's enough."

"No, I don't think it is. I'm not an idiot. I thought you weren't acting yourself, and today you proved it. I know you're worried about what lies ahead, but you weren't this downhearted even when you were being stolen from home. If you don't want to tell me why, say so, but I can't help if you won't."

She piled more wood into his arms, not meeting his gaze. The silence between them grew thicker until Ariel could barely lift her limbs against it.

"I just don't like Sienna," she said finally.

"You started as friends. What changed your mind?"

"I don't know," Ariel lied. "She's just so . . . she's bossy and she sticks her nose where it doesn't belong. And she's so worried about getting dirty or messing up her hair or—" She stopped herself before she could say anything too near the truth: Sienna was too pretty.

With vigor, she stomped a long, thin branch into pieces. She could feel Scarl's study through the satisfying snaps.

As she lifted the kindling to him, he said, "Well, all trades have unpleasant parts."

Ariel curled her lip, annoyed at the reminder that Sienna's presence had been her decision.

He continued. "I suggest you just try to ignore her."

"You don't."

The accusation slipped out. Wishing she could snatch the words back, she bent to retrieve a twig hardly large enough to bother with. The forest rustled around them, and she prayed the breeze had stolen her words before they reached Scarl's ears.

She wasn't so lucky.

"Ahhh," he murmured behind her. "Ariel, are you . . . jealous?"

She cringed. "Don't be stupid. I just don't like her as much as you do."

The wood in his arms clattered to the ground. "Come here and look at me a minute."

She only scanned for more firewood.

Scarl grabbed her elbow from behind. "At least listen to me, then," he said, irritation creeping into his voice. "I don't know what you think, or what Sienna has told you, but you're making yourself miserable for nothing. And it's affecting your work."

She stared straight ahead for several quick heartbeats before finding the courage to peek over her shoulder at him.

"That's better." His face softened. "We've been through too much together for that."

Her resistance broke. Turning, she wailed, "She says she's going to marry you! She only came with us to make you fall in love with her!"

His eyebrows shot up and a crooked smile tugged his lips. "She may be surprised, then, when we leave her in some village. Ariel, I'm a bit too old for Sienna. And she is far too wily for me."

"Sienna doesn't think so."

"Sienna is wrong."

The certainty in his voice reassured her—almost. A memory taunted her. Ariel knew she was taking a risk, but she couldn't leave that memory roaming loose in her head.

"I've seen you looking at her, though," she mumbled, "like . . . like she was a sweet that you wanted."

He stiffened and drew back, crossing his arms. Ariel was afraid to check his expression. After what felt like a long time, he exhaled hard and pointed to a hummock on the ground.

"Sit."

Hearing his terse command, she realized how hard he'd been working to hold his temper. She obeyed hastily.

He hunkered down opposite her. "I don't think I need to explain myself to you," he growled. "But I will, because I can see how upset you've made yourself, for no reason. Sienna is a tempting young woman, and you watch me too closely, but what you saw wasn't love. I don't—"

"What was it, then?" she demanded, mostly to see how honest he would be.

Perhaps he recognized that. Certainly his piercing gaze felt as though he were studying the inside of her skull. At last he said softly, "The adult word is 'lust.'" Anger still edged his voice, but his eyes had gained a glint of sympathy—or amusement. "Do you know what it means?"

A general idea was enough. She nodded quickly and cast her face down, feeling foolish and too warm all over.

"Good, because I'm not keen to explain it. But hear me sharp now, Ariel: a look is not the same as an action. I would not lay hands on Sienna for any reason. None. There are too many good reasons not to."

Ariel gulped and rubbed her knees, longing to believe him but not able. She'd been too awed by Sienna. "What if she wanted you to?"

"I would tell her she was confused. Sienna is headstrong, but she's young—in some ways she's younger than you are— and she doesn't know herself what's good for her and what's not. What you've told me speaks clearly of that. Her ambition is admirable, but the methods she uses to get what she wants are nothing I find attractive. And I do not have the stomach to get tangled in something that would surely bring us all grief."

"Really?" she breathed.

"Really." He gritted his teeth at her lingering doubt. "Imagine, Ariel, if word got around that the Finder who accompanies the Farwalker took advantage of someone like Sienna—willing or not. How long do you think we'd be welcome anywhere? And how many masters would let their apprentices walk with you ever again?"

Ariel wasn't sure how such a rumor *could* get around, unless she carried it, but she saw his point. There would be people ready to spread ugly suspicions if they saw even a shadow of wrongdoing.

Shaking his head grimly, he added, "I don't have the luxury of that kind of . . . mistake. I'm already as good as dead if I ever set foot again in Canberra Docks. One village that hates me is enough."

"You've thought about it," she observed. Her words sounded more accusatory than she intended.

"For crying out loud, Ariel, I'm human! A thought is not the same as an action, either. I wouldn't trade on Sienna's inexperience like that in any case. I know I've hardly proven my honor to you, of all people, but I do have some."

Before she could assure him she'd seen it, he continued. "It's going to be difficult enough to leave her in hands we can trust to treat her fairly for a roof and her meals. But she's an adult, by years, and this was her choice."

Mindful of Sienna's boast, Ariel ventured, "You wouldn't even kiss her?"

Looking down at his hands, he kneaded his knuckles. "It may seem to you as though Mirayna has been gone a long time," he said softly. "It doesn't seem so to me. And I did love her, Ariel, very much. There's not space in my arms or my heart for anyone else. Not yet. Nor anytime soon."

He rubbed a hand over his eyes and then looked up abruptly.

"Except you, perhaps," he added. "But that's different." He

clasped both her hands in his own. "I certainly wouldn't speak about such things with you otherwise. And I'm not going to do it ag—"

"If you can talk to me about women's bleeding," Ariel said, "you can talk to me about this."

He froze, mouth poised to speak. Then he chuckled, shaking his head.

"I can't argue with that, can I? I fear for the man that you marry, truly I do." He sobered. "But have you heard me? About Sienna, I mean?"

She nodded.

"Even if she had bewitched me completely, it wouldn't change my promise to you. Do you doubt it?"

With both his hands and his eyes pressing hers, she could hardly remember her fear. Although Ariel told him she was sorry, what she felt most was wobbly relief.

"That's all right," he said with a wry twist to his lips. "Just remember this. The next one of us to do any courting will likely be you, not me. I'll want to threaten your suitors to mind their manners and you'll want to tell me to mind my own business. That's when you can look back on this and try not to be angry with me."

Ariel giggled. The picture he painted seemed impossibly far off. Then she remembered her picnic with Nace. That hadn't been courting—had it?

Her head whirling, she restacked their firewood into Scarl's arms in silence. Her body ached with relief and leftover angst, but a long evening's rest would cure that. She could only hope that her conversation with Scarl would also drain the confusion from her feet.

CHAPTER 22

Dog Moon Speaks Up

You weren't over there, were you?" Sienna demanded, pointing. She'd been standing with Willow, clutching his mane, but she ran to grab Scarl's arm the moment he appeared. A spear of resentment flashed through Ariel before she could remind her heart that jealousy was no longer needed.

Scarl set down his firewood, and they all peered into the aspens where Sienna pointed, quite opposite where Ariel and Scarl had gathered wood.

Sienna hissed, "I saw someone in the trees! Spying on me! And I'm quite sure it wasn't old Vi!" She hugged herself, shifting from one foot to the other.

Scarl's eyes narrowed. "Just one?"

Sienna nodded. Ariel trembled and tried not even to think Elbert's name. Simple answers, she told herself. Elbert was dead.

"Build your fire," Scarl said. "Ariel, either help Sienna or do something else that will keep your eyes off those trees." He settled into the grass, drawing half his glass from his pocket.

"You really think somebody's there?" Ariel whispered. But

Vi's confused words about seeing another of them, the Far-walker's shadow, rushed back to her. As time passed, the old woman seemed ever less crazy. Ariel hoped Vi and Sienna might both have glimpsed Misha, but she'd never seen the ghost herself outside of dreams.

"I noticed something earlier that made me wonder." Scarl focused on his glass.

Ariel gulped and turned to Sienna. "Tell me how to help."

Sienna regarded her dubiously. "I'll do it myself."

So Ariel simply sat watching as Sienna arranged kindling. Shortly Scarl got back to his feet, picked up his walking stick, and crouched at Ariel's side.

"Keep on as you are," he said quietly. "I'll be back."

"Be careful!"

"Of course." He slipped his knife from its sheath and set it on the ground within easy reach of her hand. Their eyes met.

"Just in case," he added. "I'll have my staff. All right?"

Drawing a deep breath, Ariel agreed. He touched the top of her head before strolling away, headed nowhere near where Sienna had pointed. Ariel tried to ignore him. Her fingertips tickled the knife handle.

When she looked up, flames licked in the kindling and Sienna was goggling at the knife.

"You know how to use that?" Sienna asked.

"Enough."

Scarl had taught her. He would have preferred that she carry her own, but Ariel had steadfastly refused. The weight of a blade would have constantly reminded her of her unpleasant encounters with knives.

"You're sure not much like other girls," Sienna said.

It sounded like an insult, but Ariel took more pride than

offense. She wagged her head and then mumbled, "I'm sorry I've been kind of crabby."

Sienna fed her fire. "I shouldn't have told you, that's all."

Ariel rejected a number of answers before saying, "Could we pretend you didn't?"

"It's not going to change anything."

Ariel swallowed, faltering under the strength of Sienna's will. She'd seen Scarl's will proven, however, and she had to trust what he'd told her.

"I just thought it would be nicer to be friends again." Ariel shrugged. "If you don't care, fine."

Sienna sighed. "It *would* be nicer."

They both stared at the fire. Its smoke curled around them, stinging Ariel's nose. After a while Sienna scooted closer to her and gave a silly little wave with her fingers.

"Hi, I'm Sienna Flame-Mage. What's your name?" A lop-sided smile appeared on her face. "And what are you doing out here in the woods?"

Crushing a grin, Ariel introduced herself. "Don't look now," she added, "but I'm waiting for someone to run out of the trees so I can wave this knife at them."

The playfulness slipped from Sienna's voice. "You really think that might happen?"

"I hope not." Worry gnawed Ariel. Hindered by a limp, Scarl was poorly prepared for either a fight or a chase. She wished he'd return. Perhaps they were simply closer to a village than they realized and had crossed paths with a roaming Reaper or Kincaller.

When Scarl reappeared at last, however, he gripped the collar of someone in tow. Sienna groaned.

Ariel gasped. "Nace!"

The horse nickered, too. The boy walked meekly, eyes down. After a week of travel, not even Sienna was truly clean, but Nace Kincaller looked as though he'd been dragged through the dirt. He didn't even have a sweater, let alone a blanket or pack.

Scarl released the boy near the fire. "Get him something to eat, Ariel." He retrieved his knife.

She jumped to obey. Hands fumbling at the food sack, she couldn't take her eyes off Nace. He peered at her through tangled hair, a smile flickering before vanishing again. Her heart thrumming, Ariel smiled back.

"I can't believe you followed us," she marveled.

He responded with a dismissive wave and a quick point: *Not them. You.*

"Why?" she wondered, knowing the answer. His eyes swallowed hers.

"Because he's creepy," Sienna grumbled. Nace threw her a hostile glance before his gaze returned to Ariel.

"Sienna." Scarl shook his head.

Rousing herself from the lock of Nace's green eyes, Ariel brought him some dried meat and plums. Nodding a quick thanks, he tore into the food. Scarl sank beside the fire and watched him, running his knuckles thoughtfully along his stubbly jaw.

"Did you sneak up on him?" Ariel asked.

"Until he heard me," Scarl said. "He has very good ears. Fortunately I remembered his name, so he listened instead of just running."

"What's he doing *here*, though?" said Sienna.

A ghost of a smile crossed Scarl's face. "Watching pretty girls, mostly. Nothing I haven't done. He's just doing it a long way from home." But he sighed and cast Ariel a pensive look.

"Sorry," she said.

Nace snapped his fingers to draw their attention. He waved toward Ariel while looking at Scarl and shaking his head: *Don't blame her.* He tapped his own chest.

Scarl nodded. Satisfied, Nace began eating again. Yet a scowl slowly formed on Scarl's face, and from across the fire Ariel could see the muscle in the Finder's jaw working.

Softly she said, "He's not bad, Scarl. Don't be too mad at him."

Chewing, Nace shifted his gaze uncomfortably from one to the other.

"I'm not upset," the Finder replied. "It was foolish of him, but we'll deal with it. That's not what troubles me. There's something else going on here."

"What do you mean?"

Misgivings shadowed his face. "You may think I'm crazy."

"After Orion? And your cap? And my skirt?"

He snorted. "You're not comforting me. But here it is: there's a bead on your necklace—a silver teardrop."

Ariel found it with her fingers.

"Its story concerns a boy who falls in love with a wandering gazelle," he went on. "She's really a maiden, enchanted. He follows her far from home, never quite catching her."

Sienna snorted. "I wouldn't give Nace that much credit. It's only a—"

A cry escaped Ariel. She'd heard "The Enchanted Gazelle."

"You know it?" Scarl asked.

She nodded and whispered, "But . . ."

Scarl lifted his hands helplessly. "I wouldn't even have thought of it—except that it's in your necklace."

"Spooky." Ariel pulled her arms tight to her ribs to stop the shiver crawling under her skin.

When Sienna questioned them, Scarl explained, "When the boy loses her, he throws himself over a waterfall. His sacrifice frees the girl from her spell. But she's so filled with remorse that she throws herself over, too."

Ariel caught Nace's worried expression. "Don't worry," she told him. "We're not going to pitch you off any waterfall."

"What *are* we going to do with him?" Sienna wondered.

"He'll have to come with us," Scarl said. "We're much too far from Skunk to turn back now. We can drop him off when we return toward the abbey."

Sienna huffed. "Ariel said I'd have to go back by myself. Why can't he?"

"You're an adult."

Sienna's brooding scowl whisked away, replaced by a smile. "Of course. But we're already short on food, aren't we?"

"We'll get by." Scarl rose. "I'll do some finding right now."

Among his finds was a creek mottled with the shadows of fish. When he returned to get his line and hook from his pack, the others decided to join him. Sienna claimed a small pool for washing her hair and the rest traipsed upstream. Scarl threw in his line. Rather than helping Ariel pick rose hips from a bush along shore, Nace waded into the water and froze like a heron. He darted both hands below the surface and came up with a wriggling fish.

"If you can do that, why haven't you been eating better?" Scarl asked, unhooking his own catch.

Nace steepled his hands into a triangle and shook his head: *No fire*.

"You've at least found fruit, haven't you?" Ariel asked. She understood his halfhearted nod, though. Rose hips, for instance, were really best in a hot mash.

As Scarl rebaited his hook, he said, "Speaking of fruit, Ariel, I've been thinking about Vi's story and Timekeeper."

"Me, too," she said. "I think that's why my dart said we had to answer its summons by Beltane."

He nodded. "Beltane, the time of spring planting. You probably know Harvest Fest in the fall. Reapers also celebrate Lunasa—the ripening. And Lunasa is marked by the full moon in August."

Ariel nibbled tart ruby skin from a rose hip, revealing the seeds packed inside. "So you think finding the Vault is like planting the seed . . . but it won't bear ripe fruit till we prove we're worthy of it?"

"Something like that."

Grimly she studied her rose hip. When she glanced up, Nace was looking at her. Although he clearly knew nothing of what they discussed, he gave her a reassuring smile, and simply having him near made Ariel want to try harder. She tossed him a rose hip. They chomped and swallowed together.

Once her shirttail was loaded with fruit, Ariel sat on the bank, where Nace watched Scarl clean their catch. She plucked tiny daisies from the grass. Though they weren't the right kind of daisy, she couldn't resist pinching off petals, counting under her breath whether he loved her or loved her not.

With a daisy half plucked, she cried, "It was you!" She gave Nace a glare that melted into a smile. "You've been dropping flowers on my blanket every night! Haven't you?"

A sly grin lit his face. He raised his finger to his lips and mimed a tiptoe approach.

Scarl turned sober eyes on Nace. The boy's grin faded.

Trying to warm the sudden chill, Ariel added, "We thought it must be a ghost to be so sneaky. Ha!"

Scarl's lips compressed, but he only rinsed his knife in the stream and then raised it to catch the light, checking for cling-ing fish scales.

If she hadn't been anticipating some remark from him yet, Ariel would have missed what came next. With the knife still held high, Scarl lifted his gaze from the long blade to Nace, who watched as carefully as Ariel did. His face dark, the Finder held Nace's regard a long moment. Then his eyes shot to Ariel and bounced immediately back to the boy. The knife between them never lowered.

Pulling a corner of his mouth down, Nace nodded once, almost imperceptibly.

Scarl echoed that tiny nod. The shadow lifted from his face, and he wiped the blade dry on his sleeve. Only when Nace threw Ariel a look that was part shame and part defiance did she realize what had happened: Scarl had given Nace a curt warning that the boy had understood and accepted.

Ariel marveled at that soundless and almost invisible male communication. Then anger swelled inside her. Scarl didn't own her, and she didn't need that much protection. She remem-bered a conversation they'd had only hours ago. It sounded dif-ferent in her memory than it had in her ears, and this time it did not make her giggle.

"Scarl." She tried to smile to soften her words, but her mouth didn't really obey. She pushed on anyhow. "Mind your own business."

Scarl raised his eyebrows, slid his knife back into its sheath, and picked up the cleaned fish. For an instant Ariel feared she'd imagined the whole thing and now would have to explain. Embarrassment had begun to burnish her cheeks when Scarl met her gaze.

"You're fourteen," he said quietly. "You are my business." He strode past her toward camp with their dinner.

Ariel watched him retreat, feeling the prickle of Nace's eyes on her. A sound sidled in, overtopping that sensation.

Faster, fly faster. Fail full, fail, fall . . . all lost.

Ariel craned her neck wildly before she spied the moon drifting on the afternoon sky. The sinister hiss had returned.

Nace touched her, inquiring what was wrong.

"Oh, Nace . . ." She didn't know where to begin. She'd been about to ask what he knew about her yellow skirt, Scarl's cap, or Orion. The voice of the moon had made her realize how impossible it would have been for him to be involved. Scattered flowers were one thing; lost items turning up from before she'd met him were another. Like the full meaning of the moon's renewed urgings, those mysteries would not be so easily solved.

Ariel barely noticed when Nace took her hand. A strange thought rolled through her mind as though it belonged to somebody else: it was good that Scarl took responsibility for the girl, Ariel, because the Farwalker had more pressing business.

CHAPTER 23

Dog Moon, Gibbous

Tell me about my necklace, Scarl."

Ariel's commanding tone drew apprehensive looks from both Nace and Sienna. Until then, she'd said little all evening, and Scarl probably thought she was pouting. In truth, she'd simply muffled her outer senses to better listen for those she heard inside. She was determined not to stray from her correct path again.

While her companions grew drowsy around Sienna's fire, Ariel had spread her map in her lap and gazed at it, not trying to understand but rather to absorb something from it. The string of moons had caught her eye, curling along one side of the drawing like, well, a string of beads.

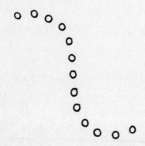

"Please," Ariel added. "It must be important. Vi thought so, too."

Scarl eyed her from across the fire and kneaded his temple. "Could you feel me thinking about it?"

"The map reminded me. What were you thinking?"

"I was recalling the story for every bead—the ones I haven't already told you—and another story as well. It's probably the first tale every Storian's apprentice learns. Do you know 'The Reflecting Abacus'?"

When she shook her head, he glanced at the others. Although Nace nodded, Sienna had not heard it, either.

"I'd better start by telling you that." Scarl reclined on his elbows, stretched out his long legs, and stared at the fire.

"Imagine this," he began. "An aged Storian had two apprentices, and in his final illness he called both to his bedside. 'Choose beads from my abacus,' he told them.

"The older apprentice immediately took the most beautiful and valuable beads. All that remained were ugly seed husks, wood, and clay. The younger apprentice, who did not care to quarrel, took what was left without protest.

"Observing their choices, the Storian said, 'Go work your trade for a week and come back to report.'

"When they returned, the older apprentice said, 'Those beads are cursed! I should have noticed how many pretty beads have stories of sorrow, evil, or greed. Each befell me. I was robbed, I went to bed hungry, and I had to sleep in the rain. I don't want this abacus after all.'

"The master took the abacus back.

"'These beads may not be much to look at,' said the younger apprentice, 'and some also have tales of sadness, but I told stories from them many times, and I am content.'

"But the master took back the ugly abacus, too. 'We will swap one for the other,' he declared. 'Go work your trade with the opposite beads, and come tell me your luck.'

"He lay abed, coughing, until their return. This time the younger apprentice spoke first.

"'These beads are so pretty, everyone asks for their stories,' he said, 'and even the sad ones hold wisdom and their own sort of beauty. I am content with this string as well.'

"The older apprentice grumbled, 'The ugly abacus is as bad as the first. People laugh. And although its stories contain happy endings, they certainly did not improve my luck. Perhaps I should start fresh with beads of my own.'

"'Perhaps you should,' said the old Storian. He gave both strings to the younger apprentice. 'But you will find the same truth. Beads reflect the Storian who bears them. Take less care for beads and more care with your heart, for that is the true source of your stories as well as your luck.' And with that the old master passed from the world."

When Scarl fell quiet, Sienna asked, "But what happened to the apprentices?"

"The first took the Storian's house and his trade, as befitted the elder, and lived a life of the sorrows and hardships in the stories he knew. The younger took the full abacus and told its stories to all who would listen. He enjoyed little wealth but much luck and love, because the younger understood what the elder had missed: The stories they knew were the same. What matters is how they are told, and how they are heard, and how they echo in our hearts."

Ariel admired the way Scarl's words seemed to linger. She finally broke the spell to ask, "And my necklace?"

He shifted and stirred the fire with a stick. The cloak of authority he slipped on for stories fell away.

"Your necklace," he murmured. "I chose the beads mostly for their appearances, because I knew the girl who would wear them has a true heart, one that reflects only courage and cheer. So nothing in those stories could hurt her. She's no Storian and won't be repeating them anyway. But . . ."

He gave her a rueful look. Embarrassed by his praise, she struggled to meet his regard.

"But that may have been foolish," he continued, "and the story I just told might be wrong. I think your little story abacus is echoing into your life. Not only with good luck or bad, but details of the stories themselves."

"What else besides the waterfall and Nace?" she asked. "The fail-safe bead, I guess, but that's about trees. And I don't really see how the bridge story—"

"Neither do I, yet. For that I am grateful. But listen: You have a bead with a story about a Flame-Mage who goes on a journey, and one sits beside you. You have a bead with a tale of moon power and divining, and we discussed that in Skunk. And do you remember when I told you 'The Selkie Stolen Away from the Sea'? Yes? But maybe you don't see something that crossed my mind when I told it: *you* were stolen away from the sea, too, and also changed, never to return to your home." He glanced at Sienna and back to Ariel. His voice dropped. "And the reason the selkie was stolen—we talked about that while collecting wood today. Didn't we?"

Ariel kept her eyes fixed on Scarl, hoping his glance hadn't revealed that she'd broken Sienna's secret. She knew exactly what he meant, though: misguided jealousy.

He added, "Those reflections make me shiver and pay attention to the rest of your necklace. Our path has a bead at each
turn."

Ariel looked down at her lap and the map's string of
dots . . . or stories. She didn't like the feeling it gave her. "Tell
the rest of the stories."

"No. Let me sleep on it first. Maybe I'm the one jumping at
phantoms, full of guilt for picking unhappy beads." Scarl rose
and slipped around the fire, extending his hand. "But I want
you to take off the necklace."

Ariel's hand flew to her throat. "No!"

"I'm not going to destroy it," he said. "Not yet, at least. But
some of those beads contain tragedies, Ariel. If I've set something
in motion I shouldn't have, it might not be too late to undo it.
Turn and let me untie it."

She cringed, shaking her head. Sympathy shone from Sienna's
face. Nace looked sorry, too, but he nudged Ariel to comply
before himself reaching for the back of her neck.

Squirming away, Ariel clutched the beads. A wordless plea
sparked in her heart.

The map speaks for itself.

She turned her face to the moon. "What?"

"You heard me," Scarl said. "I don't want to argue about
this. I'll stow it in my pack and we can see if another story mani-
fests."

"Not you, I—"

The map speaks for itself. The meaning of the words, which
Zeke had once passed along from a stone, hovered just beyond
Ariel's reach.

Scarl moved toward her again. Her mind filled with a terrible image of being held down while he ripped her necklace away. Desperate, she blurted, "You didn't pick them!"

His determined look turned quizzical.

"You can't feel guilty," she told Scarl more evenly. "You didn't pick out the beads."

"Well, nobody else did. What are you thinking?"

"Wait." Ariel's free hand smoothed the linen scrap in her lap to ease the way for understanding to come.

"Are you stalling?"

"You said you crafted my necklace in the last couple of months." She plucked at the map. "We found this last spring, way before you picked any beads. We couldn't figure it out then. But can't you feel it trying to speak when you look at it?"

His eyes narrowed. "You know I can. It's driving me mad. But—"

"It made you pick certain beads. Neither of us understood what it says, so it was trying to speak in some other way—in a language you especially know."

Scarl inhaled sharply.

"Now the map is alive," Sienna muttered.

Nace, who'd been listening with his usual intensity, gestured impatiently: *Not the map. The world.* He thought briefly and elaborated with his hands: *The heart of the world.*

"The Essence," Ariel murmured.

His eyes distant, Scarl said, "And it speaks to you through the moon, and in the language you know."

"Or the language my feet know, at least." Ariel's cheeks bloomed. "Lately I just haven't been listening as well as I might."

Scarl eyed the misshapen moon. It would swell to perfect roundness in less than a week. "Perhaps you'd better," he said.

On impulse, Ariel raised the map and pressed it to her nose as if she could inhale its meaning. It smelled of wet stones and well water and drowning. Hastily she pulled it away.

She whispered, "I'm kind of afraid, Scarl. Afraid I can't do it. And afraid of what might happen after."

He exhaled at length, but his gaze softened. "You know I'll do what I can."

The fire popped, scattering embers. Grimly, Scarl shoved the coals back into place with his boot. "I hate it when . . . Well, I wish Zeke were here so the stones could advise us."

"Me, too," Ariel murmured, feeling responsible. Then she remembered her promise to Zeke. She'd meant to plop a few rocks into their fishing hole once the fishing was done. She'd forgotten—no, been distracted. She glanced sideways at Nace. Emotions tangled inside her. Just now, she couldn't deal with those, too. She kicked at a rock near one foot, hoping that would do for tonight, and comforted herself with the cool feel of her necklace.

"You'll let me wear it, then?" she asked Scarl.

"For now. If you insist."

"Farwalkers are the strangest people I ever met," Sienna announced.

Nace, on the other hand, edged closer to Ariel. He reached as if to take one of her hands, but after a wary glance at the Finder, he settled for thumping his fist to his heart. Though she didn't really understand, his gesture still gave her strength.

She turned her face once more to the lopsided moon and begged it to wait for her coming.

CHAPTER 24

Dog Moon and Sleep

Ariel awoke the next morning with a fluttering sense that she needed to hurry. As she bolted upright and looked about in confusion, her gaze fell on Scarl. He'd curled up last night closer than usual. Now he lay with his cheek propped on his hand, waiting for her to awaken.

"You spoke in your sleep," he said. "What were you dreaming?"

"I don't remember." She shoved off her blanket. "But we need to go. I messed up bad yester—"

Her eyes fell on a worn length of rope coiled between them. The morning breeze abruptly felt chill. "What's that?"

He raised his wrist, tied with one end of the rope. "I'm surprised you don't recognize it. I woke to find it between us, but I untied your end so it might not upset you so much."

She scrambled to her feet and away. "It's not!"

"I think it is. I know my own knots." He began freeing himself from the rope that he'd once used to leash her. "I considered hiding it before you awoke, but I'm not in the habit of keeping secrets between us and I suspect this would be a poor time to start."

Ariel stared at the hated rope and tried to stop her chest from heaving. The fear inside her could not be exhaled.

"Easy." Scarl reached a hand to calm her. "I know how you feel—like the earth has turned to water beneath you and everything you know must be wrong. But none of these strange 'tracks,' as you called them, has hurt us."

"My arm hurt when it bled."

"I shouldn't have dismissed that. Forgive me. But I still think your necklace is more of a threat."

"Does it have a story about going backward in time?"

Scarl hesitated. "Backward . . . Not really. I'll have to think about that. Anyway, it seems to me that we *are* going forward. The past is just clinging to us in some unnatural way."

"Then we've got to go forward faster," she decided. "Right now. Get rid of that thing and let's get out of here."

"Done." He rolled to his feet and nudged their companions, who'd been awakened by Ariel's cry. "Up fast," he told them, ignoring Sienna's questions. Nace raised his tousled head to shoot Ariel a grin before bounding to his feet. His cheer—his very nowness—eased her anxiety. And despite the rush to leave, he managed to present her with a flower.

As they packed, Scarl's first words that morning belatedly wormed into Ariel's brain. She asked him, "What did I say in my sleep?"

"I couldn't understand most of it. But one thing was 'Walk across the waning moon.'" He glanced for Nace's whereabouts. "Another sounded like 'Don't let the moonlight burn Nace.'"

The words chimed through her head, stirring but not waking memories of the dreams. She grasped for them without success. All she could retrieve was an impression of climbing—hillsides and ladders and dozens of stairs—and the bitter taste of fear.

Seeing her puckered brow, Scarl said, "Don't fret. The same window may open again before you fall asleep tonight, and you might realize it looks out on nonsense. Just dreams."

"As long as Elbert doesn't come climbing through it," she said.

Scarl's expression turned grim, but he shook his head. "Even Orion was little more than a ghost. And if there's a bead in your necklace for Elbert, I don't see it."

"This one." She tapped her largest bead, the green glass. "Everything that happened last spring goes with this one."

His silence did not reassure her.

"Will you tell me the rest?" she asked.

"As we're walking," he agreed.

When they were ready to leave, though, Scarl drew Ariel aside. "I don't mean to doubt you," he said. "But would you be less distracted in finding your path if the three of us followed behind you, instead of all walking together?"

Ariel fought a surge of defensiveness. After her work yesterday, his question wasn't unfair.

"I'm paying attention now, honest," she said. "I was mostly distracted by junk in my head. I mean—"

"Thinking too much."

He'd advised her against that before, but she only now understood. She nodded. "I know where my feet want to go now. Please don't make me walk by myself."

"When's the last time I made you do anything?" he asked with a wry smile. "It was just a suggestion."

They forged across densely forested ridges. Despite the day's ominous start, the purposeful motion and her relief over Sienna lifted Ariel's heart higher than it had been in days. She closely attended the tug on her feet, which grew stronger until she could let her eyes wander with confidence. She had difficulty keeping them off Nace. Walking with him was like traveling with a mockingbird. Using whistles and clicks, he conversed with every sparrow, chipmunk, and cicada within earshot.

"Can you really understand them, Nace?" she wondered. "Can they understand you?"

He raised closely spaced fingers: A *little*.

"Couldn't you make up a language for talking to people with those sounds?"

He shrugged, but his face suggested he wasn't that interested in talking to people. Ariel guessed he'd had too many failures.

Struck by a sudden idea, she whirled. "Scarl!" Knowing that Nace and Sienna were both listening, however, made her tongue feel clumsy. "Never mind. I'll tell you later."

"Are you sure it can wait? We can just ask them to—"

"It's not about where we're going." She moved onward again. "Talk more to the birds, Nace. I like how it sounds."

Newly self-conscious, he cast his face toward his feet and stayed quiet a while. Eventually, though, birds drew him back into their chatter. He occasionally chirped to Ariel, too. She wanted badly to mimic the sounds back to him, but she feared he would think she was mocking. She smiled shyly instead and decided to try it some other time, when Sienna and Scarl weren't so close.

The sound of rushing water overtook Nace's chitter. The travelers shared hopeful glances. As they wove through the trees toward the sound, though, Ariel's stomach grew heavy. She knew before they saw it that they had not reached Timekeeper, but a gorge.

Where the forest broke, they stared down at the white turmoil below, which bit deeply into the earth.

"No waterfall here," Scarl said. "Upstream or downstream, Farwalker?"

The look Ariel threw him smacked of despair. "Neither! We need to cross it, not follow along." The urge to get across and beyond burned in her almost like hunger. The gorge was narrow enough to be tempting—less distance than Ariel's fall from the roof—but too risky to jump. "I knew it. I knew I screwed up."

Sienna plopped her hands on her hips. "I thought Farwalkers found ways around this sort of mess."

"We'll just have to detour until we can ford it." Scarl rummaged for his broken glass. "I'll find the nearest safe crossing."

"We don't have time!" Ariel could feel the impatience in her feet. Even the rushing water advised her: *Hasten, hasten.* Or perhaps it was an echo from the unseen, growing moon. She moaned. "We might as well stop here. I know it. We'll get there too late."

Nace tugged on her sleeve. He pointed across the chasm and slightly upstream to what looked like an odd ladder dangling over the side of the far cliff.

"A swinging bridge." Scarl squinted. "It must be left from the old days."

"Like it matters," said Sienna. "It's broken. Besides, after Scarl's story, if you think I'm crossing any bridge I can fall from, you're crazy."

Scarl grunted and Ariel shuddered. Nace scowled at it, too—and then sprinted upstream.

"Nace!" Ariel cried. When he didn't slow, she gave chase, glad to flee her losing battle with tears.

A short way along the gorge, Nace stopped. Bolts jutted from the stone at his feet, anchors for the end of the bridge that had broken. Behind them, a pair of thin metal ropes that had once served as handrails dangled from the trunks of two large trees. Bark had grown over the loops circling the trees. One line had frayed and snapped short, but the other must have given way on the far side, for its length hung over the near edge of the chasm. Nace hauled it up. The end featured several metal gadgets and clamps, which had presumably once fastened a loop on the other side, too. But now the handrail was useless.

"Sienna's right, Nace." Hot tears surged into Ariel's throat. She had to whisper to speak without letting them out. "Thanks for trying to help, but I blew it."

He gestured impatiently: *Wait*. Critically he studied the trees and the remnants of bridge. Then he flung the cable over a sturdy branch overhead that extended out across the chasm. As the loose end swooped toward him again, he caught it and tested his weight against it.

"Oh, Nace, no!" She peered at the boulders in the river and blanched. "If you fall . . ."

Nace waved aside her fear and backed up for a running start.

"Ariel?" Scarl called through the trees. "Ready when you are. And we do have a long stretch before any ford, so . . ."

His words faded in Ariel's ears as Nace dashed to the edge of the chasm and launched. Her heart seemed to come unanchored, too. The cable squeaked on the branch, bark crumbs raining down, as Nace swung over the river and past the far bank. A curse and Scarl's drumming boots sounded downstream. Nace swung back. He released the cable to drop to his feet before his momentum could pull him back over the gulf.

Ariel rushed to him. Nace spread his hands, palms up: *Ta-da!*

Scarl grabbed his arm and spun him so hard that Nace would have fallen if the Finder had not yanked him upright.

"Have you lost your senses?" Scarl demanded. "This may not be the Enchanted Gazelle's waterfall, but it's bloody well close enough! If that hadn't worked, you'd be smashed on the rocks. The very last thing I want is to have to haul your corpse back to your mother and explain how I let it happen!"

Nace dropped his eyes, looking contrite, but Ariel could tell he was only giving Scarl's anger time to burn itself out.

"Oh, never mind. We'd have no way to retrieve you!" Scarl added. "But you'd bleed in Ariel's nightmares for weeks. Did you think of that?" He swore again, turned his back, and took a few labored breaths.

Her eyes round, Sienna crept forward through the trees. Willow trailed her, blowing through his nostrils in an unwitting imitation of Scarl.

Torn by doubt, Ariel cast Nace a questioning look. He made a sign of reassurance, tapped himself on the chest, swept one arm in a gesture inclusive of her, and nodded toward the dangling cable.

"Scarl?" Ariel asked.

"Sorry." He turned. "That caught me by surprise. I shouldn't have gone off quite so hard. But truly, Nace . . ."

"Scarl, if I talk, will you listen a minute?" Ariel had already told him how Nace had swung her in Skunk, and he'd been impressed, so she got straight to the point. "If Nace swings us all across the gorge, it might save my mistake. He can—"

"Oh, no," said Sienna. "Not this Flame-Mage. No."

"He can do it," Ariel pressed. "But if we have to go around, we might as well give up now. We've only got a few days till full moon, and it's been nagging at me to go faster. And that's *without* any detour. So we can swing, or we can stop now. I say we swing."

Scarl ran his hand through his hair and sighed, briefly closing his eyes. "The horse, Ariel. Don't tell me he can get the horse across, too. If we give up Willow to haul our own gear, we might not get where we're going in time anyhow."

Nace clapped his hands for attention and squatted to draw in the dirt. It took a great deal of patience, but eventually he helped them all understand that he could ask the horse to run downstream to the ford and catch up with them on the far side.

Scarl laughed, the sound hollow. "I know you're a Kincaller, Nace, but please. He's not nearly that smart."

Anger flashed in Nace's face. He clucked to the horse. Willow whinnied and stepped forward to pluck at Scarl's hair with his lips. Only Scarl's direct apology stopped him at last.

"Maybe I'm the one who isn't so smart," Scarl muttered. He gripped the back of his neck and dubiously studied the cable and the branch where it dangled.

"No, Scarl," Sienna said, biting her nails. "You can't be thinking about this. We can just go around."

"I will make you a deal, Farwalker." Scarl's eyes bored through Ariel. "If Nace can swing *me* over safely, over and back, I will let him swing you. I weigh twice as much. If the branch and his grip will support me as well, fine. If not, you sacrifice both of us to find out."

Ariel felt the blood drain from her face. She really would throw herself in if the two of them fell.

"Is it worth that much risk?" Scarl pressed.

Nace touched her arm and nodded.

"Are you sure?" she asked him, her voice tight with fear. But the voice of the water below drowned her own: *Hasten, hasten, hasten, hasten* . . .

Ariel thought of the Vault and the stones' threat that Zeke might lose his trade. She remembered Vi's story of the fail-safe, her suggestion that people might never be ready—and the example of the uncaring men who had driven her off. And Ariel heard again all the threats of the moon, as well as the warning the cherry tree at the abbey had given to Ash: *They can't wait much longer, or all she has done will be undone.*

All lost. Ariel didn't have any choice.

CHAPTER 25

Dog Moon and Luck

Nace took a deep breath, rubbed his palms together, and gripped the cable. Scarl's hands grasped it just above Nace's.

"I'm going to put as much weight on you as I can with my legs," Scarl said. He'd already tested the branch himself. "If I do break your grip, my legs wrapped around you should give you a chance to regain it."

Nace nodded, but his knuckles gleamed white. A sweat broke on Ariel's skin.

As the pair pulled back for their swing, Ariel lost the contents of her stomach. When she spat and looked up, they were swinging back toward her, a knot of limbs and strained faces. They landed and fell over each other, entwined. Nace slapped Scarl's shoulder. Scarl cuffed the back of Nace's head. They both grinned.

"All right," Scarl said, disentangling himself. "Let's get this over with."

Ariel whooped. Sienna whimpered.

In a rush of sympathy, Ariel asked her, "Want to ride Willow and meet us instead?"

"Alone? What if—"

"No. We're not splitting up." Scarl shook his head. "I'll risk losing the horse. Not one of you."

Sienna grasped his arm. "Scarl, please. If I have to do this, will you take me? Nace will drop me on purpose."

Nace smirked and tapped one finger on his lips as if contemplating the option. Ariel elbowed him.

"I might ask if you've given him reason," Scarl told Sienna. "But it'll be easier just to say yes."

"Wait, Scarl. Can you?" Ariel asked. "I mean, your bad foot—"

Scarl shook his head. "There's nowhere to put feet. This is all arms. Which is why Nace will take you—and don't argue if you were thinking of swinging yourself. You've got your own strengths, but biceps aren't among them."

Ariel frowned. She didn't like limits, but she knew most of her power lay in her legs, not her grip. Besides, Nace had skills she didn't.

"I wanted to be sure he had enough strength, and then some," Scarl went on. "But there's no point in taxing him needlessly, either. I'll ferry Sienna."

They put one night's gear into Scarl's pack; everything else, including his walking stick and all of Sienna's trade tools, went on Willow. Cheek to cheek with the horse, Nace made small noises, his eyes closed. Then he pulled back and clapped. The horse whirled and ran.

A twinge crossed Scarl's face. "I hope you're right about his ability to understand what you've asked, Nace."

"I'm going to throttle you if he doesn't," Sienna told Nace.

"Let's just go," Ariel urged.

"You first," said the Flame-Mage.

Nace grabbed the cable. Ariel edged up to him, more frightened than she'd expected to be. Unlike in Skunk, there was no soft mud to fall into here.

"Are you going to drop, Nace, or come back with the cable?" Scarl asked.

Nace gestured: *Back.*

"Why?" Ariel asked. Nace pointed to the branch over the gorge. If the cable had been hanging straight down, they wouldn't have been able to reach it.

"So we won't have to reel it in and start over," Scarl said. "Here." He braced Nace while Ariel wrapped her body and soul around the boy. "That means you have to let go of him, Ariel, once you're across. Keep your eyes open. Don't let go too soon or too late and slip off the edge."

"I won't." Steeling herself, she turned her gaze toward the gorge.

"Keep her safe, Nace." Scarl's hands dropped.

Nace grunted as he pushed off. Ariel squeaked, crushed Nace in her arms, and prayed that the rocks at the bottom wouldn't hurt much. A heartbeat later, earth rose beneath her again, not the black-and-white river but brown duff and moss. She let go and thumped to the ground.

Nace swung away and landed safe on the other side once more. Adrenaline hit Ariel, sour in her stomach.

"Perfect," Scarl said. "Another just like that, Sienna." He drew the cable into position. "Be ready to catch her," he called to Ariel. "I'll come back for the pack, and then Nace and I can both swing together."

Poor Sienna shook hard enough for Ariel to see it across the gorge. "Don't worry," she called. She started to add that it wasn't as bad as it looked, but decided that might be a lie.

Scarl hoisted Sienna and she clung to his chest, eyes squeezed tight. Her shriek lasted even once she'd reached the other side and Ariel grabbed her.

"Let go!" Ariel cried. "Sienna, let—" All three of them were dragged back toward the edge. Ariel dug in her heels. Her boots slipped. Scarl's feet, too, scrambled for purchase, and he yelped as his lame one skidded over a tree root. At the last moment, he released the cable and all three dropped to the ground on the brink of the gorge.

Ariel flopped back toward safety. "Oh, oh," she panted. "That was bad. Why didn't you let go?"

"Are we alive?" Sienna raised her head.

"Barely!"

Scarl shoved her farther from the edge and wiggled out from beneath her. Wounds tore his palms where their combined weight had jerked the cable through his grip.

"Oh, I'm so terribly sorry!" Sienna began to cry. "I was just too, too frightened!"

"It's all right." He rose, wincing when he weighted his right foot.

Ariel looked anxiously toward Nace. Slowed and lacking momentum, the cable had not swung back far enough for him to catch it. Instead he was hauling it down off the branch.

"You're going to have to bring the pack yourself, Nace," Scarl called. "Sorry."

Nace flapped his hand disdainfully, shouldered the pack, and threw the free end of the cable back over the branch.

Ariel hustled Sienna out of the way. Her smile rose to greet Nace as he swung.

Two-thirds of the way through his arc, the branch cracked.

A startled look flashed in Nace's eyes. His body jerked

several feet lower. Ariel watched in disbelief as the tree branch gave way and tumbled into the gorge. Still flying toward her, Nace vanished below the cliff's edge.

"Nace!" She heard a sickening thud as he slammed against the stone face below. A dreadful scraping followed. The cable flopped down against the far side of the gorge, empty and limp. Its twang echoed.

"Nooo!" Ariel screamed and scrambled toward the edge.

Scarl tackled her. He flung her to Sienna, who fought to keep Ariel from the brink. By the time Ariel clawed free, Scarl was staring over the cliff and cursing under his breath.

He grabbed her as she raced to peep over the side. "Stop!" he hissed. "He's alive! Let me figure out how to help him!"

"He can't be!" But fate had supplied Nace a chance, and surely only his experience on swings had allowed him to grab it. He clung by one hand and one foot to the slats of the dangling bridge deck. It swayed with his impact. His head drooped and what Ariel could see of his face was bloody and cramped with pain.

"Hang on, Nace," Scarl called, his voice more reassuring than his expression. "We'll get you."

Ariel moaned. "How? He's got the rope in the pack."

Scarl shook her. "Hear me," he whispered fiercely. "You are going to kneel on the edge and keep talking to him. He's got to hold on until I can get him, and you've got to believe it yourself to convince him. Understand?"

"I'll help." Sienna crawled up and began speaking to Nace as if encouraging him to do nothing more desperate than hang on to a kite in a boisterous wind. Her breath coming in sobs, Ariel joined in.

On a second viewing, it didn't look quite so bad. Nace dangled no more than eight feet below, his left fist clenched over a bridge slat. His chest rose and fell in jerks, but they were reasonably steady. And the blood in his hair was already clotting. Ariel chattered about how they'd stitch up his wounds, if need be, and perhaps create a song about his most daring trick yet. Her heart leaped when his lips parted and he opened his eyes. Praising that effort, she whirled to see what was taking Scarl so long.

He'd found a sturdy tree branch, and now he wound his sore hands with swaths ripped from his shirttail.

"We'll have you up in a minute," Ariel told Nace. She prayed it would be true.

Scarl gave Ariel and Sienna quick instructions. Then he lay down and extended the branch over the edge. Nace's weight pressed the floppy bridge tight to the brink, but with Ariel's help, Scarl worked the branch between the stone and the bridge cables to put a few inches of space between them.

"Good," Scarl puffed. "I think I can get my fingers around those slats now." He sat up and braced one boot sole on each of the anchors. He bent forward and hooked his swaddled hands over a slat.

"Wait, can't Sienna and I pull, too?" Ariel asked.

"Do you see room for more hands? You'll just be in the way. I'd give a lot right now for a rope and the horse. But I'll have to do." Raising his voice, he called, "This might jounce you, Nace. Hold tight. Almost done, though. Here goes."

Scarl took a deep breath and pulled backward as if he were rowing a boat. His whole body strained. When he could not tip back much farther, he flashed one hand forward to a new grip, pulling hand over hand from one slat to the next and reeling the bridge, and Nace, upward. The tendons in Scarl's hands and wrists strained tight. He looked much like a Fisher hauling a net from the water—a net filled to bursting with fish.

Ariel alternated between clutching Sienna and encouraging Nace. As a loop of bridge coiled on the ground beside Scarl, she jumped to haul on that slack, trying to take a little weight off him.

"Leave it!" he growled through clenched teeth. "If I lose it, it'll catapult you into the gorge."

Wailing in helplessness, Ariel flopped on her belly at the edge. She exclaimed. Nace had risen nearly to the top. His face tipped up and his desperate gaze found hers.

"I can almost grab him!" She reached down. A grunt flew from her as Sienna sat on her legs to serve as an anchor.

A few scrambling hands, kicking feet, and awkward groans later, Nace spilled onto firm ground again.

CHAPTER 26

Dog Moon and a Loan

While Scarl lay panting in the dirt, Sienna and Ariel tended Nace. He managed a feeble smile. Scrapes and bruises marked his skin, but the cut on his scalp wasn't so bad. His right shoulder, on the other hand, looked so wrong it made Ariel's knees weak. She avoided it, digging carefully in the pack for a jar of water to wash the blood from his face. Although several jars had busted, a few were still whole.

Scarl took one look at Nace's shoulder and groaned. He hunkered next to the boy.

"Your arm's out of joint, Nace. This is going to hurt at least as much as it did coming out, but we've got to pop it back in."

Nace nodded miserably. The Finder eased the pack off Nace's arms, ripped his collar open, and probed the injury gently. Ariel winced at the unnatural lump under the skin. Then Scarl gripped Nace's shoulder with one hand and his upper arm with the other, long fingers reaching over the lump.

"On three, all right?" he said. "One—"

Scarl's hands jerked. Nace convulsed. He cried out, too, but only with a raspy huff. Ariel whimpered for him.

"I'm sorry." Scarl cupped his hands over the injury, rubbing. "I needed you off guard so your muscles might not be so tense. But it should feel better than it did. Ariel can bind it up for you." He glanced at her. "And we can all probably use a few pain-numbing plants."

She nodded, already making a sling from her sweater. Once Nace caught his breath, some of the tension leaked from his face, and color began flowing back in. He grabbed Scarl's hand with his good one. The boy glanced toward the tangle of bridge on the cliff's edge and pressed Scarl's hand to his heart, gratitude on his face.

"You're welcome," Scarl said. "I'm just glad you survived the slam on the rock, so you were still hanging on there to save."

Nace patted the backpack, twisting his body to show that it had taken most of the impact.

"But what happened?" Ariel tucked Nace's sling into place. "Why did we make it, but he didn't?"

"The friction on the branch?" Sienna suggested.

"It may have worn down with each swing," Scarl said. "Or he may have been less careful about how far out from the trunk he threw the cable than he was the first time."

Nace glanced ruefully across the gorge at the tree.

"Or it could have been that cursed bridge story," Ariel muttered. She fingered her necklace.

"We are very, very lucky that he didn't cross this one out of the world," Scarl replied. "Are you ready to take that off yet?"

She gave him an agonized look. "Do you really think it will matter?"

He hesitated. "Honestly? No. I think your hunch that they're linked to the map is correct."

"I'll wear it a while," said Sienna. "If you like."

Ariel snapped her head around, a denial sharp on her lips. It never departed. Once she got past her reflexive reaction, the idea was strangely attractive. And Sienna had earned her respect by swinging over the gorge despite her obvious fear. Ariel owed her for not putting up more of a fuss.

Her conflict must have shown on her face. "Not to keep," Sienna assured her. "Only until you want it again. I promise."

Timidly Ariel asked Scarl, "Would you feel bad?"

"No, I'd feel better. Not that I don't care about your safety, Sienna," he added hastily. "I'd just like to believe that its power might wane in the possession of somebody else."

"I'm not worried," said Sienna. "No offense, but I think you're both seeing ghosts in the shadows."

Ariel didn't argue. She merely reached to untie her satin cord. She had to admit that the necklace looked lovely on Sienna's long neck. Ariel could see the beads better, too. Still, she missed its weight on her throat. She didn't think it would be long before she asked for it back.

Everyone was anxious to get away from the gorge, so Ariel led them on right away, keeping a lookout for healing herbs she knew. Scarl limped worse than usual, and Nace's chirps had been silenced by aches. Although the responsibility for those pains gnawed at her, an immense relief buoyed Ariel, too. Her sense of urgency wasn't so desperate as it had been that morning, and their heading felt right. She fervently hoped the river crossing would be the only penalty she would pay for straying before.

After several miles, Sienna asked, "Does anyone know a song? I could use cheering up."

"Oh, forget that," Ariel said. "Scarl, you promised the stories today."

He made a face. "I was thinking earlier that it might be better—safer, somehow—if you don't know them. But after the gorge, I'm changing my mind. Maybe hearing them all could help us avoid another disaster."

He told two more stories that day, both of which Ariel had already heard. The first told of a Flame-Mage who went in search of a dragon, hoping to steal his fire. Though the dragon she found wasn't friendly, her bravery so astonished the beast that he didn't eat her. In the end she charmed him into sharing his flame and they lived happily ever after together.

"I'd love to see a dragon breathe fire," Sienna said. "That would be almost as good as lectrick."

"What's lectrick?" Ariel asked.

"You've never heard of it? It's this special fire, almost like lightning. Supposedly it doesn't burn anything up. That's the trick."

"Oh! Fire through a string?" Ariel and Zeke had once tried to make it, with alarming results.

"That's what some people call it." Sienna's voice held a hint of disdain. "They say people had it before the Blind War, but, frankly, it's easier for me to believe in dragons. I mean, alligators are real, so dragons might be, too. I don't want to marry one, though!"

"The babies sure would be ugly." Ariel giggled. "But I doubt we'll meet a dragon."

"Sienna's quest might turn up something even more hostile," Scarl said.

"The Flame-Mage story has a happy ending, though," Ariel retorted. He'd already told her several that didn't, but the second story he told that day ended well, too. In that one, a man with a selfish heart became stuck in the same day of his life.

Every morning, when he awoke, he was horrified to discover that everyone around him said and did exactly the same as they'd done the previous day. Eventually compassion, friendship, and love released him back into the proper flow of time, as well as a better life.

"Stuck in a loop," Ariel said. "And I walked in a loop yesterday. Think that's how this story echoes to us?"

"I don't think it's that simple," Scarl replied. "You said yourself that your map is not just a map to a place. It's a map to a time."

"Yeah, but not Groundhog's Day. It's summer, not the end of winter."

"Groundhog's Day is a cross-quarter day, halfway between winter solstice and the spring equinox. Just as Lunasa falls midway between summer and fall. It's a turning point, where winter gives way to spring, or it doesn't, and winter appears to continue. A crossroad. That might be echo enough. But this is not the only story in your necklace where time goes awry."

Ariel scowled, afraid to ponder their own evidence of a disturbance in time. "He gets unstuck, though," she said. "Happily ever after. I bet that's what counts."

Happy endings occupied all of their minds as the day dwindled without sign of Willow. Since Scarl believed the ford must be fairly distant downriver, Nace remained reassuring when they hadn't seen the horse by nightfall. By late the second afternoon, though, unspoken worry kept pace with them all. The Kincaller frequently cast puzzled expressions over his shoulder, and Sienna muttered under her breath.

"I'm starved," Sienna announced finally. "It's bad enough that I'll probably never see my tools again, thanks to Nace. But what are we supposed to eat?"

"Let's pause here, and I'll find something," Scarl said. At Ariel's expression, he added, "We'll move faster with food in our bellies. You can't starve them *and* drive them, Ariel."

Her own hunger gnawed, too, but did not argue as loudly as her restless feet. She felt fine as long as they kept moving, but she could hardly bear the anxiety that burbled into her during even brief stops.

Nace caught their attention. Nobody understood his gestures this time. He rolled his eyes and ran off.

"Wait!" Ariel cried.

"Let him go," said Sienna. "I mean, I'm glad he's not dead, but he's not my favorite person right now. Or ever."

Ariel bristled. "What is your problem with him, Sienna?"

"I know him better than you do, that's all."

"What, did you ask *him* to marry you, and he laughed?"

A bark of outrage left Sienna. "Never! Not if—"

"Stop it," Scarl said. "Let's not get at each other's throats. We'll all feel better with some food. Give me a chance."

Sienna slumped on a log, and Ariel soon regretted her cranky outburst. "I'm sorry," she murmured. "I can't blame you for being worried about your tools."

After a struggle for words, Sienna said, "I'm sorry, too. But, Ariel, he spies on people. Follows. This is not the first time."

"I don't think he means anything. He just—"

"No. It's more than shyness or not being able to talk. It's disturbing. I know you like him, though. I'll try to keep my mouth shut."

Scarl directed them toward a berry patch he suspected lay not far ahead.

"What about Nace?" Ariel said.

"He tracked us for days, remember?" Scarl replied. "He'll catch up."

"Just like Willow," grumbled Sienna.

She ate her words not two hours later when Nace ran up behind them. His arm sling bulged with walnuts and gooey clumps of honeycomb.

"Ooh, I take back half of the mean things I've ever said about you, Nace." Sienna gave Ariel a pointed glance. "Not all of them, but half."

While they cracked the nuts, Ariel played Too Many Questions with Nace to learn how he'd gathered the food. The eventual answer impressed her: he'd goaded a squirrel so intensely that she'd flung most of her larder at him. By night-fall, Scarl was wishing aloud that Willow had listened to Nace as well as the squirrel had.

CHAPTER 27

Dog Moon and Lightning

The threatening clouds rolling overhead bore more than rain.

"You know the August moon as Dog Moon," Scarl told Ariel as he watched them that evening. "To me, it's called Lightning Moon. I'm sorry to see that my name is right."

Ariel admired the flashes and nudged Sienna. "The lectrick is coming."

"I wish," said the Flame-Mage. "We'd better find somewhere to hide."

The discovery of cozy bedding spots did not seem to be among Ariel's Farwalker instincts, however, and the scrubby slopes where they now traveled offered little shelter. Too soon, raindrops pummeled them. They huddled like wet sheep in the twilight while Scarl worked to find somewhere decent to sleep.

He didn't bother with his broken glass. Dropping to his haunches, he merely cupped one hand and gazed into it as if the glass rested there. Rain filled it instead. Nace looked on, fascinated. Shortly Scarl led them to a hump of exposed bedrock with a dusty cleft beneath. It was a tight space for four, with no room for a fire. Still, it was dry, once they'd ducked past the rain sheeting off the overhang. Grateful, Ariel patted the bedrock for Zeke.

As they jostled against the rock and each other, Nace caught her eye. He pointed at Scarl and signed until she realized what he wanted.

"Scarl," she said, "Nace wants to know about finding."

"I'd like to, also," Sienna added.

"You've tried it; you can probably say more than I can," Scarl told Ariel. "It's hard to explain something you do mostly by instinct."

Ariel described the lesson Scarl once had given her: focusing on the glass alone, without thinking of the food she had craved, and then having her attention jarred loose so the location of something to eat flowed into her mind without conscious thought. She'd found only a lizard, but once roasted, it had helped curb her hunger. The memory prompted a question of her own.

"You know how you always say you can't find what doesn't exist?" To the others, Ariel explained, "It's his favorite saying. I've heard it two hundred times. But some things exist and don't exist at the same time. Or they exist in more than one way. Like if you tried to find Misha, would you find his ghost or his bones or nothing at all?"

Scarl winced. He tried to hide it by turning to stare out through their curtain of rain. "Nothing at all."

It took Ariel a moment to interpret his pained expression and realize it had nothing to do with the ghost of Tree-Singer Abbey. "Oh, Scarl," she breathed. "You've tried to find Mirayna."

The muscles in his jaw jumped. She longed to ask questions, but she could almost touch the cloak of shamed silence he'd pulled over himself, and she knew he wouldn't answer.

"Who's Mirayna?" asked Sienna.

Ariel held her breath, aching for the pain she'd unintentionally stirred. If only her thoughts would stay ahead of her mouth!

"Is she somebody in one of your stories?" Sienna pressed.

"Sienna—," Ariel began.

"She was someone I cared about. I'm going out to hunt for Willow." Scarl grabbed his coat and slipped back into the blustery dark.

Sienna erupted with questions.

"Scarl wanted to marry her," Ariel said, with a certain satisfaction overridden by sadness. "But she left the world last spring."

"How?"

Ariel gnawed her lip. The whole story was long and unpleasant, and she didn't want to be caught midway when Scarl returned. She said merely, "She had a disease that stopped her body a bit at a time."

"That sounds dreadful. What was she like?"

"She was an Allcraft. She—" Ariel's tongue tangled in her own sorrow and a guilt she'd never admitted to anyone, not even Zeke. Mirayna had left the world some days sooner than she might have, and Ariel could never be certain whether different decisions on her part may have given Scarl a little more time with his love. She couldn't think of Mirayna without regret.

Nace touched Ariel's arm, sympathy on his face.

"What else?" When Ariel didn't go on, Sienna said, "I'll ask him, then, when he comes back."

"Don't, Sienna. It makes him sad."

"He just needs some sympathy," the older girl replied. "And maybe a hug."

Nace *tsk*ed and Ariel's heart filled with dread. Obviously Sienna had never lost someone she loved.

By the time the Finder returned, catching the others a wink shy of sleep, he had apparently lost his coat and looked soaked but much more composed. He announced that Willow had caught them at last. The horse had met Scarl not far away, forlorn and stumbling with weariness. Scarl had hobbled him where he could graze and draped him with the coat to help keep their gear and the horse a bit drier.

They cheered.

Once the echoes stopped bouncing off the rock, Sienna said, "I'm sorry if I asked a dumb question. About Mirayna, I mean. Ariel told me. Please forgive me."

"No apology," Scarl replied. "You couldn't know."

"I'd like to, though," Sienna said. "I'd like to know more about you and her."

Taken aback, Scarl glanced at Ariel and fingered one cheekbone. "Well, I'm not going to discuss it," he said. "You can ask Ariel for more tomorrow. She knows enough to satisfy your curiosity."

"It's not idle curiosity," Sienna protested. Haltingly, she added, "I'm interested in you."

Ariel choked. Couldn't the Flame-Mage feel his discomfort? She almost wished they'd made camp in the rattling rain so the four of them wouldn't be so trapped together. Nace kept his eyes low and rubbed his sore shoulder.

Scarl looked at Sienna for long seconds without a trace of a smile. Familiar with that unblinking regard, Ariel guessed he was debating how to answer.

Sienna saw only irritation. She blushed and picked at her

nails. Though not long ago Ariel would have been pleased, now she felt sorry for her.

"I'm sure you mean it kindly, Sienna," Scarl said at last, "but that's a little too much interest. I'm here to serve the Vault and to make Ariel's farwalking easier, and that includes helping those she decides should walk with her—like you. I don't want to sound unfriendly, but that's really all you need to know about me."

Sienna gulped. "It does sound unfriendly."

"I'm sorry you feel that," he replied. "You've just stumbled on a topic that's difficult for me. Why don't we talk about something else . . . how we can help you when we reach a village, for instance. You said you were keen to be married, if I remember correctly. Should Ariel say so?"

"Or I could just tell them you wanted a new place to be a Flame-Mage," Ariel threw in. "So you can pick out a husband without the whole village knowing."

Sienna shot Ariel a look of reproach.

When she didn't otherwise reply, Scarl said, "I could probably find the worthiest men, Sienna, and point them out for you to consider. Or if any fellow catches your eye while we're still there, I would try to learn something about him, with your permission. I don't want to feel as though we've left you defenseless. There are some in the world even more unkind than me."

Ariel and Nace both hid smirks.

"You think I'm silly," Sienna grumbled.

"I didn't say that at all," Scarl replied. "I think you know what you want and are not afraid to try to get it. Those are rare and admirable traits. But you've never been away from people you know, and I—we—would like to help you get what you really want, and not something false."

"I think I can judge pretty well for myself," she said.

He dipped his head reluctantly. "As you like."

Wondering if Sienna still clung to her first plan, Ariel asked, "Do you want somebody cute or somebody rich?" She thought it was obvious that Scarl was neither.

Nace clasped both hands audibly over his heart, adding love to Ariel's list. It didn't aid her immediate purpose, but it pleased her nonetheless.

Sienna drew her fingertips through the dust alongside one knee. "What I want most," she said finally, "is somebody new. Somebody or something. At home I felt like a tired coal that needed a blast of fresh air to fire me up."

Ariel snorted. "New things or new people? No matter where we go, you'll get both. I can promise."

"Actually, I'm already getting both." A weak smile returned to Sienna's face. "It's not quite what I expected, but . . . I'm still glad I came."

They sank more comfortably into stillness. Before sleep won her, Ariel's thoughts returned to the notion that the Finder had sought his beloved's spirit. She recalled his confidence about finding the bridge out of the world. Troubled, she hoped that in another mood he'd be willing to tell her more. She'd like to ask, gently, if a Finder couldn't simply find a new love.

Yet that possibility worried her, too. She wasn't sure there'd be room in his life for both a love and a farwalking daughter. She did not want to need him, but she did. It made her feel childish. Even more, though, it scared her—because one thing Ariel already knew was that even things she desperately needed could be lost.

Her anxiety followed her into her sleep, or she followed it somewhere else. Sometime in the night Ariel awoke, the close blackness confusing until she remembered where they'd taken shelter. Nace lay curled beside her. She turned her head for Sienna and found only the dark, which seemed odd given the tight quarters; their limbs had nearly tangled before. Gently she reached out, not wanting to awaken anyone but needing assurance they all were still there. Her hand patted not earth but dry straw. When her fingers identified it, she realized it prickled beneath her as well.

Ariel sat up so quickly she should have bumped her head. The surprise that she hadn't stayed with her for only an instant. Scarl was gone, too, and it was not Nace sleeping beside her at all. It was Zeke. The wall at her back was flat—cut stone, not bedrock—and the stuffy air smelled of animal dung. She wasn't far southeast of the abbey, but just beneath it, in the Tree-Singers' goat pen.

Her breathing fast and jagged, she closed and opened her eyes several times, hoping to pull herself back to the cleft in the bedrock where she knew she should be. Giving up, she nudged Zeke, hissing his name. He didn't respond. When she tried harder and his body remained limp, she became gripped by a conviction that his corpse lay beside her.

Wailing, Ariel scrambled away toward the pen's wooden doorway and straight into rain. She slipped in mud and fell to her knees.

A hand grabbed her. Someone laughed. "Princess!"

"No!" She ripped away, squealing, from Elbert's hateful voice. He caught the back of her sweater and then one leg. She could not fight free. Her thrashing muffled the voice rising over the beat of the rain. Only after most of his weight pinned her down could she make out more words—and a new voice.

"Ariel! Stop! It's all right!"

The voice at her ear now was different. Though a Finder's, it belonged not to Elbert but to Scarl. She cried his name and forced her eyes to make out the planes of his face. Recognizing sooner his lean body, she clutched him and shuddered uncontrollably in the mud.

Slowly he eased up. "What is it? What scared you? Are you even awake? I felt you sit up and stir, but then you bolted like your socks were afire."

He tried to set her upright, but her muscles no longer seemed to work, and she sagged. She couldn't catch her breath, either. "Nace!" she gasped. "Zeke! And I thought he was dead!"

Scarl wiped her muddy hair back from her eyes. "Nace is right here. You woke him when you shook him. See?" He turned her head with his hand, and she saw pale ovals where both Nace and Sienna peeped out from the gloom. With soothing clucks, Nace rushed to her. Together he and Scarl drew her back into their shelter.

It was darker there, and Ariel kept a grip on both Scarl's arm and Nace's fingers, afraid to let go lest she lose them again. They waited for her trembling to ease. When she tried to explain, they assured her they'd all been touched by her or had whispered to her, without a response, before she had fled.

"I knew it must be an awful nightmare," said Sienna. "When I asked if you were all right, you only moaned." She leaned over Nace to give Ariel a hug.

"I am now," Ariel said, her voice quavering. She yearned to go home, though. Zeke was surely safe at the abbey, asleep, but after finding him lifeless, falsely or not, she longed to be certain. She rapped her knuckles on the bedrock and whispered, "Please tell Zeke I miss him. I'm worried about him. Please make sure the stones near the abbey keep him safe." Once she'd started, she couldn't stop banging the rock; stopping would let in her doubts, and the bedrock might turn to a goat pen again.

Scarl caught her hand before her knuckles bled. "Easy. I'm sure he's well."

They all lay back again, Ariel making sure her companions pressed close against her. As her racing heart calmed and sleep reclaimed first Sienna and then Nace, Ariel found a fistful of straw stuck to her blanket. Certain he was still awake with her, she pressed it into Scarl's hand and whispered, "Tracks from the past. Clinging . . . or catching us like a wave from behind. I got pulled under this time."

He crushed it in his fist, flung it into the rain, and murmured, "I knew it wasn't a nightmare. It seems to be getting worse."

"It is." Struggling against despair, Ariel added, "But I think the only way out is forward."

He agreed. His hand covered hers. "Try to rest now, though."

Instead Ariel listened to the falling water outside and imagined first a waterfall and then a great flood, and a Noah who built not a boat but a Vault, and she wondered how Timekeeper might gleam under the approaching full moon. She hoped she would see it and do what had to be done before the strange waters rising around her could drown her.

CHAPTER 28

Dog Moon, Thirteen Days Old

Rising early the next morning into freshly washed sunshine, Ariel felt she'd been given a rainbow of promise and hope. Cheered by birdsong, she and her companions greeted Willow with a double measure of petting before they set off. Ariel's feet scampered, pleased to be moving, and she ignored the only shadow on their timely departure: wet rocks steaming in the sun reminded her too much of the dank smell of the map.

Soon, rocks were not all that was steaming. Circling a large hill, the travelers walked into char. A wildfire had swept through; the rain must have quenched it. The blackened debris was still warm. Hissing clouds rose from their boots.

Sienna's eyes lit. "Look! My master talked about this, but I didn't really believe it! See how the grass burned near the roots and the stems fell over, unharmed? You can tell where the fire started from that—the grass points back to its source."

"We must be on the trail of your dragon," Ariel teased.

"Good!"

Scarl's expression was a great deal less enthusiastic.

"Think it started with lightning?" Ariel added.

Sienna's nose wrinkled. "It must have. But . . . some of the signs are confusing. And I've only heard about wildfire like this. I've never seen it. It takes a lot to start a wildfire back home in the swamp."

Once they'd walked well into the destruction, Ariel found it disturbing. Cinders crunched underfoot. The stench made breathing unpleasant, and the wind swirled ash into the air. Willow kept spooking at gusts until Nace left Ariel's side to keep the horse quiet. The skeletons of trees, some scorched more than others, stood black against the sky like warnings. As they passed, branches or trunks sometimes crashed down, spooking them all.

It didn't lighten the mood to find the burnt carcass of a deer at the base of a slope.

"Flame really swept fast up this hill," Sienna murmured. She cast uneasy glances at the steep terrain.

Spying the end of the blackness at last, Ariel charged toward it. Near the boundary, Nace pointed out a burned snag just off their path. A hollow had been chipped in the charred trunk. Staring out from the niche was a gleaming human skull. Unlike the ruined bridge, it had not been there long.

"That didn't get there by itself." Sienna's voice trembled.

They shot nervous glances toward the ridgelines. Nace voiced the mood by pretending to slash his own throat.

"I doubt it," Scarl told him. "The work of animals, perhaps."

Dubiously Nace reached to pull it down. Scarl stopped him.

"Let it be, Nace," he said. "I know what you're thinking, but it might be a shrine. A dead hero or someone beloved who left the world in a fire. We shouldn't disturb it."

"Only if someone lives around here," Ariel said.

"A village could be tucked behind any of these hills," Scarl replied. "Whether your feet take us to it or—"

Ariel exclaimed. She'd glimpsed a movement high on a ridge. By the time her roving eyes focused, they picked out only trees and rough land. But her imagination suggested that, for an instant, a human figure had stood there. Perhaps two.

"I thought I saw somebody," she explained.

"A village must be close, then!" Sienna said. "My village, I guess. I'm excited. Let's go."

They hurried away. Soothing green foliage had embraced them for more than a mile when they came upon a partial view of the narrow valley below their path. Ariel glanced down, half expecting tendrils of smoke from the hearth fires of a thriving community.

"Oh." The dread in Sienna's voice caught everyone's attention. They followed her gaze. Past the far side of the valley, a huge column of smoke boiled. Darker than the billowing clouds, it looked like a furious storm belched from the earth. Several twisting gullies opened into the valley, some green and some charred, and it was hard to tell which land now burned.

"It was pouring last night!" Ariel protested.

"Rain can be spotty, especially in storms," Scarl said. "Can you tell which direction it's going, Sienna?"

Sienna folded her hands at her chin and solemnly studied the smoke. She checked the wind, made visible by shuddering branches.

"I don't want to scare you, but we need to be careful," she said. "Let me watch a minute longer. I want to be sure."

At last she relaxed. "It's mostly moving away, and back north," she said. "We should be fine if we keep on in the direction we're going. Safer than going back, anyway."

Ariel exhaled, as relieved to avoid a detour as she was to hear that the fire was no threat.

Her relief was short-lived. Topping a ridge, they entered another burnt landscape. Purple fireweed dotted these slopes, bright against the char.

"This one's a year or two old," Sienna said. "See the saplings?" Alder sprouts pushed through the ash.

"It's still creepy," Ariel told her.

"These hills must attract thunderstorms," Scarl said.

"Maybe." Sienna's doubt hummed.

They crossed the scorched earth until the land dropped and became green again, although the burnt stink would not leave Ariel's nose. Then they spilled down a ravine and into a sloped meadow. Although scattered with shrubs and small trees, the meadow offered a sudden view—but not a distant one. A curtain of smoke hung below them. A livid red streak pulsed and leaped at its base.

Ariel recoiled. "Another!" She spun to face uphill. Palisades topped the slope the full length of the curving ridge, the rock as steep as a wall and twice as tall as Tree-Singer Abbey.

Scarl cursed. It frightened Ariel more when an oath fell from Sienna's lips, too.

"We're in trouble," said the Flame-Mage.

"How could lightning start so many fires at once?" Ariel demanded.

"I don't think it was lightning. Never mind. Later." Sienna whirled to gauge the fire's speed and potential escape routes. "If we have a later."

The wind gusted, carrying the roar and crackle—and heat—of the fire below. Flames leaped on the breeze from one tree or grass clump to the next. Willow reared. One armed, Nace barely kept him. Scarl helped.

"We'll have to retreat up the ravine," Scarl said.

"No." Sienna bit off the words. "Fire loves ravines. They're chimneys. If we could reach the fireweed we passed, I'd do it. We'd be safe there in the char. But I don't think we have time. Not uphill." She hurried forward.

"We can't hope to cross past it unless the wind shifts!" Scarl said. The open space was already narrowing as the fire clawed uphill. He jumped to grab Sienna's arm.

She yanked from his grip. "Listen to me! I know more about this than any of you, even if it is just head-learning. It doesn't matter if the wind shifts. We're in a bowl, uphill and updraft. We've got maybe ten minutes—less. We've got to find somewhere to hunker."

Scarl dropped to his knees. "We've seen lots of water today. I'll find a creek. Or a pond." He stared at one clenched fist.

Sienna turned to watch the fire and scan the still-unburned hillside. The flames snarled and gnashed, sweeping closer. With a stone in her belly, Ariel reached to help Nace with the horse.

Sienna moaned. "Our best bet might be—"

Hot air blasted them, nearly knocking Ariel down. It hurt to breathe.

"Get near the ground!" Sienna dropped into a crouch. "Scarl! Time's up!"

His face grim, he pointed downslope. "There's a hollow just past that rise." A wooded hump sat between them and the fire. "It's not much—it might be only a seep in the trees, but it's all the water that's close." He tugged Ariel toward it.

"No!" Sienna grabbed Ariel, too, yanking painfully. "Too

much fuel around it. If it isn't knee-deep, it'll boil us alive. We'd be better off running down through the flames!"

Scarl drew a tense breath. His voice came out even, but his grip on Ariel hurt. "Is that what you suggest then, Sienna? Through the fire to land that's already black?"

She gazed downhill and swallowed hard. "Last resort," she whispered. She spun. "I think we should do this instead. See that bare patch? Come on." She ran toward it, bent low to the ground. Unsure what else to do, the others crouched and scrambled after her.

"What are we doing?" Ariel panted.

"Scrape it clear of fuel, best we can. Dig ourselves in. Mostly grass is around it. That'll flare fast and not too hot. If we're lucky."

Willow squealed and tried to bolt. Scarl stopped to help Nace control him.

"Let him go," Sienna cried. "He can maybe outrun it. We can't."

Scarl grabbed Willow's bridle. "No. You and Ariel mount. He can carry you away, too."

"We all can ride!" Ariel said. "If we squish. There's no way I'm going without you."

Nace shook his head.

Scarl closed his eyes and said quietly, "I don't think he can outrun it carrying four."

"Maybe not even two," said Sienna. "Let him go. There's no need for him to . . ." Her voice trailed off.

"Die," Ariel whispered.

"No," Sienna snapped, regaining resolve. "We won't. Not if we get into that dirt. Let him go now, Nace. *Now*. We can hunker, but running is his only hope. If he'll listen, tell him to go that way and *downhill*." She gestured ahead. The fire was slightly more distant in the direction she pointed, the slope gentler, and the spindly trees farther apart.

Scarl snatched his coat from Willow's gear and released him, but Nace grabbed the horse's upper lip and twisted hard enough to get the animal's attention. The Kincaller made some sound, too, although the fire's growling drowned it. He yanked the bridle off so the reins couldn't hang up. Willow bunched his hindquarters and tore away, chunks of earth flying. Ariel hoped they'd made the right decision. The crackling in the air was so loud she had to keep checking to be sure the rushing flames weren't already upon them.

"Hurry." Sienna led them to a dimple in the slope filled mostly with shale, windblown twigs, and dead leaves. With both her hands and her feet, Sienna swept aside everything down to bare dirt.

"Do this! The fire will jump over."

"Here. A hoe." Scarl tossed each of them plate-sized slabs of shale to scrape over the ground in great swaths. They soon had a clearing twenty feet across. Ash and embers, still glowing, rained upon them. The smoke overhead made noon look like night. Flames bloomed in grass all around their bare spot.

Sienna yelped and whisked an ember out of her hair. "Trenches would be good." She panted, whirling her face toward the fire every few seconds. "To lie in. Cooler air. Here." She plowed the dirt with three mighty drags of her shale. She grabbed Ariel and shoved her to the ground. "In. Belly down. Pull your shirt over your face. Cover your head with your arms. I'll bury you some. It'll protect you from the heat. That's more danger than flames."

The roaring threat sounded enormous, as though one

continuous and boiling-hot sea wave were crashing over their heads. Too terrified not to obey, Ariel did.

"Scarl!" She peeked as Sienna dragged dirt and rocks over her back.

"I'm right here." His voice sounded too calm. He'd already widened her trench. He thrust Nace in, too, nearly atop Ariel. Nace grabbed her hand.

She wailed, "You don't have a trench!" Sienna did not, either, of course.

Ariel grunted in surprise and discomfort as the Flame-Mage dropped full-length atop her. By the time she understood, she could see Scarl's body crushing Nace's as well.

"We think alike, Sienna," he shouted and dragged his coat over everyone's heads. He must have shifted sideways, too, because even more pressure squashed Ariel into the dirt.

Talking stopped. The roar was too loud, the air too hot. Ariel buried her face against Nace in the stifling dark.

CHAPTER 29

Dog Moon and Fire

Ariel's limbs shuddered uncontrollably. She thought she couldn't get any more scared—and then she stopped being able to breathe. Sucking against fabric, she tried to drag in the searing air. Her lungs didn't recognize it. Her chest heaved. No breath seemed to come. Her muscles twitched. She fought a swell of panic, a demand to get up and run.

She felt Nace jerk and strain to push himself up. The weight above her shifted and slammed the boy back to the dirt. Ariel gave up even trying to inhale.

Her heart pounded, counting time, her thoughts swirling too loud in her head. A dreadful image flashed in her mind: she and Nace, baked like potatoes in coals while the potato skins blackened and crisped. Wanting to moan but without breath to do so, she waited for the secrets of death.

The buzz in her head was louder than the fire's roar when the weight on her eased. Flames were lifting them all into the sky like embers, she thought dully, surprised it didn't hurt more. As the buzz grew more distant and faded, she realized she was breathing again—hot air, but air her lungs would accept. The fire's roar receded to crackles.

For a long moment, she did nothing but breathe, still too frightened to feel any relief. Some of the weight on her shifted and rolled off. Nace raised himself slightly. Sienna slid from Ariel's back, an elbow poking down as she moved. Ariel couldn't unclench her eyelids. She felt a touch at her shoulder and then a tiny shake.

Her eyes cracked open. A blizzard of ash fell about them. Flames still licked above, beyond their clear space, but the fire was burning itself out against the stone palisades—except in the ravine they'd descended, where it raged more ferociously than ever. Ariel had to look away from that brilliant inferno.

"Careful," came Scarl's voice, hoarse. "Stay low. Breathe."

At that welcome sound, Ariel flipped over and lunged for him, on his knees alongside Nace. She buried her face in the Finder's dirty shirt.

"I thought you were going to—" She couldn't say it.

He brushed dirt from her cheek with his thumb. "We owe Sienna an unpayable debt. I never would have known what to do."

Ariel turned to embrace Sienna, too. She stopped. Sienna sat in the dirt, staring at nothing and trembling. Fierce blisters covered the backs of her calves. Ariel's exclamation hurt her raw throat.

"My fault," Scarl said. "I was so concerned about covering your heads that I forgot her legs were completely bare."

"It's okay," Sienna whispered, her voice distant. "It worked. It . . . I never thought . . . It hurts, though."

Nobody else had more than pounding headaches and

scorched clothes, which smelled so much like fresh ironing that Ariel wanted to laugh. She stuffed it back, afraid hysteria might snatch her. The heat eased in the wind, and Scarl helped Sienna stand. The young woman winced as her legs bent and straightened, and she clung to Scarl, whimpering. The transformation from her authority just moments before was startling.

"Come, Ariel, Nace," Scarl said. "Let's see if any of the water I found remains cool."

The motion revived Sienna, and by the time they reached evidence of a spring, she had lifted her head and quashed the sounds of her pain. The mushy ground was indeed scalding, though. Ariel could see the spring's tiny upwelling, pulsing and probably cool, but the water soaked into the ground rather than flowing away as a stream, so she couldn't get anywhere near without burning her feet.

"It's going to be a little while before we can get past hot mud," she told Scarl.

"I'll be all right," Sienna said weakly. "Let's find real water where I can dunk my legs in."

Ariel propped Sienna, stroking her arm, while Scarl concentrated on finding. Nace took Sienna's other hand. Words of thanks seemed completely inadequate.

"You were amazing," Ariel whispered.

Sienna managed a smile. "I guess I'm truly not an apprentice anymore. A fire-trial like that should definitely earn me mastery. Don't you think?"

Nace nodded hard.

"And then some," Ariel added.

Charred snags toppled not far away. Sienna gazed at the burnt landscape as if seeing it for the first time. "Goodness," she said. "I can't believe we survived that. And I can't believe I remembered what to do, either. I never dreamed I'd need that lesson, not ever. It all just came back, like a little cheat in my ear." She tipped her head thoughtfully. "But I think I'm supposed to give this back to you now." She slid her hand from Nace's grasp and reached to untie Ariel's necklace.

Ariel's fingers flashed up to stop her. Despite the cramp of reluctance squeezing her heart, she forced words from her mouth. She'd gained a whole new sense of what was important.

"No, Sienna," she said. "You . . . you keep it. If you want. We'd all be dead if it weren't for you. And it's my fault we walked into it. I should have been able to steer us around it."

"Oh, piffle," Sienna replied. "The first thing hammered into a Flame-Mage is that fire doesn't always behave. If we can't predict it, I don't know why you should be able to. Silly." She hugged Ariel. "No. It's yours." She drew back, removed the necklace, and tied it once more around Ariel's neck. "But I enjoyed wearing it. Thank you."

Ariel ran her fingers over her beads. If her dehydrated body had contained moisture to spare, she would have cried. Instead her eyes only burned. The necklace meant even more to her now. And although she did not understand how the moon could have known this, clearly Sienna had been exactly what Ariel had needed from Skunk.

And yet . . .

Nace reached to flick ash out of Ariel's hair, combing his fingers through it to make sure it was gone and not burning. He gave her a strained smile. She rubbed his arm in its sling. She wouldn't be here right now without him, either.

"How's your shoulder?" she asked. He shrugged, but lifted only the good shoulder. Her friends were taking a beating. She hoped she could make it up to them somehow.

Scarl got their attention and they shuffled downhill. A substantial creek wasn't far; the fire simply had already jumped it and stood between when they needed a haven. Everyone waded in, grateful to be cool. Sienna's pain eased a little. Ariel searched for submerged marshyellow or water aloe. She found none. Scarl had no better luck.

"As soon as we can get somewhere not burned," Ariel promised Sienna, "we'll find something to poultice your legs with."

Sienna sighed. "I had burn cream in my bag, if I'd thought to grab it. Oh, well."

They all wanted to linger and recover, and they did so for more than an hour. But without any food or supplies, they soon had little choice but to seek somewhere unravaged by fire so Scarl might find them something to eat. They followed the creek, which suited Ariel's feet anyway. After passing by several sweeping ridge views, however, it became clear that it would take all day to reach anywhere lush. Green hills rose in the distance, but before them, black ground, or black dotted with green, stretched for miles in every direction.

"I don't understand," said Sienna. "It's like a quilt of different fires stitched together, as if each burns to the edge of an old one, and then another starts somewhere else where there's fuel. I've never heard of anything like it."

"I have," Scarl muttered. "I'm just having a hard time believing it on a scale this big."

He told them of Reapers who used fire to flush animals from hiding or drive them over cliffs.

Nace expressed outrage.

"It doesn't sound fair to me, either," Scarl told him. "But I suppose that depends on how hungry your family is."

"That fits," said Sienna. "I haven't seen anything that looked like a lightning strike. But I did see hints of fires that did not want to burn and were coaxed."

Ariel gazed around them. "Even a whole village of Reapers couldn't need to burn this much for hunting, though. Besides, they'd get meat, but what about fruit and mushrooms and nuts and healing plants and everything else?"

No one had an answer. Nor had they yet seen any sign of a village.

"The only other reason," Scarl said, "would be to wage war." Feeling suddenly hunted themselves, they glanced into the black shadows and hushed.

Not too much later, however, they were all overjoyed to spy Willow splashing along the creek toward them, still bearing the packs. He whinnied in greeting. Embers had caught in his mane and among the folds of the packs, singeing both, but he seemed mostly unharmed. For a moment, Ariel thought Nace might cry.

Tears did slide down Sienna's cheeks as she put her cream on her legs. Scarl shot Ariel several hesitant looks. She could guess what he was thinking. But it was only midafternoon.

Ariel exhaled hard. "You want to camp here and rest, don't you?" she asked him. "Since Willow brought us food and our gear."

"It might be a kindness to your traveling companions," he said quietly. "It's been a trying day—several, in fact—and unlike you, we're not all . . ."

"You can say it," she muttered. "Obsessed."

"I was thinking more along the lines of trail-tough. Or even . . . Farwalkers."

She didn't know how to explain that she wanted to rest as

much as any of them. She was simply afraid to—particularly if she really *had* seen someone spying on them.

But Sienna overheard them. "I would love to stop," she said. "Don't get that wrong. But I'll do what you need to do, Ariel. I don't understand everything you and Scarl talk about, the moon and your map and all that. But I didn't just save your life so something else dreadful can happen to you, and it's obvious that you think it will, if we go too slow. It's all over your face every afternoon. Like it is now. And I can't think about the pain quite so much when we move. So we can keep going. If you ask me. Which you didn't."

Ariel's heart swelled, but she felt even worse about wanting to push on. "How about just one more hour?" she asked. "Maybe . . . two?"

They ended up walking for three more hours, drawn on by a swath of enticing green and the turquoise jewel just behind it. At first glimpse Ariel thought the vast water might be an arm of the sea, but as they drew closer she could smell the algae and mud of a lake. It curled around the feet of a small mountain at its far shore—one untouched by fire. The water stretched farther into the distance in both directions than Ariel's eyes could follow, curling away from the fringe of unscorched woods that embraced the travelers at last.

They made camp on the beach. Bleached snags and downed trees rimmed a high-water mark, with a wide strand of pebbles below. Minnows darted in the shallows. Scarl fished, Ariel made a poultice for Sienna's swollen legs, and Nace seemed preoccupied with the flotsam at the water's edge. They all fell asleep before dusk, so Ariel did not see that the moon was shaved only slightly out of round.

She dreamed of Zeke as he'd been last spring. Still expecting to become a Tree-Singer, he'd been worried that his favorite tree had stopped speaking to him. Ariel was gripped by the dream, so real that she fretted with him. She could feel the weight of the bucket dangling between them and smell the green tang of the creek water inside. Pollywogs squirmed beneath its sloshing surface.

Then, bucket gone, she and Zeke sprinted together into the woods toward his maple. Ariel wanted to help Zeke with the tree, if she could. She was late, though, very late, and did not heed where her feet went. She tripped on an exposed root and flew sprawling.

Her fall seemed to take a long time, as though she'd fallen from high in the tree and not merely over its gnarled root. Down, tumbling down, she whisked through swirling air thick with leaves and the mossy smell of the forest. Twigs slapped her face. Her hands and arms flailed to catch hold without the slightest success. With a chill certainty, Ariel knew she was going to hit the ground much too—

She jerked. The falling was gone. The air against her skin, the feel of her weight on the ground had a presence, a brighter reality that told her she'd only dreamed of a fall and now lay awake. For an instant, relief drove out her dread. A bad dream was over. She hadn't fallen. She could open her eyes—

No. Her lids wouldn't open. None of her muscles responded to her urgings to move. Cold and hard, her body pressed the earth like a stone. Ariel could still smell the forest, still feel the tree branches stinging her skin. Her ears filled again with the rush of her own motion and the banging of her heart. She could also hear someone or something moving nearby, though: footsteps, rustling fabric, a snatch of a female voice. Her mother? Those sounds rose and faded, in and out like a surf, first nearby, now distant.

Bewildered, Ariel tried harder to lever her body to action. It ignored her commands. Her mouth was not even shut; it was slightly agape, but forcing words toward her lips only tightened her throat and built pressure in her head that pounded in time with her heart.

Her confusion was roaring toward panic when a thought pierced her: maybe she'd hit the ground after all. Perhaps this was the prison of a badly broken body. She felt no pain but little else now, either, except a dull heaviness and the ground, unyielding against her claylike limbs. She might even be under that ground, part of it now, in her grave.

Wishing to scream and unable, except in her mind, Ariel snapped to mental silence at a new sensation—*any* sensation. Something squirmed at her ribs. Worms, gnawing her corpse? No, too clustered, too firm . . . Fingers. It had to be fingers. Focusing there, counting the points of contact, feeling them wiggle helped her push back her panic. Tickling, that's what the fingers were doing. Ariel grasped at that realization and followed the touch like a beacon, pulling herself out of the darkness, ribs first.

Her eyelids, long prying, flew open.

"Ha. You must have been even more worn-out than me."

The voice drew Ariel's gaze, and she rejoiced that her neck turned. A woman crouched beside her, but it wasn't her mother. Too young. Shocking red hair; that was wrong, too. And a face showing strain, the kind Ariel had seen on people in pain.

"I've never seen anyone sleep that hard," the woman added. "I thought even tickling wasn't going to work."

Confused, Ariel wanted to blink her eyes but feared they'd stick if she closed them again. Instead she stared. Red hair, fiery hair, fire . . .

"Sienna!" The name leaped from her throat, all her effort to speak loosed at once.

"Don't blame me. Scarl said I ought to wake you."

Scarl. At his name. Ariel knew where she was again and with whom. She sat up, or tried to. Her limbs were clumsy and slow as though her body still balked at returning to the wakeful world. She nearly flopped sideways and only stayed upright by flinging one hand to the side to brace herself.

"Sorry," she mumbled. "I was dreaming. Too real. And I couldn't remember at first who you were. I only knew you weren't my mother."

"Oh, I'm not that old!"

Ariel didn't manage to return Sienna's smile. She stuck her feet in her boots and rose to hurry away from her deathly dream. The expanse of green water at the lake's edge welcomed her. She distracted herself from her dank unease by throwing stones into the lake until her arm hurt. The stones were a penance, too, of a sort. She'd missed keeping her promise to Zeke yesterday.

Besides, she needed an anchor, something physical to grab and command, whose effect she could count on. The musical plop of the rocks held her in place. But Ariel could feel her dream hovering, waiting for her eyes to close once more, ready to drag her back from one part of her life into another—one that, right at the end, turned to nightmare. Nor was it merely a dream, she was sure. It was a path that she'd walked and that somehow wound before her again. If she strayed from the one she was on, the two might be tangled and she'd become lost.

Sienna's difficulty in rousing her weighed on Ariel's heart. She feared the next night—sure to come and nearer than ever to August full moon. If Ariel went to sleep under that ominous eye, she wasn't sure she could return.

CHAPTER 30

Dog Moon, One Day Shy

Ariel thought for a moment that her feet would insist on splashing right into the lake toward the far shore. They veered at the last minute, however, and she led her friends along the shoreline's long arc.

"Can you leave the world through a dream, Scarl?" Ariel asked, trying to sound nonchalant.

"People certainly leave the world in their sleep," he replied. "Hard to know if they were dreaming, though. Or whether they dreamed they were crossing the bridge."

"Ever have a dream where you're falling?" Sienna asked. "I used to a lot, with all the ladders back home. And that stupid tree swing." She shot a sly look at Nace, but he didn't rise to the bait. "I always, you know, jerked awake. But I've heard that if you land in a dream like that, you'll die."

Ariel held her face very still. She could feel Scarl's eyes upon her, though, as pointed as any question.

"I keep dreaming of falling," she murmured. "I don't like it."

After gazing at her a while longer, he replied, "You've risked bad falls more than once in the last few weeks. It would probably be wiser to keep your feet on the ground. Whether there's a waterfall to plunge over or not."

"I'll try." She hoped her dreams and Timekeeper both would comply. At least in her vision of the waterfall, she'd stood at its base. "But that reminds me. There's one more bead in my necklace. The gold one. You haven't told us that story yet."

"Its story is called 'Golden Seeds,' and here's why. In a place not far away, there lived a Reaper with a flourishing garden. One day she discovered a pea vine growing out of place among carrots. Its single pod split apart at her touch and, to her amazement, golden coins tumbled out."

"Lucky," Ariel said.

"Indeed. Needless to say, the woman carefully tended the pea vine. It grew slowly, but every pod held a row of gold coins. She traded them for fine clothes, tasty treats, beautiful furnishings, and a servant to do her most unpleasant chores. She lived like a princess all summer and never set foot in her garden again except to keep watch on her pea vine and harvest her gold."

"She didn't even collect her vegetables?" Sienna asked.

"Nope. She became lazy and the plants were overrun by weeds. She didn't care. Only one thing troubled her: the more nice things she had, the more she feared losing them. The pea vine could wither, a thief might steal her goods, or her house could burn.

"Fretting endlessly, she went by the glow of the full moon to the village well. For it is said that the light of a full moon shining into a well will reflect not the moon but the future—the face of a true love, the gender of a baby still in the womb, or the path to be taken when leaving the world."

"A well." Ariel thought of the watery scent of the map a few nights ago.

"Yes. The woman bent backward over its edge with her hair streaming down, because everyone knows you can only see your future in a well if you look upside down. And she spied a reflection that wasn't the moon's. She saw herself as an old woman, surrounded by grandchildren. She saw a prince who had heard of the pea vine and would come to ask her hand in marriage. She saw—"

"Why would she marry someone who only wanted her gold?" Ariel asked. She didn't like to interrupt him, but this was important.

"Well, he was a prince," Sienna said.

"He should have his own gold, then."

"I didn't make it up, Ariel," Scarl said. "I only tell it. Can I go on?"

She frowned at the dancing reflections on the lake alongside them. "Can we change it so he came for the gold and she told him no, but then they fell in love anyway and he let her keep all the gold for herself?"

Scarl laughed despite himself. "I suppose. And while we're at it, we'll say she also saw herself feeding everyone in the village, so no one would want."

"Good," Ariel agreed.

"I'm so relieved you approve," he said. "The woman bent over the well felt much relief, too, at those happy reflections. As she raised herself upright, though, she heard a soft voice. She knew it must be the voice of the well sprite.

" 'But for all this future to pass,' said that voice, 'you must drop in a gold coin for me before the moon sleeps tonight.'

" 'Why should I throw my gold into a well?' the woman asked. 'It will be wasted.'

" 'Did you plant gold in the soil before your vine sprouted

there?' asked the sprite. When the woman admitted that she certainly had not, the sprite went on. 'Then you owe a debt to the earth. Plant a gold seed in the well so your future can grow.'

"Checking her pocket, the Reaper found one small coin. As she drew it out, though, a fit of greed seized her. 'No,' she declared. 'I have the vine and gold now. The future is already mine.' She kept the coin in her fist and hurried home.

"To her horror, she found everything changed. Her beautiful things had all vanished. Her rooms were barren and her cupboards were bare. Worst of all, her garden contained nothing but dirt.

"She ran back to the well and begged the sprite for forgiveness. The sprite did not answer. Her heart in her throat, the woman relinquished her last possession, the gold coin in her fist. It sank into the well—"

Splash! Their heads jerked around. Nace grinned. Ripples spread from the rock he'd tossed into the lake.

"Just so," Scarl said. "Still the sprite did not speak."

"She blew it," Ariel said.

"Yes. But the sprite felt the tears that dripped into the water, and even angry sprites may be moved. When the woman gave up and returned to her house, the rooms and her cupboards still echoed. But her garden grew once more in the moonlight. In time, its lone pea vine again bore gold coins.

"The woman took her lesson to heart. She shared her fortune with any in need, and although it hadn't been asked, she dropped another coin into the well at every full moon. People jeered that she threw them away, but she didn't mind. She'd discovered, you see, that the path from yesterday to tomorrow may not always be straight. Sometimes seeds sown for the future can sprout and bear fruit in the past."

Sienna scoffed.

Ariel waited until she was sure Scarl was done before she ventured, "It's a good story, but it seems to me that it's mostly about not making well sprites mad."

"Even simpler," said Sienna. "It's a rather silly way to say, 'Don't be stingy.'"

"Stories may be understood many ways," Scarl replied. "I'm more concerned about the full moon in this one, and the disappearance of wealth, since we've already surmised there's a risk to the Vault."

"Plus a well, maybe," Ariel reminded him. "If Lamala was right about my map."

"Indeed. And again, trouble with time, a confusion between present, future, and past." Meaningfully he slid a thumb beneath the strap circling Willow's ears. The horse's skin was becoming chafed by Orion's undersized bridle.

Ariel shivered. The incongruous things from their past still unnerved her, but at least Scarl shared those with her. In her nightmares, she fell alone.

"I wouldn't mind a little mix-up in time if it brought us some gold," said Sienna. "But I still think they're only stories. You could pick a few details from any—"

Nace clapped, startling them all. He pointed.

A distant shape shimmered through the haze over the lake. Though it appeared to be limestone or granite, its stark lines could not be a natural formation. Stretched from one shore to the other, it looked like a monstrous bridge.

"Forget the gold," said Sienna. "If that's the bridge to the land of the dead, I'm stopping right here."

"I'm not sure it's a bridge at all." Scarl squinted. "It looks like it touches the water."

"There isn't flame beneath it, at least," Ariel added. "Come on."

As the day progressed and they drew nearer, she gave a cry of recognition. "It's some kind of dike! A wall to hold back the water. We had one in Canberra Docks."

"I was thinking beaver dam," Scarl said. Nace nodded vigorously. "But not built by beavers."

"There must be a village nearby," said Sienna. "Maybe it was their Reapers setting the fires."

"Maybe." Doubt filled Scarl's voice.

"It's from before, isn't it?" Ariel asked him, her excitement growing. "How could anyone now build something so huge?"

"There are stories of such things," he replied. "I thought all were destroyed. But I didn't expect Tattler, either."

Ariel increased their pace. The dike was farther away than it looked, and the sun dropped behind the hills early, but reflected glow let them continue. They'd closed to within half a mile when a distraction emerged from the twilight to greet them: another skull lay against the base of a boulder.

This time, Scarl did not stop Nace from taking a closer look, saying, "This one's been here a long while." The Finder raised his eyes to the water wall. "Although certainly not so long as that."

Ariel eased past Nace and the skull. "Put it down, Nace. It's creepy."

He chased her with it, clacking his teeth. She scrambled away.

"One might be a shrine, but two is a warning." Sienna planted her feet. "Do we have to go this way?"

"Unless you want to swim," Ariel said. "I'd like to get to the wall before we camp. I'll sleep better if I can see what's on the other side."

"I'd sleep better if we weren't surrounded by death," Sienna retorted.

Nace flung the skull into the lake, where it sank with a splash.

"We haven't seen anything to fear yet." Scarl drew Sienna forward to Ariel's side. "There's nothing threatening about bones by themselves."

Ariel was the only one who knew him well enough to hear his misgivings.

Soon the nearest end of the water wall loomed over them, higher than any building, a stark shadow in the dusk. Awed, Ariel and her friends craned their necks as they approached.

Light flared. They froze. Bright fires, a dozen or more, had burst along the wall's top at precisely the same instant.

Ariel rubbed goose bumps from her arms. "Bridge or not, Sienna, there's your flame."

"Odd flames." The Flame-Mage peered at the evenly spaced glows. They sent up no smoke, had no visible tender, and seemed to burn nothing but air. The unwavering fires shone like miniature suns.

"We must not be alone," said Scarl. "Though I still don't see any—"

Sienna gasped. "I think—no. It can't be! Can it? If that's lectrick . . ." She hurried forward. "I've got to get up there."

"Stop where you are!" ordered a loud male voice. "If you value your heads."

"People!" Sienna veered toward the voice.

Ariel lunged to yank her back. "Are you deaf?" She'd been

greeted often enough with surprise, but never before with a threat.

"We come in goodwill." Scarl thrust his staff and Willow's reins at Nace and stepped around Ariel to the front. When only silence replied, he added, "And half our group are only apprentices. Won't you welcome us?"

They stared into the gloom, searching for a face.

Scarl muttered to Nace, "Get the girls on the horse." Although Ariel had no intention of obeying, Sienna was mounted before the gruff voice came again.

"Name yourselves."

Scarl spoke for them all. "Scarl Finder, Ariel Farwalker, Sienna—"

"Farwalker? We don't take kindly to Farwalkers here. We've had strife with their kind in the past."

Scarl and Ariel shared a look of surprise. Murmuring floated to their ears. As Nace vainly tugged Ariel toward the horse, her eyes finally picked out two dark, mobile shapes against the paler gray of the shore. They were hard to distinguish with the bright lectrick fires beyond.

Scarl started to give an assurance that they meant no harm.

"Y'ave two females there, don't ya?" The question came on a woman's voice, no less surly than the first.

"Yes," Sienna called from over their heads, her voice clear. "Please, we only want somewhere to sleep for the night."

Scarl jerked a hand at Sienna to be quiet.

Though she understood, Ariel's instincts chimed with Sienna's impulse to speak up. She said, "We could greet you again in the morning, when we can all see."

More lengthy murmuring ensued.

At last the man called, "We'll haul you inside, where we

can keep a close eye on you and find out what mischief you bring." Boots shuffled and the shadows approached.

"Inside?" Scarl's knife left its sheath.

Ariel's confidence sagged. She drew so near to Scarl that she knew she'd be in the way if a struggle commenced. She couldn't help it. Having spent enough time as a captive, she wasn't about to try it again.

Feeling her at his elbow, he pushed her an arm's length back toward Willow.

"Aye, inside to our halls," came the woman's voice again. "We can get a good look at each other, and Mo will stop acting like he's about to crack your heads."

"That don't mean we're friendly," the man added sternly. "But if you'll mind manners for a moment, so can we."

The hostility had already worn through Scarl's meager patience. Ariel could see from his posture that he meant to reply with hot words. She clutched his arm to stop him, sorry the darkness prevented them from communicating with only their faces.

He pulled free and growled, "This doesn't feel right to me."

"I'm scared, too," she whispered. "But I think we should go with them. At least, that's what my feet want to do."

CHAPTER 31

Dog Moon and Strife

Ariel knew Scarl had never doubted her more, but after a long hesitation he returned his knife to its sheath. His hand on its hilt, he waited silently for what happened next. She held her breath but stood her ground as the two shadows neared them.

The man and woman stopped just beyond the reach of a handshake. The bare-chested man was hefty and hairy and much younger than the thin, careworn woman. He gripped a formidable metal pipe that rested on his shoulder, but she clasped her hands almost in pleading.

"You see," she murmured to the man. "They're people like us. A family, mayhap."

"Odd family." His face almost lost in an orange beard, he peered up at Sienna. "That the Farwalker, on the beast?"

Ariel spoke fast. "No. Me."

Both strangers regarded her like an unfamiliar bug that might bite.

"Meet the boogeyman face-to-face," the woman said, "and it isn't so bad."

"We'll see," he muttered. "How'd you get past the Reapers?"

Ariel's mind raced. "You mean where everything was burned? So your people did that?"

"Not ours, exactly," said the woman. "We let 'em in during winter. They bring meat. And their work helps protect us."

The man snorted. "They're like fleas on a dog. Worse. Never mind. Since they must not 'a reaped you, it ain't none of your business. Come on."

"We've given our names." Scarl's voice held an edge. "Will you let us have yours?"

"Time for that inside, in the light."

"My son Mo, and I'm Trisha," said the woman. "Fishers. Come along." She turned to lead them. The man stepped aside so he could take up the rear. Scarl motioned Nace into the front with Willow and Sienna. Then he nudged Ariel and fell in behind her.

"If we step off the path that you feel in your feet," he growled in her ear, "I want to know the instant it happens."

Ariel nodded. She returned Mo's frank stare as she passed him. Though it felt like a fib, she flashed him an amiable grin. He flinched.

They climbed up an outcrop of rock and a few moments later stood at a convergence of the water wall and the slope. The wall was as thick as the largest house Ariel had ever seen. At the far edge, beyond a fence of metal pipe not unlike Mo's club, she could feel the vacant air of a steep drop. In the near end of the wall stood a door. Sienna couldn't keep her eyes off the tiny, bright fire in a jar hanging over the doorway. Amazement and questions, both barely contained, flittered over her face.

Scarl studied the door and the building and gave Ariel a grim look.

"We have to," she said under her breath. His reluctance frightened her more than the door. In fact, if she'd dared to open it herself, she would have. Both her curiosity and her path called her forward. Required to wait, her toes curled in her boots.

"That thing is too big to go in." Trisha gestured at Willow.

"Haven't you ever heard of a horse?" Ariel asked. She'd visited places that kept few animals, but even villagers without horses of their own had known what they were.

A scowl compressed the woman's face.

Regretting her question, Ariel pushed a wry smile to her lips. "He's a good horse, but he probably wouldn't go in even if we wanted him to."

Through clenched teeth, Scarl said, "We can tie him here to the rail."

Sienna slid down. While Nace secured Willow's reins, the Finder moved to unlash their bags.

"Never mind that," Mo told him. "You won't need nothing you've got there inside. I said don't!"

Scarl spun. Mo took a step back and brandished his pipe.

"Look," Scarl said, his voice quiet but deadly. "I'm wearing the only weapon we have, and we've gotten this far without testing mine against yours. There are things here we don't want to lose. We'll bring them."

Unable to remain still in the wave of tension that followed, Sienna quivered and clutched Ariel's arm. Nace didn't even glance up from his hands, frozen in midknot. Yet his entire body went taut, ready to spring.

Afraid the slightest motion would set the men off, Ariel barely parted her lips to point out, "We've done everything else that you've asked." She was more concerned about Scarl than their gear, but she knew she couldn't ask him to back down again.

Looking equally worried, Trisha murmured Mo's name.

The big redhead's fingers tightened on his pipe. Its tip bounced in the air. Yet Scarl must have seen something in Mo's eyes that reassured him enough to turn one shoulder, if not his back. He reached again for the lashings holding their gear. The pipe remained poised, but it stilled. The travelers each soon hefted their packs, save Nace, who had none. Too heavy to eas- ily carry, Sienna's trade gear was left on the horse.

Trisha reached for the door handle. The door opened on a small, bright space made of the same gray stone as the exterior walls. Remarkably flat and smooth, the room looked to Ariel more like the inside of a sand castle than anything built of stone. It was nearly as empty. The space held nothing but chunky stairs that descended immediately beyond the door.

Scarl gripped Ariel's shoulder from behind. She didn't need to see him to know he questioned entering a place that would obviously be so difficult to escape from. She didn't think Mo and Trisha offered any choice, short of a fight. But she took a deep breath and confirmed the sense in her feet: Go. She jerked a tiny nod before she stepped forward from under Scarl's fingers.

She ducked through the doorway and followed Trisha down the stairs. Coming last, Mo yanked the door shut behind them. It banged like the lid to a tomb.

They descended, it seemed, to the center of the earth. Ariel had never seen so many stairs, which twisted a corner every dozen steps. Hollow echoes rose behind them. The way stretched wide enough to descend two by two, and she welcomed the tight grasp of Sienna's hand. She could see Sienna trying not to wince at each bend of her burned, weeping legs.

They reached a landing with a door. Looking down over a rail, Ariel saw more landings below. This door opened on a huge, echoing hallway like a great cave. But the walls were smooth and flat, their corners square, and lectrick fires dotted the ceiling. Along one side sat a row of rounded metal shapes as big as cottages. Ariel gasped. Tucked between them, behind curtains and lean-to walls, people lived. Ariel saw no hearths, garden plots, or livestock, but at least two dozen families filled the strange cavern.

"The whole village is down here?" Ariel asked. Voices murmured from corners, and the smell of cooked fish awoke a growl in her stomach.

"Haven't you ever heard of a dam?" sneered Trisha.

"Sure, with beavers living in it," Sienna said under her breath. "Not people."

Though she had to agree, Ariel hoped to win over Trisha. She said, "No, but it looks nice. Is that what you call your village? Dam?"

Trish snorted. "No, goose girl, this is the dam." She waved at the structure around them. "The name is Electron."

"Lectrick," echoed Sienna.

A shadow fell over Trisha's face. She urged them forward and called to the first adult she saw. "Run and hail the master. We found strangers."

The word "strangers" flashed through Electron like lightning. By the time the group reached the middle of the great hall, flocks of children and adults lined their path. Despite what seemed a warm and dry place to live, or maybe because of it, their clothing was skimpy and ragged. Like Mo, most of the men went bare chested. Everyone's skin was quite pale, almost bleached, except for rosy cheeks. They were thin, though. The only decoration or jewelry Ariel noticed were fishhooks through earlobes. Those looked like they'd hurt.

Although the crowd's attention included no smiles, her fear receded. She heard Scarl, behind Sienna, exhale a lungful of tension as well. They were both accustomed to a curious mob. And although the vast hall and its strange shapes in no way resembled a normal village, the presence of children lifted some of the threat.

Nobody dared to touch, but the onlookers raked the newcomers with sharp eyes. Questions and unkind remarks flew. Trisha and Mo ignored the hubbub completely. Ariel smiled hard and told the friendlier faces that they were visitors from far away. Sienna, who glowed in the attention, had fewer qualms. Scarl had to keep prodding her forward as she lagged to introduce herself, especially to young men.

Nace only hung on Ariel's heels—until abruptly he whirled.

"What's your problem?" asked a boy of similar age in the crowd. He glided forward to meet Nace's glare. "You got trouble with the word 'scarface,' mayhap?"

Nace curled his upper lip. Ariel, who had also heard the mean words about her, reached for his arm. He'd slipped the wounded one out of his sling.

The Electron boy crooned, "S'matter? Cat got your tongue?"

Scarl pushed his way over, but not quickly enough. The boy flicked Nace in the cheek with a finger. Nace smacked the boy's arm down. The boy lunged. His sneering lips met the Kincaller's fist.

Ariel's hands flew up to stop them, but she tangled in a flurry of elbows and curses. Village boys surged into the action.

Something hard caught her temple. Reeling, she felt a yank from behind. Scarl shoved past her into the fray.

Pulled out of harm's way, she caught a glint of Mo's club as it drew back to swing.

"Don't!" She flung herself toward him.

If she thought at all, it was to catch Mo's arm before he could deliver his blow, but instinct forced her to duck her head out of its path. She fell about his legs, clutching his knees. Mo lurched and then recovered his balance. Ariel clung, her eyelids squeezed tight, dreading the thud of that pipe on flesh.

Instead, she felt it tap her ribs. She cracked open her eyes. Scowling down at her, Mo jerked his head for her to get off his feet.

Holding on through the weakness of relief, Ariel spun her face toward the fight. Nace wasn't large and he had limited use of one arm, but he'd pounded the bigger boy back. A hail of blows thrown by others rained at him from either side, though. At last Scarl yanked him bodily out of the melee. Nace's feet scraped and stumbled as the Finder spun him away and beyond the reach of any swing Mo still decided to take. A few of his opponent's comrades gave chase. They backed off the instant Mo's pipe raised again.

Nace squirmed so hard to escape Scarl's grip that the Finder jerked him to the floor and pinned him there, shouting his name. Nace's face formed a mask of frustrated fury, the more disturbing for its eerie silence. He gestured wildly toward the Electron boy, who mopped blood from his nose with the heel of his hand.

Scarl slapped down Nace's gesture. "I don't care!" he snarled. "You're putting all of us in more danger—including her!"

That finally quelled Nace's storm. Shortly Scarl helped him back to his feet. When he was sure punching would not start again, the Finder shoved Nace toward Sienna. She caught him and clutched, partly to keep him close and partly to soothe him. Breathing hard, he tipped his face to the floor, his eyes closed and his jaw clenched.

Scarl turned to Mo. Only then did Ariel release the man's legs and scramble to her feet. Startled to discover her there, Scarl shot her a glare nearly equal to what he'd shown Nace.

"Thank you for your restraint," he told Mo. "I'm indebted."

"Like I said, strife." Mo glowered at Nace. "Consider yourself lucky you still own a head, boy."

"Yeah, you dumb—"

Mo spun to interrupt. "Your mouth began this, and don't think I don't know it," he told Nace's opponent. "I wouldn't have let him whale on you as long as he did elsewise. Sounds to me like you're asking for more. Or d'you want to be cast out with the Reapers?"

When the boy looked away, dabbing the corner of his mouth, Mo turned back to Scarl. "As for yours—"

"I have rope," Scarl said quickly. "I'll bind him if you'd feel better."

"I'd rather you beat him."

"Beating never fixed a brawler, and he's still just a boy." Scarl eyed Mo and then added, "I'm guessing you had your share of fistfights."

The two men shared an almost friendly look. "Aye."

A shrill whistle split the hall. When it died, a voice hollered from the far end. "Here, Mo! What's going on?"

"Just gettin' acquainted," Mo grumbled. He jerked his

head and herded them forward once more. A white-haired, chiseled man awaited, his hands on his hips. A beaver or mink fur draped his shoulders.

"Ennis Allcraft," Mo murmured behind them. "Master of Electron. You seem to have a fair hand, Finder, so I'll give you advice: be more humble with him than you have been with me."

Even the people watching looked nervous now.

CHAPTER 32

Dog Moon and Grace

The master of Electron turned and strode before them. They reached the end of the great cavern, turned corners, climbed many steps, and passed through a much narrower hall. This one, frightening in its blankness, seemed to squeeze down upon Ariel before at last they reached another door at its end.

Trisha rushed forward to open it for Ennis. When it swung outward, he swept past.

Ariel stopped in her tracks. Scarl stumbled into her. The inner side of that door bore a section from her map.

Before she got more than a glimpse, Mo urged them into the room. Once inside, Ariel spun, but Mo closed the door, set his back to it, and folded his arms. His bulk blocked her view. With a twitch of his head, he directed her to face Ennis.

Too many other wonders vied for her attention. One wall was scattered with tiny colored lights like glowing berries, plus half circles with arrows and squares marked with symbols. A large section sat dark and still, but the rest reminded her of the flagstones at Tree-Singer Abbey, if the marks on the stones could have come to life, blinking and moving. The opposite wall, mostly glass, looked down a dizzy drop onto the great hall. Many people below had their faces turned upward as if awaiting what occurred there.

The white-haired master seated himself on a throne at a far corner of the room, crossing his arms. Trisha murmured in his ear and they both turned their gazes first on Ariel, then Scarl.

"Did the Finder guide the Farwalker here, or t'other way 'round?" Ennis's voice was both sharper and colder than Ariel expected from a man of his years.

"Neither," Scarl answered. "She walks where her feet take her. I just help as I can because she's not yet of age." He licked his lips, choosing words carefully. "But we've visited many places together, and I beg you to welcome her and hear the news she brings."

Ennis scoffed. "Electron once had a room called a visitor's center. But we haven't had visitors since the days of my grand-father's father. And the last met his fate on the spillway. The only thing I would hear from you, Farwalker, is why you should be any different."

Afraid to say the wrong thing, Ariel shot a look at Scarl. He clamped his jaw and gave her an encouraging nod. He'd told her often that for farwalking matters, he trusted her instincts more than his own tongue.

Feeling like an ant about to be crushed by a boot, Ariel took a deep breath. By the time the air flowed back out, she'd decided not to say anything just yet. Although she thought briefly of the eel skull in her pack, her fingers reached to her new hair clips. Unfastening them, she stepped forward to give them to Ennis.

He narrowed his eyes at the glass in her hand and shot sus-picious glances toward Trisha and Mo. They shrugged, baffled.

"We mostly bring gifts," Ariel said. "These are almost the color of your lake and they'd look nice in your white hair. Will you accept them?"

A quizzical look flashed over his face. He looked askance once more at Mo.

The bearded man flapped one hand. "They're strange."

Except for a tremble in her outstretched fingers that she knew he could see, Ariel stood like a stone while Ennis stared her down. Although they were blue, his eyes might have belonged to a serpent for all of their warmth. Fighting a panicky impulse to retreat out of reach, she finally had to drop her gaze. But she kept her hand out.

At last Ennis plucked the glass from her palm. He inspected the clips, scorn on his face.

"I made those," Sienna whispered.

Scarl twitched. Ariel knew he would silence Sienna if he dared. For the second time in an hour, though, Ariel thought the young woman's instincts for when to be quiet and when to speak up might be considerably better than Scarl's.

"Tell me, then, Flame-Mage," Ennis said in a soft, venomous voice, "why I would want a girl's hair pretties."

Ariel heard the dry click in Sienna's throat from three feet away.

"Because . . . even a place that has the lectrick needs beauty?" Sienna twisted her hands together and went on, more firmly. "They might be my best work so far, and you can't say it's not beautiful glass. Even if the master of Electron doesn't want them, you must know a girl or woman here who would."

Ennis pursed his lips.

Ariel saw the narrow opening. "We mean no harm to anyone," she told him. "We'll keep walking if you don't want to speak with us, but we bring only goodwill from other villages and the news that the Vault has been found. But perhaps you—"

"I care nothing about any Vault or your news. As for villages, we keep to ourselves for a reason." The longer he talked, though, the less his voice slithered. He glanced at Mo. "It's troubling that they got past the black lands. The Reapers will answer for that."

"I've been trying to tell you, them Reapers do more harm than good," Mo muttered.

"Did Farwalkers in the past try to convince you to leave here?" Scarl wondered. "Or talk of destruction?"

The white-haired man only stared back, stone-faced.

"The water gives the lectrick," Trisha muttered, as though the words had been said many times, "and we'll let nobody take it away."

"Nobody wants to," Scarl assured them. "The Forgetting is over. Ariel walks for remembering."

"And, please, I'd so love to learn about your lectrick!" Sienna said. "Do you need a Flame-Mage? I—" Scarl caught her eye, and she stopped.

Ennis's gaze roved from one to the next, stopping on Nace.

"Nothing from that one but fists," Ennis observed. "Why?"

Never raising his eyes from the floor, Nace tapped his lips and shook his head. Ennis's white eyebrows bunched. Ariel could see that he thought Nace refused to answer.

She opened her mouth to explain.

"He means no disrespect," Sienna said, faster. "His name is Nace Kincaller. I've known him since the day he was born. He speaks to the kin because he can't speak to us."

"He hears well enough, apparently. Look at me while you do it, boy."

Nace's head came up immediately, though he did not hide the resentment in his eyes. Years of experience with unkind stares perhaps helped him meet the master's regard. To Ariel, it seemed to last painfully long. Abruptly puckering his lips, Nace released a stream of pure notes, not just whistles but an entire birdsong. He stopped as quickly, never breaking the stare.

Ennis slowly cranked his head toward Mo, his eyes leaving Nace only once his head had stopped moving.

"I believe they all may be crazy," he said. "They're too strange even to drown; they'd poison the water. I'd like to put them in a zoo, but I don't want to feed them. Send them on."

"You don't want to hear anything I have to share?" Although she couldn't deny a rush of relief, disappointment—desperation—crowded in behind. Ariel had begun to believe they would win him over, but more importantly, she needed to ask questions here. Surely someone had answers about the map on the back of the door. "Can't we at least stay this evening to talk?"

"If the people of Electron wish to hear your voice, fine. I don't care. Just stay out of my way and leave here by morning."

"Please—" Sienna flung herself onto her knees at his feet, her hands clasped before her. "I came with the Farwalker to find somewhere new. And I so want to know how to craft the lectrick. I'd trade anything for it. Anything. Please, would you let me stay here and learn it? I won't be any trouble, I promise."

Ariel goggled. The agreement had been to deliver Sienna to the first village they reached, but she never would have insisted on leaving the Flame-Mage in such an odd place, even if the people hadn't been so unfriendly.

She and Scarl swapped a bemused look. He shrugged ever so slightly.

Ennis looked down on Sienna almost long enough to count the hairs on her head.

"Well, she's not hard to look at," he said, to no one in particular. "And she must have some skill." Only then did Ariel realize he'd slipped her hair clips into his pocket. Her heart cringed at their loss, but she knew they'd been traded for something more valuable, possibly including their lives.

"Maybe she could talk sense to the Reapers," said Mo. "They only seem to know one use for flame."

Ennis heaved a great sigh. "I suppose," he told Sienna. "If you can find someone to keep you from begging your dinner, remain with my grace. If not, you'd best depart with your friends. We don't tolerate mooches or thieves. No matter how pretty." He rose, stepped around Sienna and her thanks as if she might be contagious, and left through a door opposite the one they had entered.

Everyone else remained frozen.

"Never seen that," Trisha said to Mo, her eyes round. "Never seen him so flummoxed."

If that had been flummoxed, Ariel decided, she never wanted to see Ennis angry. Actually, she never wanted to see him again at all. She thought he might have been right: Sienna, at least, was crazy.

"You brought us down here expecting to kill us, didn't you?" Scarl demanded of Mo.

"Didn't know what to expect," Mo said. "Hasn't happened while I've been alive. Just following the steps I was taught."

Ariel touched Scarl's clenched fist, hoping to pass some calm into him. "Never mind," she whispered. "Did you see what's on the door?"

CHAPTER 33

Dog Moon Over the Spillway

Ariel stuck her nose close to the thin glass that covered the image. The paint and the surface beneath had cracked and spotted with age. Although this drawing included details that did not appear on her map, and the scale seemed off, there was no mistaking the focus of this one:

Ariel had long thought this part her map looked like a slug with its tentacles alert.

Trisha jostled her out of the way to shove open the door.

"What does this mean?" Ariel asked. She pointed.

The woman craned her head back to check. "It's the lake. And the dam. As if you were a bird looking down."

Ariel's chest squeezed so tight with excitement, she barely

could breathe. So the map *did* show a place as well as a time—and they'd finally found themselves on it! She traced her finger along the marks for the dam.

" 'Walk across the waning moon,' " Scarl said behind her. Her own nighttime words gave her a shiver. "The lake is a crescent, too, like the moon. Waning. The dam must be how we cross it."

"Where does the river go?" Ariel asked Trisha. This drawing didn't extend much beyond the lake's boundaries, a few tributary creeks, and a short stretch of river downstream. Her map seemed to follow that outflow.

"Where all rivers go, I suppose. To some sea." Trisha's tone implied that following a river was the silliest thing someone could do.

"There's a waterfall somewhere, though, isn't there?"

"No idea. Come on outta here. If Ennis comes back and you're still in his room, we all might be sorry."

Swallowing more questions, Ariel and her friends obeyed.

"It ain't a waterfall, exactly, but there's the spillway," Mo told her, once he'd shut the door behind them. When she asked what he meant, he said, "I can show you."

On their way back to the great hall, Trisha poked Ariel. "You said gifts. I only seen one. What else you got?"

Ariel blew a frustrated breath. Rather than proceed with routine farwalking duties as if this trip and this village were like any other, she yearned to look at her map, talk to Scarl, and see what a spillway might be.

"Let us rest a minute and eat," she pleaded, "and then I'll have several things for you."

"Don't know any as will share their supper," Trisha replied.

Ariel rolled her eyes. "We've got our own."

For the next few hours, she felt like a pollywog in a bucket, gaped at and chased after and fingered. The worst moment, even more unpleasant than the meeting with Ennis, came early. A trio of small boys dashed up as Ariel was introducing herself to the crowd. Goading one another, they shouted:

Kill the Farwalkers! Kill them all!
Toss 'em over the spillway wall!
Suppose one comes back from the dead?
Knock him down and bust his head!

Shocked, Ariel fought to swallow a sudden lump in her throat. Scarl gathered himself as if he thought somebody might try to follow the rhyming suggestion.

"Go on, now," chided Trisha, who hovered nearby. "You could say hello first."

Ariel wondered if it was the hateful chanting or the killing that Trisha felt should begin with "hello." Then one little boy stuck out his tongue. That homey insult, which made him look even younger than his half dozen years, flipped Ariel's heart like a pancake. Her laughter burst out where tears had just threatened.

She reached into her pack. Her retort rose in her mind only just before the words hit her lips:

You'd better kill me pretty quick
Before I hit you with a stick.
'Cause I could beat you black and blue
Or—look what I could do to you!

Her rummaging fingers yanked out her eel skull and held it high.

The boys screamed, the adults—most of them—laughed nervously, and a few older children crowed and shoved closer. She let them all have a good look. When she heard a few more snatches of rhyme from the crowd, she offered the skull as a prize to whoever could sing the most verses.

It must have been a very old and well-known ditty. The girl who won, probably nearly as old as Ariel herself, sang ten more verses. By then, Ariel could have joined her on several. Most told how Farwalkers were ugly, hateful strangers who went places they shouldn't, knew things they shouldn't, and would steal the lectrick if they got half a chance. Ariel noticed, however, that several verses weren't exactly untrue:

> They find the treasures of the dead
> That should be left alone instead.
> They're outside time, and nature, too;
> They're friends with ghosts, but not with you.
> So if you want your life to last
> You'll catch 'em quick and kill 'em fast.

She *had* befriended a ghost and found treasures left by people long dead. As she considered it, though, the winner sang a few lesser-known verses that stopped Ariel's thoughts cold:

> There ain't no fail-safe we can make
> That they can't take apart or break.
> They'll wreck the dam and cause a flood
> That won't leave nothing left but mud.
> Old Noah says to save him strife:
> Just finish a Farwalker's life.

The girl beamed. The crowd nodded its approval. Just then, nobody had more verses to offer.

Ariel found her voice. "You know what the fail-safe is?"

The reactions she received ranged from pity and bemusement to alarmed stares. "We got all sorts of fail-safes here," Trisha told her, with a nervous glance at the others as if she expected someone to stop her. "Couldn't keep the dam working at all without 'em."

"But what are they? What do you do with them?"

"Relief valves, switchovers, shunts . . ." Most of the words Trisha used meant nothing to Ariel.

"It may have been a common idea before the war," Scarl told her. "The tools people used then were complex."

"Could we see one?" she asked. Nearly everyone around her tensed. Their trust of a Farwalker didn't stretch that far. Not yet. For the moment, Ariel stuffed back her need to know more and awarded her eel skull to the contest's winner.

All evening afterward, more verses of the song popped from people's memories. Ariel even recognized a few verses from rope-skipping songs she knew, except with "sea monsters" replaced by "Farwalkers." It felt very strange to discover a place where the boogeyman turned out to be not a fright like Tattler, but you. Yet it was comforting, too. If she was the worst monster the world could dish up, any others could not be that bad.

The people of Electron seemed to agree, and most of them warmed to their guests. The gifts Ariel had brought from Skunk didn't hurt. She passed along requests for Healtouches and Storians, just as she had before, although with much less hope that anyone might volunteer. She also mentioned Skunk's plea for good-looking husbands. That generated more interest. As the crowd buzzed, Ariel realized that Electron had a surplus of young men and boys.

"Are their girls pretty?" someone asked.

"Well, Sienna is from there," Ariel said. She wasn't sure that reply was quite fair, but when they heard it, at least four young men, including one not older than Nace, offered to go right away. Ariel stammered.

"I can tell you about them and Skunk," offered Sienna, who'd been listening. She shot a glance toward Ariel. "If that's okay?"

"Sure." Ariel waved her ahead, glad for time to recover. When she stepped back to make way for Sienna, she overheard Mo speaking in low tones with Scarl nearby.

". . . not enough girls," he was telling the Finder. "Big problem for us. It's part of the reason there's Reapers and black lands at all. Too many bucks fighting over the few girls we got. The troublemakers get tossed out to fend for themselves."

"So you have a gang of young men running wild out there?" Scarl shook his head.

Mo nodded sourly. "Some of us have been working on Ennis to change it. It ain't right. And it certainly ain't birthing us any more girls." He elbowed Scarl. "You might get a chuckle to know that the first thing half this lot wondered when they saw you, I guarantee you, was why you was lucky enough to have two."

Scarl snorted. Then he noticed Ariel listening. He asked, "How much can I get in trade for the pair of them, Mo?"

Making a face at him, Ariel turned back to the volunteer husbands. They'd begun to clamor for more about the journey.

"You'll have to ask your parents and master, if you're still an apprentice," she said. A few faces fell. "And I can't take you just yet. I have somewhere else to go first. But I'll return for any of you who still want to go . . . well, pretty soon. If Ennis will let me."

"Oh, he'll allow it," Mo said behind her. "If you'd told him that first thing, he'd be in here arranging it personally."

Scarl kept a close eye on Nace and the older boys in the crowd, but no more trouble arose. Trisha proved wrong about dinner, too. Several families offered food. One bubbled over with children, and Sienna soon began charming their parents, hoping they'd be willing to feed her in exchange for a nanny while she established her trade. Ariel couldn't believe anyone would choose to stay in this place.

She said as much to Sienna as they went together to Electron's strange outhouse. "Even their outhouse is inside," Ariel said as they pushed through the door. "How weird can you get?"

"I think it's rather . . ." They stared around the large and well-lit tiled room. Their reflections stared back from a monstrous looking glass on one wall.

". . . pleasant," Sienna finished faintly. "Warm, fewer bugs . . . and what a marvelous glass!" She flirted with herself in it.

Ariel gazed in dismay at the row of basins below. "These can't be the drop-holes or chamber pots . . . can they? I don't want to see myself the whole time."

Sienna peered into a basin. "Too high. These look more like washbasins to me. Except they've got holes in the bottom." She pulled what looked like a dipper handle. Water spurted. Sienna squealed and leaped back.

Ariel laughed. With much trepidation and giggling, between them they figured out the correct use of the various closets and basins. At least, they hoped so.

"See?" Sienna said. "This place is odd, I'll admit, but I do want to stay. So many new things are exciting, don't you think?"

Fond of novelty herself, Ariel had to agree.

"Besides," Sienna added, "the lectrick is worth it. All this time I've thought you and Scarl have been . . . well, rather silly about your necklace, whatever messed up Willow's bridle, all that. I thought you both let your imaginations run wild. And now right before my eyes is something straight out of a fable, way better than gold or a dragon. It makes me wonder what else I believe that is wrong, but I'm tingling just thinking about it."

"Okay," Ariel said. "I just wanted to check, 'cause I wouldn't leave you if you hated it here." She reached for the door.

"Ariel, wait. I want to say something private."

When Ariel turned back, Sienna would not meet her eyes. Instead, she traced the tiles around the washbasins. "Please don't take this wrong. I care about you, and I don't want you hurt."

"Is this about Nace?"

"Hear me out," Sienna said. "A couple years back, I was out in the trees with a fellow I liked, and we got sort of . . . friendly. Until Nace burst from a bush, raising a ruckus, and he ran home and riled up my parents, and it was just a disaster."

"Maybe he . . ." Ariel didn't enjoy this idea, but she pushed on. "Maybe he liked you himself and got jealous."

Sienna barked a laugh. "Hardly. But you don't get it. It's not that he got me in trouble. That all came from the girl my friend had promised to marry."

Ariel worked to keep her face blank, but Sienna never paused. "Nace could only have known I was there if he'd been following me. Spying. And it wasn't just once. I can't tell you how many— All right. I'll be totally honest. I've done a few things I probably shouldn't. I just got so bored. And Nace always found out. *Every single time.* He kept most of my secrets, but he let me know that he knew. At first I thought animals told him, or birds, but no Kincaller's that good, and why would they care? I started wondering if Tattler whined to him somehow, but that was ridiculous, too. And then twice Nace showed up to stop me *before.* Like he knew in advance. It's bizarre."

Ariel wondered just how naughty Sienna had been, but that wasn't the point. "His mother's a Judge, though. He's probably got some of that skill. And he's pretty observant."

Sienna huffed. "Fine. Don't say I didn't warn you."

"Sienna! If you hadn't done anything bad, there'd be nothing to tell me!"

Sienna's face worked, and she stalked to the far end of the room. Ariel groaned. She didn't want to leave with hard feelings between them. "Oh, Sienna . . ."

The Flame-Mage spun and strode back, pulling a lock of her hair between her teeth. She spun again, pacing. "I hate being embarrassed. You know? Hate it. I suppose I could be . . . blaming that feeling on him. When it's all my own fault."

Ariel stepped forward to soothe her. "I only meant—"

"No. You might be right. Partly." Sienna gnawed her hair. "He's just a—a better person than me. And that makes me—"

"That's not true. You're just different. We've all done things we shouldn't have."

Sienna's hopeful expression tugged at Ariel's heart. "You think so?"

"I know so."

"Well . . . okay." Sienna tucked her hair back into place. "Maybe I've been unfair. Don't be surprised if you can't keep a secret from him, though. Any secret. He's not a Kincaller; he's a mouse, always skittering out where you least expect him."

Ariel laughed, remembering her first startling contacts with Nace. "Maybe. But I'd be more scared of Electron, and you're not, so we made a good trade."

"We sure did. Even if we both got surprises." Sienna managed a wry smile and linked arms with Ariel to leave. "It didn't all work out like I'd hoped, but I get the lectrick instead, and a big pack of new men to choose from. They're a little . . . undressed, but I can fix that."

The scanty clothing was explained later by Electron's Storian, Bess. Scarl had tracked her down to learn what he could about the dam, and Ariel sat with them. The crotchety old woman was not very forthcoming. She claimed that most of the dam's workings were secrets held only by Ennis and his most favored apprentices. But she did explain that the entire village was descended from those who'd been working at the dam when the Blind War struck.

"They just holed up inside for a long while," she said. "Went out dusk and dawn only, when the fishing is best. Brought forth babies and got by. When the sight finally came back, they let visitors in. Farwalkers, mostly." Bess eyed Ariel suspiciously. "But then the visitors started yammering about getting rid of the lectrick. So them in charge got rid of visitors instead. That's when we first started burning, to better see strangers approach."

"Life must be hard, though, without anything from the forest," Scarl said.

She shrugged. "The lectrick keeps us warm, so we don't need much. We eat mostly fish and what we can reap from the south shore—the green one. No visitor ever came from that way; the war destruction yonder was too great. So the Reapers never bothered to burn it. We trade meat and skins from them a few times a year. There's talk of bringing them back in more regular. Parts of the dam have been failing more often. Even Ennis can't always fix it. And some folk is nervous we couldn't get by without it."

Scarl smiled. "The rest of us do."

"Aye. The Reapers know how. They could teach us. We'll see. I do get mighty tired of fish."

"Or maybe what's in the Vault could help fix the dam," Ariel said.

Scarl nodded. "If Ennis will join with us, we might do even better and spread the lectrick to others. Electron would be full of heroes, Ennis chief among them."

Bess hooted. "Keep me in the world long enough to see that! I'll tell him you said so. But Ennis ain't much for sharing."

Bess couldn't give them what Ariel wanted most, either. Although Electron had its own Noah story, the old woman didn't know the version they'd heard from Vi, and she scowled in confusion at Ariel's map.

"That's the lake and the dam, surely," she said. "The rest don't make much sense. If it led you here, though, I suppose it served well enough."

"But it seems to keep going," Ariel noted. More importantly, her feet were not content to stop.

Bess tossed the linen back into Ariel's lap. "Why would you want to keep going? I always figured Electron was the Vault. It's just as good. Better, 'cause it ain't never been lost. Not for us, nohow. As long as it lasts, the lectrick's all we need."

Ariel kept her mouth shut, but she thought of one or two things Electron could use—a Tree-Singer, for instance. She'd hoped to trade pine seeds for news of Zeke or the abbey, but

Electron had no one to ask. That seemed strange only until she remembered the Reapers' fires and the fact that nothing green grew in Electron at all.

Once Bess hobbled off to bed, Ariel asked Scarl, "Do you think lectrick's a good thing? I wouldn't want anywhere else to become more like this place."

"I know what you mean," he replied, "but I think it's like everything else in the Vault. Or for that matter, a story. The good or evil is not in the thing but in how we all share it. Don't give up on them yet. They've stretched a long way just since our arrival."

Exhaustion weighed on Ariel by the time interest waned and people began drifting away for the night. Mo escorted Nace outside to bed down Willow while Scarl went to locate Sienna, who'd last been seen cuddling a baby. Waiting for him to return, Ariel lay curled in a corner. The building thrummed like a living thing. There'd been no chance for Mo to show her the spillway—presumably the same one she might have been tossed over.

Scarl came back without Sienna, who was wasting no time wiggling herself into Electron. When Mo returned, too, Ariel jumped up and reminded him of his promise. He rolled his bushy head back in exasperation, but waved for her to follow. With Nace staying behind to keep an eye on their things, Scarl accompanied them.

Without a guide, even the Farwalker would have become lost in the maze of hallways and stairwells, but shortly they stepped through a door that opened on cool night air. They walked along the crest of the dam. On one side, the lake stretched dark and smooth. The other fell away like a cliff, but in the moonlight Ariel could see the gleam of the river below. As Mo led them, she happened to think that in him and Trisha, as in Scarl's bridge story, a man and a much older woman guarded this bridge.

It had a hole in it, too, of a sort. Mo stopped at a railing, leaned over, and pointed. Near the center of the dam, the wall had a breach. A sheer curtain of water slid down the steep ramp below.

"Not much spill now," Mo said. "Low water in summer. Other times it looks more like a falls."

Ariel sidled up to the rail. Scarl clamped a hand on her arm. She flashed him a long-suffering look. His attention, though, remained fixed on Mo. He wasn't afraid Ariel might fall; he was making sure Mo couldn't act on a well-concealed plan. Too aware of the hulking man alongside her, she was suddenly glad Scarl was there.

A crooked grin wiggled through Mo's beard. "Stand down, Finder. We may be a lot of things here, but we ain't sneaky."

Scarl's grip relaxed. Before he could voice the apology on his face, Ariel said, "He just thinks I'm clumsy, that's all." It made her uneasy to feel so dependent on him.

She peered over the edge and imagined what it would have been like to bounce and scrape all that way before being swallowed by the churning river below. The cool damp air gave her goose bumps.

"Timekeeper?" asked Scarl.

She shook her head. Even if it had roared with spring flow, this was not what she'd seen when they'd broken his glass.

"You asked about fail-safes," Mo said, his voice low. "Don't tell no one I told you. Ennis would flay me. But I can't see how you could break it, so . . . the spillway is one."

"It is?" Ariel gazed at it anew. "What does it do? How does it make sure there's not a mistake?"

"If the lake gets too high, see, in spring rains or storms, that could be a big problem. The whole dam could break. This lets the worst of the high-water spill."

"It works by itself?"

"Pretty much."

Ariel gave Scarl a bewildered look. She didn't know how such a thing could apply to the Vault or the calling she felt.

"I don't know," Scarl said quietly. "But I think it's encouraging that it works by itself. Perhaps making the trip will suffice."

Ariel watched the water slide down. Nothing about this trip felt that easy to her—not so easy as falling.

She regretted that thought immediately. A dizziness swept through her, too familiar, like dropping. She jerked back against Scarl, glad he still held her arm, and lifted her gaze. The moon stared back. Only a day short of full, it rammed a bolt of worry through her chest.

Scarl steadied her with an inquiring murmur.

The dizziness passed. The dread didn't. "If I weren't so tired, I'd keep walking tonight," Ariel told him. "The moon's bright enough."

"Shy moon, I'd say. Almost full." Scarl rubbed weariness from his face. "You could ride, if you really think we need to."

Ariel studied the dark land that awaited. Abrupt hills rose like ant piles, the river having long since carved the easiest route through them. She considered a rush to gather their things, say farewell to Sienna, and set off along its banks in the dark. She could barely summon the energy to think it.

"Dawn will be soon enough." She hoped it was true.

When they got back inside the great hall, only two lectrick fires remained burning, one at each end. Nace lifted her spirits with a flower he'd picked while outside. The waxy white blossom oozed a peppery scent.

She yearned to thank him with a hug. They'd enjoyed no secret twining of fingers since the fire; they'd been too busy and too wary of Scarl's disapproval. Still, Nace's willingness to champion her earlier had filled her with a strange, conflicted joy, and she longed to show him how she felt. Scarl and Mo looked on from too close, though. She settled for words, adding, "I've never seen one like this."

"Moonflower," offered Mo. "Only blooms under full moon and the cusp day either side—shy moon to spilled moon. They're unlucky, though."

With dismay, Nace reached to retrieve the flower from Ariel.

She dodged. "Why? They're not poisonous, are they?"

"Nah. Worse," said Mo. "Good thing your knucklehead only took one. They say that following moonflowers to pick them will lead you out of the world."

CHAPTER 34

Dog Moon and Good-byes

When Mo left them for bed, Ariel, Scarl, and Nace all lay down near a wall. Soon Nace's soft snoring joined the hum that vibrated the floor.

Ariel tugged her blanket one way, then another, so tired she couldn't find the doorway to sleep. She wasn't sure she wanted to pass through it, anyway. It seemed silly to be scared of night-mares, but she dreaded another like last night's.

After she heaved an especially deep sigh, Scarl's whisper came out of the shadows. "You all right?"

She squirmed around until she could see his face in the low light. "No."

"Want to tell me?"

"I don't know what to say. I'm just worried."

"About . . . ?"

"I said I don't know!"

His eyebrows lifted, he reached toward her shoulder. She pulled away from his touch. His hand hovered an instant, then drew back to rest on the floor between them.

"All right," he murmured. "Anything I can do?"

Ariel flopped onto her back, stinging from the flare of her own irritation. "Just get us out of here fast in the morning."

After a moment she rolled over to see if he was still looking at her. He was.

"If I kissed Nace, would you hurt him?" she whispered.

He raised his head. "That's what you're worried about?"

"No! I mean, yes, but it's not why we need to get down the river."

Scarl rested his head again. "Is that where we're going?"

"Answer me," she growled. "Would you?"

"I'm pretty sure I pulled every muscle I have saving his hide a few days ago. And I fully expected . . . Well, let's just say I was surprised when all four of us survived the fire."

She moaned. "I know that! But why won't you answer my question?"

"Ariel . . ." He sighed, rubbing one eyebrow. "I wouldn't hurt Nace for any reason, short of him hurting you. But I remember what it's like to be a young man his age. It's annoying to know someone is watching, but trust me, it helps."

"He wouldn't do anything wrong."

Scarl opened his mouth, reconsidered, and closed his eyes to choose different words. Finally he said, "Kiss him if you feel you must. A kiss is a very fine thing. Just realize that once you wade into that current, it can be tough to get out. And it may be even tougher for Nace. Okay?"

Ariel could see cautions and concerns piling up behind his eyes, but he held them back. She could guess that most of what he wanted to say matched secret fears of her own. She nodded. "Okay."

He smiled and wondered, "How did I get this job?"

"You snatched me." She'd meant to grin back, but her words

recalled the night it had happened—the night her mother had been murdered by Elbert. The memory would never come without pain. It reflected onto Ariel's face.

Wincing, Scarl cast his gaze to the floor. "Forgive me. I'm wrong to complain, even in jest."

"I didn't mean it like that." Frustrated by her own emotions, she reached to grip one of his fingers. He curled it and hers into his palm.

"I didn't mean to give away part of my First Day present, either," she added.

"But it worked." His grin reappeared. "You really confused him. I suspect that's not easy to do."

"Do you think Sienna will be okay here?"

He nodded. "Mo gave me his word he'll look out for her, and he's big enough to enforce it. Besides, they're not cruel. Just afraid. Sienna will be good for them. And she'll have her pick of the bunch."

"Maybe we can come back and check. We're almost to the end of the map, did you see? Except I couldn't find anything in that drawing on the door that looks like a waterfall."

"No. But there's a fair stretch of the map after the dam. It might not represent any particular distance, but if it does, I don't think we'll cover it all before the moon starts to wane."

Ariel brushed her nose with her limp moonflower. "We have to try."

"I know."

The eerie hum of Electron surrounded them.

"'Outside time, and nature, too,'" Scarl said, quoting Electron's disparaging ode to Farwalkers. "Even the wildest stories usually contain seeds of truth. The Storian in me wonders where that rhyme might have sprouted."

Ariel rubbed her eyes until she saw sparks. Her mind was too tired to explore Scarl's words. "This place is outside of nature, if you ask me. But maybe we'll find out tomorrow. Full moon."

"Perhaps. Best get to sleep now, though." He squeezed her hand and let go.

"Scarl?"

She could hear him try to hang on to his patience. "Yes?"

Ariel closed her eyes, embarrassed to ask it. "Would you . . . would you hold my hand while I fall asleep? I'm afraid of my nightmares."

He simply reached to tuck her blanket around her. Her heart plummeted, taking that as a no. But then he drew her, blanket and all, into the shelter of his arm. "Or this?"

"This." She tipped her head against him.

"No kicking," he said, a smile in his voice.

"I'll try," she replied. "I don't want to sleep long, though. In here, it'll be impossible to know where the sun is."

"I'll wake early," he promised. "This floor is hard and cold enough to make sure of that."

Ariel needn't have worried. The dreamless sleep that fell on her didn't last, and she woke the moment children began stirring. Not much later, the lectrick fires lit again, by themselves as far as she could tell.

Scarl groaned awake. When he checked to see if she still slept, his glance lingered.

Self-conscious, she wiped her face. "Is something wrong?"

"Guess not," he replied. "Sleep all right?"

"Not really. But I'm ready to leave anyway."

While Scarl roused Nace, Ariel made her way back to Electron's strange outhouse. By the time she returned, early risers had approached to see what the strangers did next. A few members of Sienna's adopted family went with Scarl to help retrieve her goods from the horse. Nace offered Ariel bites of a breakfast someone had shared. Soon they were saying good-bye.

Sienna embraced Ariel so hard it hurt.

"Last chance to come somewhere else with us," Ariel said from within the hug.

"No. Ellie Fisher is kind, and I adore her kids. I'd probably stay even if they didn't have lectrick."

"Is there someone to take care of your burns?" Ariel couldn't remember if she'd met a Healtouch last night or not.

Sienna nodded. "I know this sounds strange, but now that they don't hurt so bad, I'm kind of glad."

"What?"

"When I first saw the scar on your cheek, I thought, 'How awful.' But then I got to know you. You're so smart and brave. You made me brave. Smarter, too, or at least I tried harder. And every time I notice my scars, I'll think of you."

"Sienna!" Dismayed, Ariel tried to pull back. Sienna's arms tightened to hold her in place.

"No, it's a good thing! Because the scar's just the smoke. The important part is the fire. But you can't have one without the other." She kissed Ariel's forehead. "Except for lectrick, I guess. I'll find out."

Ariel's breath became short, and not only because of the tight hug. "I'll come back as soon as I can," she whispered. "If you get sick of this place, I'll help you leave. I owe you a lot more than one trip."

"I'll count days till your visit. Be sure to walk where it's already burned when you come back, and you'll be all right. But you always are, aren't you?"

After a final squeeze, Ariel stepped back. With an uncertain look on his face, Nace offered Sienna his good hand. After an instant of hesitation, she slapped it aside to hug him instead.

"I'll miss you, Nace," Sienna told him. "Never thought I'd say that. I don't . . . I don't understand you, but I'm starting to think I was wrong about some things. Help take care of her, okay?"

He nodded, drew back, and pulled something from his pocket—a necklace. He'd strung a fishline with short lengths of striped grass stem, seedpods, and what looked like a hummingbird egg. The egg was set off by beautiful feathers that had graced his own armband, now gone. Although quite different from Ariel's, the strand was lovely. Tears welled into Sienna's eyes as Nace slipped it over her head.

"Did you help with that?" Ariel whispered to Scarl. If she hadn't been so pleased for Sienna, she might have been jealous. But then Nace retreated to slide furtive fingers into Ariel's hand.

"Only the fishline."

Scarl waited until Sienna whisked the tears from her face, and then he clasped both her hands. "Sienna." She looked into his eyes. As usual, Scarl let those do most of his speaking. Sienna's color rose the whole time. Keeping his voice low, he finally said, "Promise me that if you become unhappy here, you'll get help from Mo or await our return. I don't want you trying to get back to Skunk and running into those Reapers alone."

"I promise," Sienna said. "But I don't think I'll want to leave. Scarl?"

"Yes?"

After a nervous glance at the onlookers, Sienna leaned quickly to kiss his lips. She backed away even faster, pulling her hands free, before he could either return it or recoil.

"I promised myself I'd do that," she said, her cheeks bright. She threw Ariel a rueful glance and busied her hands with her necklace. "I keep my promises, that's all."

Ariel didn't dare look at Scarl's face, but surprise and amusement contoured his voice. "I'm not sure I understand, Sienna, but thank you. For everything. Good-bye, goodwill, and good luck."

The words repeated through the great hall, following them out. Ariel clung to the echoes, especially the ones for good luck. She thought they would need it. The dread of being too late had started to swamp her again.

Mo took them outside the way they'd come in and then around to a path that Willow could travel over the top of the dam. The horse took some coaxing on the unfamiliar surface, but soon the clopping of hooves echoed through the cool morning air. Though the sun hadn't heaved itself over the hill yet, the sky glowed with anticipation of dawn.

Nace skittered ahead to gaze over the rail at the spillway.

"Don't jump," Ariel teased. "I'm not a gazelle."

He grinned and swung himself up onto the rail. Her stomach flopped.

Scarl grabbed Nace's collar. "Quit being foolhardy. Have you already forgotten that things break?"

"That's where we cast thieves," Mo added. "As far as I know, none has survived. I don't expect you will neither, boy, unless you grow some more brains."

Nace dropped lightly back down and hung his head, but only until the men's attention shifted elsewhere. Then he cast Ariel a wink.

She and her friends stepped onto the far lakeshore, waved to Mo, and angled eagerly down toward the river. Perhaps

Ariel let herself ponder Scarl's bridge story too much, because their footsteps seemed to clatter unnaturally loud in her ears. Nace trod alongside her, providing company but not conversation. She missed Sienna's chatting.

The river, when they reached it, proved even more troubling. Though Ariel could see it tumble and spray over rocks, no burble or swish reached her ears. It flowed without sound. The matted brambles and stubby trees on their side of the river did not sigh at the touch of the wind. The arid sweeps on the other side, although unburned, looked barren.

"It's awfully quiet here," she said.

Nace whistled, paused, and tried again. No bird or chipmunk responded.

"I noticed, too," Scarl replied. "And so has Willow." The horse's ears pressed tight to his head. His eyes rolled as if predators stalked him on all sides.

Nace slipped back to stroke Willow's nose, his temple tipped against the wide jaw as if listening there.

"Think he's smelling wolves or a lion on the prowl?" Scarl asked.

Nace turned his face into the breeze to inhale it. He shook his head. Then he waved at their surroundings and wrung his hands as though squeezing a dishcloth: *Twisted*.

Scarl agreed. "There might still be places tainted from the war. I've been surprised to find anything as large as Tattler or the dam intact. Maybe the destruction here took some other form."

Ariel eyed the nearby trees, which looked stunted and forlorn. "Could it still hurt us?"

"Would you walk somewhere else if I told you it might?"

Ariel watched the gravel under her feet. "No," she replied. There was only one path to where she was going.

She sang her Farwalker's song to dispel the eerie hush. Nace whistled the tune on her last several verses. That cheered her.

"You sing something, Scarl," she suggested, once they'd gone through hers twice. "You must know a few songs."

He refused.

"Come on. You can hum any parts you forget."

"There's only one song I can sing with any grace," he said. "But it's a very old war song, and too gloomy for traveling."

She pestered him until he gave in.

"Remember," he warned, "you insisted." Then he lifted his voice for the song:

You take the high road and I'll walk through shadow
And I'll reach our homeland before you.
The rain and the cold wind will bother me no more
But arms won't hold me close again like yours do.

You take the low road and I'll walk through sunshine,
But I'll rest a while here to mourn you.
Your love and your young ones will shun the news I'll bring.
Their tears, I know, will rip at me like thorns do.

Scarl's voice was richer than Ariel had expected, but he hadn't been wrong about the song's mood. Nace signaled his approval anyway. Ariel walked silently a while, then piped up with a third verse:

You take the high road and I'll grab your coattails,
And I'll cling through danger or bad weather.
Our task still awaits us; it won't take too much time.
We'll both return to lands we love together.

Nace's clapping echoed.

"Perhaps there was something to your days as a Fool, Ariel," Scarl said. "You certainly could have made up songs for your supper. Sing it again so I can remember it."

Pleased, she complied. Her heart jumped higher when Nace shot Scarl a wary glance and then sidled close enough to grab her hand. Every inch of her skin burned, knowing Scarl could see, but when she summoned the nerve to peek over her shoulder, he pretended not to notice either the clasped fingers or her look.

Nace withdrew his hand all too soon. The longer they walked, the more balky Willow became. He planted his hooves, danced sideways from invisible threats, or rushed forward, nearly treading on someone. Eventually Nace mounted in front of their pack load, lay forward with his cheek against Willow's long neck, and soothed him with constant murmurs and pats. Only then could they calmly move on.

Ariel thought she knew how the horse felt when they reached the dead forest.

CHAPTER 35

Dog Moon, Full

From a distance, the hillside looked as though heavy snow had fallen in summer. As they drew near, Ariel realized that the trees gleamed white because only gaunt trunks and a few curling branches remained. Leaves, twigs, and bark had fallen away, leaving a forest of bones. Pale, cracked mud coated the ground beneath.

"They couldn't have burned," she said. They'd passed through plenty of char, but this wood was bleached.

"A landslide, I think." Scarl pointed to a vast scar on the hillside.

They picked their way through the rubble strewn on the bank. The dead trees loomed alongside, sinister. She'd never heard a tree's voice the way Tree-Singers did, but these wooden ghosts seemed to groan at her just below the threshold of hearing.

She sighed in relief when they left the bone forest behind. Even thinking felt easier once they'd escaped it. Indeed, a fact burst in Ariel's mind so hard she stopped in her tracks.

"This can't be right," she told Scarl. "I should have noticed before. We're walking downstream. But when I saw it, Time-keeper poured toward me."

"We'll just come to the top of the falls instead of the bottom."

She shook her head. "No. It falls toward us. It has to."

Nace cast a glum look back the long way they had come, but Scarl gestured toward the hills on their right. "Your falls empty into this river as a tributary, then," he said. "I used my glass last night, Ariel—half of it, anyway—and I'm sure we're headed in the right direction."

"Oh! You know where Timekeeper is?"

"More or less. So far, I agree with your feet. Trust your sense of direction and stop thinking. It won't serve for this."

Ariel's legs moved again. Her soles felt sore in her boots, but her heart lightened.

Then her mind tracked back over Scarl's words. "When did you have time with your glass last night?" she asked.

"After you fell asleep. Nace?"

The boy raised his head from Willow's neck.

Scarl hesitated. "Forgive me if this question sounds cruel. I don't mean it to. But would you still be a Kincaller if you could speak?"

Nace nodded immediately. Ariel wondered at Scarl's abrupt change of subject.

"Would you tell me why, if you think you can make me understand?" he asked.

With clear trepidation, Nace sat up. Willow halted. Making sure he had Scarl's full attention, the boy signaled a bit at a time until they correctly guessed his meaning: *I hear animals inside my head. I can speak with them inside my head.*

He finished with a grimace and a twirl of his finger by his temple: *Crazy?*

"No, I suspected as much," Scarl said. "You can hear people the same way, can't you?"

Nace shot Ariel a look of misgiving. Reluctantly he replied: *A little.*

"Ohhh," Ariel said. "That's how you followed us so easily from Skunk! And why Sienna thought you knew things you shouldn't. She's right."

Alarm filled Nace's face. He made gestures of protest and hurried to explain: *Tracks. Willow. I hear.* Most of his other waving was too complicated, and too agitated, for her to understand.

"It's all right," she said. "I don't have things to hide." Even as she spoke, though, implications unfurled before her. Her conscience generally kept her out of much trouble, but all people had embarrassing things in their lives, mistakes to forget, faults to work on, or feelings they didn't want others to see. She gasped. "Wait. If you hear thoughts . . . My thoughts, too?" Had opinions of him crossed her mind lately?

He shook his head, but he couldn't suppress a sly grin. Ariel covered her burning cheeks with her hands.

With effort—and helpful guessing from Scarl—Nace assured her that he didn't hear single thoughts, but the noise and pitch of emotions.

Ariel wasn't sure whether to believe him. "So you don't hear exactly what I think about you?"

"He doesn't need to hear thoughts for that." A smile tugged at Scarl's lips.

Ariel groaned and hurried forward.

Scarl chuckled, but Nace chirped sharply at her. She could barely meet his gaze, afraid of what thoughts might leak out to be gathered by him. He did something remarkable, though. He reached a hand toward her, palm up, and for an instant she felt the plea on his face, and the reassurance he wanted to give her, echo through her own heart and mind. The unexpected connection—closer than touch—warmed her enough to melt the fear of being known rather too well.

"I hear you," she said softly. She had to look away, but she could guess how the foxes they'd watched together had known that Nace wouldn't hurt them.

He ducked his face, too, blushing, and coaxed the horse into walking again.

"I'm sorry I stirred up a storm, Nace," Scarl said, "but the reason I wondered is this: if Ariel became separated from us, would you be able to hear if she was still al— Still all right?"

Ariel heard the stumble and knew what he'd started to say. Ignoring Nace's confident nod, she asked, "Why?"

Scarl blew an unhappy breath. "Just trying to think ahead."

"To what?"

Looking aslant at her, he said nothing. Already flustered, she battled more turmoil rising inside.

"You're scaring me," she told him, as evenly as she could. "What do you know?"

He stared out over the river. "Maybe nothing," he said, "but when you talk in your sleep, Ariel, it wakes me. And it may be foolish, but I pay attention. The Essence flows through us all, and I think it can speak once our bodies and minds become silent enough. No doubt that's what women attuned to the moon really hear."

"I said something after I fell asleep?"

"We had a whole conversation a few hours later. You remember nothing, I take it?"

"What did I say?" When he wouldn't answer, she added, "I'm the one who said it—I should get to know."

"No. You advised me not to repeat it, and I'm going to honor that."

"I told you not to tell *me* what *I* said?" she demanded. "You're making this up."

"If you like," he replied.

She spent much of the afternoon feeling as though a stranger had stowed away in her skin and that everyone else knew her thoughts better than she did. The creepy sensation added to the burden of silence hanging over their way.

Yet pulling her through the gloom was one bright hope that she'd kept to herself now for days. Reminded again by Nace's labored gestures, she finally broached her idea with Scarl when they stopped for a meal. The Kincaller had hurried away, looking determined, after the Finder remarked on their dwindling food supply, which had not been replenished in Electron. Ariel made use of his absence.

"Scarl, I've been thinking," she said. "When we go back to the abbey, we could take Nace with us. Couldn't we? He could care for the goats, and the Storians there could teach him the symbol writing. Then he could talk, even without a voice!"

Scarl took a long draft from the water jar in his hands and swirled what was left.

Her heart fell. "You don't think that's a good idea."

"Have you already spoken to him about it?"

When she shook her head, relief eased the tired creases around his eyes.

"It may be a fine idea, if he thinks so," he said. "It would open a new world for him. But I can see at least three reasons it may not be wise. First off, he'd be awfully far from his family."

"He's far away now," Ariel argued.

"I very much doubt he asked anyone what they thought,

though, or considered it carefully himself. He's almost too old to beg permission, but he may decide he's needed at home."

"What other reasons?"

He studied her briefly and then offered her the jar. "I'll stop at one. It's not really my place."

She ignored the water. "You started with three! Tell me."

Ruefully, he set the jar aside. "Well, he may hope to draw you into his life, instead of being drawn into yours. And what if you tire of him? And don't you think Zeke might be jealous?"

"Zeke?" The notion hit her like a splash: first a shock, then a disquieting dribble.

Crushing a smile, Scarl flung up his hands. "I may be wrong. Like I said, not my place."

"Zeke." She poked at that strange idea. She and Zeke had been through difficult times together, and she certainly loved him. When he'd first returned home to Canberra Docks after helping to discover the Vault, it had quickly become clear that too much had changed for Ezekiel Stone-Singer to live again with his family. She'd been overjoyed when he rejoined her and Scarl at the abbey. But it had never occurred to Ariel that he could be any more than a surrogate brother.

"You really think . . . Zeke?" she wondered, low.

Scarl's face cramped. "I'm sorry I said anything."

"I'm not." But now she felt completely confused.

When Nace returned, he bore only a few grass seed heads for Willow. Ariel wasn't surprised. They'd passed thickets of berries before the charred lands, but none since. She hadn't seen so much as a honeybee on this side of the dam. So she ate tasteless dried fish with her friends, chewing in thoughtful silence and measuring memories of Zeke against a new yardstick. She longed to see him again; she missed his amiable wit and she needed to know he was well. Yet when she glanced up and her eyes met with Nace's, his bottomless regard drowned everything else.

Only the need to keep walking could break through, stronger than hunger.

Poor Willow ended the day bearing them all. The moon rose, swollen, before twilight had leaked from the sky. Seeing it, Ariel quailed and nudged the horse on with her legs.

Scarl insisted on stopping once the moon had crested and begun sinking again. "I've been telling myself 'just another hour' for four hours," he said. "We don't know what lies ahead, and we all need sleep, Willow included. We'll have even less hope of succeeding tomorrow if we don't."

Ariel argued for walking until dawn.

"No," he told her. "I don't think we'd reach the falls by then, anyway. It doesn't feel that close to me yet. And we'll cover more ground in two hours of daylight. If the light of the full moon itself is important to whatever awaits us, we can come back next August. It'll be easier once we know where we're going and why."

She couldn't budge him. Ariel fell into sleep with the weight of failure dragging her under—and a nightmare awaiting her there.

CHAPTER 36

Dog Moon Dream

What if a branch breaks?" Zeke cried. "The wind's starting to blow. Come down."

Already much higher in his maple tree than she had intended to go, Ariel glanced down. The space between her and the ground seemed to throb. Still, she reached for the next slender branch. She would retreat once she'd proven that she was not scared.

A gust shook the tree. Its limbs swayed and bent, swimming beneath her. Ariel's body pitched toward her hands. One foot slipped and too much weight dropped on the other. Wood snapped. She fell.

Flailing down past Zeke, Ariel grasped for a hold. She scraped along branches but only twisted herself awkwardly, now dropping nearly headfirst. The earth rushed to greet her. Through a roar in her head, she heard Zeke shout her name—or did that voice belong to somebody else?

An image flashed into her mind. Everyone said your life flicked before your eyes as you left the world, but this view was not from her past. It was a man, a stranger whose name she nonetheless knew. His fingers held a shiny brass shaft. She'd never seen one, but she'd heard stories, so she thought it might be a telling dart. The device had once been used to send messages. And the man's name—

Ariel hit the ground. A spasm went through her body, but it was not caused by pain. The jolt felt more like slipping down two or three stairs when she'd meant to descend only one. It scattered her thoughts. She opened her eyes, but for a moment the colors and movement they showed her did not speak a language she knew. Only slowly did awareness reconnect out of chaos: *Huh?* Woods . . . Oh, the woods. Daytime. Alone. Leaves above, branches, sky . . . tree. And a fall.

Once she'd earned back that fragile understanding, dread flowed back, too. Ariel remembered how she'd gotten there on the ground. The complete lack of pain scared her more than it reassured her. She tensed, expecting pain to answer from somewhere, and could feel nothing at all—no hurting, no movement, not even the earth beneath her. Instead, her effort to move stirred the leaves and sky overhead. They spun, blurred together, and faded away. Silence crushed her. It was not just the hush of a startled forest. She lay in a dead quiet, empty of her own breathing and heartbeat—empty of life.

"Ariel! Ariel!"

Although distant, the sound of her name gave her a fix in the blankness. She grasped at the low cry that followed. Two hands clutched at her torso and shook her. Surprised to feel them, so firm and close, she struggled anew to gain understanding. She was certain she'd been lying on her back, gazing up at the sky, but now the hands flopped her over and pulled the wrong way as if dragging her into the earth. That terrified her. Nothing good grabbed you from out of the earth.

Ariel strained to fight, but her body remained limp, apparently broken beyond all response. As the hands tumbled her once more—or still—onto her back, a blur slid again into view, confirming that her eyes were open. She focused. Other than the blue of a blank sky, what she saw confused her yet more. The woods did not appear here at all. A man shook her. Now came the pain as she rattled in his grip. A strange boy crowded in at the man's shoulder. The boy would have been cute if his face hadn't been so twisted in horror. His hands reached to her . . . hands she knew. Hands she'd touched. She'd seen them on a rope and felt them on her fa—

With a tangible snap, Ariel's memories returned. She gasped. Her limbs jerked—she'd regained their control. Her stomach heaved at the shift. Through sheer will, she kept its contents inside. Swallowing hard, she flung herself forward against Scarl's chest, her arms rising to clasp him.

"It's all right!" she cried. "I'm awake now. I'm here."

He crushed her in his embrace and then eased her back to examine her face. Tears stood in his eyes. "Bloody hell! I thought you were dead."

"No," she said, her voice shaky. "Just stuck in a nightmare."

Scarl exhaled with a force that seemed to suck the bones from his body. "That was no sleep." He gave her over to Nace, who brushed her hair back from her eyes. The tension in their features drained only slowly.

"Your eyes were staring and blank," Scarl added. "You were cold. I didn't think you were breathing."

"I don't think I was sleeping, either. Not really. More like . . . I don't know . . ." She found herself distracted by Nace's touch. "Like closing my eyes and opening them somewhere else."

Scarl drew Nace's hand from her face, but without reproach. "Just a minute, Nace. Where?"

"Home. Canberra Docks, I mean. I keep dreaming of the same day—the day I found my telling dart. Before then, though. And I keep falling." Even the thought of that fall from Zeke's maple sent her heart hammering. "It keeps getting more awful, Scarl. Harder to wake up. If I do it again, I'm pretty sure I won't wake up here at all."

Scarl dragged one hand through his curls. A soft curse slid from him. Nace went back to petting Ariel's hair.

"Perhaps you're just exhausted," Scarl said faintly. "Or ill."

"I don't think so." Her queasy stomach had calmed. As she assessed how her other parts felt, she expected to stumble on last night's despair. Instead, the desire to walk surged through her, stronger than ever. Her feet, at least, felt that time had not quite run out.

"I'm not sick," Ariel added. "Just late." The sun throbbed on her shoulders. She glanced up, dismayed by how high it rode in the sky. Jostling Nace, she reached for her boots, slid her feet in, and rose. "We'd better go."

"Not so fast," Scarl said.

She whirled on him. "Yes! Fast! I don't want to talk about not waking up next time! You wouldn't let me keep going last night. This might be my last chance. Let's go!"

He stared, drew a hand over his mouth, and then turned to his own gear. Nace scrambled to follow suit and helped secure the load on the horse. Their task complete, Scarl gestured limply for Ariel to lead on, but without meeting her eyes.

She softened. "I'm sorry. It's not your fault. It's just . . . I don't want that nightmare again. I have to escape it. Any way I can. Please help me."

Anguish twisted his face. "I'm trying. I don't know what to do but follow."

"That's enough."

She fled from one kind of fall and toward another until they reached a stream. It drained the uplands on their right into the river on their left. The wide streambed was littered with flood-wood and rocks, but now the water meandered at a summertime low. Ariel turned to climb alongside it, sure it flowed from the waterfall somewhere above.

Willow refused to proceed.

As Nace tried to coax him, Ariel bounced from one foot to the other. The sun roasted the top of her head through her hair. Around them, the forest had thickened, drapes of ghoulish moss cloaking the stillness. They couldn't see far through the trees, but nothing tangible threatened. Still, Willow blew through splayed nostrils and locked all four legs, trembling.

Miming, Nace suggested blindfolding the horse.

"He's not sure-footed enough on such rough ground," Scarl said, "and it looks to get worse. Will we return this way, Ariel? I could hobble him here."

Ariel could no longer see past the going to imagine returning. Tomorrow and the day after were as distant and blank as the sky. When she tried to envision climbing back down this hill, her journey complete, what came instead were glimpses of tree branches, ground rushing too close, the sensation of falling.

To cover a shudder, she said, "If anything wants to eat Willow, though, he won't have a chance."

Nace snorted. She realized he was right, unless the stunted trees pulled up their roots to chase Willow. Nothing else lived here.

The hobbled horse began stumping back the way they had

come the moment Scarl released him. With an unhappy squint, the Finder watched Willow go.

"We might not catch him, if he keeps that up. I hope this is worth it."

"Do you think Vi's story was only a rant?" Ariel asked. "I might be as crazy as she is."

A wisp of a smile eased the strain on Scarl's face. "Oh . . . you've been crazy before, and that worked out well. I'm counting on this being the same."

Although she plunged onward, she murmured, "It's more frightening this time." She wished Scarl would hold her hand while they walked. He'd probably oblige her, but she couldn't bring herself to ask for something so childish, not in front of Nace. Holding Nace's hand wouldn't feel childish, but that would cause a nervousness of its own.

She thought of a third choice. "Could I carry your glass, Scarl? It would make me feel safer."

Confusion flickered over his features, but he immediately pulled out the pieces. "Don't cut yourself."

Mindful of the raw edges, she curled her fingers around one piece in each hand. Although—or because—they were sharp, they made her feel more attached to both Scarl and the world, as well as the sparkling Essence she'd occasionally glimpsed in their depths. Clutching them, she stormed the hill.

Since they now had to haul it themselves, it was fortunate their food stock had grown light. The companions scrambled over strewn logs and boulders, breathing hard and carving switchbacks on slopes too steep to climb straight up. Spring flood debris slid out from under their feet or thrust up to trip them.

As she stumbled ahead, something hard clunked between Ariel's anklebone and her boot. Shifting both halves of Scarl's glass to one hand, she poked a finger into her boot top after the stone that must have slipped in.

Her fingertip struck metal. She pinched it and pulled. A telling dart rose in her hand. The symbols on the brass shaft were familiar, as familiar as the idea of stashing it in her boot. She'd slid it there for safekeeping more than once last spring. The very first time had been the day she'd found it in Zeke's tree.

She wailed and recoiled, flinging it like a spider to the dirt.

Looking puzzled, Nace bent to retrieve it. When he straightened and opened his palm, what lay there was a stick.

"It was my dart!" Ariel cried. "The old one! Did you grab the wrong thing? I—" Her head whipped as her eyes scoured the uneven ground. No dart shone from among the wood litter, either.

Scarl stopped her frantic search. "I think your first instinct was right. It doesn't belong with you now, anyway."

Ariel stood trembling while Nace snapped the offending stick into pieces and tossed them away. Then she turned numbly uphill and continued.

Her blood pounding, she descended into a daze almost like fever. A mantra began circling her mind in time with her labored breath: *Cross one moon, follow many, climb more.* It didn't make sense, but it would not go away.

Oblivious to scratches and scrapes, she soon pocketed the halves of Scarl's glass so she could use her hands to pull herself along. *Cross one moon, follow many, climb more.* Ariel took shortcuts, ducking under or leaping across obstacles when it would have been safer to go around. Even with longer legs, her companions worked to keep up.

Scarl stopped her when he spotted tears on her cheeks. She hadn't known they were there until he pointed them out.

"It doesn't matter." Her voice tightened as she held back a sob. "We're almost there."

"We won't make it at all if you break a leg," he replied. "It hurts me to watch you. You've got to calm down and take more care."

Cross one moon, follow many, climb more. "I'll be okay. Let me go."

Scarl did not release her arm. "Nace," he asked, "if Ariel were an animal, could you do something to calm her?"

After a startled pause, the Kincaller grinned. He raised his good hand and drew it downward, petting as though Ariel were beneath it.

"That's what I was afraid of," Scarl said. "Never mind."

Nace's grin drooped and he kicked his toes against a log. Then he raised his palm: *Wait.* He thrust his good hand behind his back and closed the distance between himself and Ariel. He stopped a few inches short and tapped his eye socket. Resisting an urge to lean forward against him, Ariel looked into his eyes. They caught her as surely as Scarl's grip, which he now released.

Nace inhaled deeply and exhaled hard, three times. A fourth. Acutely aware of his body as well as his breath, Ariel found herself following his pattern. He nodded and smiled. His eyelids closed.

She followed suit.

Nace opened his own eyes again, concentration replacing his smile. His deep breaths rolled on, drawing hers. With fingers splayed briefly toward Scarl to stay him, he reached to lift Ariel's hands. He slid them under the edge of his sling to press against his heart.

Ariel's breathing lurched and her eyelids threatened to open. Nace *tsked* gently, squeezing her hands.

From behind the red-black veil of her lids, Ariel could feel him before her like a roaring fire. She tried to listen for his voice in her mind, for a flash of the connection she'd felt yesterday. It was impossible to think of anything but his chest, taut and warm beneath his shift. At first that sensation made Ariel's heart flutter, but soon she noticed the steadier beat under her hands. Gradually his heart's patient rhythm anchored her own and slowed it. Tension melted from her limbs.

She wasn't sure how long they stood motionless, their blood pulsing and breath twining together, before Nace's fingers stroked the backs of her hands. Ariel's skin wanted to jump off her body, perhaps onto his, but a drowsy warmth made the rest of her sway.

"That'll do, Nace," Scarl said softly.

The boy gave Ariel a few chirps that rang with regret. Then he released her hands and stepped back. She lingered a moment in bliss before she opened her eyes.

Nace couldn't meet them. He turned away.

Scarl caught his arm and leaned in. If the forest had not been so unnaturally silent, Ariel would never have picked up what he said.

"You've earned my respect twice," he murmured to Nace. "Once as a Kincaller. Once as a man. I'm sure that wasn't easy for you."

Nace shrugged off Scarl's praise along with his grip. Ariel followed him with her gaze. If her heart hadn't already been lost, it was now.

With effort, Scarl got her attention, tilting his head up the slope. "Continue more gently?"

She sighed, feeling as though her last breath were leaving

her lungs, but such a good breath that she didn't mind. She nodded.

Her tranquillity stretched until late afternoon, when they pushed through clinging tree boughs and finally emerged at the base of the waterfall she had known would be there. It looked exactly as Ariel had envisioned, except that a jumble of boulders and storm-ravaged trees speared into the ground at its base, preventing too close an approach. Dripping slime on the cliff suggested that during most of the year the flow raged much wider and with ten times the force. Despite this proof of fury, the water fell with unnerving quiet, much like the muffled river below.

The travelers gazed upward while mist collected on their faces. No thunder clapped. No Noah stepped out to greet them; no flood worthy of his name burst forth to drown them. Nothing marked their arrival at all.

"Timekeeper?" Scarl asked.

"Time waster, maybe." Ariel slumped. At long last, her feet wanted only to rest. But she had no idea what to do next.

CHAPTER 37

Dog Moon, Spilled

I expected something to happen," Ariel admitted. The endless welling of nothing but water bewildered her. "Maybe we're supposed to go up it," she added, without feeling much impulse to do so.

A choked sound escaped Scarl. "Look at it, dear one! A mountain goat couldn't scale that cliff." When she opened her mouth to debate, he continued more harshly. "What's not slick is sharp, and one misstep will break every bone. I'll not do it, and I'll not let you try. Not this time."

Nace wagged his head in agreement.

"Don't forget 'The Enchanted Gazelle,'" Scarl said more kindly. "If you think we need to get to the top, we'll have to backtrack and find some way around."

She shook her head and sank to a damp, mossy rock. Spray condensed on her cheeks like weak tears. Backtracking wasn't the answer.

"I won't let you sleep tonight, either," Scarl added, "if that's what you're worried about."

She started, wondering if he knew, somehow, that the

longer they'd traveled upstream, the more each step had echoed to her not of mounting a slope but of climbing a treacherous tree.

"We'll stay up with your accursed moon, and you can sleep when dawn breaks," he explained. "I'll watch over you then. So I can snap you awake if you so much as whimper."

Nace assured her that he would help, too. Ariel still feared no sunrise would come.

While Scarl worked to find supper, Nace clambered to the base of the waterfall. Ariel watched, flipping half of Scarl's glass in her palm like a worry stone. *Cross one moon, follow many, climb more.* She'd crossed one moon at the dam, and certainly followed the urging of many. But where were the rest?

After the Finder had moved out of sight, Nace explored a few places that might yield a path up. Ariel tensed as he jumped for handholds and scrabbled with his feet, yet ached each time he dropped back. At last he gave up. If Nace, agile as a cat, couldn't do it, she and her gimpy guardian certainly could not. The tiny wood violet the boy brought her didn't make her feel any better.

Night swirled around the fall. Scarl struggled in the damp to catch a small fire for roasting the fungus he'd found. Though he assured his companions that he'd eaten the same thing before with no ill effect, it was too slimy and ugly to choke down raw. They dried chunks on a stick until Ariel could pretend she was eating ill-shaped but nutty cookies.

Once their bellies were full, Scarl let the sickly flames die. They all thought of Sienna.

The spilled moon, a day past full, drifted over the tops of the trees to peer down. Ariel glared back. The right edge, nibbled barely out of round, mocked her.

Scarl asked to see her map. Listless, she handed it over, but as he mulled it, a flare of frustration moved her tongue.

"Don't you know that hideous thing by heart?" she demanded. "Cross the bridge over the lake where it looks like a slug's horns and follow the river from there. The broken line is the falls, or the stream flowing into the river. There's nothing beyond that but wintertime moons. We've missed the full Dog Moon. Too late."

He folded the cloth. "We don't even know Dog Moon is on here, not really. The idea of Lunasa made sense to me, but we're going on nothing but speculation and instinct. We might be mistaken, wildly so. Don't feel so bad. I'm not sure what we'll find on our return to the abbey—"

Unable to stop herself from imagining destruction and death, Ariel cringed.

"—but even the loss of the Vault would not bring the world to an end." Scarl said it firmly, defying disaster. "You've made new friends in intriguing places. And Electron may teach us a lot, once Sienna shows them that visitors aren't always a threat. We'll stay here a few days, if I can find enough to eat, to make sure we're not missing something. We can try again next summer, too, if you like, starting sooner and taking more time."

"No, we can't." She rested her chin on her bent knees. "Look at the map. There are two big circles of seasons, one inside the other. Two Augusts. Two chances. We found it last June, and remember what the stone said to Zeke? It told us to leave. We didn't understand soon enough. We should have come then, right away, but we didn't. *That's* why my dart said, 'No later than Beltane,' Scarl. We only had so long to get here. We got one second chance, one more Lunasa. This is our last chance."

Unable to argue, Scarl stroked her hair. "We'll try anyhow. You might be wrong."

He and Nace built a shelter of dead boughs against the waterfall's spray. Ariel ignored it, preferring to shiver. Dread hung on her, pinned down with exhaustion. She feared falling asleep despite her companions' best efforts. Once dreaming, she'd need only a moment to fall out of a tree. If she did it again, she didn't expect to survive—not in this time and place, and not in the other.

She might have found the solution herself if she hadn't been so discouraged. Nace wandered away briefly, probably to add his body's own waste to the damp rot all around. He returned quickly. Though he was pinching a moonflower in two fingers, he didn't give it to Ariel. He only thrust it under her nose, tugged on Scarl's sleeve, and gestured for them both to follow.

Eager for any distraction, Ariel got to her feet.

Scarl groaned. "I'm tired, Nace. What is it?"

Nace twirled the flower. He didn't attempt any other answer, but he wouldn't let Scarl stay behind, either. They picked along the cliff, aided by moonshine. They'd almost left sight of the falls when Nace pointed out a patch of moonflowers at the base of the bluff. Near the end of their short lives, some blossoms had wilted. But enough tattered petals remained to faintly glow in the moonlight.

Scarl took one look, managed a perfunctory nod, and turned back toward their shelter.

"Pretty, Nace." Ariel sighed. She took a step closer—and saw. She lunged after Scarl.

By the time she turned him around, Nace was standing over their heads on the side of the cliff. He'd followed a sparse path paved in moonflowers. It twisted up the rumpled stone, barely wide enough to accommodate feet.

"It's the way up!" Ariel cried. "Cross one moon, follow many . . ." From where she stood, the trail seemed to disappear above into sheer rock and moss, but it reemerged each time, always trending up and back toward the top of the falls. A missing piece of her heart settled back into place. She knew again what to do. "We've got to follow and see what's up there."

Ariel expected Scarl to mutter about breaking their necks. He merely dropped his forehead into his hand.

"You told me last night I had to let you walk the path once you found it," he said. "This must be what you meant. It goes against all my judgment, Ariel, but I can't stand against the forces behind you."

He raised his gaze. "You can do it, Nace, but can she? Would you risk her life up there?"

Nace snapped his fingers: *Easy*. He scrambled down to them and back up right away, though the path was already fading where he'd trampled the flowers. He extended his hand to Ariel.

His face grim, Scarl waved for her to proceed.

The moonflower staircase was neither smooth nor straightforward, but nobody stumbled. Nace led, gripping Ariel's hand and helping her balance. Hindered by his bad foot, Scarl sometimes lagged, but he always seemed to be right behind whenever she needed another steadying touch. Remembering Mo's remark about following moonflowers out of the world, Ariel could only promise herself she wouldn't pick any. Turning back was out of the question.

The path grew more treacherous, and they slowed as they reached a slick area where water must have gushed most of the year. Even in August, rain might have stopped them. As it was, a sheet of falling water soon cut off their path. Both the top of the falls and the bottom were lost in shimmering mist. The trio pressed against the rock face, exposed. Their trail seemed to have ended.

Then Ariel spotted a glimmer behind the curtain of water. Sidling around Nace, she plunged her free hand into the icy blast. Not stone but cool air met her touch.

"Hang on to me, Nace." Before anyone could protest, she doused her head and shoulders into the downpour and past it.

Roaring assaulted her ears. The falls thundered here, their noise more stunning for the hush on the other side. Gasping at the cold flood down her back, Ariel blinked until she could make out the source of the gleam. A stone alcove hid there behind the waterfall, glowing moonflowers coating its walls. It looked like the inside of a sunlit seashell.

Ariel stepped forward—and yanked up short. Nace held her too tightly. She spluttered back through the deluge to urge her friends in behind her.

They all pushed through the gushing water. At the rear of the alcove, the ceiling disappeared upward. Except for the flower-glow and the moss-scented air, Ariel felt as if she'd crept into a fireplace to stare up the chimney. Fresh air floated down and moonlight gleamed on the close walls above, so clearly the breach opened to the sky. Half circles of gnarled root thrust from the wall below, forming curved ladder rungs in the stone. They led up.

"Look!" Ariel shouted over the roar of the falls. "More moons, for climbing. I've got to go up." She gripped a rung—and only then noticed the moss clinging to the stone just below. The moss grew in no random patch but a symbol, yellow-green against the black rock. Though drawn oddly backward, the Farwalker symbol sent a thrill of recognition through her.

Scarl reached to slow her. A tiny, bright jag of lightning passed between them at the touch. It stung. They both flinched.

"Did you feel that?" he hollered.

"Like winter shock!"

As she spoke, the hairs on her arms and neck lifted. Soon her bangs also stuck out from her head. Nace grinned, reaching intentionally to give her that startling zing.

Impatient with his teasing, she lifted one foot onto the rungs in the wall.

"Wait," Scarl yelled. "Those may not hold weight." He grabbed the rung over her head to test it. With a curse, he jerked back so fast his forearm smacked Ariel's head.

"It bit me!" He shook his pained hand. "Like the winter shock, but—" Realizing that she was already gripping the next lower rung, he reached alongside her hand. He swore louder at the second nasty shock.

"I don't feel anything," she said. "But look." She toed the Farwalker symbol near her knees.

Nace moved forward to try.

"Don't, Nace—," Scarl began. The boy also yanked back his fingers and thrust their tips into his mouth.

"I don't think you can come with me," Ariel said.

"Let me go back for a rope," Scarl replied. "We'll tie it around you. When you get to the top you can—"

"No. You can't help me with this."

Scowling, Scarl smoothed the raised hairs on the back of his neck. He didn't like it, but he knew she was right.

Ariel let go of the ladder long enough to throw her arms around him. They both ignored the resulting zap.

"I'll be okay," she said into his shirt, almost certain he wouldn't hear it over the noise of the fall. "Wait for me."

"Slow down," he said. "Let's—"

"No. This is right." Releasing him, she turned to Nace. She meant to give him more than a hug, but when their eyes locked, she lost her nerve.

Nace took it up for her. He extended his hands. They both flinched at the small shock when she put her fingers in his. He drew her forward, the thin space between them melting sweetly. His lips met hers without either of them seeming to cause it.

A jolt considerably more potent than winter shock coursed through her. Ariel recoiled, needing to see into Nace's eyes at his thoughts. His lips chased hers for an instant before he straightened his neck and let her go. Unable to draw in a breath, she stared at the wild glint in his gaze. One corner of his mouth pulled into a crooked smile, softening an intensity that weakened her legs.

She leaned forward again, their lips not quite matching in an awkward but breathtaking way. Then she stepped back before the roar in her head could drown all thoughts of the moon-shaped rungs that awaited.

"Wait for me." She added a sweet-name she hadn't known until Scarl had applied it to her earlier: "Dear ones."

She was most of the way up the ladder before her thoughts connected one to the next well enough for her to recall the confusing soft-and-hardness of Nace's lips or the spicy scent of his damp skin. By then, Ariel was no longer in the same world as the boy she'd just kissed.

CHAPTER 38

Moon in the Well

Ariel pulled herself up through the tight space, staring only at the next higher rung. At first she feared that if she glanced down, the sight of upturned faces might squash her intention and she'd descend, too scared to leave Scarl and Nace. After a few moments of climbing, she supposed that if she peeked down at all, her body would realize how far she could fall. Her arms and knees would start shaking, and a nightmare might wrench loose her grip.

She reached the moonbeam in the chimney. It cast shadows of her hands on the stone. The hole yawned a goodly way farther up, though. Swallowing hard, Ariel clasped the next grip. She wished she'd thought to count rungs. Her palms and fingers grew sore.

The echo of her panting made her feel alone. She decided to pretend her friends were following behind her so she'd have someone else to help bear her tension.

"Almost there," she told them.

Her forearms ached by the time she poked her head into clear air. In the last few yards of her climb, the stone had curved, smooth, as though hands and not nature had shaped it. When she broke into moonlight, she saw why. Though she'd begun in a crack through the bedrock, she'd emerged from a mortared stone ring like the mouth of a well.

Gripping it, she pulled herself out. Once her feet felt solid ground, a spurt of adrenaline left her dizzy and weak. She leaned on the rocks.

"That was a long way to climb," she said to her absent companions. "Way taller than a tree."

A circle of standing stones guarded the well, each rising over her head. Beyond those loomed a row of evenly spaced but dead trees. Although their skeletal branches clawed at stars in the clear sky overhead, mist rose between them to swirl at Ariel's knees. Stepping past the sentinel stones and two trees, Ariel could see only a cottony blanket of fog in the moonshine. The abrupt downward slope under her feet told her the trees stood atop a sharp hill. Only its peak breached the fog. No sound rose from below. The waterfall must lie somewhere down to her left, but she couldn't hear it through the chimney or spy any spray.

"Now what?" She stepped back toward the well stones to hail Scarl and Nace, if her voice would carry that far.

Looking down, Ariel yelped in surprise. Dark water filled the hole to within a foot of the rim.

Her chest tightened. The chimney couldn't possibly have filled with water behind her. No amount of sudden rain could have filled the crack in the stone, the alcove, and the whole land below it. Other than its rock rim, the well she gazed into now bore no connection to the place where she'd climbed. The moon reflected in water that lay still and stagnant; scum clung against the stone on one side. With a skittering heart, Ariel remembered the wet smell of the map.

She touched the water to make sure it was real. The reflected moon rippled. She knelt, gritted her teeth, and plunged her arm in to her shoulder, feeling for the first rung. All the way around, her hand met nothing but water and rock. She drew it out, dripping.

"Guess I'm not going back that way."

Trying to swallow the lump in her throat, Ariel scowled at the water. As it stilled, she noticed her reflection. She bent closer. Her hand rose to one cheek, then both. The skin there was smooth. With a grunt of confusion, she shoved up her wet sleeve. No scar marred her left forearm, either. Her fingertips coursed back and forth between her elbow and wrist as though they might find what her eyes couldn't.

She looked up to the moon, wondering if its light were playing some trick. It gleamed as bright as the pearl on her necklace. Yet now that she studied it, this moon was wrong. An hour ago, the waning moon in the sky had shown a crumbling edge. This moon shone perfectly full.

Ariel slumped against the side of the well, clutching the arm that had long borne a scar and staring at that wrongly round moon. After a while, another disturbing fact worked its way through her thoughts. This moon didn't move. Her viewpoint placed it near the silhouette of a tree branch, but the moon never drew farther away from that branch. Certain she must be mistaken, she rested her cheek on the edge of the well to keep herself still and recited the multiplication of numbers from one to fifteen. It took her nearly ten minutes, and the moon should have rolled its whole width farther along in the sky. Instead, it was frozen. A chill rattled Ariel's core. If she wasn't in the land of the dead, she had climbed outside of time.

"Scarl?" She couldn't repress the whine in her voice. The

thought of him helped, though. She gripped the lip of the well with both hands and tried to slow her uneven breathing. If he were here, what would he do? She imagined it very carefully to keep the panic away. He would wander the circle of stones and the larger circle of trees, looking for hints as to what they should do. He would rub the stubble on his jaw while he considered. He might drop a hand on her shoulder to shush the tremble in her breathing. Then he would tell her, she supposed, to stop thinking and let her instincts guide her.

Ariel rose. Her knees wobbled. She pressed her feet into the ground to stop the weakness and walked toward the nearest tree. Its bark glistened as though speckled with frost in the moonlight. With one finger, she touched it.

The branches of several trees swayed overhead, clacking and rubbing together. Ariel jumped back, half expecting one to reach down and swat her. No hint of wind disturbed the fog near her feet.

"So the moon doesn't move, but the trees do?" She shuddered with them.

The trees stilled. Their sound stopped. Then one tree alone trembled and hissed with a noise like a breeze through invisible leaves. Another scraped two creaking branches together. Ariel got the distinct sense they were speaking to her.

"I'm not a Tree-Singer," she called. "I can't understand you."

The trees stilled and the silence returned, empty even of a slithering wind. Ariel waited, and when no more trees moved, she slowly traversed them. For a moment, she'd felt less alone in this bewildering place. But now the trees seemed to stare.

"Sorry," she murmured. "I'm trying."

She turned her attention instead to the standing stones nearer the well. These, too, made her wish she weren't here alone. Surely Zeke Stone-Singer could have helped her right now. The imposing slabs all stood silent, each as tall and wide as a great door. Though they appeared to be uncut, they were so well matched they made Ariel think too much of headstones or coffins. She tried shoving one over simply to see what might happen. She couldn't budge it.

In the eerie silence, a sound caught her attention. It seemed to come from the well. She approached and bent over its rim.

Voices echoed from its watery depths, low but rising. Her heart leaped as she thought she heard Scarl and Nace. Then she frowned. The next voice, overlapping, belonged to her mother. A louder call she recognized with a sickening jolt: it belonged to her dead enemy, Elbert. The echoes were so thick and distorted, she could make out no more than a few words from each, but the voices themselves came through clearly. Tears sprang to her eyes when she heard Zeke plea for her to come down from the roof.

Her heart begged to respond, but she knew those voices burbled up from her past. There was nobody down there to answer.

Still, the sounds drifting upward reminded her that a bead in her necklace carried a story of a well. With new confidence and purpose, Ariel bent backward over the rim, the rocks scraping her back and her hair dunking in the water. That stilled the voices. She cranked her neck sideways to eye the wavering reflection of the moon.

It hadn't been in Scarl's story, but she recited a rhyme that she knew:

Here I dangle in the well;
Show what only time will tell.

Her strained position made her struggle to breathe, but her discomfort vanished when the moonface wavered and twisted. Ariel watched it reshape itself into the open throat of a well. She saw herself there beside it, but the girl in the reflection didn't arch backward, headfirst. Instead she sat on the edge, threw her feet over, and slipped soundlessly into the water.

Ariel stared. Perhaps some friendly well sprite was showing her how to get back to her friends. But the girl in the well merely sank like a stone. Ariel held her own breath. After an ominous absence, the girl bobbed back to the surface, her neck limp, her eyes closed, and her face bloated in death.

With a cry, Ariel flung herself up and away from the image of drowning. Landing hard alongside the well, she curled her legs to her chest. Could that be her true future?

Sobs rose from the water. Mockery followed.

"April Fool!"

"Scarface."

"You're lazy enough, and a goof, too."

No longer thinking, Ariel clapped her hands over her ears, jumped up, and fled toward the trees. She aimed past them. The fog tricked her. Where freedom had beckoned, dead branches clawed her. She fought them, only to collide with trunks and stumble over uneven ground. A root hidden by mist sent her sprawling. Picking herself up, she backtracked and crossed the circle to try the far side instead.

She'd just passed the well when another insult echoed behind her.

"Foolish girl! Where would you go?"

As if Scarl had reached from the past to clout her, Ariel skidded to a halt. When he'd actually snarled those words, long ago, she'd been his and Elbert's prisoner and she'd tried to escape. He'd slapped her then, too. Her cheek burned at the memory, and her heart chafed with old resentment she hadn't known she still carried. Its bitterness flowed toward the forces that blocked her escape now.

She whirled. "I'm not foolish!"

"Prove it." Though she recognized that voice from Skunk, she wondered if some of the gurgles from the well were not random at all.

She stalked back to its rim with an impulse to throw something in. A splash would end the rude echoes, at least for a moment, as well as defy the evil picture she'd seen there. Without so much garble in her ears, she could think more calmly and perhaps figure out why she'd been led here. Otherwise, the well's taunts would be true. The Farwalker would become a Fool.

Casting about, she found only barren ground. The rocks of the well were too firmly fixed to break loose. Although she considered snapping the end of a tree branch, she quickly rejected that option. For all she knew, these trees might snap her bones in return.

As she stood fuming, trying to ignore the voices and toying with whether to simply slap at the water, another phrase came through clearly.

"It's disrespectful to climb trees!"

"Oh, Zeke." She dropped her face into her hands, doubting she'd ever see him again. The words and the day when he'd said them sat fresh in her mind, recalled more than once by her nightmare. Perhaps she should simply lie down and await its return. Her heart knew that if she dreamed it again, especially with no one to wake her, it would be the last dream she ever had. Yet even that might be better than drowning herself in the well.

"It's disrespectful to climb trees . . . to climb trees . . . to climb trees. . . ." The words pushed through other jumbled echoes of her past.

"I got it," she grumbled. "You can go on to something else now."

"Climb treessclimb treeeesss." The voice grew more sibilant, no longer Zeke's at all. It sounded, in fact, like a watery swish. Ariel jumped when a splash flew over the rim of the well. She didn't dare approach to see what had stirred it.

"Cli'treesss. Cl'tree—"

"Oh!" She regarded the trees. "That's not advice, is it?"

The rattle of branches drowned out the well's voice.

Ariel approached the skeletal trees slowly. "But . . . it's disrespectful. Isn't it?" The idea of climbing one of these bony husks, putting herself in its clutches, chilled her.

The rustling dwindled until only one tree still trembled. Ariel laid her hand flat on its bark. Its vibration passed through her, too, before stopping.

She raised her arm to pull gently against the lowest branch, testing. Even if they were not strictly dead, the dry branches might break. And a fall from one of these trees might be as deadly as the fall in her dream.

But she had to do something, and she was out of ideas of her own.

When her Farwalker's feet lifted her onto her toes, she said, "All right. If that's what you want."

CHAPTER 39

Moon Out of Time

Ariel took off her boots. It seemed less rude that way and, besides, she'd need to cling with her toes. The wrinkles in the tree's bark were too fine to serve as footholds or grips.

For a moment she wasn't sure she'd be able to climb it at all. The lowest branch arched over her head. Finally she wrapped her hands around it from both sides, let herself hang to make sure it would hold her, and then swung and scrambled her feet up the trunk until she could wrap her legs, too, around the same branch. From there, she squirmed and levered herself until at last she twisted atop the branch and upright.

"Oh!" she said to the tree. "You're not helping much, are you?" Panting, she peered up. The next branches were distant, a confusion of pale bark and slashing moon shadows. She couldn't see so much as a dead leaf trapped in a fork, so she wasn't sure what she was meant to accomplish—unless the idea was to fall.

A moonlit glint to her left caught her eye. A telling dart lay atop the nearest standing stone.

Ariel stared, not trusting what she saw. Brass gleamed from

the top of each stone. If she'd been taller, she might have spied the darts from the ground, or at least from the rim of the well.

"Thank you," she sighed. Then she frowned. The tops of the stones all rose over her reach, and they'd already refused to be toppled. A friend to boost her—that's all she needed—but the trees stood too far away. She couldn't contemplate breaking a branch. Ariel fingered her necklace, racking her brain. A dragon could reach them, or a bridge, but neither helped here. She had nothing but the clothes on her back.

So she slid out of the tree and out of her shirt and pants, too.

"Like the selkie in the story slid out of its fur," she decided. She tied a sleeve to one pant leg and flopped the length over the stone like a lasso. She pulled. The clothes dropped. The dart remained out of sight. Repeat attempts also failed. While she could hear the dart rattle, her clothes could not drag it off—or at least, she had too little patience to manage it once, let alone with every stone in the circle.

"Fine." She yanked her clothes back on and glanced up at the moon. "Here I come again." With her arms outstretched, she could just embrace the stone's expanse, so she gripped both corners and hoisted herself up. Unlike the stones of the abbey, this one offered no cracks for her fingers. She simply clamped it between her hands and feet and pressed her body to its cold surface, clinging through sheer strength and friction and squirming up like a bear cub shimmying up a tree. Fortunately, the stone wasn't terribly tall. Still, by the time she pulled herself atop, her skin stung with scrapes and her muscles groaned.

The dart that awaited appeared to be blank, but she didn't examine it carefully now. Instead Ariel clenched it in her fist and stood unsteadily, shaking the strain from her legs and eyeing the next stone on the circle. She would have liked more than one stride to launch from, but she thought this was a leap she could make.

Ariel glanced down. By contrast, the next stone looked close. She jumped.

Ariel stumbled twice on the route, both times cracking her knees and nearly tumbling before catching herself, but soon she was sitting atop the last stone, a bundle of darts in her fist. Rolling onto her belly, she eased her legs over the edge. She was too tired to even attempt to climb down, but with her legs dangling, the drop was less than six feet. She pushed off.

The stupidity of letting go occurred to her too late.

Ariel fell. The earth did not meet her. She flailed, spun, and tumbled, empty space whistling past her ears. Leafy branches brushed at her legs, at her face. A scream trailed from her throat. She heard Zeke cry her name.

When the ground slammed against her at last, the pain came as a relief. At least it was solid. A broken cry burst from her lips, but she was still glad the falling was over. Her body too shocked to inhale, Ariel wallowed in the earth and the scent of decomposed leaves before slipping into yet greater darkness.

The blackness spat her back out. Voices murmured nearby. Alarm arced through her body and her eyes opened. She lay flat on her back with the full moon ogling her from above. Ariel squinted, only slowly connecting what she saw. She was not in the woods near Zeke's maple. She lay instead near the base of the stone she'd abandoned. The voices spoke from the well. Ariel groaned.

Before her next breath, the moon swirled, as its reflection had done when she'd asked for her future. She blinked, supposing tears caused the blur. It spun faster. With a wince, she realized why. She was not dangling upside down, strictly speaking, but she was staring into a well in the sky. The stones in her peripheral vision formed a rim, framing the moon. Stars glittered around it as if on the surface of water.

"You've already shown me one death," she whispered. "I'm not certain I'm not a ghost now. How many more deaths can I have?"

She regretted the question. The twisting moon slowed to form the face of a corpse. Though pallid and disfigured, it was a face she knew well: Scarl's.

"No!" Her eyelids clamped shut. She cringed and rolled away before she'd even known she could move. She couldn't trust anything here. Yet her traitorous heart whispered a truth: sooner or later, the Finder would pass from the world. Even if she remained trapped out of time, Scarl's death would eventually come.

A sob of dismay pulled her upright, awakening bruises and aches. Yet the thought of her guardian renewed her will. She'd face his loss when it came, since she hadn't a choice. But despair could only speed its arrival. She had to escape this place somehow, or all of her friends would be dead to her now.

Telling darts lay scattered around her. Wondering how long she'd lain senseless, she pulled on her boots and gathered the darts. To be sure she missed none in the fog, she counted the stones: thirteen, the same number as moons on the map. The same number as—

Tiny glints flickered between her fingers precisely as the realization struck her. Ariel's eyes darted quickly enough to catch the last of the symbols still forming on the darts in her hand. They were no longer blank. A different trade mark appeared on each dart, showing who was supposed to receive it. The other marks on the stems were the same between darts, and familiar.

A bolt of understanding hit Ariel so hard it sickened her stomach. She had received one of these darts. Not one *like* them—one of the very darts in her fist. They'd come not from her world but from a place out of time, a place where the moon froze and night reigned and her only future was death. The darts had no mark on them identifying the sender. She supposed that was because they had not yet been sent, but the mapstone had led her to the sender after all: Ariel herself was the sender.

With that, she knew what she must do here, and why. She had to send out those darts. They had to be launched into time, upstream from the Timekeeper where she'd stepped out. If she didn't, she'd never find a dart near Canberra Docks or take up her path as a Farwalker. She'd merely fall to her death on a fateful day in Zeke's tree. That day was the crossroads, and the strange echoes that had bled through from her past all depended on it. If she erred now, her life would already be over.

Fighting to hold on to her courage, Ariel paced. Her only chance was to send out the darts. Yet she faced a problem: while she knew how to open a telling dart and close it again, she'd never learned how to send one.

Maybe it was as simple as wanting it so. Certainly the darts had known, almost before she did, who they should go to and what they must say. Consciously, at least, she had not guided them. Sending them might be the same. What had Vi told her? Something about having a purposeful thought. Ariel opened her hand wide and wished the darts gone.

The darts did not move from her palm.

"Fly," she said. "Send. Go. Go away. Um . . . be off. Carry the message. Deliver?" She ran out of words. Desperately seeking an insight, she tried to block out the mutters still bubbling up from the well.

Wait—perhaps those echoes might help her again. "How do I do it?" she called into the water. "How do I send the darts? Anyone? Please tell me."

The sounds from the well rose and fell, now a giggle, now wailing. Her ear caught a reference to scorpions and snatches of stories. The words did not string together into anything that could be done with a dart.

Of course, she'd heard of darts that could be thrown in a game, not only the kind that bore messages. Grimly, Ariel set her burden on the ground to take up just one, starting with the dart for the Fool. If any were to be lost, that was her choice. Meeting Gustav Fool last year in the desert, suffering his threats and abuse, had been vile. She preferred not to invite him again. In fact, she would have left that dart unsent intentionally, if she hadn't been afraid of meddling with events that had already happened. Moving to the edge of the circle of trees and wishing they didn't watch her so closely, she pumped her hand near her ear to work up her nerve. She aimed into the dark, drew a taut breath, and threw the dart as hard as she could.

Her eyes lost its track, but she heard a dull *thunk* from quite close.

Turning her head, she spied the telling dart stuck in a tree, quite an odd angle away from the direction she'd thrown.

She tried again. Soon she'd proven only that no strength or steady hand could fling the darts past the trees, even if she stepped beyond them to throw. She saw no tree move, but somehow they drew in the darts and caught them.

Befuddled, Ariel collected the thrown darts once more. A dozen she held in her left hand; the Farwalker's dart she gripped in her right. She closed her eyes and moved her awareness into her feet, asking them to find her path. One slow step at a time, they carried her back to the well and its maddening garble.

The well. She pondered the bead in her necklace, the gold one, whose story had featured a well. The name of that story had been "Golden Seeds."

Ariel shuffled the darts in both hands, uncertain. But thinking would not make a difference, not here. She reached over the rim, took a deep breath, and splayed her fingers. The darts dropped into the water with nary a splash.

Expecting them to shoot like arrows back into the sky, Ariel leaned away from the rim. She listened to silence and the wild beating of her heart for several long moments before she realized the voices had stopped. Yet the darts did not fly up and out.

Praying that the water might be gone now, she peeked over the edge. Her hope sank. The moon stared back from the water's surface as before. Ariel looked away fast, still stinging from the scene of her death that reflection had shown her.

If she'd lingered, she might have glimpsed her own future again, the view entirely changed by her release of the darts. But Ariel moved too quickly for the moonlight to reveal it.

"I hope that was right," she mumbled. "If not, it's too late." Weary beyond measure of feeling too late, Ariel rolled her head on her neck. It occurred to her that even if her instincts were sound, she had ensured only that the Vault would be found. Her own path might still end here and now.

A thunderous crash sounded behind her. She whirled. A standing stone had toppled onto its back. Another dropped, shaking the ground, while she watched. Ariel cringed against the well as a third and a fourth, two at once, and then the whole circle fell.

The soil alongside them first trembled, then heaved. Spidery roots sprang from the earth, squirming up the sides of the stones. Larger roots followed to swarm over and bind them, growing with the speed of flames rising. Ariel gulped and glanced at her feet. The ground where she stood was still solid, but perhaps not for long. Roots crawled toward the well. She raced between stones toward the trees.

No sooner had she passed beyond the circle of stones than, with a terrible groan, the ground split and the roots dragged them into the earth. Dirt flew. Fisted tight, the roots yanked and wrestled. Ariel wanted to cling to a tree trunk, but she was afraid of the trees, too, for she knew where the tangled roots came from. Her common sense urged her to run, but she couldn't tear her gaze from the burial.

First one fallen stone and then another was sucked down completely. When only churned dirt was left, the roots pulled the well in on itself. The rimstones fell in with a splash. Soon nothing remained on the hilltop but Ariel and the circle of trees. The earth between them rippled languidly, smoothing itself, like swells on a mild summer sea.

Hence, walker. Whole.

She looked up, surprised by the voice.

Well, all well. Time, trees, twisted . . . tired.

Ariel eyed the circle of trees and remembered what Ash had said before her trip started: trees had done people a vast favor already. Somehow transcending time, they'd helped tend the failsafe. She hoped she could see their compassion both earned and repaid.

Leave, lead, heed. Hence.

"Thank you," Ariel told the trees. "I'll go now, if that's all right." Wary for a root coiling over her feet, she edged past the circle. The trees let her go.

Engulfed swiftly in fog, Ariel skidded down the steep hill, trusting her feet to avoid unseen hazards. The clammy silence of mist weighed upon her, deadening the sound of her boots. The farther she descended, the thicker the fog grew, until even her own body faded from view. As she lost sight, she began calling Scarl and Nace. She didn't really expect any answer. She only did it to prevent herself from vanishing altogether. When her voice became hoarse and she'd stumped downhill for what seemed to her sore knees like days, she whispered her Farwalker's song under her breath. Her head and eyelids both drooped, but the words kept her going.

Her shuffle had grown hitched and painful by the time she heard anything beyond her own whisper. Sharp voices barely roused her. As blind as if the fog had seeped into her eyes, she whimpered and shrank. Despite the moon's final whispers, Ariel feared she was only imagining others, ghostly guides to ease her travel the remaining way out of the world.

She jerked at a touch. Arms lifted her, solid and too strong to resist. Only the familiar and welcome smell of his sweat told Ariel the arms had to be Scarl's. She buried her face against him and let the fog claim her, never more grateful that he was a Finder.

CHAPTER 40

Dog Moon, Waning

When Ariel's eyes opened a few hours later, they darted in confusion. Dead tree bones loomed all around. No moon stared back when she turned her face up, and for that she was grateful. But despite the hammering sun and heartfelt embraces from Scarl and Nace, who were resting beside her, the ghostly white forest gave her a chill.

"Why'd you bring me here?"

She was stunned to learn that they hadn't. Though she'd walked a long way in the fog, the chimney behind the waterfall couldn't possibly have emerged above the dead forest, nearly two days of travel away. Yet that's where Ariel's friends had found her, wandering aimlessly among the skeletal trees. They'd never seen any fog. So they'd remained on the spot, watching over her while she slept.

"Next time we find a path marked with a Farwalker sign, I'm tying you with a leash, like old times," Scarl said. "Don't ever disappear like that on me again."

"How did you find me?" she wondered, resting in his arms.

"Nace went wild almost as soon as you'd climbed out of

sight," Scarl told her. "He was sure you were dead, though we couldn't see how. He tried to climb after you."

"Didn't it hurt?"

Nace ducked his face, but Scarl grabbed the boy's good wrist and turned up the palm. An angry stripe slashed across it.

"It would have been worse, but the moment he grabbed one and held it, the rungs pulled into the stone, like eels slipping into the sand. We spent a while trying to find another way up or around on the outside. I'm not sure why we're alive. We both took desperate skids down that cliff."

Nace mimed a fall. Ariel had to look away.

"When we gave up on climbing and got to the bottom, I kept trying to find you without feeling a thing." Scarl's voice dropped and he shuddered. "Not *anything*. I should have been able to locate your body, at least, when I stopped seeking you and instead sought your lifeless remains. Only the fact that I couldn't do it let me hang on to hope."

"The ladder was—I don't know—some kind of shortcut." Ariel described what she'd found on the hilltop. Scarl listened intently. She did not mention the face of his corpse.

When she told him how she'd dropped the darts into the well, he said, "Hmm. I have something to show you." He unwound his arms from her to reach for her pack, which she'd left behind at their camp.

"First tell me how you got here." Insecure without somebody's touch, she twined her fingers with Nace's, mindful of his sore palm. A smile lifted the boy's tired face.

"Not long before dawn I finally caught a sense of you," Scarl said. "It was hard to believe you'd gotten so far, but it was all we had. With my cursed foot, we'd still be a long way off if Nace hadn't shouldered most of our gear and I hadn't found Willow hock-deep in the river near where we'd left him. That horse ran an incredible way bearing us both when Nace asked him."

Ariel didn't press for more details. Her friends' faces told her they had traveled hard with no sleep. She embraced them again, too grateful their paths had reunited to feel nervous about hugging Nace.

"But that reminds me," Scarl said. "Willow's bridle is back."

Ariel clapped a palm to her cheek. She shoved up her left sleeve. The creases in her skin stirred a wave of relief that threatened to spill into tears. They weren't lovely, but those scars were hers, returned to their proper places and time.

"That's good, don't you think?" she asked Scarl.

"I do. And there's this." Scarl flapped a certain bit of linen before her. She goggled. The lines on her map had faded, and Ariel didn't have to be at the abbey to guess that the mapstone itself was now blank, too.

"Oh! Do you think the whole Vault's disappeared?" She didn't know how, but at least marks could vanish without an earthquake or landslide, so the abbey's inhabitants might still be safe.

"When I first noticed, I feared that." He shook his head. "But after hearing that you are the sender, I'm sure it only means that the fail-safe is no longer needed. Its work—*your* work—is done. You've proven that the Vault's discovery was not a mistake, so the fail-safe no longer exists."

Awed, Ariel said, "I had plenty of help."

"I'm sure cooperation was what the fail-safe intended. It's a wonder the little you had was enough."

"Not so little," she replied, thinking back on her path. It was littered with unwitting insights and information in shreds, yet the encouragement and knowledge she needed had all mounted up.

She wanted more help right now, though, from Scarl and Nace. She ached to escape the bone woods. Its eerie breath on her face disturbed her, especially as the sun rolled toward home. But her companions and Willow all looked worn-out. Strung with guilt, she wondered aloud if they could bear just a little more travel.

"Slowly, perhaps, if you're up to it," Scarl said. "The thought of a night under these trees makes my skin crawl."

When they began lurching downhill toward the river, she felt a clunk against her leg. She reached into her pocket. What she found froze her feet.

"Scarl," she said, choking, "remember how you gave me your glass? In two pieces?" She drew her hand from her pocket. His Finder's glass lay on her palm, round and whole.

Nace whistled. Scarl started, but then took it from her. The glass bore no hint of its days asunder.

"How could it do that?" she mumbled. "And why?"

Frowning, he gave no reply. They walked on. Scarl muttered, mostly to himself, about whether it had mended or never broken in the first place.

After much thought, he said, "I'm only supposing, but suppose the fail-safe bent time in a loop." He raised one of Willow's reins so the end dropped toward the ground, and then he pinched a floppy circle from its length. "You copied the mapstone in that loop. My glass broke there, too, as we tried to understand the map." He wiggled his free hand within the circle. "Both actions were linked to the cause of the loop. When you dropped the darts into the past"—his fingers released, the leather fell straight, and his free hand fluttered away—"the loop fell away and so did a few things that rested inside it, things that time no longer needed."

"And if I hadn't," Ariel said, "I'd still be trapped in the loop. You would never have found me."

"I suspect I would never have met you." Scarl briefly folded the loop back into place, marking its extent with his fingers. "We've reached the leather at the end of the loop. If you'd not sent the darts, we may have come back to the start. We both might have awakened from a vivid dream of darts and the Vault. You'd still be living in Canberra Docks. I expect that's why the stones told Zeke he would not be a Stone-Singer long if you failed. He would become Zeke Tree-Singer instead, as he'd planned. And you might have become a Healtouch after all."

"No." She shook her head. Zeke may have kept his original trade as Scarl was suggesting, but Ariel was quite sure she'd be dead from a fall. A barb tore at her heart. "But my mother . . ."

"Or perhaps not," he added hastily. "The Tree-Singers would have us believe we cannot dodge our fates very long. If you hadn't dropped the darts into the past—and our future—we may not have had one. All three of us may have fallen ill and died."

"Fallen," Ariel agreed. "But not ill." She shuddered.

Nace rubbed the goose bumps from her arm. She shot him a grateful look before adding, "And I bet Nace and everyone else would have fallen asleep, tonight or tomorrow, to wake in a world where the Vault had never been found and none of them ever had met us."

"Likely," Scarl told her. "Regardless, it's done."

"Are you sure?" Though she'd slept safely enough just that day, the thought of closing her eyes again made her tense. She feared she would awaken in a circle of trees in the fog. "What if we're going around and around in the loop and can't get out?"

Scarl mulled her words. "If so, I don't think we'd know it. But where do your instincts call you now?"

She inhaled, considered well, and smiled for the first time in two days. "To the abbey."

His brow furrowed. "To discover the Vault? Or to make sure it's safe?"

"Neither," she replied. "Simply to see Zeke again and relish the feeling of home."

CHAPTER 41

Waning Moon, Waxing Hearts

When they reached the river, Scarl called for a halt. Ariel yearned to push on upstream past the edge of the bony white forest. Nace suggested a third option: crossing the river.

They studied the water. It wasn't a torrent, but it was impossible to tell how deep it ran or what hazards might lie beneath. Reluctantly Scarl agreed, provided they remain on the horse.

Carrying them all, Willow waded in, more willing to cross than to continue either direction along the shore. He faltered only when depth lifted him off his feet. Ignoring Scarl's provision, Nace slipped off to hold the bridle and swim alongside the horse's great head. Ariel clung madly as Willow's legs thrust beneath her, but they were all carried downstream until his hooves found purchase again. The horse jumped out, stumbling on rocks but as eager for solid ground as his riders.

Even the fading sun felt different on this side of the river. A breeze shushed through the dry grass. Nace whistled, long and loud, for the joy of the noise. A soaring hawk answered. Ariel spied a prairie dog hole.

"I feel like we're round again instead of flat!" she said. The first words in her mind, in fact, had been "living" and "dead," but she didn't want to say those aloud.

"I still feel flat," Scarl replied wearily. "Let's camp here."

Nace stretched to dry in the waning sun and fell asleep immediately. Seated nearby, Ariel didn't realize how openly she was studying him until Scarl spoke.

"We pushed hard after you, harder than I've ever traveled," he said, perhaps misinterpreting her gaze. "And he was terrified that we'd lost you. Fear is exhausting. I'm surprised you're not asleep again yourself for the same reason."

She thought back over her own fearful moments, especially the scene in the well of her drowning. Clearly the future she'd seen had been false—or was it true until she changed it by sending the darts? The death she had seen in the face of the moon, though, was certain to pass eventually.

"I'm too glad to be in the world to sleep yet." Ariel's mind shied from any more thoughts of the future. Instead it lurched to one of the well's taunts from the past. In the circle of trees, it had spurred her defiance, but now the memory festered.

"But, Scarl?" She turned to gain his full attention. "Don't ever hit me again."

"What are you talking about? I wouldn't hit you."

"You slapped me, hard. When I tried to escape."

"When you . . ." His frown deepened, then slid to regret. "Oh—in the beech wood that day with Elbert. I remember." He canted his head. "What made you think of that, more than a year gone now?"

"Why did you do it?"

He met her eyes with unusual difficulty. "I could tell you I hoped it would stay Elbert from giving you a much sounder beating, but that would be a wobbly excuse. In truth? I was angry and worried, and you had proven beyond doubt that nothing was under my control. Including my temper, obviously. I rued it the moment I did it. It seems rather late to beg your forgiveness, but I will. Would you give it?"

"No." With the old scab ripped off, what lay under it hurt.

Taken aback, Scarl rubbed his jaw. "Would you have some penance of me?"

She considered but was too tired to think of anything fitting.

In her silence, he said, "I'm sorry. It's your right to begrudge it, I guess—but it happened a long while ago, and I hope I've proven myself better since. Why is it troubling you now?" When she still didn't reply, he added quietly, "If I didn't know better, Ariel, I'd think you were just trying to make us both feel bad."

Plunking her hands on her hips, she thrust her chin out to deny it. But his words struck a chord in her conscience. Her arms dropped.

"Maybe I am," she admitted.

"Can I ask why?"

Her mouth worked, empty. At the well, she'd been able to think of little but getting back to Scarl and Nace. Once she left the circle of trees, she would have walked until she met them or fell dead. Now she'd finally quenched the call of the map and the moon to return to a land of texture and sound. So why, indeed, pick a fight now?

She had something to lose again, that's why. She whispered, "I'm afraid to care about you too much."

His face cramped and he nodded. "It hurts terribly, doesn't it? Losing people you love. Even for a short while."

"It's not always a short while," she said flatly. "It's sometimes forever."

He rose and resettled awkwardly beside her to cradle her shoulders. "So it seems."

"How can you stand it?" she asked, not thinking of anyone in particular, just desperately needing the adult in her life to have an answer.

He rested his chin on her head. "You can't," he whispered into her hair. "You can't stand it, Ariel. You pretend, that's all."

"But why?"

"Because others are pretending, too, I suppose. You do it for them."

As she opened her mouth to question, he unsnarled a twig from her hair. The gesture made his point better than all argument.

"You pretend for me and I'll pretend for you?" she murmured.

"Exactly." He smiled unconvincingly. "And when one of us leaves the world, the other will find someone else to pretend for. That's what people do. Because the world is pretend, Ariel, all of it. It's one long and layered make-believe tale—just a bead on a very big abacus."

Ariel pondered his words. So much pretending seemed like a lot of trouble, and inside out, somehow. She could feel, too, that he was trying to skip over his own loneliness and doubt. That was what he meant, she supposed, by "pretending," and the fact that he needed to do it hurt her, but it also showed that he loved her and was trying to comfort her. She sighed and rested her head on his shoulder, unaware of how much her motion comforted him.

He touched the beads at her throat. "You have many stories

to live yet, and plenty of people to love. Even if they aren't here on your necklace today."

Her fingertips rose to her abacus, too. She recalled a Flame-Mage and bridges, dragon's fire and lectrick. She saw a sheaf of brass flowers slipping into a well, seeds for the past. One of those darts would find her; it already had. If the world was only a story, as Scarl claimed—and she suspected his words contained truth—it was filled with genuine magic as well as pretending.

That notion cheered her. She poked Scarl in the chest. "If I have to pretend anyway, I'd rather pretend not to like you."

He smiled. "As you will. Shall I slap you more often?"

"You better not!"

"Just trying to help."

They held their embrace in companionable silence until she slipped free a few moments later. The Finder rubbed his lame foot.

"If I sleep, will you still be here when I wake up?" he wondered, not entirely joking.

"Not if I find another ladder," Ariel retorted, but she added, "I might lie down, too."

She stretched out but did not close her eyes. She wasn't aware, exactly, that she was waiting for Scarl to drop off, but when she recognized the shift in his breathing, she sat up and crept closer to Nace. In sleep, his relaxed face looked young. Sitting cross-legged alongside him, Ariel gazed at his jaw, her fingers itching to feel the fine, soft start of a beard there. To stop them, she had to trap her hands in the crooks of her knees.

The temptation to do something else, though, grew too great. Her heart began banging so loud she was sure he'd awaken anyway. Wishing with all of the throb in her chest for the magic of another old story, Ariel carefully bent forward to brush her lips against his—just in case he might awaken and speak.

Nace woke, all right, jerking hard enough that their teeth bumped behind their lips. Ariel flinched back. He didn't speak as she'd hoped, but merely blinked and offered her a groggy smile. He fingered his banged lip. A bit of the softness slid from his face as he pieced together just how she'd roused him. His green eyes sharpened on her in a way that sent a tingle through Ariel's core, and his hand rose from his lip to the back of her arm. With the slightest pressure of fingers, Nace asked her to bend her face close again.

She obeyed. Neither of them could mistake this kiss for a simple token of good-bye or good luck. He tasted of river water and hunger and sunlight, and Ariel's lips would burn for hours afterward with the rush.

When she thought she'd die if she couldn't stop feeling so much in a rather small part of her skin, she leaned back. Nace did not want to let her. His hand had slipped to the back of her neck, and in pulling against his reluctance Ariel flashed on Scarl's warning about stepping into that enticing sea. Awash in a flood of sensation, she understood for the first time what he'd meant. She still felt in control, but she drew a quivering breath and looked forward to being swept off someday.

For now, she curled up next to Nace and fell asleep with her cheek on his chest.

Later, after they'd both had more sleep, Ariel took out the cloth that had once wrapped her necklace. Finally she had time—and enough sense of the future—to show Nace the symbols and explain what each meant. Grasping at once how he could use them, he immediately began pestering Scarl to teach more. The Finder obliged, and Nace became an apt student.

Soon symbols in the dirt weren't enough. When they stopped by Electron to check on Sienna, Nace bartered with her. He followed bees to a hive near the dam, returning with wax that the Flame-Mage could use to make candles. Excited to be plying her trade, she gave him charcoal-tipped sticks that would draw on a thin flake of slate. Before Ariel set off with her companions once more, she had also collected three young men who still wanted to be guided to Skunk. One of them joined Nace in learning the symbols, and they pushed one another. By the time they all reached the swamp, Ariel often had to ask Scarl to explain the marks Nace had drawn for her.

Ariel's favorite message from Nace, though, was only one symbol. They perfected it together, or left it in flower petals for the other to find. Sometimes in the evenings, Nace would trace it over and over into Ariel's palm. It was a symbol from Scarl's First Day note, the one that meant "love." Though Nace's fingertip never left any mark, it somehow balanced the scars left on Ariel's skin by another hand's unfriendly knife.

As they traveled, she worked him into her song, sharing Sienna's verse with him, too:

Walk toward the morning sun,
Guiding Sienna.
New friends make travel fun
Walk, talk, and laugh.

Heart laughing, feet move fast.
New friends meet old ones.
Moon smiles silently.
Sending is done.

Scarl on one side of me,
Nace on the other,
Zeke waits to welcome us—
Home, here we come.

Ariel had another verse about Nace, but she was too shy to sing it aloud.

The second time she and Scarl bid Skunk good-bye, Nace hugged his mother and accompanied them home. In the end, the invitation had come from the Finder. Having grown too afraid the boy would refuse, Ariel couldn't bear to ask him herself. She needn't have worried. Nace had already followed her to an edge of the world; a few more peaks and valleys could hardly have stopped him. Plus, his passion for learning made him almost as happy to see the Vault as Ariel was to find the abbey's residents safe. The Kincaller would inhabit the Tree-Singers' home and Ariel's life for a long while to come. As Scarl had predicted, sparks would strike between Nace and Zeke Stone-Singer, but that tale has a bead of its own.

Ariel would live that story and more before her wandering was through, but she never walked far enough to outpace certain echoes. A mute boy's green-eyed gaze and the thrill of his kiss rang through any silence, reflecting Zeke's voice and Scarl's scent and the half-forgotten feel of her mother's embrace. The circles and lines drawn on the mapstone had faded, but like the Far-walker symbol that directed Ariel's feet, the mark of love had been etched not just onto her palm but indelibly into her heart.

CODA

I wish we still had one of those first thirteen telling darts," Scarl said to Ariel somewhere between Electron and Skunk. "Perhaps the next time we travel northeast, I can find one. I'd love to see if the blank place for the sender's mark now shows they were sent by a Farwalker."

"We can check the one we took from the mouth of the mountain," she told him. The first thirteen darts had led to the one she spoke of now, and its sender's mark had been absent, too. "It's back home at the abbey."

"That wasn't sent," Scarl said. "That one was placed, and it sat waiting for you a long time. Someone must have stashed it at the start of the war, after hiding the Vault. Perhaps Noah himself."

Ariel gazed at the curl of moon sailing before them on the bright morning sky. It did not speak to her now and would never again, but it reminded her of the cycles of time.

"You could be right," Ariel said with a grin. "But maybe you're not. Maybe I just haven't put it there yet."